Fire with Fire

Book 3
of
The Chronicles of Crett

By

L R Attridge

Grosvenor House
Publishing Limited

This book is published by
Grosvenor House Publishing Ltd
Link House
140 The Broadway, Tolworth, Surrey, KT6 7HT.
www.grosvenorhousepublishing.co.uk

This book is a work of fiction. Any resemblance to
people or events, past or present, is purely coincidental.

A CIP record for this book
is available from the British Library

Paperback ISBN 978-1-83615-445-7
Hardback ISBN 978-1-83615-444-0
eBook ISBN 978-1-83615-446-4

Acknowledgements

Thanks to my brother Colin for his suggestions and patience

Also available by the same author

Rumours of Magic, book one of the Chronicles of Crett

Chasing the Magic, book two of the Chronicles of Crett

1

Haggitt Mulderbish cursed the weather. He'd climbed this mountain every year for the past eighteen years on the anniversary of his father's disappearance, for no other reason than his father had told him to. Though he trusted that one day the reason would become clear. His father had been insistent, yet vague, about this duty.

Haggitt was just a lad at the time, only twelve years old, and he didn't know any better. But now, coming up to thirty years old, he felt a bit of an idiot. *What would people think?* He wondered, *a fully qualified wizard in his prime, beard still not grey, climbing a mountain in the middle of the night, his hair plastered to his face with rain. Why couldn't the man have gone in the morning? Or the afternoon? At least I would've had daylight*, he complained to himself.

He kicked a stone. *Oh gods*, he thought. A flash of lightning lit the sky and was followed almost immediately by a crash of thunder. 'Alright, alright,' he murmured, looking up at the heavy clouds, just in case any gods were actually listening to him. His angular face was peppered by a shower. It seemed the only god paying him any attention was the one in charge of rain.

He pulled his robe tighter around him. A difficult move when carrying a staff in one hand, and anyway the wind soon undid it again, and his hood slipped back off his head. 'Damn it!' he growled, and jerked it back up. Another flash of lightning lit up the sky and illuminated the rain-soaked mountainside.

What was that? he wondered. There was a dark shape to his right. A rock, perhaps? Or something he'd rather not meet? It didn't move. That was a relief. But something did. Just momentarily, then it vanished.

Haggitt strained his eyes. His forehead creased in concentration. Another fork of lightning struck a stunted tree to his left. It burned momentarily before the wind snuffed it out, but it was enough for Haggitt to see the dark shape was a cave mouth. He wiped the rain from his eyes with a wet sleeve, pulled his hood forward and held it in place with his free hand. He'd climbed far enough on this foul night. 'Sorry, Father,' he muttered. 'But you're gonna have to wait. I'm bloody soaked.'

He ducked inside the cave, let his hood slip back onto his shoulders and looked around. Not that he could see a lot. Outside, the thunder marched across the sky again; lightning touched the rocky landscape with fingers of fire. Haggitt shuddered with the cold and sat down on the cave floor against a wall, cradling his staff in the crook of an arm while he rubbed his hands together to get rid of the numbness.

The rain had stopped and snow took its place. At least it was quieter, and the wind died down too. He shrugged his shoulders and sighed. *Looks like I might be here for a while.* He made a complicated hand gesture in the air. A torch appeared on the wall and spluttered into life, illuminating the cave. Fire-raising spells were the first things the wizards taught the new students at the university, apart from showing them where the privies were.

Haggitt had a fairly good time at the university. He was quick to learn and not overly ambitious. Ambition in student wizards tended to make the staff wary. His father was also a wizard. It often ran in families, though most never married, and most were ostensibly celibate. It was an anomaly without being a mystery. Most wizards chose to work at the university or nearby after graduation, but Haggitt's father was inclined to wander off in search of adventure. It was probably one of those adventures that resulted in Haggitt's existence.

His father spent a lot of time with the barbarians on the Yellow Grass Plain, mainly because once he'd learned his trade in wizardry, he'd got bored with it and looked for something else to do. He'd found a group of barbarians that he could bend to his will. They didn't mind, because he was good at forecasting the weather. And for them there was nothing worse than chasing after a caravan guarded by half an army in unexpected pouring rain. Haggitt shook the worst off his clothes regretting that he hadn't inherited his father's gift.

The night ground on and the snow dissolved as it touched the sodden slopes, adding to the numerous rivulets streaming down into the valley. Haggitt rubbed his hands together, and huffed on them. Then the light bulb of an idea appeared above his head. *Why not light a fire?*

A quick glance around the cave soon told him that it was sadly lacking in the wood department. Apart from a small rivet-studded, black door behind him. Without turning his head, he raised a hand and snapped his fingers. The torch rose out of the bracket and floated into his waiting hand. When you have that level of ability it tends to make you lazy, but he still had to stand up by himself.

Haggitt moved quietly to the door and examined it by the light of the torch. Some of the rivets seemed to form the features of a face, and it was staring back at him. He ignored it and continued to eye the door critically. It wasn't like other doors. Lower than most, but more different than just that.

There was no handle, no knocker or even a keyhole. Its hinges were invisible too. He reached out with the torch and placed it in a bracket beside the door that he'd not noticed before, and touched the door lightly with his fingertips. It was icy cold and steam rose from the film of condensation where he'd touched it. He pushed gently with his hand inside his sleeve, not knowing what to expect, but half expecting it not to move. He was half right. It didn't. *I suppose the next best thing to walking away,* he thought, *is knocking.*

He tapped lightly and listened, resisting the urge to press his ear to it in case it stuck. Not a sound. He grew even more curious. He hefted his staff and took a step back to give himself room to swing it, but thought better of it and used it to tap lightly three times, right in the middle of the 'face'.

The door moved back half an inch with a sound like the lid coming off an airtight jar, then swept silently back. Haggitt shielded his eyes from the unexpected glare that rushed out at him, and he took a step back. Apart from that, nothing happened.

He allowed his eyes time to adjust and warily ducked inside under the low portal. Then, the door closed. He silently cursed. The inside of the door was even more featureless than the outside. He looked at his new surroundings. The room was shaped like a tetrahedron, its walls as black as coal and shiny as an oil slick. Obviously, in a pyramidal room, there is no ceiling, but more disturbingly the room had no visible light source. In the centre of the floor was a raised triangular slab, and on it was a shiny, black pyramid about the size of a fist. Haggitt stared at it for a moment, then, with his curiosity overriding his lack of courage, he moved closer.

He leaned over the pyramid and mouthed a protective spell for himself before extending a hand. The thing was cold, but not as cold as the door, and when he looked closely, he saw tiny points of light in its black depths. *It's some sort of crystal,* he thought. It began to turn under the pressure of his fingers, and he snatched his hand away.

The strange object continued to rotate. Quite unexpectedly the room darkened. Though the pinpoints of light within the crystal were still sufficient to light the room. Haggitt stood back not knowing what to do, and worse, not knowing what to expect. The crystal stopped turning and its three sides spread out slowly, like the petals of an exotic flower. He was mesmerised – and alarmed when the raised triangular slab on which the pyramid sat, slid to one side with hardly a sound, exposing a narrow spiral staircase. Cautiously, he stepped forward and peered in, only to jump back in fright, clutching his chest where he thought his heart should be.

A head emerged from the semi-darkness of the stairwell and swivelled around until it spotted Haggitt, who was about to slide to the floor.

* * *

2

'It's about bloody time!' snapped the head, climbing into the room with the aid of a body. 'Do you know how long I've been in there?' he pointed an accusing finger, first at Haggitt then at the stairwell. Haggitt didn't answer. He had the distinct impression that whoever this was, was going to tell him.

'Well, I'll tell you,' the man started, 'nearly eighteen bloody years! That's how long.'

Haggitt side-stepped the tirade. He eased himself up, regaining his composure 'Who are *you*?'

'Oh, you've got a tongue in yer head, then.'

Haggitt didn't answer.

'I'm Gi Mulderbish. Not that it's any concern of yours.'

Haggitt ran the name across his mind. Repeatedly, in fact, wondering how likely it was. 'Gi Mulderbish, the *wizard*?'

The small man in the brightly coloured rags unfolded, and attempted to stand up straight. There were grunts and sighs, and the sounds of vertebrae clicking into places they hadn't been for a long time.

Eventually Gi was about as tall as he was going to get. 'You've heard of me?' he said, slowly, warily, as though something from his past was about to catch up with him.

'Yes, Father.'

A momentary pause. Gi scuttled across the room, and squinted icily into Haggitt's eyes. He stepped back, held out a hand about waist high, then raised it slowly till it was above his head and level with the top of Haggitt's.

'You've grown,' he decided, looking him up and down.

'Grown?' said Haggitt. 'Of course I've damn well grown. I was twelve years old when you disappeared.' Then added as an afterthought. 'Almost.'

'Is that right? Twelve years old, eh?'

'Yes.'

The older wizard's face mellowed slightly. 'Well...' he began, uneasily, 'how are you?'

Haggitt held out his arms. 'Look at me. I'm bloody soaked, that's how I am!'

'Oh,' was all Gi could think of to say.

As father-and-son reunions went, this was about as awkward as one could get. Neither was good at this emotional stuff. Not at expressing it, anyway. They both felt it keenly enough, but lacked the vocabulary. And in the short, pained silence, an emotional truce surfaced, as they each recognised and honoured the other's difficulty.

Gi tried to sound matter-of-fact, but choked faintly when he said, 'Well, let's get out of here then, shall we?'

Haggitt looked around the room, and settled his gaze back on his father. 'Any ideas?'

Gi looked around and came to the same conclusion. 'Well, there must be a way... Striper got out,' he said, thoughtfully, stroking his unkempt beard.

'Striper? Who's Striper?'

'Baron Striper, you know? Lord of Gremanos.'

'What's he got to do with this?'

'I'll tell you later,' said Gi, 'it's a long story. A *very* long story.'

Haggitt shrugged, he wanted to pursue it, but he knew that from his father's tone there was no point. For want of a better idea, he turned his attention to the black, crystal pyramid. 'Perhaps this thing operates both exits.' He reached out and touched it. It turned at his touch, as before, and the raised triangular slab of rock on which it sat, slid back across the stairwell with barely a sound.

'How does it do that?' said Haggitt, intrigued.

'I'm guessing it's magic,' said the older wizard to the younger, a little sarcastically. 'And, nice one. Now we can't go down either.'

Haggitt ignored him. He thought it was more mechanical than magical, but didn't argue. The room darkened again. Lit only by the tiny pinpoints of light from the pyramid. Haggitt didn't hesitate. He touched the device again and this time the door opened, and a shaft of flickering torchlight widened across the floor. 'As I thought,' he said. 'It's set up to operate them in sequence. Once it's worked the door it will work the stairwell, and vice versa.'

'Hmm,' Gi snorted. 'I would've thought of that. Like I said, it's magical.'

Haggitt was even more certain it was mechanical. Not that it mattered. What mattered was the door was open. 'Well?' he said, 'are you coming? Or do you want to stay in here for another eighteen years.' Haggitt ducked down and went outside.

* * *

Outside, the sun was glaring down from a clear blue dome of sky. Haggitt breathed deeply and looked around. Sand. Everywhere. It stretched uninterrupted to every horizon. The only thing on it, apart from themselves, was the black pyramid behind them.

'Any idea where the sea is?' said Gi, sarcastically.

Haggitt thought for a moment. 'I think this must be a desert.'

Gi looked up at the blue yonder and rolled his eyes.

'But I climbed a bloody mountain in pouring bloody rain last night!' Haggitt snapped.

'It seems to have stopped,' said Gi, flatly, holding out a palm up as if checking.

'And you're going to tell me that the mountain got washed away, are you?'

'Don't be ridiculous,' said Gi. 'Somebody's moved it.'

The bitter humour was beginning to irritate. Haggitt didn't remember his father being like this. He didn't remember him being much like anything, really. Eighteen years ago he'd seemed distant and a bit domineering, but that was probably how most kids saw their fathers. And eighteen years locked away was enough to make anyone cynical, or worse. Haggitt made an effort to cool his anger. Though physically he was getting hotter. 'Any idea where we are?'

'I've been in that...' he pointed behind him just as the tetrahedron vanished, 'for...' he paused, 'oh... it doesn't matter now.'

Haggitt looked around. Apart from the black prison not being there anymore, nothing had changed. 'Okay, which way?'

'Seriously?' Gi shrugged.

'Well, if we don't find shade soon, we'll fry.'

He looked up at the sun and sneezed. 'We'll go that way,' he said, pointing them away from walking directly into the sun.

Gi gestured and mumbled something that materialised his wizard's pointy hat. He pulled it down low over his eyes and started to walk.

The top sand was loose and the going was slow. Haggitt had an idea. 'We're both wizards. There's surely something we can manifest that will help us more than hats?'

Gi paused and searched his son's face. 'Magic uses energy, boy. You should know that. And we may not have much to spare before we're done here. Don't they teach you these things anymore?'

Haggitt felt a moment's nostalgia at being chastened. He even smiled to himself as he caught up with his father, who'd strutted off – especially over being called a boy at almost thirty.

They hadn't gone more than a mile before Haggitt could feel the heat of the sand coming up through the soles of his pointy-toed boots. The sun was high and nightfall was a long way off. *Like the horizon*, he thought, scanning it as he trudged onwards. The horizon was indistinct in the heat. He was about to avert his eyes when he noticed something way over to his right. He tapped his father's arm and pointed it out – a dark smudge on the distant sand that was growing like it was coming towards them.

'What do you think?' said Haggitt.

'Knowing my luck,' said Gi, 'it's probably a sandstorm.'

'No. There's no wind.'

'Not this side of it,' said Gi, ignorant of how sandstorms work, 'It'll be pushing it along.'

'Wha...? I think it's riders. We may be in luck.'

'Or not.'

'Yes, you can just make them out.' A dark line of riders was racing ahead of the dust-cloud, and at the speed they were travelling, it wouldn't be long before they were bearing down on the two wizards.

* * *

'Do you think they're friendly?' Haggitt wondered.

'We'll know in a minute,' said Gi.

As it turned out, it was almost two minutes, and the leading rider was frantically waving his free hand as he neared them. Haggitt waved back. A couple of seconds later he realised that the rider wasn't waving a greeting.

'He wants us to get out of the way!' Haggitt yelled. Gi had already worked that out and scurried a good distance before Haggitt had got his feet sorted out.

As the white-clad riders thundered by, the nearest one shouted, **'RUN!'**

'Where to?!' Haggitt yelled back. The rider reined in his horse, sending up a cloud of fine sand and dust.

'Sorry?' called the rider.

'Where to?' Haggitt repeated, stretching his arms wide to indicate there was nowhere to go.

'Wherever you like, except that way!' said the rider, looking over his shoulder. He dug his spurs into his horse's flanks and galloped off to catch his comrades.

That's when the wizards saw the next group of riders. More of a horde than a group. They were dressed in black, with hoods covering their faces, and only a narrow slit for their eyes. They arrived so fast that getting out of the way wasn't an option. Their leader brought his horse to a melodramatic halt, rearing up in front of them. And to stop his men stampeding passed or into him, he held up a hand – one of his own, thankfully, not a trophy from a previous skirmish – and the black-clad riders thundered to a dusty halt.

The leader walked his horse forward through the dust cloud he'd brought with him, and stopped in front of the wizards. Gi looked behind him, then back at the black-clad rider. 'They went that way,' he said, pointing to a receding cloud of dust behind him.

The rider ignored Gi and walked his horse around the wizards again. 'You are wizards?' he asked, sounding curious.

Gi looked at Haggitt. Haggitt nodded. He could hardly deny it; the clothes were a dead give-away. 'You can tell, can't you,' said Gi, although his sarcasm was wasted.

'Name!' demanded the rider.

'My name is Gi Mulderbish,' said Gi, defiantly. 'And this is my son, Haggitt.'

'Hmm,' the rider snorted. The eyes in the slit of his hood looked thoughtful as the name resonated with him.

'Any chance of a lift?' asked Haggitt, meekly.

'Do you know who I am?' the rider asked.

Haggitt couldn't see his face, but the man's tone and narrowed eyes told him that he was grinning menacingly in there. 'Sorry, no,' Haggitt tried, politely and honestly. 'I can't really tell.'

'I am, Catscart du Merde,' he announced, proudly. 'Centurion of Baron Striper's Black-Guards.' He nodded slightly, as if confirming his self-importance.

Gi calculated the number of riders in this Centurion's band to be only about fifty, and he took a certain amount of pleasure in pointing it out. 'Fifty?' the Centurion spluttered, and stood in his stirrups to get a better look. The dust cloud was settling. 'Fifty-six,' he said to himself. 'Alright!' he bellowed to the unit waiting patiently in the heat, 'Who's missing?' When no-one ratted on any of his mates, he turned to the man nearest him. 'Sergeant! I want those men found and standing outside my office first thing in the morning! Understand?'

'He's the Sergeant, sir.' The man pointed to an identically-clad man next to him.

The Sergeant identified himself and rolled his eyes. 'Yes, sir.'

'Now, get these wizards on horses and follow me!' du Merde reined his horse around and galloped off.

* * *

5

Baron Striper leaned back in his chair, his hands together as if in prayer, with his index fingers lightly touching his top lip. A small, hooded figure stood on the other side of the desk, shifting from foot to foot. This was Barter Stogie, the baron's eyes and ears in the city.

Barter ran a network of ne'er do wells, whose main sources of income were burglary, robbery, eaves-dropping and selling information. But in the baron's case, the information was free. Barter didn't want the Baron's Black-Guard knocking on his door in the middle of the night, or the sound of his own screams as anything the baron thought he might know, was tortured out of him.

The baron stared into the darkness of Barter's hood. 'What you're telling me,' the baron began deliberately, 'is that the pyramid is back?'

'Yes, Lord,' Barter mumbled.

'I haven't finished yet!' the baron snapped. 'The pyramid is back... and it's *empty?*'

'Yes, Lord.'

'Do you know what this means?' the baron queried.

'Nope, not a clue, Lord.'

Striper leaned forward and picked up his quill, 'I'll tell you, shall I?'

Barter remained silent and shifted onto his other foot.

'It means...' he paused, for dramatic effect, 'That Gi Mulderbish, is free.'

So what, Barter thought. The Baron dipped his quill into the ornate inkwell and held it poised over the parchment, wondering how best to phrase it to make the reader realise its urgency. *Ah*, he thought, and began to write his note.

After reading it through to dot a few i's and cross an errant t, he signed it with a flourish and folded it in four. He pulled open the bottom drawer of the desk – there was the faint clink of a bottle as it rolled against a glass – then he pulled out an envelope.

He rummaged in the desk for a few moments more, then stared grimly into the darkness of Barter's hood again.

'Yes, Lord?' said Barter, in anticipation.

'I take it you possess a box of matches?' asked the baron.

'Yes, Lord.'

Striper held out his hand, expecting Barter to hand it over. 'They're on my kitchen table, Lord,' said Barter, apologetically, and a little nervous, knowing how his Lord was likely to react.

Striper thumped his desk angrily and stood up. His chair slowly over-balanced, then clattered to the floor behind him. He stalked across the room, wrenched open the door and bellowed to his secretary. 'Pinch! Come in here!'

The secretary dropped his quill and scurried into the baron's office. 'You called? Your Lordship.'

Although Striper insisted on the pleasantries, he wasn't always very pleasant about them. 'You're here, aren't you?'

'Well... er, yes.'

'Tell me, Pinch,' said the baron. 'Do you smoke?'

'Yes, Lord, you know I do.'

'Right, what do you smoke, Pinch?'

'*Old Camel* – stranded, Lord.'

'Ah,' Striper murmured. He put his hands behind his back and walked slowly back to his desk, 'I suppose they'll have to do, then.' He picked up his chair and set it back behind the desk, sat down and held out a hand, waiting.

Pinch realised what he was getting at, and began to pat his robe. 'Here, sir.'

'Good.' The baron pulled a cigarette from the box and put it to his lips. 'Light?' Pinch offered him a box of yellow headed matches. The baron took one out and scraped it along the side of the box. He held the flame to the cigarette and puffed life into it. His eyes crossed for a moment, and he rocked back in his chair. *Bloody 'ell*, he thought, as the strength hit him. 'You may go, Pinch.'

The secretary thought about holding out his hand for the baron to give the matches back, then thought better of it. Striper leaned down and lifted a lump of sealing wax out of a drawer, struck another match and melted some of the wax over the envelope. Satisfied that there was enough to keep it securely closed, he thumped his seal into it and handed it to Barter. 'Deliver this,' he ordered.

Barter took it and ambled to the door, where he stopped and turned.

'You can go,' Striper prompted, waving him away.

'Who shall I deliver it to, Baron?' He held the letter out lamely. 'It's blank, my Lord.'

'Ah, yes. You're not a mind reader, are you?' Barter Stogie was in fact not a reader of anything, which was why the baron used his services. 'Take it to my son,' he said, then took another draw on the rapidly diminishing cigarette. *Oh God, I'll be glad when I've finished this,* he thought.

'Right, Lordship. Lord Welkin it is, then.' And he quickly made his exit.

* * *

Three-hundred miles or so from Baron Striper's castle was a small desert outpost. It was situated alongside an oasis, that in addition to supporting Catscarte du Merde's garrison, supported reptiles, small mammals and birdlife for miles around.

It was just dawn when du Merde was woken by a bird trilling outside his bedroom window. He cursed, sat up and swung his legs over the edge of his bed then fell back, dragging the pillows over his head. It was no use; he could still hear the damned bird. He threw one of his pillows at the window and sat up with his head in his hands. *What a night*, he thought. *I don't even remember getting back here.* He forced himself to his feet and staggered bleary-eyed to the washstand and poured a small amount of water, which he flinchingly splashed onto his face. At least it got his eyes to focus.

He stared into the shard of mirror propped up behind the washstand and stroked his stubbly beard. 'No, it'll go another day,' he muttered. One of the many things du Merde hated was shaving. He splashed more water on his face. He was awake now, and mentally running through the day's agenda. Outside the window, the bird had gone quiet, or flown away. Either way, it wasn't annoying him anymore.

He got dressed. He hadn't fully undressed last night, so all this meant was making himself respectable with the addition of a couple of items from his uniform wardrobe. Finally, he picked up his helmet, and from past experience, he examined it carefully before putting it on his head. 'Oh, not again,' he sighed, and emptied the contents out of the window, making a mental note to buy another pot to piss in, to replace the last one he'd hurled at the dawn chorus, the next time the tinker-man came around. He hadn't thrown out the water in the wash basin yet, so used it to rinse out his helmet.

After some vigorous shakes, he planted it firmly on his head, gave it a little twist, slung his sword over his shoulder and marched to his office. That's when he remembered one of yesterday's orders. He shouldered his way through the forty-four men he'd ordered the

Sergeant to report to him. Grabbing the Sergeant by his arm as he went passed, du Merde pushed him into the office and slammed the door behind him.

du Merde strode around to the back of his desk and sat down. 'Sergeant,' he said, quietly.

'Sir!' replied the Sergeant, snapping to attention. du Merde took a long slow breath and sighed. 'When I said I wanted these men outside my door, I didn't mean all at once... you know, a dozen at a time would be good.'

'Permission to speak, sir?'

'Well?'

'Wiv respect, sir, they 'ad the day off yesterday.'

'Why didn't you say so at the time, Sergeant?'

'Well, sir. I fought you knew, like. They 'ad put in the proper request... sir'

'What, all of them? Individually? How could I have possibly missed all that?'

'It was all done together, sir. They all went together... sir.'

'What on Crett were they all...' He trailed off, deciding he didn't really want to know what they'd been up to. 'Go and dismiss them, Sergeant. Then come back in here. Let's try and salvage what's left of the day.'

'Yes, sir!' the Sergeant saluted briskly and left. When he'd gone, du Merde sifted through the papers on his desk to see what he'd arranged for the day. Toward the bottom of the pile, he found a note the Sergeant had left regarding the two wizards. *Ah*, he thought, *this will bring a nice little bonus when I tell the baron I've got these two under lock and key.*

There was a very old and outdated warrant for the capture of Gi, which was never cancelled after Gi was captured and locked up. That still stood. Gi was now guilty of escaping the baron's pyramid prison too. *And surely*, he thought, *Haggitt must be wanted for something, helping a prisoner escape, probably,* he thought, and smiled, pleased with himself for coming up with that.

16

Having spent the night in a cell, Haggitt stared through the barred window. 'See anything?' whispered Gi, who wasn't tall enough to see out.

'Sand,' said Haggitt, 'a wall, and a lot of sky.'

'Ah, well,' said Gi, cheerfully, 'at least we're in the shade.'

'This place will be like an oven in an hour or so, Father.'

'We'll be out of here by then.'

'You plan to escape?' Haggitt whispered.

'No, of course not,' said Gi. 'Where would we go? No – I reckon du Merde will take us to the baron. Didn't you see the gold coins glistening behind his eyes when he found out who we were?'

'All we'll be doing is swapping one prison for another,' Haggitt pointed out.

'We're wizards, or have you forgotten? We could've gotten ourselves out of here last night if we'd wanted, but there was no point. When he takes us to the baron, there won't be any bars.'

'Yes, and if we'd gone last night, it would have been dark,' Haggitt mumbled.

'Let's not waste magic on these fools now, we'll need it when we get to Striper's castle. Let's just sit back and enjoy the ride.' Gi clasped his fingers behind his head and lay back on his bunk.

'Father!' Haggitt hissed, urgently. 'They're coming.'

* * *

7

It was a good day's horse ride to Lord Welkin's castle, and half a day longer by cart. Barter Stogie possessed neither. So, it was around noon on the third day when he arrived at the castle door. It was locked, but there was a note pinned to the little notice board hanging near the knocker. It read, 'Back in ten minutes', and was of no use whatsoever to Barter. He couldn't read. He knocked. There was no reply, so he gave it a good kick. Still no answer, so, dejectedly and still clutching the letter, he went home.

* * *

Three days later, back at Baron Striper's castle, Barter was standing on the mat in front of the baron's desk. 'Yes, Lord, that's what I said... he wasn't in,' said Barter, his voice slightly muffled by his hood, which kept falling across his face.

'Well?' said Striper, leaning forward. 'Did it not occur to you to wait?'

'Um...'

'Evidently not.' Striper stood up and walked to the door. 'Pinch!'

'Lord?' came a croaky voice from without.

'Are you still smoking that Camel rubbish?'

'Er... yes, Lord.'

'Oh...' Striper hesitated for a moment, then added, 'Alright I'll have one, then.'

Pinch sighed, and reluctantly parted with his last cigarette. *I can't afford to keep him in cigarettes*, he thought, *he doesn't pay me enough.*

Striper took the cigarette, and tossed the empty packet into the fireplace. 'Light?' he snapped. Pinch obliged. The baron drew deeply. 'Now,' he began, turning back to Barter. *Oh, my god*, he thought, *this is bloody awful.* He steadied himself against the desk and uncrossed his eyes. 'Go back and see if he's home yet, and if he's not... wait. Understand?'

'Yes, Lord,' Barter mumbled. 'How long?'

'Until he shows up, reads my note, and gives you an answer!' The baron sat down. 'You may go,' he said, waving him away. 'You too, Pinch.'

Pinch clenched his fingers a couple of times and stalked slowly back to his desk.

Barter followed, looking forward to the day when he could get even.

* * *

9

The journey back to Striper's castle became tedious. Gi and Haggitt had spent the last six days bumping across sand and rocks, with hardly a change of scenery, but now the terrain was just barren rocks, and dusty roads. They had the hundred man escort of Black-Guards, led by du Merde himself, who wanted to deliver them in person to take any credit and rewards that might be due.

Thinking about what might be lurking out in that desert, Haggitt was silently grateful for their company. They knew the terrain, and seemed at ease, which made him feel better about it. However, the wagon he and his father were travelling in, was like an old wooden caravan with bars across the windows. But, at least they were in the shade and not on foot having to walk, and as they didn't know where they were, there was no point wasting magic trying to escape.

The driver was quiet and seldom spoke. His mind was numbed by the gentle rocking of the wagon. So much so, that he spent most of the day sleeping. The horse was content simply to keep pace with the outriders.

The sun was high, du Merde considered it was too hot to carry on for now. He ordered a couple of his men to break out the canvas tents they carried from the supply wagon which accompanied them. This was a heavy vehicle drawn by a team of six large horses, with a driver and a guard sitting up high in front.

Much as they would all have welcomed some rain, it was good that it wasn't, because the tents were old and moth-eaten. But at least they afforded some shade.

No-one was asked to volunteer for anything in du Merde's little army; whenever there was a job to do, du Merde simply pressed whoever he thought could do a job, into doing it. Today, the task of getting the encampment organised fell to Fox Loer. Fox was a tall man with dark brown hair and blue eyes. His facial features are kindly and actually bore no resemblance to a fox. There was a hint of barbarian about him, except that he was intelligent. He was easy-going and able to look after himself in a fight.

This was the type of man du Merde kept close by him. Also pulled from the ranks to help him today was Reza Lock. Slightly shorter than Fox, but still taller than most, he was also chosen for his fighting skills. However, the talents of both men were being wasted today, erecting tents.

Reza had long golden hair that he wore in a braid that hung down his back, almost to his waist. du Merde was jealous because his own hair was thinning. He'd often thought of telling Reza to get his braid cut, but even though du Merde was his commander, he was wary of him, as Reza could be quick tempered, and didn't take kindly to personal remarks.

From this, you might gather that du Merde was not a brave man. Though he was not a coward by any means. But his inflated opinion of himself gave him a tendency to bully on occasions. He tried to bully Gi Mulderbish on the first evening of the journey, but after Gi hypnotised him into thinking his legs had turned to jelly, and he couldn't walk for a few hours, du Merde would send a lesser soldier to check on the two wizards.

A couple of hours later, when the sun had moved well past its zenith, and all the soldiers had been refreshed, du Merde considered it was cool enough to move on. Which they did until it was too dark to see. Then, they made camp for the night. Most of the soldiers carried bedrolls, and some even carried small, one-man tents.

When the fires had died down, a black-clad figure crept away from the camp, loped to the nearby rocks and ducked out of sight. The black-clad figure put his hands around his mouth, and made a poor attempt at a bird impression.

Gi Mulderbish was still awake. He nudged Haggitt, 'Did you hear that?'

'Yes, Father,' Haggitt replied. 'I wonder what stupid sod does a chicken impression in a desert in the middle of the night.'

'I think we may have a spy,' said Gi. 'I wonder why. Are we going to be ambushed? We can't be in any more trouble than we are now.'

'Well,' said Haggitt. 'I don't think there's anyone in this caravan we can't handle if we have to.'

'Let's not worry about it then, it's du Merde's problem, not ours.'

The black-clad figure cursed. He'd heard the wizards murmuring and feared it might be about his poor attempt at a bird call. He listened again. Everything was quiet. He did his chicken impression again, quieter this time. He waited a moment, and just as he was going to try again, a pebble struck the side of his helmet.

'Is that you, Gennett?' a voice hissed in the darkness.

'Yes. Were you expecting somebody else?' said Gennett.

The pebble-throwing barbarian in the darkness was Huddy Mincing. He'd been shadowing the caravan, and now he'd come to find out what his undercover man, Gennett, could tell him about it. Chiefly, was it transporting anything of value and worth stealing.

Gennett, who was sometimes the relief driver of the wagon that held the wizards, was not highly ranked in du Merde's a hundred strong army, which was why Catscart du Merde enjoyed referring to himself as a Centurion. But all Gennett knew was that they were carrying weapons for Baron Striper, supplies, and enough money to pay the soldiers for about a month. This was the time it should take to get to Baron Striper's palace-cum-castle in Gremanos.

Huddy told Gennett to return to the camp, and he'd contact him again in two nights.

* * *

10

When Huddy was far enough away from the soldiers' camp, he jumped on his horse and rode back to the barbarians' camp on the other side of the rocky hill. The chief of the barbarians was a man called Broosh Marteef. He wore more fur skins than the rest of his clan. This is mainly because there was more of him than anybody else. He was not fat; he was just a giant of a man. He wore rows of gold chains around his neck, and wide metal bracelets on his wrists, thick enough to stop a sword stroke, and judging by the gouges in them, it appeared to be their primary function.

There were white furs wrapped around his shins, bound with strips of black leather. The furs were more likely stolen, as Broosh had never travelled anywhere near where animals had white fur. When it came to cold climates, he was a bit of a wuss. He was a man who liked to look good and took pride in his appearance. His cloak was light brown, and adorned with intricate patterns stitched along the hems. However, it was rumoured that his loin cloth had been handed down by his grandmother.

Huddy Mincing rode into camp and tied his horse to a long rope that served as a hitching rail, and made his way to the camp fire.

'Ah, Huddy, you're back!' shouted Broosh. 'Come and sit by the fire. What news from Weasel?' (The soldier, Gennett, was one of Broosh's spies and was known to the barbarians as, Gennett the Weasel.)

Huddy sat down. One of the clan passed him a horn of horse beer, although, truth be told, it tasted more like horse piss. He pretended to take a sip and put it down beside him, letting most of it spill into the sand. He rubbed his hands together, like a man with good news to tell. 'Gennett says they're going to Gremanos. Carrying weapons and the soldiers' wages.'

Broosh's face lit up. 'How many soldiers?'

'Gennett said about a hundred.'

'Did you see any tents?' asked Broosh.

'Only two. But I saw two wagons Gennett didn't talk about.'

'Did you notice what was in them?'

'Well, I 'ad a quick look before I spoke to Gennett. One was real big – needed six horses to pull it. That'd be the one with the supplies and weapons in it, I reckon. The other one was smallish, just one horse, and it's got bars on the windows. Looks like they're movin' prisoners.'

Broosh gave this some thought. 'Hmm... Perhaps someone needs liberating.'

* * *

11

Barter Stogie eventually arrived with the letter a second time at Lord Welkin's castle. There was no note on the board this time, so Barter knocked and waited. He waited again. Then, he hammered on it with his fist. He cursed, because this hurt and drew a tiny amount of blood. But there was still no reply. *Perhaps they still can't hear me*, he thought. He looked around, and saw a fist sized rock by his foot. He picked it up and proceeded to smash it against the door. 'Oh, shit,' he muttered, realising he'd punched a hole in the door.

A face appeared in the hole. 'Oi! Did you just do that?' said the face. 'Lord Welkin will not be an 'appy bunny when 'e sees that.'

'Is that you, Elgett?' said Barter.

''Oo's that?' Elgett demanded.

'It's me, Barter Stogie, I 'ave a letter for Lord Welkin.'

'Where 'ave you bin, I ain't 'eard from you for ages.'

'I've been running errands for the baron. That's why I'm 'ere now. I'm delivering a letter for 'im.'

'What does it say?' asked Elgett.

'How should I know?' said Barter. 'I can't read.'

'Ah. Course you can't, that's why 'e sent *you* then, I expect.'

'Can I come in?'

'Oh, yeah, 'old on a minute,' said Elgett. Now he had to perform the ceremony of the bolts. Why castle doors had to have so many bolts, nobody seemed to know. But it was only the man who had to undo and do them up again, *who actually cared.*

This castle was built in a valley. Some called this counter-intuitive, while others settled for plain stupid. It didn't have a wonderful view from the battlements, and it didn't have the same grand, pictorial and imposing effect from ground level as those built on hilltops. It was also a lot harder to defend.

Once Barter was inside, Elgett went through the lengthy process of slamming all the bolts back in place.

The pair walked across the lawn to the small keep where Lord Welkin lived.

'Wait 'ere,' Elgett told Barter. 'I'll let 'im know you're 'ere.' Barter sat on a wooden bench beside the door at the edge of the lawn, and marvelled at the way the groundsmen had scythed patterns into the grass. He thought the one of the two dogs was exceptionally good. Then, he started to get fidgety and to think about the journey home. *What's keeping Elgett so long?*

He stood up and pushed the door. It was open, and creaked slowly back. Inside, across the room, Lord Welkin and Elgett were deep in concentration, playing some sort of board game.

'Oh, sorry, Barter. I forgot you were still out there,' said Elgett.

'Queen to knight four. Checkmate!' said Lord Welkin, taking advantage of Barter's distraction. 'Come closer,' said Lord Welkin, beckoning Barter forward. 'Elgett tells me you have a letter for me. Do you know what it says?'

'No, my Lord. I can't read,' sighed Barter, as he handed Lord Welkin the letter. Welkin took it, leaned back in his chair and read. Then, he placed the letter on the desk in front of him.

'Oh dear,' he said. 'Gi Mulderbish has escaped from the pyramid.'

'I know,' said Barter.

'I thought you couldn't read,' said Welkin.

'I can't,' said Barter, 'but your father talks while he writes and I'm not deaf.'

'Do you know what this means?' said Welkin.

'Er… yes,' said Barter. 'It means the baron talks to himself.'

'No. Not that. Now Mulderbish has escaped, he will almost certainly make his way back to Gremanos to get even with my father.'

'Really? What did the baron do to him, then?' Barter wondered.

Lord Welkin sat and thought. *Hmm… yes, what did he do? Father never said.* 'Sorry, Barter, I couldn't say.' Then something occurred to him. 'Do you think he wants me to go back to Gremanos?'

Barter said he didn't know. 'But if you write a letter, I'll take it to him and find out.'

'How long will that take?' Welkin wondered.

'Er... I don't know my Lord. How fast you can write?'

'No, how long to get it to my father?' he said, adding 'idiot' under his breath.

'Well, if I walk, about three days, but if I was to *ride...*' said Barter, throwing out an unsubtle hint, 'I could probably do it in a day.'

Lord Welkin opened the top drawer of the desk and extracted a blank sheet of parchment. Then rummaged in the next drawer for a quill and inkwell. Barter stood waiting silently, with his hood pulled down across the top of his face, which he thought made him look cool. At last, Welkin finished his letter. He didn't have any sealing wax, so he rolled it into a tube, and tied a nice blue ribbon around it. With a bow. Then passed it to Barter.

'I know you said you could get it there in three days if you walked,' said Welkin. 'But how soon could you get it there if you *ran?*'

'Wiv respect, my Lord,' said Barter. 'If you want it run there, you'd better find someone else. *I* don't do run.'

'Oh,' said Welkin, slightly deflated. 'But it's urgent!'

Barter didn't hesitate. 'Why don't you lend me a horse, my Lord?' he tried again. 'I could bring it back when the baron gives me a reply. And you'll get your answer all the quicker!'

'I've got an idea, your Lordship,' said Elgett, thinking to break the stalemate. 'Why don't you take the letter yourself?'

Lord Welkin thought about it. 'Good suggestion, Elgett,' then he looked at Barter, 'I won't have to wait for his answer, then. And *I* can use the horse.'

Welkin placed his hands on the desk and stood up, resolutely. 'Elgett! Saddle me the horse. Then wash your hands and do me a packed lunch.' He strode back to his rooms to change and pack an overnight bag.

As soon as Welkin was out of sight, Barter said, 'What did you suggest that for? I 'ad a buyer for that 'orse.'

'I think 'e may have worked that out.'

Barter thought, 'Nah, 'e ain't that bright.'

* * *

12

Gennett the Weasel sneaked back into the soldiers' camp. He crept up to the prison wagon where Gi and Haggitt were being held, and risked a peek through the bars.

'Everything alright, soldier?' asked Gi, in a soft voice.

'All's well, sir,' said Gennett. 'I'll check again later, maybe in a day or two. I may have some news for you about our progress.'

'We are a month out from Gremanos,' said Gi, trying to be patient. 'That means, in two days, we will be two days closer. That will be our progress, I imagine.'

Gennett was a little confused for the moment, but re-gathered his wits. 'I know, sir. But for now I must get back before I'm missed.'

'He seems friendly,' said Haggitt. 'Why is that, Father?'

'Because he's a susceptible soldier,' said Gi, smiling. 'I don't want to be in this wagon more than two more days, so, I hypnotized him into helping us get out.'

'Does he have the key?' asked Haggitt.

'No. But if all goes to plan; we won't need a key,' Gi whispered.

Gennett crept quietly passed the sleeping soldiers till he reached the spot in the line that he was supposed to be occupying.

'Alright, Gennett?' asked the man sitting next to him.

'Yeah, it's okay, I just needed a pee.'

The other man laid back down and turned over, soon the soft sounds of breathing hanging on the breeze began again.

It seemed that Gennett had only just closed his eyes, when the soldier with the bugle woke everyone. Lots of muffled voices filled the early-morning air, all talking at once. Most were cursing the bugler.

On the other side of the hill, Broosh Marteef silently vowed, that when the ensuing battle commenced, he would kill the bugler first.

'Come on you lot!' du Merde shouted, as he walked along the line of semi-conscious men, and kicking the occasional foot. 'Get your breakfast finished and mount up. I want to get some miles in before it gets too hot!'

Fires got poked, pots clanged, and considering the time of day, the soldiers were now all in a reasonable frame of mind.

Gennett was on duty to look after the wizards today. He stopped at the supply wagon to pick up a couple of bowls of food. He wasn't really bothered what it was, as he knew Gi would turn the grey mush in the bowl into something resembling a five-star meal. As he carried the bowls, it dawned on him that he'd forgotten to mention the two captive wizards to Huddy. *It probably doesn't matter,* he told himself. Then shrugged, and almost lost the wizards' breakfasts.

* * *

13

On the hills to the left of the strung-out column of du Merde's soldiers, two riders were discretely keeping pace with them. One of the riders was a barbarian by the name of Harvey the Bear. Not that he was particularly fierce, it was just the way he greeted everybody with open arms, crushing them to his chest. Fortunately, he knew his own strength and only crushed hard those he didn't like. Needless to say, he was a big and powerful man. He wore the compulsory barbarian bits of leather and animal skins about his person, and some iron bling on his wrists and around his neck. His choice of weapon was a double-sided battle axe. An idea he got from a dwarf that he couldn't hug – Harvey being over six feet tall.

The other rider was Huddy Mincing. He had no bling, but he carried quite an assortment of knives and daggers in the various leather straps that criss-crossed his chest and waist. His weapon of choice was sheathed in one his belts somewhere. The two riders were scouts for Broosh Marteef. Harvey was his chief scout, always keeping an eye out for any sign of trouble. Or something worth stealing. Huddy was also keeping an eye on Gennett.

Harvey kept to the ridge overlooking the column of soldiers, but Huddy had to get ahead of them to leave a sign for Gennett to meet him that night.

He rode hard for about ten minutes, all the time keeping below the skyline, and when he was sure he was far enough ahead, he reined in his horse and dismounted. His usual way of alerting Gennett that he wanted to meet him was to leave a white rock along the trail for Gennett to spot, and hopefully remember to pick up again for future use.

Huddy knew Gennett would be on the left side of the column, so he found a flattish boulder tall enough to stand the white rock on. Satisfied that it was in a noticeable place, he remounted and walked his horse back far enough to be out of sight. Then waited for the soldiers to pass.

Minutes later, as the column of men came in sight around a bend, Huddy mounted and walked his horse back to where he'd left the white rock. It was gone. He always had a warm feeling when things went right.

But Gennett was concerned. He was supposed to meet Huddy the following night. Why had he brought the meeting forward, he wondered.

When Harvey the Bear and Huddy arrived back at the barbarian's camp, they strode purposely to Broosh's tent. They waited, listening for any sounds before they went in. It was quiet, apart from the clinking of crockery, and the sound of a kettle coming to the boil. Then a female voice said, 'Do you take sugar?'

Harvey slapped a hand over his mouth to stifle a laugh that was threatening to explode. Huddy quickly decided they'd better come back in an hour or so. He grabbed Harvey's arm and pulled him away.

Back at the campfire, Huddy poured himself and Harvey a drink. The two men sat and stared into the fire in total silence, hardly daring to think about what they'd just heard, or even look at each other for fear of breaking down into fits of laughter.

After about two hours, the flap on Broosh's tent was slowly drawn aside, and a naked young woman sneaked out, carrying her clothes. 'I don't think she made very good tea,' said Harvey, 'or she'd 'ave been in there all night.'

'I didn't know Broosh liked tea,' remarked Huddy.

'He doesn't. It's a little game he plays, so we don't think he's doin' it,' Harvey grinned.

'Doin' it?' said Huddy. 'Doin' what? I'm sure I heard that girl ask him if he took sugar.'

'She did, and I expect she gave him a couple of spoonfuls too, but judging by the time she was in there, she had no staying power.' Harvey grinned broadly.

Moments later, Broosh came out of his tent, tightening the belt on his loin cloth. 'Ah, you're back!' he called as he walked over to the two men.

31

He sat down between them, causing Huddy to move along a bit. 'Anything happening?' said Broosh, genially.

'We followed the column for a few miles,' said Huddy, 'but there was not much goin' on. I left the rock to let Gennett know I want to see him later tonight, though.'

'What about you, Bear?' Broosh asked the big man.

'I scouted ahead and found a narrow pass, Broosh, with high sides, but not so steep that we can't get down.'

'Any large rocks near the entrance? Anything we can roll in to stop an escape?' asked Broosh.

'Yeah. There's enough laying around to stop *anything* getting out of there,' Harvey assured him.

'Okay,' said Broosh. 'Let's make a plan. How many soldiers are there? Huddy – get the exact numbers when you see Gennett tonight. I also need to know who is in that prison wagon, and if they're worth anything to us.'

'What about the weapons, and the soldiers' wages?' asked Huddy.

'Find out what weapons they have… they may not be any use if they're too heavy. We probably have enough already, but if the opportunity arises to take the supply wagon, we will.'

Harvey had just been listening; now he had something to say. 'I think we should grab the supply wagon, then see what's in it when we get it away from the column.'

'Can you do that, Harvey?' asked Broosh. 'How many men would you need?'

'I saw only two with the wagon. One driving the team, and one guard. Though, I'd expect more to show up when they see us coming for it,' grinned Harvey.

'Right. We'll wait and see what news Huddy brings back later, and if it still looks like a good plan, we'll attack them in the pass.'

* * *

14

In the failing light of evening, Huddy watched from among a group of rocks as the column came to a standstill for the night. Fires were lit, and the aroma of food began to hang in the air. The strongest smell was bacon sandwiches. *Everyone* loves the smell of bacon sandwiches.

When all had quietened down, Gennett slipped away from the camp, found somewhere out of sight and tried his terrible chicken impression again. There was no reply. Huddy was hanging back to see if it drew any attention from the camp before he broke cover. Nothing happened, so he picked up a small pebble and very accurately threw it at Gennett's head. It struck with a dull clonk.

'Damn,' cursed Gennett, almost failing to keep his voice down. 'I wish you wouldn't do that. It stings.'

'Sorry,' Huddy grinned. 'Just letting you know I'm here. Now, what have you got for me? Broosh wants to know exactly how many soldiers there are, and who's in that prison wagon.'

Gennett hesitated. He was still slightly hampered by Gi's hypnotic block, and struggled to get his thoughts in order. 'There are a hundred soldiers,' he began, slowly, 'two drivers and a cook.'

'I didn't know you had a cook,' said Huddy. 'No wonder the food here always smells so good.'

'That's about the extent of it,' said Gennett, ruefully. 'It smells good but it tastes bloody awful. I don't know how he manages it.'

'What's in the small wagon?'

'There are two wizards in there. They seem happy enough, mostly. One's called Gi Mulderbish. Not sure who the other one is.'

'Gi Mulderbish, eh? Name rings a bell – my old mum used to tell me stories about him when I was a kid. He disappeared about twenty years ago.'

'Eighteen, actually,' said Gennett. 'Then, he turned up in the desert a few days ago. du Merde recognized him from an old wanted poster, and took him prisoner. Now we're taking him to Baron Striper, in Gremanos.'

'What for?' asked Huddy.

'du Merde thinks the baron will reward him,' said Gennett.

'Huh. Anything else?'

'Not that I can think of.'

'Right. Get away from the camp tomorrow night, and wait for me to throw another stone at you. Something's going on.' The meeting over, Huddy disappeared into the night. Gennett went back into the camp to locate his helmet before their next meeting.

* * *

15

Daybreak in Broosh's camp, and one by one the barbarians were waking up. It was chilly up on the hill today, and their breath was visible as they breathed the morning air. Broosh was sitting closest to the fire with his thick cloak wrapped around his shoulders. It wasn't long before Huddy joined him, then Harvey the Bear.

Huddy related what he'd gleaned from Gennett the previous night, and Broosh sat quietly thinking about what he would do. After a few moments, he asked, 'Anybody got a stick?'

Everyone in earshot hung back.

'Oh, alright. Has anybody got anything I can draw with?'

Huddy reluctantly offered Broosh his bluntest dagger.

'Bout time you sharpened this one, Huddy,' said Broosh. 'It's not nice to stab somebody with a blunt dagger.'

'It's the one I keep for drawing in the dust,' said Huddy, chancing a little humour, which went unnoticed.

'That's good, then. Because that's exactly what I propose to do with it,' said Broosh. 'Have you scouted the area up around the pass, Harvey?'

'Yeah... it's narrow at the entrance. Just about enough room for a wagon. Then it opens out and there's enough room for soldiers to ride about ten abreast. Trouble is, it stays that wide all the way through.'

'How steep are the sides?' asked Broosh.

'The left side's not very steep, you could probably ride the horses along and down, but they would struggle to get back up. The right side's like a wall, straight up, sheer cliff. Can't utilize that at all.'

'Hmm,' breathed Broosh. 'Are there any boulders on top of the cliff side?'

'A lot, but not many big ones.'

'Well, if there are enough, we could get some men up there to wait for the column to pass by, then push the boulders over behind them. Hem them in,' said Broosh.

'Then, with some men already up ahead, we can come at them from front and side.'

Huddy had another idea. With a finger, he drew two oblong boxes in the narrow neck. 'What about waiting till the wagons are just through the narrow opening, blocking it? Then push the boulders down behind 'em. That would cut off the soldiers following behind, and we'd have less of 'em to fight to take the wagons.'

The Bear liked that idea. But Broosh stared into the remains of the fire for a moment. 'That seems like it would work. We should outnumber the soldiers quite safely then. Oh, and one other thing, Huddy. Do you know whereabouts in the column that bugler rides? I really want to kill him,' Broosh grinned.

'I'll make a point of finding him for you,' said Huddy.

'Now, who's in the other wagon? Do we know yet?'

'Yes,' said Huddy. 'Two wizards. They're being transported to Gremanos. One is Gi Mulderbish, I don't know the other one.'

Broosh looked slightly taken aback. 'Did you say, *Gi Mulderbish*? Wow! My mother used to tell me stories about him when I was a kid!' said Broosh, with a wide smile. 'Well, men. Gi Mulderbish will be liberated tomorrow!'

He reached down to the rough drawing and scraped aside the dirt in the wide length of the pass. 'Once we've dealt with the soldiers here, we can take the wagons on through and out. And we should have enough men to hold the exit long enough to get both wagons away.'

'Excellent.' said the Bear.

Huddy smiled. He thought it would work like clockwork.

'Right, Huddy. Get back down there and tell Gennett what's going on. He'll have to quietly defect as soon as the fighting starts.'

'I'll have him out long before then, Broosh.'

*

Huddy followed the column at a safe distance for the rest of the day. He kept to the side of them. He'd tried following from behind, but found he was eating dust all day, and whilst he could not be seen, he might be heard coughing and choking from a considerable distance.

That evening when the last of the campfires died away, Huddy crept into the soldiers' camp to look for Gennett. He found him sitting by the embers of a dying fire. 'Gennett...' he whispered, trying not to spook him. 'Get your stuff, you're leaving. Come on.'

'Stuff? What stuff? I ain't got no stuff,' said Gennett, a little irate.

'Well, just come then, or you might get killed.'

'What? Is Broosh going to attack?'

'Yeah, in the morning, when the column gets into the pass up ahead,' said Huddy. 'Now, get up and move!' he hissed, urgently.

They slipped unnoticed from the camp.

'Didn't they put anyone on watch tonight?' said Huddy, who couldn't believe how easily he'd got in and out.

'Yeah me,' said Gennett.

* * *

16

High on the hill overlooking the pass, Broosh Marteef and some of his barbarians watched the column of soldiers and the two wagons enter the pass. Things were quiet for a short time while Broosh's men waited for the second wagon to enter the pass's narrow neck.

When Broosh was sure the second wagon was in, he gave the signal to start the avalanche. Small rocks were kicked out from beneath the pile of larger rocks, and began tumbling down the steep slope towards the soldiers at the rear of the column. Small stones rained down on the soldiers, catching them on their heads and shoulders.

They looked up to see what was happening and caught sight of some barbarians levering a rather large boulder over the edge. The soldiers rode on regardless. Except one who saw there was no way they'd get far enough through to avoid the rocks with the wagons slowing them down.

'Turn back, men!' he shouted. 'It's an ambush!' As the boulder began crashing and bouncing down the slope, there was panic as the men turned their horses in the narrow entrance and charged out. The rock shook the ground barely inches from the hooves of the rider who'd raised the alarm. 'Everyone alright?!' he called, as he joined his shaken companions.

'Just a few scratches, that's all,' said one, speaking for all, a little breathlessly.

The soldier whose quick wits had saved the men was Fox Loer. When one of them related what had just happened to their superiors, Fox would probably get a medal for this day's work.

'How many are we?' he called.

'Only twenty, Fox,' said one, who'd taken a quick tally to see what their strength was.

'Okay. We need to join the others, fast.' He studied the area around the pass.

'The entrance is partially blocked, and we'll be easy targets if we try to pick our way through. We don't have time to circle round. We need to check out the terrain from up there before we do anything else. Can one of you climb up that cliff and take a look?'

'I'll do it,' said Sivad Snod, a young soldier Fox regarded highly.

'Thanks, Sivad. Be careful, there might be more of them up there.'

Sivad unbuckled his sword belt and passed it to Fox. He spat on both palms and started to climb the steep face. It took the young soldier about fifteen minutes, and when he pulled himself onto the clifftop, much to his relief, he was alone. He stood and surveyed the scene along the pass, and on either side. *Now, where are we*, he thought. *Steep wall this side. Can't get horses up that way*. To his left, there was what looked like a manageable slope about half a mile back. *That could be okay to get the men up here. Then what?*

There was no other feasible route. He turned and walked back to where he'd climbed up. *Hmm. This is going to be tricky*, he thought. He sat on the edge, and turned around. Gingerly, he put a foot down hoping for some sort of ledge or outcrop to stand on. Taking his time, and carefully picking his way, Sivad reached the bottom safely with just a few superficial cuts and grazes on his hands and knees.

'What could you see?' asked Fox, handing Sivad his sword back.

'There's a slope about half a mile along, Fox. It looks like the only way we'll get up there. And there's what looks like a slope down beyond the pass, about a mile in the direction the rest of the column's headed. But I couldn't see where it comes out. I don't think we'll catch them in time to be any help, though.'

Fox was thinking. 'Is Reza here?'

'No, Fox. He got trapped on the other side,' said one of the other soldiers.

'Did you see what was happening on the other side, Sivad?'

'No, but I could hear the sounds of battle.' He slapped a fist hard into the palm of his hand, frustrated not to be a part of it.

* * *

17

On the other side of the rockfall, the soldiers rushed to defend the wagons. But too late. Harvey the Bear, and several other barbarians had already overpowered the drivers and were now charging the wagons through the lines. More barbarians were riding down the hill. Some tumbled, but being skilled riders, they held on to their horse's reins and remounted.

At the bottom of the hill, Huddy Mincing charged forward slashing from side to side with his longest dagger. It was a wonder he didn't hurt anybody. He set about knocking soldiers off their horses, helping to clear the way for the prison wagon. Neither he nor Broosh wanted any harm to come to their prized wizards. As Huddy got closer, he saw that Gennett the Weasel had the reins, and was urging the horse on as fast as it could go. Inside the wagon, Gi and Haggitt hung on for dear life, as the wheels bounced over stones and dropped into ruts as they were thrown from side to side.

The pursuing barbarians raced as fast as their horses could carry them to reach the end of the pass before the soldiers. But Broosh already had enough men blocking the exit. His problem was that the wagons might still be among the soldiers when they got to his men.

It looked like Broosh and his barbarians at the far end, would have to change the plan slightly. He told half the men, about seventy of them, to stay where they were, and not to let the soldiers through. Or he'd be very annoyed. The other sixty or so were to go with Broosh, confront the soldiers, and force them away from the wagons. This led to much fighting. du Merde came charging to the front of his men, and tried to barge his way through. But he met an equally determined Broosh, who caught him a glancing blow to the head, knocking the Centurion off his horse. This wrong-footed the soldiers momentarily, who didn't expect their leader to go down so quickly.

The bugler blew the recall, and the soldiers retreated to rally around their flag.

'Where's Fox?' asked Reza Lock.

'He got trapped on the other side of the avalanche,' somebody answered.

'Damn!' Reza cursed. 'Where's du Merde?'

'He got hit by that big bugger with the double-handed sword.'

'Is he dead?' Reza asked.

'Don't know,' was the non-committal reply.

'Okay… In that case, until we know if he's still alive, we need a temporary Sergeant. Any offers?'

Nobody answered, as each man wondered if he was up to it, or the extra pay was worth it. Then, a voice at the back said, 'Why don't you do it, Reza. All the men respect you.'

This was met with a mumble of approval.

'Okay, but only till we get back to the barracks. Understood?' said Reza. This was also met with approval. 'Right, first I need a man to climb those rocks to see what's happening, where everyone is, and how many are still alive. Then report back to me.'

In the pass, the fighting was fierce. Soldiers and barbarians were locked in a battle that flowed one way then the other. Not that many on either side were getting seriously injured, but Broosh was getting impatient. 'Look, men, we need to get this done! Now! Get those soldiers away from these wagons and get them out of here. Try not to kill anybody, but if you must, then do it!'

The nearest soldiers heard Broosh's call to his men to go all out. One, more senior and with more sense than the others shouted, 'Retreat, men! Leave the wagons and get back down the pass!' They didn't need telling twice. Most of the soldiers had suffered cuts and bruises to some degree, which was acceptable, but if it looked like somebody might actually get killed, they knew they weren't getting paid enough. *No way.* They galloped back to where Reza was holding court and deciding what to do next. Fox was missing, du Merde might be dead, and a quarter of the men were unaccounted for.

*

Fox was still stuck on the other side of the rock slide, having discovered his options for joining the others had turned out to be about zero. All he'd managed was to travel a short and circuitous distance parallel to the pass.

'I need a volunteer to get up that hill and see what's going on.'

'I can do that, Sarge.'

Fox looked around. The voice was unfamiliar. Badger Hercop stepped forward in front of him. Fox looked the man up and down.

'How did you get in here? You're a bloody barbarian!'

'No. Not now, Sarge. I'm a changed man.'

'No, you're not, you're still dressed like a barbarian.'

'Yes, Sarge. But I want to be a soldier. You know, wiv a fancy 'at wiv feathers in, and clothes I didn't have to nick off a washing line, or skin off an animal all messy-like. And I don't want to worry where me next meal's coming from, anymore.'

'Alright, I'll give you a chance. Are you freelance? Or one of Broosh Marteef's regulars?'

'I'm not one of Broosh's men… so I must be freelance, I suppose.'

'It means you work for yourself,' Fox enlightened him.

'Okay,' said Badger. 'What would you like me up that hill for, Sarge?'

'I need to how many men I still have left alive in the pass, and whether the fighting has stopped.' Fox couldn't see anything from where he was. He could hear a lot of shouting, but there were no screams.

The barbarians had captured the wagons and were escorting them out of the pass, circling round to the higher ground that led back to Broosh's camp.

About an hour later, the triumphant horde finally drove into their camp. There were a few women waiting for them, in case there was any loot to share. There would normally have been more women, but they'd seen the column of soldiers heading in their direction, and didn't rate the barbarian's chances very highly.

The barbarians driving the wagons parked them together. Broosh and Huddy, went first to the prison wagon, keen to meet their childhood hero. 'Huddy, give me your blunt dagger, will you? I want to force this door.' Huddy didn't argue. He wasn't a small man, but Broosh was bigger and probably had the strength to tear the door off with his bare hands if need be.

Gi and Haggitt were sitting either side of the door. They heard the sound of the dagger working on the hasp holding the padlock. But for all Broosh's strength, and all his huffing and puffing, it wasn't going to break anytime soon.

'Do you think he might need help, Father?' said Haggitt.

'Probably,' whispered Gi. 'But he looks like he's having so much fun, it seems a shame to interfere.'

Haggitt wondered what on Crett was holding things up. Then he noticed a slight blue luminescence around the lock, and gave Gi a look. 'You're deliberately making it difficult for him. Why?'

Gi grinned. 'Just trying to gauge how strong he is. I'll let him have it in a minute. I promise.'

Haggitt had seen enough. He snapped his fingers and the heavy padlock snapped open and fell on Broosh's foot. *Oops.*

'I told you I would see to it,' said Gi. 'Now you've probably upset him.'

'He's just rescued us, Father. I thought it bad manners to torment him.'

Broosh yanked the door open with such force, it slammed into the side of the wagon and bounced back. 'Ow... I didn't expect that,' said Broosh, rubbing a painful red welt forming on the side of his face.

'Are you alright, Mr. Mulderbish?' said Huddy.

'Yes... thank you,' chorused the two wizards.

Huddy reached into the wagon, and pulled the wooden steps down. Gi poked his head out and looked around. His gaze fell upon Broosh. 'Who are you?' he demanded.

Huddy stepped forward and held out his hand. 'This is Broosh Marteef, our chief,' he pointed at the big man. 'And I'm Huddy Mincing.' He bowed slightly.

Gi stood in the doorway at the top of the steps. 'Are we prisoners?' he asked, before moving.

Broosh came forward. 'Certainly not, sir. We are your liberators,' he said, grinning broadly.

Gi descended the steps, saying, 'This is my son, Haggitt.'

Broosh held out his hand to greet Haggitt, and the younger wizard accepted it grudgingly, 'Nice to meet you, I think.'

Gi looked around. 'Which one of you was driving that wagon?' he asked, pointing behind him.

'Me, sir. Gennett the Weasel, at your service.' He stepped forward eagerly.

Gi looked him up and down, then said, 'Don't you ever drive like that again when I'm in there, young man, or I'll turn you into a real weasel!'

Gennett's chin dropped.

Broosh and Huddy laughed. 'Come on gentlemen, let's drink!'

They all sat around the camp fire discussing the day's events, while some of the men poured horse beer into large horns, and others were cooking a large bird on a spit over a roaring fire. It was one of those fires that cooks the outside over-efficiently while leaving the inside as raw as when they found it.

Huddy tore a leg off the bird and offered it to Gi. He took it and eyed it critically. 'Where do you get turkeys in a desert?' he wondered.

'I haven't got the faintest idea,' said Broosh. 'That's a vulture. We found it by that dead horse we passed on the way up here.'

'Hmm...' breathed Gi. 'It's not half bad,' he said, enthusiastically.

Haggitt was looking a bit green.

'My old mum used to tell me stories about you, when I was a kid,' said Broosh, 'She thought you were one of the nicest men she'd ever met.'

Haggitt nearly choked, then said, 'Did she get out much?'

'Probably not,' sighed Broosh. 'But then, there were a lot of us to look after. You know, what with dad being away all the time, fighting in some war somewhere.'

Haggitt had to ask. 'If your father was away all the time, how come there was so many of you at home?'

'I always wondered about that,' said Broosh, and turned to look back at Gi. 'Would you know anything about that, Mr. Mulderbish?'

'Call me, Gi,' said Gi. 'What's your mum's name?'

'They call her, Kirsten,' said Broosh.

'Kirsten?' said Gi, thinking aloud. 'Are there seven of you in your family?'

'That's right!' said Broosh. 'Do you remember her?'

'Er... yes. I remember her,' said Gi, mentally reminiscing those heady days. 'I helped her when Baron Striper burnt down your little hovel.'

'What? The *bastard*!' said Broosh. 'She never told me!'

Gi was still thinking about the cosy, warm nights he'd spent with Kirsten in that hovel, and he sighed deeply.

'Want some more horse beer?' asked Broosh.

'No. I don't think so, thanks,' said Gi. 'It tastes more like horse *piss* to me.'

Broosh looked at him wide eyed. 'Do you know, Gi? I've never tried *that*. No wonder people looked up to you.'

Gi didn't expect that response. 'Don't try it,' Gi told him. 'It will give you an upset stomach.' In fact, Gi had no idea what it might do to their stomachs, but he thought this lot looked daft enough to try and find out. He finished his vulture leg and tossed the remains into the fire, sending a shower of sparks into the night sky.

'Time to sleep, Haggitt,' said Gi.

Haggitt looked around, 'Where?'

'It looks like we're back in the wagon,' said Gi. 'But at least the door won't be locked tonight. Not that it ever was,' he added under his breath.

Haggitt went up the steps. *Gods, look at the state of this place*, he thought, looking inside the wagon. He raised both hands, and muttered a spell he used at home sometimes. The wooden benches that served as seats, turned into a pair of single bunk beds, with warm blankets and fancy matching covers. Curtains appeared at the windows. A small patterned rug appeared on the floor between the beds. He cast another spell and created a nice wooden chest, then conjured up some new, clean clothes to put in it. He just hoped the magic wouldn't wear off before they reached a proper place to stay. Oh, and the final touch of luxury, a pot to piss in under each bed.

Haggitt sat on a bed and swung his feet up. Almost immediately, he was asleep.

Gi said his farewells, climbed the steps and peered inside. 'Hmm, this looks alright,' he said, admiring his son's handiwork. 'Did you do this, Haggitt?'

Haggitt stirred, and opened one eye. 'Yeah,' he drawled. 'Do you like it?'

'Like it? It's bloody fantastic. Hang on I'll be back in a minute!'

Gi went outside and looked around. 'Oi!' he yelled. 'Where's Gennett the Weasel?'

'Over 'ere, sir,' Gennett replied, somewhat quieter than Gi.

'Come 'ere. I want to show you something,' said Gi.

Gennett came forward.

'Up the steps, if you don't mind.'

Gennett climbed the steps, and peered inside the wagon. 'Wow,' was all he could think of. 'You've sure done it up nice.' Then he saw Haggitt. 'Is he dead, sir?'

'No,' said Gi. 'He's sleeping. Now, young Weasel, you will be my driver. And I want you to drive very carefully. I don't want this lot buggered up. Understand?'

Weasel was taken aback at first, but he warmed to the idea.

'Er… there's something else,' said Gi. 'I want you to change the front of this wagon so it can be pulled by two horses. I think one might get a bit overworked. Can you do that?'

'I'll see to it while you sleep, sir,' said Weasel, cheerfully.

'Good. And now that's sorted out, you can call me Gi, or Master. No more sir. Alright?'

Weasel grinned. 'I like 'Master',' he said, and went off to find someone to help adapt the wagon.

* * *

Gi and Haggitt had been really tired, and slept soundly. Being in the thick of yesterday's battle was draining, even for wizards with some protective magic. The camp was still sleeping when they woke up and looked outside. A few fires were still glowing in the half-light of the early morning. It was about an hour into the sunrise, but in a desert there's not much birdsong. Well, none in fact.

Haggitt stretched and went down the steps. He walked a few paces and was surprised to run into Gennett, who seemed to be up to something.

'What's going on here?' asked Haggitt.

'Ah, mornin', sir,' said Gennett.

'It's Haggitt.'

'Right, sir. Haggitt it is, then. Master Gi asked me to do some alterations,' he said, leading Haggitt to the front of the wagon. 'I hope he likes 'em.'

Gi joined them right then. 'Perfect,' he announced. 'Now, where can we get another horse?'

'We're going to sort out the supply wagon horses when Broosh gets up, Master. It's got a team of six. I'm sure he'll let you have one,' Gennett assured him. 'And by the way – I can't believe what you've done inside. It looks... er,' he was struggling, 'posh?' he added, lamely.

As if on cue, Broosh emerged from his tent. 'Huddy! Where are you?' he called.

Huddy had company and was hoping for a lie in. 'Oh, no, not already,' he moaned. 'Sorry, my love, I've got to go. Help yourself to anything you need.' He kissed her lightly on the forehead, slipped on a light vest and ducked out of the tent.

The girl searched around the tent. 'That's just bloody typical,' she moaned. 'No money, as usual.' She put her shift dress on over her head and slithered out under the back of the tent. After a few steps, she felt something heavy swinging in her pocket. Upon inspection, she found it was a gold coin. She smiled, and almost skipped back to the tent that the camp followers used.

'Ah, there you are Huddy. Get Gi and Bear. Let's see what's in this wagon.'

'Before we start, Broosh,' said Gennett. 'I need another horse for the wizard's wagon.'

'Go see what's there,' said Broosh, 'and take your pick. I've got the one I want.' He was in a rare good mood this morning.

Harvey the Bear climbed into the supply wagon. It wasn't long before he'd raised the canvases on each side. 'Hello, what have we got here?'

A small man was hiding amongst the boxes. 'Don't hurt me,' he pleaded. 'I'm not a soldier. I'm the cook.'

Harvey was impressed. 'How'd you manage to stay in there, the way I was driving?'

'It wasn't easy. You were driving like a bloody maniac,' said the cook.

The Bear grinned. 'Broosh, I've found a cook among the supplies!'

Broosh was smiling. 'Help him down, then. There's work for him to do. We don't want any passengers.'

Harvey the Bear reached out. 'Give me your hand, cook, and let's get you out of there.'

The cook was surprised how gentle Harvey the Bear was. He felt himself being lifted effortlessly into the air and placed gently down.

'You'd better tell me which of those boxes has breakfast in it,' said Bear.

Bear clambered into the wagon, and grabbed one of the boxes the cook pointed out. Broosh took it off him and handed it to the cook. 'If you poison any of my men, I will personally kill you,' Broosh threatened. 'And if you poison me, Bear will kill you. Understand?'

Bear grinned. 'I don't think he's likely to, Broosh.'

'What else is in there, Bear? Anything useful?' asked Huddy.

'I think you'd better get up here and have a look at some of these weapons. The crossbows look good, but they may be too heavy.'

'Okay,' said Bear, 'give 'em to the bigger men.'

'The bows are long,' said Huddy. 'For archers defending battlements, and long-range stuff. Not much use for us.'

Broosh leaned on the side of the wagon, looking in. 'Take the strings off 'em, they'll be useful. And the arrows. We never seem to have enough arrows.'

'There's hundreds of 'em in 'ere, Broosh,' Huddy complained. 'I don't know where we're gonna to put 'em all.'

Broosh ignored him. 'Get some more supplies down here, the cook's waiting.'

'Right, chief. Cook! Come and get what else you need,' said Huddy.

Broosh was still scanning the contents of the wagon. 'Have you found the gold yet?'

'Not yet,' said the Bear, shifting things about.

'You won't find any gold in there,' said Gi.

'And why is that?' asked Broosh.

'I've got it in *my* wagon,' said Gi, sounding rather pleased with himself.

* * *

19

Down in the pass, some soldiers were stirring. There were no fires, no cooking smells, and worst of all, no cook.

Outside the pass, cut off by the rockfall, Fox Loer and his men stowed their bedrolls in their saddlebags in readiness to move off. Fox had been annoyed when he turned in for the night, but he'd slept well, and he was his usual calm, assured self. He wasn't the sort to stay angry for long, and it was only carelessness and unfairness that got him really worked up. The men had great respect for him.

Corporal Sivad Snod, had described a likely way around the fallen rocks at the entrance to the pass, and Fox wanted to be up and on the march again. He'd spotted Badger Hercop, the renegade barbarian he'd sent clambering over the barrier, peering over from the far side, checking on him and his men. Badger hadn't returned yet, so Fox decided not to wait, but to follow Corporal Snod's directions.

There was a narrow track about half a mile off. From there, they should be able to ride up the long slope to the ridge at the top of the pass and follow it along. He wasn't too concerned about Badger Hercop, he'd changed his allegiance before, perhaps he'd done it again.

Fox asked two of the men to scout ahead for barbarians, and any signs of life below in the pass. An hour had passed when one of the soldiers returned.

'What news, soldier?' called Fox.

'There's a few horses wandering around down there, Sarge, and a few men sitting around, I can't hear what anyone's saying, though, or tell how many, as they're sitting close under the cliff.'

'Anybody killed?' Fox asked.

'Not that we could see, Sarge. There's no bodies lying around.'

'Thanks, soldier.' Fox stood up in his stirrups and looked over his shoulder. 'I want to pick up the pace, men. There might be injured men down there.'

An hour's ride further on, parallel to the pass, they found the way down that Sivad had anticipated from his reconnaissance. It was manageable, if a little steep. They dismounted and led the horses, and once all the men and horses were safely down, Fox called them closer. 'Get your horses in the shade, men. It's going to get quite hot soon.'

'What do you think we should do, Fox?' asked Sivad. 'Wait and see who comes out, or go in and look for 'em?'

'We'll go in when the sun moves and it's cooler for us and the horses. With…'

They turned to see Badger Hercop dismounting.

'I asked that stupid barbarian to climb that rock pile into the pass to see if anyone was still alive,' said Fox. 'I thought he would have had the sense to carry on to the other end and meet us. Not climb all the way back over and then catch us up – the long way round!'

Sivad grinned, thinking *what a prize.*

Badger was quite pleased with himself, but his report added nothing to what they already knew.

Fox shaded his eyes and looked out across the baked, sterile landscape of rock and shale. The sun had hardly moved. 'Send a couple of men ahead, Sivad, hopefully they'll find whose left and let them know we're coming.'

Fox was still sitting in the shade watching, when Sivad returned. 'You know,' said Fox. 'I might have under-estimated that barbarian.'

'How's that?' asked Sivad.

'How did he get a horse over those boulders? And, where did he get it?'

*

The two soldiers picked for scouting were Maurice and Brian, a couple of seasoned regulars in the Black-Guard. They mounted up and started walking their horses back along the pass, keeping to any shade they could find. All was quiet apart from the vultures calling as they circled overhead. This was not a good sign. When the pair were out of sight, all Fox could do, was hope they made contact soon.

It wasn't long before the scouts found a few men sitting in a circle on the ground.

Maurice, rode up and dismounted. 'Anybody hurt?' he asked. When the seated soldiers ignored him, he asked again. 'Is anybody hurt?!'

'I've broke me finger,' complained one.

'I really don't care about your finger,' said Maurice. 'Perhaps I should've worded that better. Does anybody think they're going to die anytime soon?' he corrected himself. 'No? Good. Then get your horses and come with me.'

'That's gonna take a while. The buggers bolted yesterday when those barbarians came down on us. Nobody said I would 'ave to fight barbarians when I signed up,' he moaned.

Maurice was getting annoyed. 'Look, there's enough of you to round up a few horses, so get on with it!'

'Are you going to 'elp?' said the soldier.

'Nope. You lost 'em. You get 'em back.'

'I'll go and see if I can find any more.' said Brian.

'Okay, Bri. I'll get this lot up off their fat backsides and get 'em moving out.'

Catching the horses was not as simple for them as Maurice expected. The more they chased, the more they ran. Either these solders were not trying, or just plain stupid. He favoured the latter explanation. 'Do you know your horse's names?!' he yelled at them.

'Course I do,' said one. 'It's called, 'orse'.'

'Well, call it then!' yelled Maurice, in exasperation.

'Oh, yeah...' said the man. He called. It didn't work. Then they all started calling their horses, and the noise spooked them even more.

Fearing they might charge off down the pass – or worse, out of the pass – Maurice spurred his horse into the milling strays. They shied away at first, but when Maurice slowed his calm horse among them, the animals sensed it, quietened down, and followed.

'Grab your mounts!' shouted Maurice. 'And head back that way. Fox Loer's up there waiting for you!'

At the mention of Fox's name, the soldiers got to their feet and promptly caught their horses' reins. They didn't want to be on the wrong side of Fox. Likeable as he was, Fox didn't tolerate unsoldierly conduct from anyone. Maurice's report wasn't going to be good as things stood, so best not to make it worse by hanging about.

A few minutes further into the pass, Brian met some soldiers limping towards him. He reined in his horse. 'Who's in charge?'

'Well, we ain't got nobody in charge now,' said one man.

'Well, who *was* in charge?'

'Catscart du Merde!' he shouted.

Of course... thought Brian. *That pompous fool.* 'Where is he now, then?'

'He got 'it on the 'ead by a bloody great barbarian.'

'Is he dead?'

'No such luck, mate. He's got a bitta blood on 'is 'ead, an 'e finks e's gonna die. But it was just a blow from a big sword... it's rammed 'is 'elmet on so tight, 'e's gonna need a crowbar to get it off.'

Brian resisted a smirk for a second, but then joined the rest of the men in the hilarity. 'Okay men, that's enough. Can you catch your own horses, or do you want my help?'

'No,' said a senior soldier. 'We can manage, son. You go and find Reza. He's back in there somewhere.'

'Right,' said Brian. 'When you're ready, Fox is that way. I wouldn't keep him waiting too long, if I were you.' He smiled, and rode deeper into the pass.

As he rode, he met some other riders, and pointed them in the direction of Fox. When he met a few more, he was thinking that there didn't appear to be any serious casualties. That was good news; Fox would be pleased. He turned a bend in the pass and saw a larger group of men standing around listening to one man, who was standing on a rock. Brian recognised the stature and long plait of blonde hair of Reza Lock. But where was du Merde?

One or two soldiers acknowledged Brian as he approached. They were listening to Reza. 'Men... you have to catch your horses. We could be days from the nearest town,' he paused and looked about.

'A few of you have got your horses back, so you need to help get the rest. We can't sit here all day. We need to catch up with the supply wagon.' Then he saw Brian. 'Who are you soldier?' he called, when he saw Brian.

'The name's Brian. I got cut off when the barbarians blocked the entrance to the pass.'

'Just you?' Reza asked.

'No, I'm with Fox and some others. We rode around and came over that ridge.' Brian pointed to the top of the cliff. 'Fox sent me to see if there was anyone left.'

Reza stepped down off his rock and approached Brian, he walked on passed a few yards and beckoned him to follow. When they were far enough from the others, Reza said, 'How many are you?'

'Only twenty.'

'I count twenty-five here,' said Reza, glumly.

'There are some more ahead, around the next bend,' said Brian. 'I don't think those barbarians had any intentions of killing us. They just wanted our stuff.'

'You think we got off lightly, then?' said Reza, quietly.

'Well, no. They took the wagons.'

Reza swore under his breath, at the loss of the supplies. 'No need to worry about the prisoners, though,' he said. 'They'll find their own way back. Gi Mulderbish won't stay with the barbarians any longer than he wants to. We were only kidding ourselves that he was our prisoner.'

The horses hadn't strayed far. It was the same problem Maurice had dealt with, and a little cooperation and co-ordination solved it. Most of the soldiers were now on horseback. 'Will you get your men in line now, sir? Fox is waiting,' said Brian.

Reza returned to his rock and called the men around him. 'Men, the barbarians have taken the supplies, so we have to get going right now. Brian here tells me nobody's been seriously hurt, and Fox is waiting at the end of the pass. One more thing... I want a volunteer to look after du Merde, till we can get his helmet off.' This was met with silence. 'Where is he, by the way?'

'He's a bit embarrassed, Reza. He's keeping out of sight,' said one of the men.

'You'd better come out, du Merde!' said Reza, his raised voice echoing off the high walls. 'We're leaving now.'

'Alright. I'm coming,' grumbled du Merde, emerging from a cleft in the rock, as if from nowhere. The black hood of his cloak was pulled over his helmeted head. 'One-word Sergeant, and it's the stockade.'

'We don't have a stockade, du Merde, we're in a desert.'

'Get my horse. Let's get out of here,' sighed du Merde. Fortunately, his horse was among those rounded up.

'Are you in command, now Reza?' Brian asked.

'It would appear I've been saddled with that honour,' said Reza. 'At least, until du Merde is up to it again.'

The soldiers formed into two short columns and followed Reza and Brian along the pass. Around the bend they met Maurice. He was alone, and walking his horse back towards Fox in the shade that now extended to half the width of the pass.

'I see you've found the last of 'em,' Maurice observed.

'You've sent the others on?'

'Yes, they're all safely with the rest by now,' said Maurice. Then he noticed the man beside his friend. 'Is that you Reza? Thank the gods! Fox is looking for you.'

Ahead of them, Badger Hercop, in his assumed role of chief scout, rode into the camp, and reined in his horse in front of Fox. 'The rest of yer men will be 'ere in a minute,' he announced, making it sound like it was all his doing. He was about to ride off again when Fox stopped him.

Fox wanted to ask the ex-barbarian about his return. 'I saw you climb over those boulders at the other end, Badger. You were on foot. How'd you get a horse back over? Sling it over your shoulder?'

'No, Fox,' he said, as if it needed denying. 'I've known this place since I was a kid. When I got over, I could see the men were okay and there were lots of loose horses milling round. So, I caught me-self one and walked 'im back through a cave I know in the pass that comes out about half a mile back up the road. I'm a bit pissed you didn't wait for me, though.'

Fox half grinned. 'I must admit, I didn't think I'd ever see you again.'

'I told you, I'm a changed man,' said Badger, feeling slightly hurt.

'But why didn't you tell me there was a cave?' asked Fox. 'We wouldn't have risked life and limb climbing that cliff.'

'Excuse me, sir,' he said, by way of explanation. 'You asked for a volunteer to go over the rocks, and I was trying to be a good soldier, like.'

'Yes, but...' Fox decided to leave it at that. 'I take it you know this area well, then?'

'Yeah, it can't have changed much in twenty years.'

'Were you with the barbarians when they attacked?' asked Fox, pointedly.

'Yeah,' said Badger, 'but it wasn't me that pushed the rocks down. I was gonna sneak off when the fighting started and join the soldiers, but I slipped on the way down, banged me 'ead and landed on the wrong side of the rock pile.'

'I don't know why,' said Fox. 'But I believe you. And we could do with a guide who knows the area.'

'That would be me,' said Badger, quick on the uptake, and seeming to grow a couple of inches. 'What's the pay like?' he asked, hardly missing a beat.

'The going rate. But the wagons have been stolen, so, pay's on hold till we get them back,' Fox explained.

'Not much incentive, then, is there?' said Badger, then after some serious thought, he added, 'Okay... I'll do it.'

'Good man,' said Fox. 'We'll kit you out when we get to the barracks. Now, stay here while I meet the men coming in.'

It wasn't long before Reza and the rest of the stragglers arrived. du Merde, whilst still the commanding officer, had lost his nerve along with any respect he may have had from his men. The command was now held by the two men most qualified for it. Their choice of second officers was automatic, too – they chose themselves. Sivad Snod, Brian and Maurice.

Badger was made an honorary soldier on eventual full pay, and formally introduced to the men so he wasn't mistaken for the enemy. He tried to smile at his new colleagues, but they were justifiably wary.

The fact that Badger had a horse was still worrying Fox. If Badger had found it in the pass, and all the soldiers had mounts, then someone had to be missing.

'Any ideas, Brian?' asked Fox, when he expressed his thoughts.

'The cook was taken with the supply wagon,' said Brian. 'But I didn't see anyone else taken.'

'I think I know who's gone,' said Maurice. 'I saw a soldier on the prison wagon and he let his horse run free. I thought he was trying to stop them taking it, but now I reckon he was helping them. I think he must have been one of them all along.'

'Got a name?' asked Reza.

'They called him Gennett the Weasel, sir,' said Sivad.

'Well, if that's not a barbarian name, I don't know what is,' said Fox.

'Come to think of it,' said Brian, 'I did see him wandering on the edge of camp at night a couple of times, and he looked a bit shifty when I challenged him.'

'Seems we both had a defector in our midst,' said Fox. 'We've swapped Weasel for Badger.'

Reza responded with a pained expression. 'Right, everyone, I think our next move is we track these barbarians down and get our supplies back.'

'What about the wizards?' said Fox.

'If we can get into their camp and get some of our stuff back, the wizards may follow. I know Gi Mulderbish wants to get back to Gremanos for some reason.'

* * *

20

'Why have you got the gold?' said Broosh.

'Think about it...' said Gi. 'Who's gonna look in a prison wagon? Not only that, it has the only door with a lock on it.'

'Okay,' said Broosh, 'let's see what there is, shall we?'

Gi shrugged. 'I suppose so.'

'Well, aren't you interested?'

'Not really,' said Gi. 'This desert is seriously lacking in any places to spend it.'

Broosh grinned, and marched over to the prison wagon. Haggitt was sitting on his bed when they arrived.

'What's going on?' asked Haggitt, when Gi and the barbarian poked their heads in.

'Broosh wants the box with the gold in it,' said Gi.

'What? I thought it was in the supply wagon. I haven't got any boxes of gold in here,' Haggitt assured him.

'What's that, then?' said Broosh, pointing at a wooden chest under Haggitt's bed.

'That's got my clean clothes in it.'

'Pass it down,' said Broosh, suspiciously. 'I don't believe you.'

Haggitt dragged the chest out from under the bed and onto the top step of the wagon. When Broosh tried to move it, he found it a lot heavier than he expected. He left it on the step. 'Unlock it,' he demanded.

'It's not locked,' said Haggitt. 'I didn't anticipate anybody wanting to steal my clothes.' He took hold of the lid and lifted it up. 'Satisfied?' he said, when Broosh saw the neatly folded clothes and checked under them.

Gi was as surprised as Broosh. He'd noticed the box on their journey and assumed his son was one step ahead of everyone. But apparently not. 'It must be in the other wagon,' said Gi.

Broosh slammed the lid down and walked off. He vaulted into the supply wagon and started tearing the boxes open. 'Bear!' he yelled. 'Get over here. Now!'

Bear came running, and although he wasn't summoned, Huddy ran with him.

'What's wrong?' asked Bear.

'I can't find the gold!' snapped Broosh. 'Help me open these boxes! And check the weight… some of 'em may have false bottoms!'

The three men started to take the boxes apart. After a fruitless search, they sat in the bottom of the wagon looking at one another. Nobody spoke.

It was the Bear who eventually broke the silence. 'Perhaps they weren't carrying any gold, Broosh.'

'They must be,' moaned Broosh. 'They wouldn't be going to Gremanos just with supplies.' He put his head in his hands while he thought, then… 'Send the scouts out. See if there's any more wagons on the road.'

'Let 'em eat first,' suggested the Bear. 'They might be more diligent on a full stomach.'

'Let's all eat,' said Broosh, sniffing the air. 'Something smells good.'

* * *

The cook had excelled himself that morning. The barbarians actually complimented him. Though, when he thought of what they were used to eating, it wasn't difficult to do a lot better.

Broosh and the Bear decided to go with the scouts. They could think better when they were occupied and not just sitting around. Huddy walked his horse a few paces behind, thinking about the girl he'd spent the night with. *What was her name, now?* He wondered.

They left the camp almost empty. A few of the men were racing each other over short distances to pass the time, while others watched, taking bets on the outcomes.

'I need to get some more stuff from the wagon,' the cook told the man assigned to guard him. He was more intent on watching the racing, and just waved an arm in consent.

The cook took an almost empty box back to the supply wagon, then went around the back to where the prison wagon was parked. No-one was watching, so he whispered, 'Mr. Mulderbish? Are you in?'

Gi peered around the door. 'Yes? What can I do for you?'

'Can I ask you something?' He took the silence for consent. 'Are you staying with the barbarians, or will you be travelling on by yourself, sir?'

Gi gave the man a puzzled look. 'Why do you ask?'

'Well, it looks like I'm a prisoner,' said the cook. 'And I don't think I can do this.'

'What do you propose to do then,' asked Gi.

'I have to escape.' He looked around furtively, and lowered his voice more. 'And if you're planning to leave, can I go with you?'

'Maybe,' he said, answering both questions. 'They're not the greatest of company, so you have my total sympathy.' He nodded. 'We'll pick our moment.'

'How about now?' pleaded the little man. 'There aren't that many in the camp at the moment, so it's a good time… I'd only need to get a few pots and pans and things, if you could give me a hand?'

'I'll help him, Father,' said Haggitt, appearing in the doorway. 'Where are they?'

'In the supply wagon, it shouldn't take long.'

'Okay, but be quick and quiet,' said Gi, finally deciding to seize the moment. 'First, though, cook, what's your name, and can you drive a two horse wagon?'

'Not a problem, sir. My name is Muto Bright. I drove the supply wagon with a team of six.' The cook smiled.

'Might be a good idea to hitch them to the front, too, before we go,' he suggested, then stressed, *'quietly.'*

Muto nodded enthusiastically.

With a little help from Haggitt to calm the horses, Muto managed to complete the task. The barbarians were still absorbed in their games when he and Haggitt crept over to the supply wagon.

They climbed into the wagon. 'Which one is it?' asked Haggitt.

Muto looked around, then pulled back a blanket. 'This is it.'

'You get down, and I'll pass it to you.'

Haggitt was surprised how light it was. 'Are you sure this is the right one?'

'Oh, yes,' Muto assured him. 'Put it down close to the back on your side, and open it.'

Haggitt set the box down, and lifted the lid. 'It's empty.'

'I know,' said Muto, and passed Haggitt a small spade. 'Just loosen the earth around the wheel. You'll find some bags buried there.'

Muto was not wrong. Haggitt found them almost immediately. They were heavier than they looked and made a dull clinking noise when he shook them. Not a word passed between them, but each knew what the other was thinking, and smiled.

'How many should there be?'

'Eight,' said Muto, proudly. 'We should be able to manage them between us.'

Haggitt put half in the box and tested it for weight.

'Hmm... No, I don't think so,' he said. He flexed his fingers. There was a small popping noise, and when the sorry-looking smoke cloud had cleared, a small wheelbarrow stood by the box. *Not quite what I intended,* he thought, *the box was supposed to sprout wheels.* He grinned, and both men started back to the prison wagon.

'What about your pots and pans?' Haggitt asked him.

'I think we've got enough here to buy some more, don't you?' Muto grinned. 'Leave 'em for the next cook.'

'This is not *your* gold, Muto,' Haggitt pointed out, feeling a little uneasy.

'It's not theirs, either. But it does include my wages you know.'

The two men heaved the bags onto the back of the prison wagon. Gi moved Haggitt's clothes onto the bed to make room for them in the box, and placed a garment over them.

'Right. Let's go now, before Broosh gets back,' said Gi. 'Up you get, Muto. Let's see you drive this thing out of here.'

Gi got in the back and sat behind Muto, so he could direct where they were headed. From there he flung a muting spell at the horses' hooves, which baffled the creatures immensely, and on the first creak from the wagon's axels, he flung more at the floor.

The trio passed unseen and unheard down to the track that led from the camp. They came to a crossroads, and Gi decided they should go north. He thought the desert would end sooner if they went that way. The dust looked undisturbed that way, too, and he didn't want to meet Broosh and his men returning.

This made Muto suggest they brush their own tracks away. 'We don't want to get caught before we've got very far, do we?'

'Carry on driving,' said Gi. 'I'll sort the tracks out.' He moved his hands in circles, getting faster and faster, until he looked like he was holding a very small whirlwind. Then, he launched it at the track behind them. It rushed back to the crossroads and then arced back to the wagon, destroying all evidence that the wagon had ever been this way. It followed them for a few more miles, then slowed down and ceased to exist.

'That was impressive, Mr. Mulderbish, sir,' said Muto. 'I've never seen a wizard do tricks like that before.'

'I'm Gi, or Master,' said Gi. 'I'm not a knight. Probably never will be.'

'I will call you Master, then,' said Muto.

'Good,' said Gi. 'And don't ever call what I do *tricks* again. I didn't study for fifteen years to do tricks. Dogs do tricks, I do serious magic. Now, let's put plenty of miles between ourselves and that camp. Then, we will rest.'

'Yes, Master,' said Muto meekly. He gently tapped the reins across the horse's backs. It wasn't meant to make them go any faster. Just a friendly tap to let them know they weren't alone.

* * *

The prison wagon – which was no longer a prison wagon, and which had never been a prison wagon for the wizards – rolled on, as did the day. Muto had tossed some food in the personal bag he'd stowed under his seat, and shared it that evening. There was enough water in the wagon for them and the horses. There were even tufts of grass about occasionally. They hadn't given any thought to sleeping arrangements, but Muto was okay to bed down under the driver's seat.

Broosh and his party arrived back at the camp as the daylight was fading. The campfires accentuated the growing darkness. The riders tied their horses to the hitching rope and slouched toward Broosh's tent.

'That was a waste of time,' the Bear moaned. 'Nothin' for miles.'

'I'll get some drinks,' said Huddy.

Broosh just grunted. He was unusually miserable at the moment, perhaps a drink might cheer him up.

Huddy returned a moment later with a jug of horse beer and three cow's horns. He passed one to Broosh, then held up the jug. 'Say when,' he said, quietly.

'That'll do,' said Broosh as it flowed over his hand.

Huddy passed one of the other horns to the Bear, then filled his own before passing the jug for Bear to finish.

'You know, Broosh,' said Bear. 'I think it might be time to move on. Set up camp somewhere else, maybe nearer a town…'

'Nope,' said Broosh. 'It would be too open. The caravan scouts would see us coming from miles.'

'I've an idea…' said Huddy – who, as the one who'd told them the soldiers' wagon carried gold, was desperate to redeem himself. 'What if we find the next town, send in half a dozen of us posing as merchants or guides, and offer to take a caravan across the Southern desert for them? They lead it here. And then we rob them.'

'Sounds simple enough,' said Broosh, ready for almost any suggestion. 'But who could we send? None of us look like merchants.'

'What about Gi and Haggitt? They might help,' said Huddy. 'They must be getting bored sitting around here. They'd probably jump at the chance of something to do.'

'Yes... that could work,' said Broosh. 'Go and get 'em.'

Huddy stood up, and with his horn of beer in one hand, picked his way through the men sitting around their fires. Some nodded as he passed, others ignored him. Not that he was unpopular... they were already asleep.

He approached the supply wagon and walked on passed. Then he approached the space where the prison wagon had been. '*Oh, bugger,*' he muttered. 'It's gone.' He turned to go back, and spilt most of what was left of his drink when he tripped on a small wheelbarrow.

Huddy was going to find the next conversation a little difficult. He was running over the script in his mind. It was easy to remember because it only had three words. 'They've gone, Broosh,' he said quickly, and took a step back. Broosh was a big man, but he was not usually violent towards his own men, but Huddy was not prepared to take that chance.

Broosh closed his eyes, mumbled a few oaths, and seemed to be counting to himself. He'd have to get his head around a new set of problems. He was not good at that. 'They won't have got far with a wagon in tow. Wait till first light, then send a couple of men to track 'em down and bring 'em back.' No-one was about to point out that wizards' magic might be more than a match for a couple of scouts, however well-armed or competent. Broosh sighed, then got up and went into his tent. He stood still for a moment, taking in the scene. There were two women in there, one was sitting on his makeshift bed, and the other had taken the liberty of laying on it. 'I wasn't expecting you to bring a friend...' He smiled.

* * *

The next morning it was overcast, but a watery sun was trying to melt the clouds. Muto was first up and had a small fire going. Gi stretched painfully and went outside. Haggitt turned over.

'Mornin', Master,' said Muto, cheerfully.

'Why have you lit a fire?' said Gi. 'Do we have something to eat?'

'No, Master. Force of habit, I suppose,' replied Muto. 'I don't suppose you could magic something up, could you?'

Gi thought about it. 'I suppose I could. What do you feel like cooking?'

'Nothing too fancy, Master. I expect you'll want to get moving soon.'

That was exactly what Gi was thinking. Broosh and his men would know that he and Haggitt were gone by now, and he would have sent men out to look for them.

'What about eggs, bacon, sausages and a fried slice?' Gi suggested.

'The full barbarian it is then, Master.' And as an afterthought, 'A frying pan would be handy, too.' Gi made a small gesture with his hands and there was a light popping sound as a frying pan materialised in the air in front of Muto. 'Oh, nice one, Master, thank you. It'll all be ready in about ten minutes.'

'Can I smell food?' said Haggitt, appearing bleary-eyed from the back of the wagon a few minutes later. He sat on the wagon steps and saw Muto at work.

'You can indeed, Mr. Haggitt,' said Muto, cheerfully.

'Then I shall sit and wait. It smells very good.'

Shortly after, all that could be heard for a while was the sound of conjured cutlery scraping on conjured plates, as three men sat in silence eating the conjured food. Muto was thinking. *How am I going to wash this lot up out here?* When they'd finished, he stacked the plates with the cutlery on top, and sat staring at them.

'You're not honestly thinking of washing up, are you?' said Gi, frowning.

'Well, I would normally, Master.'

'Well today you can do things differently,' said Gi.

'How's that? Master.'

'See how far you can throw 'em,' said Gi. 'They'll disappear within an hour anyway.'

'Master, now I'm with you, my life just gets better and better,' said Muto, skimming plates across the sand.

'Right, we'd better get moving. We need to find food and water for the horses,' said Gi. And when Muto looked at him quizzically, he explained, 'We can't depend on magic for everything. If we keep using it for trivial things like food, that's abusing our powers, and there can be consequences.'

Food seemed hardly trivial to a cook, but Muto got the message. He scraped sand over the dying fire, and climbed back onto the wagon. Haggitt and Gi were already waiting.

'Ready?' said Muto, not expecting replies. Haggitt held on and Gi sat down. Muto tapped the horses and they started heading north. It would be easier in this direction as it would put the sun behind them for much of the day, and would provide a small amount of shade for the horses. An hour later, Muto spotted some greenery up ahead. 'Can you see that, Master?'

'It could be a mirage,' said Gi, doubtfully.

The horses sensed it and started to move quicker, so it was no mirage. They were still tired, so Muto didn't have any trouble controlling them. But as they got closer, the horses became more excited. 'I think it might be an idea to unhitch the wagon before they pull us over,' said Muto. 'We'll probably need to anyway, if there's water for them.'

When the horses had eaten and drunk their fill, and showed their gratitude by dumping fresh manure for the greenery, Muto manoeuvred them back between the shafts. He then began filling containers with water for the next leg of their journey.

The wizards had refreshed themselves and sat in the shade of some palms. Any sense of urgency put on hold for the moment. But the conversation inevitably returned to their situation.

'One thing I remember from the geography of deserts,' said Haggitt, 'is that oases tend to be around the edges of deserts, not in the really hot interiors. I think, if we keep going straight, Father, we should come to a road. Or at least a well-used track.'

'Good to know you paid some attention at the old university,' said Gi. 'More than I did from the sound of it. Apart from magic, of course. I'm ahead of you there.' Haggitt didn't argue, so he went on, 'We might meet someone who knows the way to Gremanos pretty soon, then.'

'Are you sure you want to go back there, Father. They didn't treat you very well last time, did they?'

'The people treated me just fine. It was Striper who mistreated me – and everybody else,' he said, suddenly angry.

'When are you going to tell me what happened?' said Haggitt.

Muto was almost finished with the water containers.

'I'll tell you quickly now. Then we'll move on...' Gi began. 'Many years ago, Baron Striper and I were the best of friends. At least I thought so. We owned a gold mine together. Dwarfs worked it for us. I would give those who worked in my part of the mine a good share of the gold. And I thought Striper was paying his fairly, too. But, he gave them a pittance. He took whatever they brought up for himself and hid it away, including my share when I wasn't there.

A few months later, he told me the mine had run dry and wasn't viable anymore. Next thing I knew, he told me there was a major cave-in, and my share of the gold was lost down there. The only thing wrong with that story was everything. My good friend, Long Jimmy, found out what Striper was up to. So, Striper made him disappear, and the dwarf who told me about that also met with a fatal accident. I got tricked into entering that cave with the pyramid thing in it. Now, I want to face Striper, and get my gold back. And I'm going to make sure the families of those dwarfs get the help they deserve.' Gi's chest heaved, as though he was glad at last that somebody else now knew the story.

'I'm glad I found you, Father. This is way overdue,' said Haggitt.

'You could say that. Allowing me to get that instruction to you before I vanished was the flaw in Striper's plan. But I didn't think it would take you eighteen years to find that bloody cave on the mountainside!'

'I was twelve years old,' countered Haggitt. 'I hadn't even started magic.'

Gi just grunted. 'Have you finished yet, Muto?'

'I have now, Master,' he replied.

'Good. Let's be on our way. I don't think Broosh's men will find us now.'

* * *

24

After a dozen miles trundling along in silence, Gi called out, 'Muto, find somewhere to stop for the night. It's getting dark!'

'I was going to suggest that, Master, when I saw those rocks ahead. They look like a good place to stop.' He drew up nearby and stopped the wagon.

'Stay here,' said Haggitt. 'I'll have a look to make sure it's safe.'

He jumped down from the wagon, and walked to the rocks. When he got close, for some reason – instinct, probably – he stooped down so he couldn't be seen. He reached the nearest rock, a large boulder and flattened himself against it, still crouching. He waited a minute then, satisfied that all was well, he stood up and peered over the top.

* * *

When Haggitt peered over the boulder, a face was mirroring him from the other side. 'Oh,' he said, lamely. The face smiled. *Ah, good.* Haggitt thought. *Not hostile.* The face was very pale, white in fact. Which was strange considering where they were. Even Gi had gained a good tan since he'd been freed from the cave. The figure stepped out from behind the rocks. He was tall and slim, and smartly dressed – *all in white*. Haggitt wondered about that. The man's face, though longish, was very handsome. His hair was silvery white and short enough to show his slightly pointed ears.

The man stepped forward and bowed slightly. 'My name is, Dash,' he announced, holding out a hand. Haggitt took it, expecting it to be cold – because the fellow's whole appearance made him shiver – but it was warmish.

'I am Haggitt, and that's my wagon over there,' he explained. 'My father and I thought this might be a good place to shelter for the night, but we will move on, if this your... er ... home.'

'There's not just me,' said the man. 'And it's not our home.'

Haggitt was having misgivings about this. *Not alone?* 'How many are you, then?'

'Just the two of us...' Another elf stepped out – for elves they were. She was not as tall as Dash, but she was as beautiful as he was handsome, with long silver hair, and a smile to melt the heart. 'This is Bayna ... she is my mate.'

Haggitt was struck dumb by her looks. All he could do was nod. To touch her was unthinkable, like mauling a work of art. She smiled again, and nodded back.

'I think we should move on,' said Haggitt. 'We won't disturb you any longer.'

Bayna spoke, and with a voice made of honey. 'We are happy for you to stay. I know Dash will not admit it, but we are a little lost.'

'No, my love, we are here. Perhaps a little geographically challenged, rather than lost,' said Dash.

'We are a little lost ourselves,' said Haggitt. 'We're travelling north, hoping to find a road to a town. It occurs to me though, that you are elves, and this being a desert, you must be well far from home. Where are you going?'

'We are Snow Elves,' said Dash. 'We're looking for the northern snow line; we stand out too much in this landscape. And people assume that because we are elves, we are carrying wealth of some kind. It couldn't be further from the truth.'

'How are you travelling? Do you have transport?' Haggitt asked.

'Come, I will show you,' said Bayna.

Haggitt followed her behind the rocks. And there, standing silently in the gloom of the evening shadows, was a pure white horse, and a large white stag with antlers at least two yards across. 'No wonder you don't want to be here,' said Haggitt. 'Barbarians wouldn't think twice about killing you and taking these beautiful animals.'

'So, you see our problem,' said Dash, standing behind him.

'I'll get my father. He'll want to speak to you,' said Haggitt. 'I won't be a moment.' He ventured out into the half-light and walked quickly to the wagon.

'You took your time,' said Gi.

'Father, you must come. There are two people over there, and they need our help.'

Gi wasn't impressed. He was looking forward to getting some sleep. 'Muto, take the wagon over there.' He almost yawned.

It didn't take long to cover the short distance. Muto reined in the horses and jumped down. He offered a hand to Gi and helped him down. Then the two white figures stepped out from the rocks.

'Oh, my gods...' said Gi. 'Snow elves. I haven't seen any for years.'

'You know of us?' said Dash.

'I like to think I've seen most things,' said Gi, smiling. His tiredness was leaving him and at the sight of Bayna, he was suddenly wide awake. 'But I don't think I've ever seen anything as lovely as you,' he said, walking towards her.

'He can be so embarrassing at times, Muto,' said Haggitt.

'Wha...' said Muto, who was absorbed. 'She's a fine-looking young lady... er... elf, I mean.'

Much to Dash's discomfort, Gi said, 'You two really are lost, aren't you? Vulnerable, too.' Gi looked concerned. 'You'll be wanting to get north, I would guess. Which is good, because we're heading north to find a road to the next town. You're more than welcome to travel with us.'

'Thank you. We will think and talk about it, and then tell you,' said Bayna, sweetly.

'My name is Gi Mulderbish,' he announced, 'and this is my son, Haggitt. We are wizards, in case you hadn't noticed. And that man over there is Muto. He's our cook and driver.'

'We don't usually *get* into danger,' said Haggitt. 'We get out of it. Mostly. So we can help you, I'm sure.'

'Right, Muto! What did you do with that frying pan I made you?' asked Gi.

'It's under Mr. Haggitt's bed, Master.'

'Well, make sure it's clean, and bring it here. We're going to eat again.'

Muto scurried off.

'We don't eat a lot,' said Dash. 'Just an apple will do.'

'Any particular colour?' said Gi.

They looked at him quizzically. 'How ripe do like them?'

'We like the red ones, please,' said Bayna, flashing a stunning smile.

There followed a waving of hands and a snapping of fingers, which ended with a gentle *pop*! Gi held out his hands, each contained a shiny red apple.

'I can't eat these, myself,' Gi moaned, though smiling as he passed them to the elves. 'So, it's the full barbarian for us.'

'I'm ready, Master. Get conjuring,' said Muto, happy to be cooking again.

The travellers sat around the small fire that Haggitt had summoned. The Snow Elves sat a short distance away, not comfortable with the heat. Haggitt got his father to say more about his past. The

73

more he heard, the more he disliked this Baron Striper. When the fire died, the Snow Elves joined them.

'We overheard you talking,' said Dash. 'We have seen this black pyramid you speak of.'

'It appears from nowhere. Someone gets out and it disappears again,' said Bayna. 'We don't know where it comes from, or where it goes.'

'It comes from a castle in Gremanos,' said Gi. 'Where it goes, may seem random, but it's probably being steered by the controls inside.' He glanced at Haggitt.

'It wasn't my fault, Father. I didn't know it would drop us in this desert.'

'No, I suppose not,' agreed Gi. 'But if I ever come across it again, I *will* destroy it.'

'It has appeared in our land. Our elders believe it to be interdimensional,' said Dash. 'The elders also believe it to be bad, and want it found and destroyed. It has caused much unrest.'

'We have decided to accompany you on your journey,' said Bayna. 'We need safety. And in return we will help you in any way we can.'

* * *

26

Barbarians were reluctantly waking up. This was Broosh's fault. When he was awake, everybody was awake. He'd found a discarded bugle in the pass, and was now putting it to bad use.

Huddy was awake. 'Where did he get that damn bugle?'

'Come back to bed,' said a sleepy female voice from under the rug he used as a blanket.

'Huddy!' shouted Bear, as he walked by. 'Meet me in my tent later... we need to talk.'

'It's not *me* making all the noise, Harvey,' said Huddy.

'I know who it is,' said Bear. 'Just meet me later.'

After much complaining about the noise and mumblings of 'Do you know what bloody time it is?' barbarians started congregating around their camp fires.

'Scouts! Get over here!' Broosh yelled.

Gennett the Weasel and another man scurried forward. 'What do you want, chief?' asked Gennett.

'The prison wagon's gone. The wizards have gone. And worst of all... the cook's gone with them. Get out there and find 'em.'

'Right, chief. Then what? Bring 'em back?'

'*That* sounds like a plan,' said Broosh, sarcastically. 'Of course I want you to bring 'em back.'

The scouts got to their horses and went off to follow the tracks, which ran all the way from the camp to the crossroads and stopped. 'Which way do you think they went?' said Gennett.

'Not really fussy,' said the other man, who went by the name of Smokey Kole. 'North most likely. It's cooler that way.' He had a high reedy voice that somehow matched his build.

Gennett agreed, and they spurred their horses northwards. They were some miles up the track when Smokey saw what looked like the recent signs of a heavy wagon travelling in the same direction. 'Do you think these could be what we're looking for, Gennett?'

'I hope so,' said Gennett.

'They can't be too far ahead,' said Smokey, hopefully.

'We can't ride all day; the horses won't last,' Gennett reminded him.

'Okay, I say we camp in the shade and follow when it gets dark. They'll probably stop overnight and we might even catch 'em napping.'

'Sounds good,' said Gennett.

They found a shady outcrop under a cliff where they could rest themselves and the horses till dusk. When darkness closed in, the air cooled and it was time to move.

A few miles down the road, the horses started to get restless.

'What's up now?' Smokey wondered. Then he saw the dark shapes of palms, some scrubby grass and, most welcome of all, a glint of water. 'It's a bloody oasis!' he cried joyfully. Both men gave their horses free rein, and in seconds the horses and riders were up to their knees in the water.

'We should've carried on, instead of waiting around back there all day,' complained Gennett.

'You can't plan for what you don't know,' said Smokey, almost making sense. The two men ducked their heads into the water. It felt so good they decided it was time for their annual bath.

'Top the water bottles up first!' snapped Smokey.

'Good point.' Gennett grinned, pulling his shirt off.

Moments later, both men were splashing about in the shallows.

'Did you check for crocodiles?' asked Smokey.

'Er... really?' Gennett stood up and made towards the bank, eyeing the dark water suspiciously.

'Nah, just joshin' you. You'd hardly get them here.'

'You bastard!' said Gennett, dripping with water. It was then that he realised they were going to have to spend the night in wet clothes.

'Stop whining,' said Smokey. 'We'll dry out soon enough.'

They sat down by the palms that bordered the water. 'If it wasn't so hot in the daytime, this place would be quite nice,' said Gennett.

'You know, Gennett?' said Smokey, seemingly out of the blue, 'I've been thinking. I don't specially want to stay here. But I'm not sure I want to go back to Broosh, either.'

Gennett thought about it. 'It's not as though we owe him anything, is it? Could be time to move on. If we catch up with the wagon, we could just ride on by. Or join 'em.'

'I was thinking that,' said Smokey. 'I'm fed up with the barbarian life. I've never got any money. Never know where the next meal's coming from. The ground's hard…'

'Alright…' said Gennett, 'we've talked ourselves into it. Now, let's see if we can catch up.'

* * *

27

'Those two have been gone all night, Bear,' said Broosh. 'Do you think they've found the wagon?'

'What, those two?' Bear smiled, 'no chance.'

'Why do you say that?' asked Broosh.

'They couldn't find their backsides with both hands,' Bear told him.

'Why did you let me send them out, then?'

'You're the chief,' said Bear. 'You do what you want.'

'That's not a good attitude, Bear.'

'Well… some of us have lost confidence, Broosh. We don't think you're making it worth our while anymore,' said Bear, calmly.

'So, is this a leadership challenge?'

'No, Broosh. It won't come to that. From what I hear, the men might just walk away.'

'Okay, what do you think I should do?' said Broosh.

'That's just it,' said Bear. 'You don't seem to be able to make good decisions anymore. So, why don't you ride out on your own and find another band of men.'

'Is this how you feel as well, Huddy?' said Broosh.

'Yep, sorry chief. It was fun while it lasted, but if you keep attacking caravans and soldiers who aren't carrying any valuables, we're all going to starve.'

Broosh was angry. He stood up and drew his great long sword. Huddy stood up and began to walk away. Harvey the Bear sprang from seated to upright in a single movement. Broosh swung his sword with both hands, but missed Bear by a hair's breadth, and as Broosh turned to regain his balance, Huddy stepped in and plunged his dagger into Broosh's chest. A surprised expression lit the big man's face, and the big sword slipped from his fingers as he dropped to his knees and fell face down in the dust.

'Is he dead?' said Harvey.

'I'm pretty sure,' said Huddy, kneeling over Broosh's body. He put an ear to Broosh's mouth. There was no breath. He looked up at Harvey. 'Yeah, he's dead. Now... what was it you wanted to see me about?'

'Hmm? Oh, it doesn't matter now,' said Harvey.

Some of the men had seen what had happened, and came across to investigate. One took off his cloak and laid it on the ground, while two others rolled Broosh's body onto it. Another tied the cloak closely to the body, and two more dragged it away. Huddy wiped his blade clean on the back of his leg and stuck the dagger back into its sheath.

'I thought he was going to kill you, Bear.'

'So did I,' said the Bear, 'so did I.'

The pair went back to Broosh's tent to take anything of value. They met the man who'd donated his cloak coming out of the tent with a new one. They let the men share out the rest. Broosh didn't have much. He didn't see the need.

'What shall we do with the body?' said Huddy.

'Bury him, I suppose,' said Bear. 'We don't have a boat to burn him in.'

'Oh, let's just burn him anyway, and move on,' said Huddy.

* * *

So, that's what the barbarians did. After the funeral fire, it took them a half day to pack everything up. 'Good thing we stole that supply wagon,' remarked Bear.

'Yeah, the lads are throwing out the stuff we don't need and packing the tents and stuff in it,' said Huddy.

The next morning, the barbarians left their camp of many months. And when Bear looked back as they rode out, he thought it looked like the biggest refuse tip he'd ever seen. He thought he even saw gulls swooping over it. *Gods,* he thought, *that's gonna stink when the sun gets up.*

The horde travelled at walking pace. Not because they weren't in a hurry, but they hadn't decided where to go. 'Do we still have any scouts?' asked Huddy.

Bear called the nearest man forward. 'Are there any scouts or trackers among us?' he asked.

'I know of three, Bear. I'll go find 'em.' The man wheeled his horse around and galloped back along the straggly line.

Three riders left the line and hurried to the front where Harvey the Bear was waiting. 'I realise, men, I'm supposed to know everybody in the clan, but when men leave and others join, I can't keep up.' He grinned. 'So, what do your mothers call you?'

The first rider spoke up, 'I'm Trevor,' and pointing at the other two in turn, he said, 'This is Nigel, and that's Barry, both good men.'

'Okay, Trevor. Take Barry and ride on ahead. I want to know if there are any wagons or riders ahead of us. If you see anything, one of you come back and tell me. The other man is to keep them in sight. Understood?' said Bear.

'Yep. No problem,' said Trevor, who'd assumed the role of spokesman. 'But if we haven't found anything by nightfall, we'll get back, and try again in the morning.' The two men spurred their horses on and left in a cloud of dust.

'I wish they wouldn't do that,' moaned Huddy, waving the dust away, and nudging his own horse into a steady trot. 'Seems like things are working out well for you, Bear.'

'At least the men are in good heart and sticking together now,' murmured the Bear.

A couple of miles ahead, out of sight, Trevor and Barry, slowed their horses to a walk. They weren't exactly in good heart, though they were sticking together. 'Let's hope we come across something worth reporting,' said Trevor. 'I don't fancy going back with nothing.'

'Nor me,' said Barry. 'What with Huddy killing a big man like Broosh, what chance have we got?'

'None, I shouldn't think.'

Ahead of them, the landscape sloped up for some miles, all the way to the horizon. 'Once we get to the top, we should be able to see for miles. If there's nothing to see, I say we go back and try again in the morning.'

Barry was okay with that.

It was late afternoon, with about an hour's daylight left, when the two riders crested the ridge. 'Oh… thank you, gods,' said Trevor. Below them in the valley were a cluster of small fires with men sitting around. There were no wagons, and no tents to speak of, but there were lots of horses.

They watched in silence until, 'Come on, let's get back to the Bear,' said Trevor. 'He'll be well pleased with this.' The pair turned their horses and walked them back down the long slope.

* * *

Down in the valley… 'Did you see those two riders on that rise, Fox?' asked Reza.

Fox nodded. 'Barbarian scouts, I'd say, looking for plunder.'

'We've got no supply wagon,' said Reza, 'they may be after horses.'

Fox sent for Badger Hercop.

'How's your night vision, Badger?' asked Reza, his plait of blonde hair tied in a man-bun for once, and who, for stature and bearing, looked everything that Badger didn't.

'Depends on the moon,' said Badger, candidly. 'What do you need?'

'A few minutes ago, a couple of scouts of your kind were on that rise. I want you to get after them, and find out what they're up to.'

'Gimme an hour,' said Badger, saluting in a fair parody of a soldier. He scurried off for his horse and departed.

'Sivad – get Maurice to keep an eye on him. From a safe distance, of course,' said Reza.

'You still don't trust him, do you?' said Fox.

Reza frowned. 'No, not yet.' He looked about him. 'Brian! Will you get the men assembled so we can talk to them, please? I've an idea there might be trouble.'

'Right you are, Sarge. I'm on it.'

The men congregated in the area in front of Reza and Fox's tents. Brian arrived last to confirm everyone was present. 'Men,' said Fox, 'we were being watched earlier, by a couple of scouts. Probably barbarians. I've sent Badger and Maurice to see where they went, and how far away the main body is. We need to stay alert.' A mumble of agreement went around, and after a few more comments and mumbles, Fox dismissed them.

Twenty minutes later, Maurice rode into the camp and found Fox. 'It's barbarians alright,' he said. 'They're camped a couple of miles down the track. Badger's sneaking around trying to pick up what he can. Fortunately, he blends in pretty well.'

The men exchanged a smile. Fox said, 'Stay here, now you're back. We'll see what our spy comes back with.'

Half an hour later, Badger rode into camp, excitedly. 'Fox! Reza! I heard 'em say they're gonna attack us in the morning,' he blurted out before he'd even dismounted.

'Damn,' Reza muttered. 'Now, calm down and tell me more. How many are there? What's the state of them? And get off your horse first.'

When the ex-barbarian had told them everything he could, Reza and Fox sat quietly digesting it, while Badger yawned and stretched, broadly hinting he'd like to turn in now.

Reza stirred after a while and got up. He reached behind his head and undid the knot of hair, letting his plait swing down.

'You have a plan?' said Fox, grinning.

'Of course,' said Reza. 'Have you ever known me not to? This tired barbarian is the answer. Attack them tonight while they sleep, and cut 'em down before morning. If we stay here, we're sitting ducks.'

'Whoa,' said Fox. 'Let's talk about this. We don't have the best soldiers in the world you know?'

'I do know,' Reza replied. 'But they're all we've got.'

'We got caught out last time, Sarge,' said Sivad. 'Let me and Maurice go in with five or six men and set fire to their tents. Give us a few minutes and send in half the men to attack them when they come to put the fires out. Give *them* a few minutes, then send in the rest of the men. We'll have the advantage of surprise. We can retake the wagon, and with a bit of luck, they won't know what's hit 'em till it's too late.' Sivad paused for breath. 'Once we've got the wagon, we head back to the high ground on that side.'

'Have you done this before?' Fox asked him.

'No, Fox. It's a situation my father told me about a few times. He was a bit proud of himself for leading it. Sounds like what we need to do here.'

'Did it work?' asked Reza.

'He's still alive, Sarge.' Sivad grinned.

'Get the men formed up, Maurice,' said Fox. 'And quietly. I don't want any rattling swords or harnesses when we move. Got that?'

With the men in line, Sivad looked for six volunteers to go with him and Maurice in the advance party.

'I'll go,' said Badger, promptly, sticking out his chest. 'I know my way round their camp.'

'Can't argue with that. What about you, Brian?' asked Sivad.

Brian looked surprised. 'Oh, sorry, I thought you'd already included me.'

'Three more of you, that's all I need... Come on, men,' said Sivad. 'Or this may cease to be voluntary.'

'Thank you,' said Sivad. 'Now, here's what I want you to do.'

Sivad briefed his volunteers and they rode out. The rest of the soldiers followed at a distance. As the advance party drew closer, they ditched their horses and crept the final hundred yards. A few barbarians were sleeping by their fires, but most were inside the tents.

'Badger,' Sivad whispered, 'deal with the one on watch. Then kill any you find on their own. As quietly as you can.' Badger's bared his teeth and crept forward. They heard a muffled cry. 'Maurice, follow Badger. Get the flaming wood off a fire. Wrap your hand in your cloak if you need to, but don't set yourself on fire.' Maurice said he'd try not to. 'Don't throw it inside the tent, hold it against it near the bottom, till the flames take hold. Then go along to the next one,' said Sivad. 'You men, do the same. When you've done that, get out quickly. Barbarians will be everywhere trying to beat out the flames. Once you're out of the camp, Fox will be coming in to cut them down. I'm hoping they'll leave their weapons in the tents, so it should make it easier for Fox's men to deal with them. When Fox has done his part, Reza will bring in the rest of the men to finish it. Now, get to it, and I'll see you all back here in a few minutes.'

Within moments, flames were licking the sides of most of the tents. But it took a while before the barbarians were roused enough to realise what was happening. They ran from their tents coughing and spluttering, looking for something to beat out the flames. At this point, Fox and fifty soldiers charged in with swords drawn, slashing at the men as they tried to get away from their tents.

As Sivad expected, only a few barbarians had weapons, but they were no match for the mounted soldiers coming at them out of the dark.

Fox Loer took a considerable toll of the barbarians, and some began running. Sivad and his volunteers made it safely back to their mounts just as Reza went in with the rest of the men. Badger was still darting about adding to the mayhem.

'Badger! Get out of there before you get yourself killed. Take Maurice and Brian with you!' Reza shouted. He dug his spurs into his horse's flanks, put his head down, and with his sword held out in front of him, he charged into the camp. 'Follow me, men!'

As more barbarians were cut down, more began fleeing. Only a few stood their ground. Fox and Reza hadn't lost a single man so far, but two of the barbarians still standing were Huddy Mincing and Harvey the Bear, who looked intent on inflicting damage. Two others stood behind them, forming a square. The soldiers formed a circle around them. There was no means of escape. And it could get bloody.

Reza dismounted and walked forward. 'There's no disgrace in yielding to a superior force, men,' he said, quietly. 'Put down your weapons, or I will kill you where you stand.' Threats can be more menacing when uttered quietly.

'What, just you, or all your fancy soldiers?' said the Bear.

'Just me,' Reza assured him, flicking his blonde plait over his shoulder, not intimidated by the huge barbarian.

The Bear lifted his axe and growled his intentions.

'Have it your way,' said Reza, raising his sword.

Bear charged wildly, axe raised and cursing. At the last second, Reza simply stepped aside and tripped him.

The Bear sprawled in the dust. Reza waited for him to get up, then beckoned him forward. Bear rushed again, and again Reza sidestepped. The more Reza taunted him the more careless the Bear became. But, the big man didn't go down after his next charge, and he swung his axe at Reza's head.

Bear was tiring, and the double-headed axe was feeling heavier now. He wielded it slowly enough for the agile Reza to easily avoid it. Reza was beginning to lose patience with this barbarian, who was all bluster and no skill. Bear recovered from the momentum of his swing, and lifted the axe to bring it down on Reza's head, with the intention of splitting him in two.

When the Bear had his axe raised ready to strike, Reza stepped in close and slashed Bear's throat with a single sweep of his sword. The axe fell behind the barbarian, and his head lolled forward onto his chest before leaving his body and falling into the dust. The headless body stood motionless for a moment, then crashed forward.

'Now, who's next?' Reza asked, a little too cheerfully.

The three men dropped their weapons. Huddy stepped forward. 'If the Bear couldn't beat you,' he said, 'we're not going to try.'

'You have a choice...' Reza began. 'You can run... I'll give you a start as far as those rocks. Or, you can join my men as soldiers.'

Huddy and the other two men looked at each other. 'Is that a good deal?' said one.

'We get paid in the army,' said the other.

'Yeah... but we could end up fighting barbarians.'

Huddy said, 'How far do you think we'll get on foot?' Silence. Then Huddy asked, 'Do we get horses if we decide to run?'

Reza grinned, 'As many as you need, friend.'

'Okay... Three.' Then, he thought again. 'No... I think we'll join the army.'

'Good choice,' said Reza. 'Hand your weapons to my men, and take up positions behind the supply wagon.'

'Rather not do that,' said Huddy, incautiously.

'You don't have a choice,' Reza told him.

'You expect us to eat dust all day?'

Reza pointed out that it was still dark.

'Okay,' said Huddy, 'in the morning, then.'

'You don't have to *swallow* it.' Reza swung his blonde plait over his shoulder and put his hands on his hips – a clear preparation for action – and the conversation ended abruptly.

'I'll take them to the wagon,' said Fox. 'Tie them to a wheel for the night in case they get any bright ideas.'

'Okay, Fox. Take Sivad with you. I'll get Maurice and Brian to relieve you in a couple of hours,' said Reza.

When the three barbarians were out of Reza's sight, behind the wagon, one of them made a grab for Sivad's knife. Fox didn't hesitate. With frightening speed, his own dagger was in hand and in the back of the barbarian's head. The man slumped to the ground. Fox spun round…

'Whoa…!' said Huddy, hands raised in front of him. 'That was not *my* idea.'

'Shall I kill him, Fox?' asked Sivad.

'No, not yet. I've a better idea. Take the pair of them back to Reza and I'll tell him what I have in mind.'

* * *

When Reza heard what Fox had in mind for the prisoners, he frowned. 'That's a bit dangerous, Fox.'

'Of course it is! They were prepared to kill our men. They're getting off lightly.'

'Okay...' said Reza, repeating it back: 'Put them on horses, facing backwards. Tie their hands behind them and tie one foot in a stirrup. Blindfold them and stampede their horses. Is that what you want?'

'Yes, it is,' said Fox, and Sivad nodded in agreement.

'Oh... alright, then,' Reza concurred, adding, 'I just hope I never get on the wrong side of *you*.'

Fox didn't waste time. Within minutes there was the sound of two horses being slapped and bolting headlong in to the darkness. He looked back at Reza. 'Well,' he said, sounding satisfied, 'at least now we don't have any prisoners.'

'I don't like prisoners either,' said Reza. 'They slow us down.'

'Speaking of prisoners, I wonder where those wizards are?' said Fox.

'I don't really care,' said Reza. 'It was du Merde's idea to take them back to Striper. Probably best that they got away. I don't want to get involved in a wizard's feud.'

'Is Striper a wizard?' asked Sivad.

'Oh, yes,' said Reza. 'A dangerous one. Wizards' sons are mostly wizards, too. Though Striper's son's not even what I would call a man, in the true sense of the word, either. Always seemed a little slow on the uptake to me.'

'Who's his son?' asked Sivad.

'My, you've got a lot of questions tonight, young man,' said Reza. 'Lord Welkin. I'm surprised Striper ever lets him out on his own. Even he must realise that the boy needs someone to hold his hand. Anyway, enough about him for tonight, let's go see what's left in that supply wagon.'

Reza, Fox and Sivad walked casually along the line of soldiers, sitting about or stretched out from fatigue. Fox jumped up onto the back-board and looked inside. *Bloody 'ell*, he thought. *I'm not going in there without a torch*. He leaned round the side of the wagon. 'Someone get me a torch!' Moments later, Maurice appeared with a flaming stick.

Fox had a cursory look at all the broken boxes and various weapons strewn everywhere, but there was no sign of the box that contained the soldiers' pay. He stepped out and jumped down. 'Let's not start shifting stuff around tonight. Sivad, post a couple of trusted guards and we'll search it in the morning.'

* * *

A face appeared low at the window of the old prison wagon.

'Are you awake, Master?' said Muto. 'I'm just starting breakfast.'

'Mm...?' mumbled Gi. 'Is it that time already?'

'What time, Master? I only know it's light.'

'Where's Haggitt?'

'He's talking to Dash and Bayna, Master. He's already conjured breakfast for them.'

'Tell him it's his turn do it for us as well, then. I'm going back to sleep.'

Suddenly he sat bolt upright. 'Who the hell are Dash and Bayna?'

'They're the snow elves, Master. You must remember them. *Lovely* people,' said Muto.

The mental fog of sleep cleared. 'Ah... yes, I remember. That's the beautiful girl with the sing-song voice, and the other one that turned up here yesterday...'

'Yes, Master, they're the ones. Mr. Haggitt's chatting with them now.'

Gi put his feet on the rug between the beds. 'This was a good idea of young Haggitt's, putting a mat down. Nothing worse than getting out of bed and having to stand on an ice-cold floor. Unless you're a snow elf, I suppose.' He stood up and pushed his tatty wizard's hat back out of his eyes. 'Do I look decent, Muto?'

'Always, Master,' he smiled. 'I wouldn't have you any other way.'

Gi stepped off the wagon. 'Ah... there you are,' he said, walking a bit lopsidedly, still working on his coordination, towards Haggitt and the two elves. 'What have you been plotting?'

'Plotting, Father? I don't know what you mean,' said Haggitt. 'We were wondering what direction to go. I think directly north, like we said yesterday.'

'We need to get started soon,' said Dash. 'We've lost a night's travelling.'

'Do you know who, exactly, is tracking you?' asked Gi.

'No. One looked like a small demon. One is taller, and wears an ornate robe with lots of pockets in it,' Bayna told him.

'Any idea who that is, Father?' asked Haggitt.

'Only two of them? I thought you had a whole posse after you.' Gi seemed almost disappointed. 'No, I don't know who they are. But the taller one could be a wizard. Do you know why he's chasing you?'

'We think it's what you said yesterday,' said Dash. 'He believes we are carrying valuables, or our animals have magical powers.'

'Have they?' said Gi.

'No, they're just unusual. There's nothing magical about them,' said Bayna.

'Where did you see this wizard and his demon?' asked Haggitt.

'They came up out of the snow, in our dimension,' said Dash. 'The demon tried to steal my horse, and when I told it to stop, it attacked me.'

'I hit it with a large icicle,' said Bayna. 'But it just kept coming.'

'We got on our animals and fled,' said Dash. 'And as we did, a portal opened in front of us and we found ourselves in this dimension.'

'...And they followed you through,' said Gi, completing the story.

'No. The portal closed behind us, stopping them from coming through,' said Dash.

'Well, at least we're safe for now, but we don't belong here,' said Bayna.

'Well, you've got us to help you now, so when we've eaten we'll move on,' said Gi.

* * *

Two ex-barbarians were riding slowly along the desert track, following the wheel-marks left by Gi's wagon. Gennett sniffed the air. 'Is there such a thing as a smell-mirage?' he wondered aloud.

'Never heard of one,' replied Smokey.

'That means I can smell breakfast,' said Gennett, feeling saliva moistening his mouth.

'I think you're right,' said Smokey, spurring his horse into a gallop.

'Whoa… Hold on!' shouted Gennett, seeing a wisp of smoke.

'It's coming from behind those rocks. Look! The wagon's there as well.' Smokey sounded almost happy.

'I think we'd better go slowly and give 'em some warning we're coming.'

'Good idea,' said Smokey. 'No point risking a fireball in the face is there?'

As they approached, Haggitt left the cover of the rocks and confronted them. 'What do you want?!' he called.

'We're hungry and we smelt food, sir,' said Gennett. 'We mean you no harm.'

Haggitt looked them over and smiled. 'I wouldn't try.'

Dash and Bayna stood up. They were holding bows pointed at Gennett and Smokey. The two men raised their hands away from their weapons and dismounted somewhat awkwardly.

'Keep your hands high and come forward,' said Haggitt. 'We don't want to harm you, but try anything and my friends here *will* shoot you.'

'We don't wish us any harm, either,' said Smokey.

'Let them in,' said Gi. 'If they misbehave, I'll turn them into something edible.'

Haggitt frowned at the thought, but Muto was thinking he might need a bigger pan.

'I know how this looks,' said Smokey. 'But we're not barbarians. We were, yesterday, but last night we talked it over and decided it wasn't for us anymore. We realised we could do better.'

'Sounds a bit lame to me,' said Haggitt. 'Where are you going?'

'Gremanos,' said Gennett. 'Where I can find work.'

Smokey laughed. 'What? You? A proper job? What can you do?'

'Actually, Smokey, I'm a carpenter by trade,' Gennett told him.

'No wonder you were a rubbish barbarian,' said Smokey, still pouring scorn on his companion. 'You were going to saw people to death, were you?'

'I think that'll be enough,' said Haggitt. The ex-barbarian's reedy voice and truculence was starting to irritate. 'If you're coming with us, we don't want you two bickering all the way.'

'Do you know the way to Gremanos?' asked Gi.

'Yeah, course I do,' said Gennett. 'It's north of here, then west when you get to the River.'

'What river?' asked Gi.

'The one that's north of 'ere. It don't have a name, we just call it the River,' said Gennett. 'No point giving a river a name – it won't come if you call it.'

'Good point,' said Gi. 'Just the River, then. Give these men some food, Muto. And if either of them speaks out of turn, put an arrow in them, Dash. I'm not here to be messed about.'

'Can I just say something first?' said Gennett, a little urgently.

'What's that?' asked Haggitt.

'Have you noticed that great cloud of dust coming towards us?'

Gi climbed up onto the wagon and shielded his eyes from the sun. 'Oh, bugger. Soldiers,' he groaned.

'It's not the same lot as last time is it, Father?' said Haggitt.

'It looks that way,' said Gi. 'But I'm not going with them this time,' he vowed. 'I've had enough of them. And we don't need them anymore.'

'Just keep down and stay quiet, Master,' said Muto, 'they may pass by.'

'No chance,' said Smokey. 'They'll have seen you already. They'll be Striper's men going to Gremanos.'

Gi used up another bugger. 'Oh, no. If that fool, du Merde is with them, I will have to turn him into something small enough to tread on.'

'You might be able to get him on your side, Master,' said Muto.

'And how's that?' asked Gi.

'When the barbarians attacked, du Merde rushed at Broosh Marteef to try and kill him. Oh, he was *so brave*, Master. His helmet gleaming in the sunlight, and the sunshine reflecting off his sword, he made such an impressive sight.'

'Well, what happened?' asked Gi.

'Broosh hit him on the head with his huge sword, and rammed his helmet down so hard he hasn't been able to get it off since, Master.'

Gi laughed so much he thought he would wet himself. 'That's the best story I've heard in years.'

'Perhaps you could use your magic to stretch his helmet, Master.'

'No,' said Gi, still grinning. 'I think I'll shrink his head.'

'That works for me,' said Smokey.

'Get on with your breakfast,' snapped Haggitt.

'They're getting close, Master,' said Muto. 'What shall we do?'

'We'll wait. I'm not going out to meet them. They can come to me,' said Gi.

* * *

The soldiers weren't exactly hurrying, and it was ages before they arrived at Gi's little camp amongst the rocks.

The snow elves and Muto kept out of sight and the two ex-barbarians sat on the ground, watched by Haggitt. Gi told him to hit them with a fireball if either made a noise.

'Are you looking for me?' Gi called out, stepping from behind the rocks.

At the unexpected sight of someone suddenly appearing in front of them, the first two horses reared and shied away.

Then, Fox Loer rode up to Gi and dismounted. 'Good morning. And no, we're not looking for anybody. Especially you, Mr. Mulderbish. We're on our way to Gremanos.'

'I remember you...' said Gi. 'You were one of the better ones, with that other one with the hair. What's his name... something to do with doors...?'

Fox thought for a moment. 'Ah, Reza Lock!'

'That's the one. Is he with you?'

'Yes, Reza and I are now in command of the column. So, no harm will come to you and your party,' Fox assured him.

Gi smiled. 'You don't know who I've got in my party, do you?'

Fox studied Gi's face, and wondered if *he* should be worried. 'I'm sure they're all good people,' he said, trying to smile.

'Oh, they are,' Gi assured him. 'Now then, is du Merde with you? I need to have a laugh at his expense.'

Fox smiled. 'So, you've heard?'

'Yes. I do *so* hope it's true.'

'It is.' Fox grinned and turned in his saddle. 'Brian, go and bring du Merde up here. Someone wants to see him.'

'Will do, Sarge.' Brian smiled wickedly and rode off. He was back a moment later, leading a horse with a rider hiding his head deep in the hood of his cloak.

'Has he been complaining and whining about it?' Gi asked Fox.

'You have no idea.' Fox smirked. 'From the time he wakes up. That's why we keep him at the back of the column.'

'Do you want me to get his helmet off?'

'It would be good,' said Fox. 'I think he's suffered enough, now.'

'I'll only do it if he promises not to command these soldiers ever again,' said Gi.

'The men won't follow him now, anyway,' said Fox. 'du Merde! Come here. There's someone who can get your helmet off.'

du Merde nudged his horse forward grudgingly, and dismounted.

He peered with difficulty from under his rucked-up face mask. 'So, it's you. We've caught up with you again, at last,' said du Merde. 'Arrest this man and tie him up.'

Fox came forward. 'That's not going to happen, du Merde. This man is a wizard with the power to get your helmet off. He'll not be harmed.'

'Just as well,' said Gi. 'I have two of my people behind that rock with arrows trained on you.'

'I doubt it, wizard!' said du Merde. 'Nobody in their right mind would help you.'

'Look, it's going to be difficult enough getting your stupid helmet off without hurting you,' said Gi. 'But it won't be nearly as painful as me enjoying pulling an arrow out of you.'

'Just let the man deal with it, du Merde,' said Fox. 'Or stay like that. But if you do, you're on your own. I'm not even leaving you with a horse. Understand?'

'You can't do that to me!'

'No?' said Fox. 'Watch me.'

After very little thought, du Merde agreed. 'Don't hurt me, Mulderbish, or I *will* scream, you know.'

'I won't hurt you... much. Probably.' Gi grinned. 'Ready?' And before du Merde could reply, there was a pop! And the helmet fell in two pieces.

'I wasn't ready!' snapped du Merde. '... You bastard.'

'That's no way to speak to our friend, du Merde,' said Fox. 'After what he's done for you.'

'Exactly, said Gi, keeping a straight face. 'I took the risk of splitting your head in two with that untried spell.'

The colour may have drained from du Merde's face, but it was already so pale from lack of sun. 'Well, it doesn't hurt anymore,' said du Merde, then grudgingly he added. 'Thank you. Perhaps we can let the past go? What do you say?'

'I can let it go,' said Gi. 'But you're not to be Centurion over these men anymore. Fox and Reza will lead them now. Is that understood?'

He hung his head. 'Then it seems I am just a soldier again.'

Gi didn't feel sorry for him. 'Soldiering is a noble calling. You can work your way back up again. Probably. But you can't be a literal Centurion anymore, because three of your men have gone – changed sides, in fact' said Gi.

'Changed sides? Deserted you mean?' said du Merde.

'Not really. You never paid them, so they considered themselves free agents.'

'Barbarians stole the money,' du Merde insisted.

'Yes, they did. And now I've got it,' said Gi. 'But they don't know that. They're with me because I've treated them well.'

Fox perked up. 'Do you really have the money?'

'You'd better believe it,' said Gi. 'Are these your men who were attacked?'

'Yes, but we went after the barbarians last night. Now their leaders and most of the others are dead,' said Fox.

Gi called Fox to his wagon alone and showed him the soldiers' gold. 'I will look after it until we get to the next town,' said Gi. 'It's safe where it is and well-guarded.'

'I see you have a couple of barbarian spies with you,' said Fox, indicating Gennett and Smokey.

'They claim they've given up that lifestyle now, Fox. They're looking to join me on the road to Gremanos.'

'I wouldn't be too quick to trust them yet, Gi. It's a long way to Gremanos,' said Fox. 'There may be more bandits along the way they might decide to side with. So, don't give those two any weapons.'

'I have something else to show you,' said Gi, 'And if anyone tries to steal or harm these, *I* will kill them with a lightning bolt, or a fireball, depending on how I feel at the time. I'm not one for all that messy stuff with daggers.'

Fox followed Gi to where the wagon was parked. There he saw the white horse and the beautiful white stag. 'What wonders are those?' he said. 'Can you protect them?'

'Up to a point,' said Gi. 'But these two can. Dash! Come out here please.'

Both elves appeared as if from nowhere.

'This is Dash, and this is Bayna. The creatures belong to them. They'll be travelling with us as far as the northern snowline.'

Fox was immediately struck by the beauty of the silver haired elves. He also took in the fact that they were both carrying bows of sufficient length to be used on horseback, and both had quivers of arrows on their backs. He also noticed the additional quivers attached to the saddles of their animals.

'Dash, Bayna, this is Fox Loer. He is joint-leader of these soldiers with another good man called Reza Lock,' said Gi. The two elves nodded. Fox nodded back. 'We're going to be travelling with them to Gremanos.'

Fox smiled amiably. 'Fine by me. And maybe we can take our prison wagon back when we reach the barracks.'

'Oh, and we rescued your cook, too. He's with us now.'

Fox seemed amused. 'Anything else I should know?'

'I don't think so.'

'I will see you later, then,' said Fox. 'I need to find shade for the horses.'

'We look forward to your company,' said Dash.

'Just what we need,' said Gi, rubbing his hands together. 'Our own private army.'

'Can we trust them, Father?' Haggitt wondered.

'You were with me in that prison wagon. You know you can trust Fox and Reza. Not du Merde, of course. But he's been neutralised for now.'

'Have you forgotten, Master,' said Muto, who'd been keeping out of the way, 'You haven't had breakfast yet?'

'Oh… I'll eat it later. We need to get started now. Dash and Bayna are even less comfortable in this desert than we are, so are their animals.'

Muto sighed. 'I'll share it between those two barbarians, and do you a fresh meal when you're ready.'

'Try to keep yourselves in the shade of the wagon,' Gi told the elves. 'It's not very high, but it does cast a shadow.'

'I'll tell Fox we're moving out. If he wants to stay here longer, he can catch us up,' said Haggitt.

Fox listened sympathetically to what Haggitt told him about the snow elves and their need to leave straight away. 'Would you like a couple of my men to go with you, till we catch up?'

'My father might be glad of their company,' agreed Haggitt.

'Give me a moment.' He walked a few paces and found Sivad. 'Get Maurice and Brian up here, please?'

Fox told them he wanted them to accompany Gi and Haggitt until the column caught up.

'Sure, Sarge. Are they prisoners again?' asked Maurice.

'No. You'll see why when you meet them. Come with me,' said Fox.

The two soldiers' chins dropped in awe. 'What beautiful animals,' said Brian. 'No wonder you need an escort. Where did you find them, Mr. Mulderbish?'

'If only,' said Gi. 'They're not mine. They belong to these fine people.'

'Snow Elves?' said Maurice. 'I thought they were a myth!'

'No, they're quite real. And they need our help,' said Gi.

'They've got it,' snapped Brian.

'You don't know what you'll be doing, yet,' said Gi.

'Don't matter. We're not gonna miss the chance to ride with snow elves, are we Brian?' said Maurice, who was not usually this excited about anything.

Gi looked about. 'We look ready to go.'

'Our animals don't travel well in the dark,' said Dash. 'So, that's when we'll rest.'

'Suits us. Muto! Get those two barbarian drop-outs on their horses and let's move out,' said Gi.

'The two soldiers fell in behind the wagon, where they could keep an eye on everyone. 'Stay wide, or you'll be eating dust all day,' said Muto, loving the bit of authority Gi had given him. And the soldiers were happy to humour him. For now, anyway.

* * *

34

The wizards and their company travelled north, and soon saw an end to the sand and rocks of the desert. Patches of green appeared and there was a noticeable dip in the temperature.

'You know what I'm gonna do when we reach that lush proper grass, Master?'

'What's that, Muto?' said Gi.

'I'm gonna roll in it, and let the horses eat as much as they can.'

'If I was younger,' grinned Gi. 'I'd run around like a mad thing.'

Brian rode up beside the wagon. 'Mr. Mulderbish!' he called, 'there are riders keeping pace with us, over there on the right.' He pointed to the rise where the desert ended and the grassy plain began.

'Any ideas, Brian?' asked Haggitt.

'Could be bandits. There aren't that many, though.'

'I count seven,' said Gi. 'And they're brazen enough to show themselves.'

'The odds aren't in their favour, though,' said Maurice, joining them. 'They'd be foolish to start anything. Shall I go see what they want?'

'I'll go, too,' insisted Dash, eager to make himself useful.

'Okay. But change horses with Brian before you go,' said Gi.

Dash agreed it might be safer, and dismounted. 'He is not good with strangers, Brian. You may need to hold on tightly.' The soldier mounted gingerly and looked pleased with himself sitting astride such a fine animal.

'You don't get to keep it, soldier,' said Gi, amused.

Maurice and Dash cantered up to their followers and challenged them. 'We've been watching you following us,' said Maurice. 'What do you want?'

A scar faced man walked his horse towards them. 'Well now...' he said. 'I see a wagon with two outriders and four guards. I thought, what might they be carrying, then?'

'We're not carrying anything,' Maurice told them. 'Just travellers going to Gremanos.'

'That's a long way,' said Scar-face, sneering. On closer acquaintance, he made a barbarian seem refined. 'You've gotta be carrying something of value.'

'I would suggest you leave the wagon alone, sir. There is nothing of value for you,' Maurice assured him.

'I like the look of the woman with the silver hair...' He smirked. 'What say you, lads?' The rest of the band laughed with their leader.

'Okay,' said Maurice, 'come with me. I'll introduce you.'

'What are you doing?' whispered Dash.

'I arranged with Gi that if they looked like trouble, I'd bring them in, so he could deal with them,' Maurice whispered.

*

'Oh dear,' said Haggitt. 'They're bringing them here.'

'How are your fireballs, son?' Gi grinned.

'Fine, I think, thank you, Father,' Haggitt replied, checking himself and assuming a puzzled expression.

'I'm talking about your magic!' said Gi.

Sitting in earshot on the wagon, Muto chuckled.

'Get ready,' said Gi. 'When they're closer, Haggitt, you take the one on the right. I'll take the one on the left.' Moments later, he ordered, 'Stop the wagon, Muto!'

The bandits were riding towards them in a loose bunch. Dash and Maurice were slightly ahead, and as they closed on the wagon, the elf and soldier veered away, which was the signal for Gi and Haggitt to work their magic.

'Now!' Two balls of fire sped through the air, catching their targets full in the chest.

'Wizards!' shouted Scar-face. 'Take cover, men!'

'Where?' The nearest man screamed. 'We're in open country, you fool.'

'Send the signal!' shouted Scar-face. 'Get the rest of the men here!'

A man broke away from the group, and started galloping away.

'Stop him, Dash! He's going for reinforcements!' shouted Maurice.

As Dash raised his bow, the rider fell to the ground with two arrows in his back, striking with such force that the arrowheads protruded through the man's chest.

'How did you do that?' asked Maurice.

'I didn't,' said Dash. 'That's one of Bayna's tricks. I haven't mastered firing two at once yet!' The elf took quick aim and brought another bandit down. Now there were three.

'Do you want to let the rest go, Father?' asked Haggitt.

'No. They'll only come back with more. Kill them all, and free the horses,' said Gi, as he released two more fireballs, creating two more corpses. Left on his own, Scar-face dug his heels into his horse's flanks and turned tail. A few strides later, he was on the ground. One arrow in his head, and one in his back.

Dash and Maurice returned to the wagon, where Brian reluctantly exchanged horses with Dash again.

'What are we going to do with all the bodies, Father?' said Haggitt.

'What bodies?' said Gi. 'I see only crow food.'

'Shall I check them for valuables?' asked Brian. A soldier was always on the lookout for booty.

'No, they're poorer than you,' said Gi. 'If they had anything, I doubt they'd be trying to rob us.'

'I like the way you said, *trying*, Mr. Mulderbish. Though they didn't really, did they?' said Maurice.

Dash went straight to Bayna to make sure she was alright. The two elves nodded and hugged, emotionally.

'That might not be the end of it, Mr. Mulderbish,' said Maurice. 'If there are more of them, they'll be missed. And those horses might find their way back.'

'Well, the fact that they're rider-less, will tell them we're not to be messed with,' said Gi.

'Can we move on, Master?' suggested Muto.

'We might as well, Muto. Give 'em a slap.' Muto tapped the horses and the journey continued. Brian and Maurice fell in beside the wagon. Two ex-barbarians, who'd been told to stay put throughout the incident, took their places at the rear, feeling curiously safer and more at risk at the same time.

* * *

35

'Did you see what those wizards did back there?' said Maurice.

'Yeah, and I'm thinking they could've escaped from the wagon whenever they felt like it. I wonder why they stayed?' said Brian.

Dash overheard and rode to join them. 'I can answer your question, Brian,' he said. 'The wizards do not have a good sense of direction. Neither did they have transport. They want to get to Gremanos, where you are going, so why walk when they can ride with someone who knows the way?'

'I think we're lucky to be alive,' said Brian. 'They could've killed us all.'

Maurice smiled. 'Better not upset 'em then, eh?'

The rest of the day was quiet, except for flocks of crows heading in the opposite direction.

'We should stop soon,' said Dash. 'It's getting dark. Our animals will not be able to see.'

'Muto, find somewhere to stop, please,' said Gi.

'This place is as good as any, Master. Shall I start getting food ready?'

'Good idea, but don't let the horses wander too far. I'm just going for a quick run round on the lush grass like a mad thing, I won't be long.' He paused, when he saw the look on Muto's face. 'No, not really.' Gi smiled.

'Ah.' Muto ginned widely. 'I'll get Mr. Haggitt to sort out food for Dash and Bayna, Master. If you conjure up five full barbarians, I'll do the rest.'

Later, when the darkness had descended and they were sitting round the campfire, 'You know...' said Brian, 'this food is excellent. How does Muto do it? He only ever served up crap when he was cooking for du Merde.'

'I know, but he's cooking for Gi, now, and long may it last,' said Maurice.

Earlier that afternoon, when the sun was still westering overhead, Fox and Reza got the column moving again. 'We should be able to catch up by nightfall,' said Reza. 'I think it would be a good idea, if we split up. You take Sivad and about thirty men, and head on. The rest of us will keep pace with the supply wagon.'

Fox thought about it. 'Yeah, that should leave you with enough men to protect the wagon, and I should be able to catch up with Gi before he gets into trouble.'

'Right,' said Reza. 'Get your men together, and we'll see you later tonight.'

Fox got Sivad to muster thirty men, and the young soldier jumped into action with a hearty 'Yes sir!' He was a good man, and Fox loved his enthusiasm. Within minutes, there were two columns of fifteen men following Fox and him along the tracks left by Gi's wagon and his company.

As they galloped along at a reasonable pace, they were hit by the pungent smell of burnt and decaying flesh.

'That's awful,' said Sivad, screwing his nose up.

'Not nice at all,' said Fox. 'And judging by the crows, I'd say we've found a few dead people.'

'Oh, no. Not zombies!'

'No such thing,' Fox assured him, then added, 'Probably.' And laughed. As they got closer the smell worsened. They saw the overly long arrows and the large burns that decorated the bodies.

'Looks like some have been hit with fireballs. The others were killed by elves, I'd say,' he said, gravely.

'Elves?' queried Sivad.

'Yes, Gi's got two elves with him. And by the look of this lot, they're a useful addition to his group,' said Fox.

'You've seen them?'

'Yes, very striking folk, but try not to gape when you meet them,' Fox advised. The column had slowed as the soldiers gawped. 'Come on, men! You've seen bodies before. We've got a wagon to catch. Preferably before it gets dark.'

The column broke into a canter again, and within the hour, as the sun set, they could see the greyish white rectangle of the roof of the wagon.

Upon hearing the rumble of hooves, Dash stood up. 'Riders,' he said.

'Can you make out who it is?' asked Gi, peering into the night alongside him.

'It must be the soldiers,' said Dash.

A few yards away, a voice in the long grass muttered, 'Oh, bugger.'

The grass started to bend and sway as two bandit scouts scrambled to get away before Fox and his men arrived.

When they considered themselves to be far enough away, one whispered, 'Did you 'ear 'im say lots of soldiers? That's plural, innit? So, what's lots of 'em?'

'Dunno. More than two, I 'spect,' came the reply.

'I don't fink we should 'ang around then, do you?'

'No,' replied the other one, standing up and coming face to face with an elf.

'Oh shit... 'Ow'd you get 'ere?' was the last thing he said before an arrow went through his neck.

The other bandit cowered on the ground. 'Get up!' said Dash. The man slowly got to his feet. 'Go to the wagon,' Dash ordered, motioning with his bow. The man moved forward with his back to the elf. He was drawing a knife from his belt – secretly, he thought, until he suddenly yelped with pain and dropped it. His forearm had gained an arrow. Bayna waved at Dash and smiled, her lips mouthing, *You owe me.*

Dash cut the feathers from the arrow and pulled it through the man's arm. Fortunately for him, the flight feathers were nearest his flesh. The scream would have been louder and longer if Dash had pulled it back out the way it went in. He prodded him in the back, shoving the man forward.

'What have we got here?' said Gi.

'He was spying on us from the long grass, Gi. Probably a scout for bandits. We may have to torture some information out of him.'

When the bandit heard that and saw the look on the wizard's face, he fell to his knees. 'What do you want to know? I'll tell you anything.'

'Damn,' said Gi, 'you're no fun, are you? I've a good mind to torture you anyway, for being so annoyingly cooperative.'

The man looked confused. 'No, don't 'urt me. I wouldn't like that,' he pleaded.

'Oh, alright,' said Gi, grudgingly.

'Are there any more of you out there?' asked Haggitt.

'Lots of 'em.'

'How many is lots?' asked Gi. 'And how far?'

'I dunno, mister. I can't count. But not far.'

'Okay, which way to their camp?' asked Gi.

The bandit pointed with his good arm. Dash thought he was probably telling the truth. He clambered to the top of the wagon for a better view, and saw the faint glow of campfires in the distance.

'Going by the number of fires, we are outnumbered, even with the soldiers.'

Gi mumbled a curse. He seemed to be doing it a lot lately. And he thought he caught the flicker of a smile on the bandit scout's face.

* * *

36

The thunder of hooves arriving made the ground shake. Fox and his soldiers rode into Gi's camp. Fox raised a hand, for the men behind him to stop. It was dark and the men at the back of the column nearly didn't make it.

'Fox!' said Dash. 'We're so pleased you've arrived. There are many bandits camped over there.'

'We have one of their spies,' said Bayna, 'but the other one seems dead.'

Sivad tried to stop gaping. The elves were just too much for him to take in. They were beautiful, especially Bayna, and she spoke as if singing. 'Sivad!' called Fox, 'come and meet Dash, and his mate, Bayna. And close your mouth,' he whispered. Dash nodded, Bayna smiled. Sivad nodded, and contemplated bowing.

'Do not bow, Sivad. We are not royalty,' said Dash, with a wry smile.

'Ah... you've met the snow elves, then,' said Brian, coming to greet Fox. 'They look amazing, and they can fight as well,' he added.

'We saw proof of that back on the trail,' said Fox. 'Did you sustain any casualties?'

'No, not even a scratch,' said Maurice, joining them.

'Fox,' said Gi, 'It would be good to know how many bandits we're dealing with.'

'Have you questioned the prisoner?' asked Fox.

'Yes, it was fruitless. He can't count,' said Haggitt.

'Well, he must know how much room they take up,' said Fox.

'Shall I take Maurice, and have a look, Fox?' asked Sivad.

'No, get Badger, he's dressed for the part. Maurice can go with him and keep out of sight in case Badger gets seen,' said Fox. 'If you're not back by the time I'm tired of waiting, I'll send some more men.'

'Shall I go, Fox?' said Dash, ever eager to help.

'No, you will definitely be seen,' said Fox. 'And if we see these two running back with a lot of men chasing them, you'll be a useful member of the welcoming committee.'

Dash nodded.

'Ready?' said Badger. 'Let's do it.'

Both men stooped low and disappeared into the long grass.

The rest of them could only sit and wait. Either for their safe return, or pursued by a pack of bandits with big swords. It seemed hours before they returned.

'Where have you been?' asked Fox, who was seriously considering sending someone after them.

'It's further than it looks,' said Badger.

'Okay, what have you got?' asked Fox.

'There's a hundred or so,' said Maurice. 'Certainly not more.'

'Are they well-armed?'

'Swords mainly, and a few have lances,' said Badger.

'Oh,' said Fox. 'When Reza gets here, we'll plan our attack. He's not keen on lances, so those will have to be taken out first. Anything else we need to know, Badger?'

'I think I saw a few of the men that rode with Broosh Marteef, but I didn't know any of them,' said Badger.

'And they aren't the best fighters we've come across,' said Fox. 'I expect they'll be the first to run when it hots up.'

'Any idea when Reza will arrive?' asked Brian.

'Be patient. We're not in any hurry to die, are we?' said Fox, calmly.

'No, Fox,' said Brian, matching his tone. 'I've developed a taste for fighting on the winning side, though.'

'You can help by riding back to hurry them up. They may have camped for the night.'

He left immediately. Thankfully, he found them not far down the track, and got Reza to pick up the pace.

Reza's troops rode into camp to smiling faces. The supply wagon followed as fast as it could. Reza was greeted by Fox. He thought he'd been fully updated by Brian about the situation until he saw the elves' animals.

'Are those yours?' he said, in awe.

'The horse belongs to Dash, and the stag is Bayna's,' said Fox. 'Haven't you seen them before?'

'I'd certainly remember seeing *those* before,' said Reza. 'And I'll always remember them now. *Beautiful* creatures. All of them!'

'Come and see Gi,' said Fox, 'we need to agree on what to do.'

'What does Gi *want* to do?'

'Well, we can't outrun them, so we're considering attacking them at first light.'

They reached the wagon and joined others, sitting around in a circle outside. Gi sat with Haggitt on his left, and Dash and Bayna on his right. Fox, Reza, Brian, Maurice and Badger completed the circle.

'What ideas are on the table?' asked Reza, starting the conversation.

'Nothing firm,' said Fox. 'But we know there are about a hundred bandits out there.'

'Some of them have lances,' said Maurice.

'How many?' asked Reza, wincing.

'A half dozen, maybe,' volunteered Maurice.

'Right,' said Reza. 'First, we take out the lancers. They'll be leading any charge. And seriously dangerous. Any ideas?'

'Bayna and I will do that,' said Dash, adding without a trace of conceit, 'but we need to get close.'

'We don't want you seen,' Haggitt warned him. 'I have spare cloaks in the wagon. They might disguise you enough to get close.'

'That leaves about ninety-five,' said Reza.

'I can't guarantee to kill them all,' said Gi. 'But I'll rain lightning bolts down on them. A bit hit and miss I know, but I should get some, and it will panic them.'

'What about you, Fox. Any ideas?' asked Reza.

'If Gi can do his stuff, and the elves can take out the lancers, I believe I can circle around with half our men and drive what's left of the bandits towards the wagons. If you line up the rest of the men there, they can charge forward and cut them down when they come,' said Fox.

'Some of the other bandits will be mounted. Not just the lancers,' said Reza.

'Good point,' said Fox. 'Before this battle gets underway, Brian and Maurice need to find the horses and stampede them. That should ensure they're all on foot. Though the lancers may keep theirs away from the communal paddock, and bed down beside them.'

'Let's hope there aren't too many guards on the paddock,' said Brian.

'I doubt there'd be more than two,' said Fox.

Reza turned to Gi. 'When they come running this way, before our men go in, I want you to hit them with as many fireballs as you can. That'll make it a fairer fight for us.' He looked at Fox, then around the circle. 'Does that sound like a plan?'

'All in favour say "Aye",' said Gi.

After the chorus of 'Ayes', Reza said, 'One more thing – we don't take prisoners.'

There was another chorus of 'agreed.'

'Good. We start in one hour,' said Reza. 'Gi, did I hear you say you had a spy?'

'He's tied to the wagon.'

'Alright,' said Reza. 'I'll take care of him.'

'No need,' said Bayna. 'I put an arrow through him earlier.'

'That only went through his arm, my love,' said Dash.

Bayna smiled, this time baring the fangs at the corners of her slightly open mouth. 'That was the first one, my dear.'

Dash grinned, and Reza mouthed an 'O'.

'An hour, then,' said Gi, breaking up the meeting.

* * *

37

The bandit's campfires had long gone out, and a pre-dawn stillness had settled over the camp.

Haggitt had raided his clothes chest and found cloaks for the elves, who quickly put them on and pulled the hoods over their heads. They took their bows and disappeared into the night. 'Try not to get them dirty,' Haggitt called after them. 'They're a bugger to clean.' Then he heard whispering in the long grass.

'What are you doing here, Badger? I almost killed you,' said Dash.

'I heard noises, so I crept out to have a look.'

'Anything?' said Bayna.

'Two more spies, but don't worry I got 'em both,' Badger whispered.

'Thank you. Go back and stay with the wizards. You've done your bit for now,' Dash whispered. He watched Badger climb onto the wagon, then the two elves moved silently into the darkness.

'Why, Mr. Badger...' said Muto. 'You've got blood on your hands. Show me. I'll clean it up for you.'

'It's alright. I'm not in any pain, so I don't think it's mine,' said Badger.

'Nevertheless, I will look,' insisted Muto.

'Ouch! That hurt,' cried Badger.

'See, you have a cut. It needs a stitch.'

'No. No. No. It'll get bet...' he didn't finish because he was now unconscious, Muto having administered a fist-anaesthetic between the eyes.

Muto looked in the little bag always attached to his belt, and found a needle and a short length of thread. He sterilised the needle with the flame from one of the yellow-headed matches he carried, and it wasn't long before there were three neat stitches closing the cut on the back of Badger's hand.

Then, Muto slapped Badger's face a few times. 'Come on, Mr. Badger, wake up, we'll need you in a minute.'

Badger stirred. 'Did you just hit me?'

'*Me?*' said the little cook, 'What makes you think I'm capable of hitting anybody? You passed out from the pain, I expect.'

Badger looked at his hand. The dried blood had been cleaned away and a neat row of stitches was holding the skin together. He flexed his fingers and grimaced, but they did work. 'Thanks, Muto. I owe you.'

'We'll see,' said Muto.

Brian and Maurice had already set out. They'd located the horses and there was only one guard. 'I'll deal with him,' Maurice whispered. 'You cut the horses loose.'

A few quiet steps and the guard died from a deep knife wound to his throat. On hearing the horses running away, the two elves moved in close and dispatched the men with the lances, who were bedded down away from the communal paddock with their own steeds, as Fox had predicted. Maurice and Brian crept over and recovered the lances.

The bandits were stirring. They were hardly awake when the sky lit up with forked lightning, which rained down on them. As they started to scatter, Fox yelled 'Charge!' and thirty mounted soldiers galloped headlong into the camp. Fox slashed the heads off at least six men, and Sivad took out another four before they'd gone far. The mounted soldiers pursued and headed off the bandits that were running away from the wagons and shepherded them back with the others. It was crucial that all the bandits were heading towards the wagons.

Fox's men pushed them forward as best they could, but the long grass impeded the horses' progress. 'Slow down, men! Wait here.'

The soldiers fanned out behind the bandits, effectively cutting off any retreat. The scene lit up again as multiple fireballs seared the air into the pack of bandits heading toward the wagons. Many of them fell, while others tried to run back to their camp.

Reza shouted at Gi and Haggitt to stop, and led his men at full gallop to slay the rest of the approaching bandits. Those who weren't cut down were trampled to death. As he said, Reza took no prisoners.

When all was quiet, Maurice, Brian and the two elves walked back into camp.

'I don't think I've ever seen so many bodies at once,' said Brian.

'Nor me,' said Maurice, sounding thoughtful. 'Makes you wonder why.'

'We know why,' Brian came back. 'We did it because we didn't want that to be us.'

A short silence later, Maurice said, 'Yup.'

'We'd better report back to Fox, and see what's next. I just hope he doesn't ask us to clean this lot up,' said Brian.

Badger walked out to meet them. 'Well done everybody,' he grinned.

'What's happened to your face?' asked Brian, walking back.

'What do you mean?' asked Badger.

'You've got a big bruise on your forehead,' Brian told him.

'I got a cut hand,' said Badger, holding it up.

'Sorry?' said Brian. 'You cut your hand and you got a bruise on you head?'

'I'm not sure,' said Badger. 'But I think Muto hit me.'

'Did you upset him?' said Dash.

'No, he said I needed stitches in my hand, and I don't like needles. He told me I passed out with the pain. The little bugger,' said Badger.

They couldn't help laughing. But Maurice put a comforting arm round Badger's shoulder and led him back to the wagon. The ex-barbarian had certainly earned his place among the soldiers after this morning.

'Are you better?' grinned Muto, when they got back to the wagon.

'I don't want to talk about it,' snapped Badger.

Then Gi appeared. 'It's good to see you all back safely,' he said, but there was concern in his voice.

'Have you seen Fox, Mr. Mulderbish?' Brian asked him.

115

'He was walking with Reza just now. Planning something, I expect,' said Gi.

'Thanks, come on Maurice, let's go find him.' The two soldiers took a walk around, seeing who was where. 'Do you think we lost anybody?' said Brian. 'It was pretty hectic out there.'

'It would be surprising if we didn't,' replied Maurice. 'But I sure hope not.'

'I'm going to ask Fox if he would mind if I rode with Gi, till we get to Gremanos,' said Brian. 'I need time to clear my head.'

'I know what you mean,' said Maurice. 'Maybe we can come up with a reason to stay with the wizards. But with their power and the two elves, we can't really claim that they need protecting, can we?'

The two men didn't find Fox and Reza on their stroll, so they went back to Gi's wagon. 'Are you in there, Mr. Mulderbish?' Brian called out.

'What can I do for you?' asked Gi.

'Would you mind if we sleep under your wagon, till we all pull out?' said Brian. 'The sun's coming up and it'll shade us.'

'Not at all. Unless you snore, then you'll be told to go. Probably not politely, either,' Gi warned them.

'Understood, Mr. Mulderbish.'

* * *

38

After the exertions of the pre-dawn fighting, they all turned in as dawn broke. The sun had risen when Muto gave Brian a nudge. 'Come on, soldiers. Wakey, wakey. Master wants you up now. It's time for breakfast.'

'Hmm?' Brian grunted.

'Please get up,' said Muto. 'Master Gi wants to be well away from here before all those bodies start to rot.'

'Oh, gods,' said Maurice, suddenly conscious. 'I'd forgotten about those.'

'I don't suppose you're responsible for *all* of them, Mr. Maurice,' said Muto, but it didn't help.

'Is your Master up yet?' asked Brian.

'I'm here,' said Gi, appearing from around the wagon.

'We were wondering, me and Maurice that is, if you'd like us to accompany you the rest of the way to Gremanos?'

'I think it's a sensible idea, yes,' agreed Gi.

'Would you mind asking Fox, then? He may refuse if we ask him,' said Brian.

'I have already spoken to Fox about escorting us, and he thinks it'll be best if he accompanies us with the whole troop,' said Gi. 'But I think two wagons travelling with a hundred-soldier escort is going to attract attention, don't you?'

Brian and Maurice looked crest fallen. Gi went on, 'I'm going to tell Fox, that just a couple of men with the wagon and a bigger force about a mile behind, is probably safer.'

'I like that,' said Maurice. 'It makes more sense. If there's any problems, we know help is only a few minutes away.'

Later, Fox let Gi know that the soldiers were ready to move out. Gi related the conversation with Brian and Maurice, and Fox gave it the okay.

They were out of the desert now, and the weather was cooler. There was no need to worry about what time of day they travelled.

But after a few miles of hanging back behind the wagon, Fox grew impatient. He and Sivad had caught up with Gi on several occasions during the day.

'Tomorrow,' said Fox, 'we'll go ahead and you can follow us. Reza and some men are further back with the supply wagon, so he can keep an eye on you from behind.'

'Let's talk it through tonight,' said Gi, but thinking it didn't sound negotiable. When Fox was out of earshot, Gi said, 'I don't like that idea much, Brian. I think he intends to leave us behind.'

'It looks that way, Mr. Mulderbish. But I like Fox. I doubt he'd leave us stranded.'

Gi wasn't so sure. 'Let's see how it goes tonight. Right now, I need to speak to Muto.'

Brian and Maurice strolled off, and Gi climbed up into the wagon, 'Muto, can you remember what was in that supply wagon?' Gi asked, keeping his voice down.

'Most of it, Master, yes.'

'Were there any weapons?' asked Gi.

'Oh, yes, Master. Bows, arrows, spare strings, crossbows with those little arrowy things.'

'Bolts,' said Gi.

'*Really*, Master,' said Muto, hiding his sarcasm well.

'Do you know how to use one?' Gi asked him.

'Master, you offend me. I'm possibly the greatest crossbowman the world has ever seen,' said Muto, proudly.

'Don't give me that bullshit, Muto,' Gi smiled.

'Alright, Master. I didn't say I *was* the greatest in the world: I said *possibly*. I know how to load one, and how hard can it be to point it and fire it? Look, all I've done for you on this journey is cook and drive, Master. Let me do something really useful.'

'See if you can get into the supply wagon and get a couple of crossbows then, and some bolts. Take Haggitt with you, and meet me back here. I'm not going anywhere.'

'Come on, Mr. Haggitt,' said Muto, beaming.

The wizards' party had paused so long that the supply wagon had caught up. It had drawn to a halt not far behind, waiting for them to move.

Haggitt and Muto walked back and weren't even challenged when they went to look inside.

'Give me a leg up, Mr. Haggitt.' Muto grinned.

'Can't you step on the wheel?' said Haggitt.

'I can,' said Muto. 'But it won't be half as much fun.'

Haggitt was beginning to worry about Muto, but he kept his thoughts to himself. Just then, Muto called, 'Mr. Haggitt! Take this box, please, and put it on the ground.'

'Why?'

'Because I need you to take these as well.' He passed down two crossbows. 'Now help me down, please.'

Back on the ground again, Muto asked Haggitt if he could hide the crossbows under his robe. 'I can now,' he said, having muttered a spell he remembered from Seventh-Level classes, which temporarily reduced things.

When Muto got over that, he grabbed the box of bolts.

Again, they weren't challenged. Muto gave the driver a cheery wave as they left.

'Don't you think they'll miss these?' said Haggitt.

'Nobody saw us take them,' said Muto, 'so they'll think the barbarians did. Don't worry so, Mr. Haggitt.'

* * *

'Ah, good. You've got them. Well done, Muto,' said Gi. And as an afterthought, added, 'You too, son. Now hide them in the wagon. Quickly.'

'We timed that just right,' said Muto. 'Reza's soldiers are getting ready to move out.'

Fox's men had left and were already some distance ahead. 'So much for discussing whether they should lead,' said Gi, moodily. 'Alright. Let's go.'

'Master,' said Muto, with some urgency. 'The left front wheel is dragging badly.'

'Okay,' Gi sighed. 'Get down and see what's happened.'

He passed the reins to Gi and jumped down. 'Oh dear, Master, we forgot to cut that man loose that Bayna killed.'

'Get Gennett and Smokey to deal with it. They've done nothing to help so far.'

'I'll deal with it, Master. Those two left and joined Reza's group,' Muto told him.

'Oh, good,' said Gi.

'Not really, Master. It means I've got this nasty mess to scrape off the wheel,' moaned Muto. 'And before you say it, Brian and Maurice can't help. They rode back to check with Reza that they can ride with us.'

'Haggitt, go and help him, please,' said Gi. 'Be quick, though, because Reza's men will be moving soon.'

'He has an answer for everything, Muto,' Haggitt grumbled.

'I *know*,' said Muto. 'Isn't he wonderful?'

It was almost half an hour before Haggitt and Muto climbed back onto the wagon. Gi was napping inside, so Haggitt rode up front with Muto.

Brian and Maurice joined them with a message from Reza to get a move on – which was the polite version.

'Thank you, Brian,' said Muto. 'Dash wants you two to guard that side now. Gennett and Smokey are riding with Reza.'

'Yeah, we saw them,' said Maurice. 'They kept out of our way, though. A bit odd, if you ask me.'

'Do you think Reza's up to something?' asked Brian.

'Not sure. Let's not say anything to Gi until after the meeting tonight,' said Maurice.

Not long into the day, a rider came galloping back from Fox's troop. 'Stop the wagon! Fox is in trouble; I'm going to get Reza!' He dug his spurs in and galloped off.

'Should we stop, Master?' said Muto, unhappy taking orders from anyone else.

'No,' said Gi. 'Wait until Reza has taken his men to help Fox, then I think we should get off this road as soon as we can.'

'Are Brian and Maurice staying with us, Master?'

'Yes,' said Gi. 'And with Dash and Bayna, we should be able to look after ourselves.'

In minutes, Reza's column drew up alongside. 'Stay here till I send for you!' Reza shouted.

Gi just waved a hand, thinking *not on your life, soldier.* But he said, 'Okay, but don't be too long!'

* * *

With Fox's troop in trouble somewhere up ahead, and Reza's men being fetched from behind to aid them, Muto took the first opportunity to leave the track, as Gi had instructed him. Muto turned the horses in the direction of what was possibly a river. There was no track to follow, but sizing up the terrain he felt it safe to assume that a river came down from the mountains ahead. He wanted to get out of sight before Reza went by, but the going was rough and slowed them down. And when they reached the safety of the foothills there was no sign of a river.

'Perhaps it's further up, Master,' said Muto.

'Ever the optimist,' Maurice grinned.

'There's a gap through there,' said Brian, standing in the stirrups and pointing.

'Yes, go that way, Muto,' said Gi. 'There's something I need to do.'

He clambered into the back of the wagon and started waving his hands in circles, getting quicker and quicker, creating a small whirlwind which, when he was satisfied it would do the job, he aimed it at the tracks left by the wagon and riders. As before, it wiped out all signs of the wagon's trail. 'Hmm,' he breathed, 'same old magic.' He moved back up with Muto. He was at peace with the world for a moment, but wise enough to know that it wouldn't last.

'Could there be trolls around here?' Haggitt wondered, scanning the rough landscape.

'What makes you think that?' said Gi.

'Might be their kind of place, that's all,' said Haggitt.

'Probably not. They like to be higher where there's no grass,' said Gi, the new troll expert.

Haggitt dismissed the thought and tried to think of something else.

'Do you know how to load a crossbow, Mr. Haggitt?' asked Muto.

'You know, Muto?' said Haggitt, 'it's something I've never had cause to try. But I don't suppose it can be that difficult, can it?'

'No,' said Muto. 'But I'll show you anyway. Can you get one from the back, please?'

Haggitt left and, moments later, returned with a crossbow.

'Good,' said Muto, teasing. 'You still remember what they look like. Now, see this lever here, well that comes off and this bit swings about a bit. You fit it just here, in front of the string and lever it back till it catches on that bit there. Mind your fingers, Mr. Haggitt! Then you take a bolt and slide it into that groove so it catches on the string. Now all you have to do is point it and pull the trigger. That's all there is to it.'

'Where shall I point it?' asked Haggitt.

'Always at the ground, when not in use, please,' said Muto, pushing the pointy end away. 'You'll have to wait until we stop if you want target practice.'

'Brian!' Gi called. 'There must be a town or a village nearby. I can smell wood smoke.'

'I can smell it too, Mr. Mulderbish. I'll ride ahead and take a look,' said Brian, the volunteer.

Brian rode to the top of the rise ahead and stopped. There were a few run-down plank houses, a tavern, a shop, and what looked like a small hotel. But where were all the people? A chimney was smoking, so there had to be someone around. Brian trotted back and reported what he'd seen.

* * *

'What? Nobody? Not even a sound?' asked Gi.

'No, Mr. Mulderbish, I didn't see a soul.'

'I think it's an ambush,' said Maurice. 'Do we really need to walk into it?'

'Maybe just two of us,' said Gi, 'while the rest wait back a little way.'

'With respect, Mr. Mulderbish, I think we should leave Dash and Bayna here, till we've made sure it's safe,' said Maurice.

'You're probably right. Are you two okay with that?' asked Gi.

The two elves agreed. Whilst their animals were commonplace in their own dimension, they were rare and highly prized in this one.

Muto drove the wagon down the slope to the group of buildings. The first place he passed was a tavern, confirmed by the sign over the door. He drove on at walking pace. They passed a two-storey wooden building, possibly a hotel, with a staircase on the outside leading to a veranda with doors to the upstairs rooms. On the other side of the street was a general store. Then came a row of five detached wood-planked houses. All had shuttered windows, with slits in the shape of crosses cut into them.

'I don't like the look of this place one bit,' said Maurice.

'Gives me the creeps,' Brian agreed. 'The shop's not open. There's no noise coming from the tavern. Where is everybody? Hello!' he yelled. 'Anybody there!'

There was an echo he didn't expect. And somewhere behind him, a door slammed. All six of them turned to see that someone had appeared.

A thin, almost emaciated, white-faced man was standing in the middle of the street, leaning on a pitch fork. He looked odd, but harmless. Brian turned his horse around and trotted back towards him.

The man looked afraid. 'What do you want?' he asked, abruptly. 'Whatever it is, make it quick, and leave this place.'

'Sir, you don't look at all well, are you alright?' Brian asked him.

'Please… take what you need and go,' the man insisted. 'This is no place for you.'

Brian dismounted. 'Are you alone here, sir? Perhaps we can help you.'

'No, not alone. There are thirty-eight of us left,' croaked the man.

Brian looked around. 'Can we see them?'

'They're all hiding in the tavern. You will have to go in there. They will not come out,' said the man, starting to shake.

'Gi, Muto! Bring up the wagon!' shouted Brian.

Maurice rode up and tethered his mount outside the tavern.

'He seems to be in fear for his life, Maurice. He's trying to get us into the tavern, where the rest of them are. There's something not right,' said Brian.

'No kidding,' said Maurice. 'Let's get them to come out. There may be someone or something in there holding them.'

Brian turned to the pale man. 'We're not going in there until we've seen more of your people out here.'

The man looked even more afraid. 'I will ask them,' he muttered, shuffling over and pushing the tavern door open.

There were still no sounds coming from inside, but two females of indeterminate age, wearing long white dresses with low necklines came out. Their complexions were paler than the man's – though not strikingly white like snow elves – and there were bruises and small puncture wounds on their necks and shoulders. Their eyes were glazed, and it didn't look even worth trying to speak to them.

The three on the wagon had watched in silence. Gi climbed down and went to look at the women. He breathed deeply, and sighed. 'I've seen this before – years ago,' he said, quietly.

'What's the matter with them, Father?' asked Haggitt.

'They're being kept like animals to feed upon their blood, and whatever is doing it only comes at night,' said Gi, sadly.

'Is there anything we can do?'

'Not unless they ask us,' said Gi.

'I'm asking,' said the thin man, plaintively.

125

'Does he come every night?' Gi asked.'

'Whenever the moon appears,' said the man. 'He asks for volunteers, but if none offer, he chooses.'

'I have an idea,' said Gi. 'Brian, go and bring Bayna and Dash. They're safe enough here.'

*

Gi explained what he wanted from the elves, mainly Bayna, but Dash would need to be on hand if anything went wrong.

'When this thing comes tonight,' said Gi, to the pale man. 'I want you to tell him that a beautiful young woman has come into town and she is staying at the hotel. In the first room on the veranda. Can you do that?' asked Gi.

The pale man nodded, and ushered the two sick-looking women back inside the tavern.

Muto turned the wagon back to the hotel. Usefully, there was a water trough outside for the horses. Then he picked up a crossbow and a handful of bolts, and went into the hotel to wait.

Bayna went to the room above him, and Dash occupied the room next door to her. It looked like being a clear night. When the thing came to the hotel, Muto was to bang lightly on the ceiling to warn her.

When darkness fell over the small town and the moon stood high, the adrenalin began to flow. All except Bayna scanned the night sky for the creature. She lay still, her heart pounding. Just as the tension was getting unbearable, a shadow flew across Muto's window and the sound of leathery wings flapped to slow a descent. It settled outside the tavern and the pale man approached it warily. After a brief conversation, the thing made for the hotel steps. The man had played his part. Muto tapped on the ceiling and looked out the window, just in time to see a man-like shape, cloaked in black, climbing the stairs outside. The thing stopped at Bayna's door and listened before going in. She was lying on the bed, awake, and beckoned him to her. The man allowed his cloak to slip to the floor and he perched on the edge of the bed.

He slid his arm under her head and laid a hand on her waist as he bent forward to kiss her. He was completely entranced by her beauty until Bayna bared her fangs. Before he could react, she sank them into his neck. A quick shake and his throat hung from her mouth. She spat it out and wiped the blood from her chin, then banged on the wall for Dash to come in. He opened the door and fired an arrow through the thing's heart for good measure. Then, he grabbed the body with distaste and dumped it unceremoniously over the veranda rail into the street for Brian and Maurice to secure it where it would be in full sunlight the next morning, as Gi had instructed.

Dash and Bayna descended the steps. They were holding hands, looking relieved and very pleased with their night's work. 'Gi, I think we may have freed these people for a long time to come,' said Dash. 'And only the one man – I suppose it was a man – died,' said Dash.

'I'm not sure if you can actually kill these things. But even if it does survive somehow, I'm sure it will leave these people alone,' said Gi. 'It might even revert back to eating animals, like they did years ago.'

The pale faced man came out of the tavern and saw Brian securing the body of their tormentor. He hobbled inside to tell the rest of his people.

One by one the people filed into the street. They were happier than they had the strength to express, but their eyes appeared to be smiling.

The pale faced man approached Gi with tears in his eyes. 'How can we thank you?' he asked.

Gi looked around at the poor state of everything and took the man's hand. 'I don't think you can,' he said. 'Thank yourselves for surviving, and put your community back together again.' Gi paused for a moment, then... 'Is the bar open?'

'The bar never closed,' the man told him. 'There's nothing to drink.'

Gi pushed the tavern door open and went inside. The man was right; the shelves *were* empty. 'What happened in here?'

'Soldiers,' was all the man said.

Gi was not happy. 'How many?' he wanted to know.

'About thirty, maybe more.'

'Go outside,' said Gi. 'I'll call you in a minute.'

The man shuffled away obediently and stood outside. Then he jumped when he saw bright flashes of light coming from the windows and around the door. The sounds of bottles being moved around filled the air. Then there was silence.

'You can come in, now!' called Gi.

The man walked into the bar. It had been totally re-stocked. 'I don't know what it's going to taste like,' Gi warned him, 'but it's better than nothing.'

The man's face brightened. He went outside and told the people what Gi had done and they started to wander back in.

Gi was waiting by the door. Every one of them touched his hand as they passed. And, once all the people of the village were inside, Muto, Brian and Maurice went in.

'Where are the elves?' asked Gi.

'They don't drink alcohol, Master,' said Muto. 'Mr. Haggitt is conjuring something suitable for them.'

'Get yourself a drink, Muto, and come and sit with me in the corner,' said Gi. The invitation was friendly, but his face was stern.

Muto returned with two bottles, and sat down next to Gi, 'What's the matter, Master?'

'I think Reza brought his men through here. They cleared out all the stock and I've seen no sign of them paying for any of it. Even worse, they made no attempt to help these people, just took advantage on them.'

'It doesn't sound like him, Master. But he has changed lately,' said Muto.

'I'm glad I'm not the only one who's noticed,' said Gi.

'Brian and Maurice have lost faith in him too. That's why they want to ride with us.' The little cook looked puzzled, though. 'In Reza's defence, I don't see how he could have got here before us. He was behind us when we turned off. Surely him and his men couldn't have got here and drunk the tavern dry before us.'

Gi wasn't deterred. 'We came by the cross-country route, Muto. They must have used the proper track further up the road. They know the road, remember. It's their regular route to Gremanos. Even though they were rushing to help Fox, I'm guessing Reza didn't want to miss an opportunity to stock the supply wagon with drink. It's about the morale of his men.'

'Ah,' said Muto, nodding.

'Well, I can't see my way clear to letting Reza get away with it. I'm of a mind to recompense these people from the bags of gold you and Haggitt stole from them,' said Gi.

'Not stole, Master. We stopped them from wasting it,' Muto insisted.

'Of course you did. So, I think one bag should be enough, don't you?' said Gi.

'Master, whatever you do is fine with me.'

'Good. Go and get Haggitt. Tell him what's happened, and bring *one* bag to me in here. And keep it out of sight when you come back,' said Gi.

Muto left discretely. Once out on the street, he called Haggitt to him. Haggitt followed, as did the elves.

At the wagon, Muto explained, 'The Master wants one of the bags from the bottom of the chest.'

'Do you know why?' asked Haggitt.

'Yes,' said Muto, 'so pass one down, please.'

'Are you going to tell me?' Haggitt asked him.

'No. The Master will tell you when he's ready, I expect.'

'But it's not his, Muto,' Haggitt argued.

'No, and it's not ours either.' Muto took the bag and clutched it under his coat as they made their way back to the tavern.

Muto slid onto the chair next to Gi, making Haggitt sit across the table with his back to the bar.

'What are you up to, Father?' said Haggitt.

'I think Reza's men were here, and they took the ale,' said Gi. 'And I've yet to find any evidence of them paying for it.'

'Ah… I see,' said Haggitt. 'Now I understand. Do you think one bag will be enough?' he whispered.

'What?' said Gi, feeling stung. 'I don't see that giving them any more will make life better, but it might ease it a bit.'

'Shall I call the man over, Master?' offered Muto. 'The pale one we saw when we arrived?'

'Yes,' said Gi, 'but do it discreetly.'

Muto disappeared momentarily, and came back with the pale-faced man. 'I've found him, Master. Among all the other pale-faced people.'

'Sit down, please,' said Gi. 'We will be leaving in the morning, probably before you and your people rise. And my companions and I have decided to give you the money the soldiers should have paid you for your stock,' said Gi.

'Thank you,' said the man, looking tearful again. 'I will pay the tavern keeper his dues and distribute the rest among the people.' He picked up the bag, struggled for a moment under the unexpected weight, then made his way to the man standing behind the bar.

There was a lot of secret whispering, which stopped abruptly when the tavern keeper banged on the counter for everyone's attention. He was as poorly as the rest of them, and spoke quietly for a man slightly larger than the rest. But Gi could pull together the threads of what he was saying and decided to stay and make sure the man followed through on his promises. A cheer went up and Gi could see the pale faced man was giving everybody a share of the money. The tavern owner had refused to take any money for what had been taken, as Gi had magically re-stocked the bar for him. He took the same share as everybody else. Gi was content; the night had gone well.

'Come, Haggitt, Muto, let's get some sleep. Brian! Maurice! Don't stay up too late. We leave early.'

The wizards and the cook walked up the street in the direction of the wagon.

Dash and Bayna were waiting. 'Good to see you, gentlemen,' said Dash.

'We've come to sleep, now' said Gi. 'Where do you two sleep?'

'I will show you.' Bayna smiled. She told the horse and the stag to lie down. There was enough room between the two animals for the elves to lay between them.

'Aren't you worried somebody might try to steal them?' asked Haggitt.

'All the time,' said Dash. 'Snow – that's my horse – is usually quiet, unless I tell him to be otherwise. But Ice – the stag – will attack without hesitation. His antlers are lethal.'

'I'll be careful,' said Haggitt, moving gingerly around the animal as he climbed up into the wagon. He held out his hand to Gi, and pulled him up. Muto made himself comfortable under the driver's seat.

* * *

42

The next morning, Gi's party were awakened by a bright sun and a cock crowing somewhere. A few villagers had stirred and the village felt happy, if such a thing can be said of a place. Brian went to make sure the dead thing he and Maurice had secured the previous night was still there. It had gone, but not altogether. There was a heap of white powder where it had been.

Gi appeared at his shoulder. 'Did you know this would happen when the sun came up, Mr. Mulderbish?'

'I wasn't certain,' said Gi, stooping to examine the powder. 'I'd heard stories. Have we got a broom?'

'No,' said Brian. 'But I know where there is one.'

The young soldier crossed to the general store where a broom was leaning beside the door.

'Right,' said Gi. 'Sweep the powder in different directions until you lose sight of it.'

Brian did even better. He swept briskly so a lot of the dust rose up and was carried away on the light breeze.

Satisfied, Gi called, 'Muto! Time for breakfast. I want to be out of here within the hour.'

'If one of you wizards would conjure up something nice, please…'

Gi directed him to the general store.

* * *

Over breakfast, they weighed their options. They could get back on the regular route to Gremanos using the track out of the village. Or they could continue cross-country and keep out of the way of the soldiers. The owner of the general store said the cross-country route was doable, even with a wagon. There was a bit of a track. And he confirmed they would eventually reach a river.

Muto drove the wagon out of the village and headed for the river, trying to keep to level ground as much as possible. Dash and Bayna rode at the rear, and as they were travelling across an expanse of grass, the wagon and horses weren't kicking up dust. Brian and Maurice took up stations each side of the horses pulling the wagon where Gi could see them. And the day was going well.

'How far did he say the river is?' asked Haggitt.

'Three or four miles,' said Brian. 'But you know how these village folk can be with distances. So, I'd double that.'

'It can't be that far, Mr. Haggitt,' said Muto. 'There are lots of birds in the sky ahead.'

'Then we will go where the birds are,' said Gi.

'Trust me, Master.' Muto smiled. 'Look. Herons. Water birds. We must be going the right way.'

'What do they taste like?' Gi wondered.'

'Chicken, probably, Master. I've never tried one.'

'Nor me... probably need a bloody great pot to cook them in, though,' said Gi.

'Not chicken,' said Haggitt. 'Fish. That's all they eat. Please don't try and catch one, I hate fish.'

'That's got to be strange,' said Muto. 'Eating a bird that tastes like fish. Not so bad the other way round, though. I think I could handle that.'

He turned his attention back to the road ahead. 'That tree line ahead looks more like a forest, Master. Do you want to find the track through, or shall we go around?'

'We'll go through,' said Gi.

They found a suitable gap. Brian and Maurice moved to the front of the wagon as the route was narrow.

It was pleasant. The wind was cool and sighed occasionally as it rustled the leaves. The sun was high and its rays through the canopy highlighted the dust and seeds floating in the air.

'If we come to a clearing, Muto, we'll stop for a while,' said Gi. 'And give the horses a rest. I'm sure Dash's animals would like a break, too.'

'Yes, Master. Shall I get a picnic ready as well?'

'Don't be sarcastic, Muto. It doesn't become you,' said Gi.

'Sorry, Master. I didn't mean it like that.'

'Apology accepted,' said Gi. 'You're right. I think we should eat as well.'

Progress was slow. It was warm, and the animals were showing signs of discomfort. It was getting on for midday before they found a suitable place to stop. They heard a stream, probably a tributary of the river they were heading towards, and diverted through the trees to find a stretch of clear ground along the banks.

'Dash, you and Bayna take your animals and let them drink; we'll see to our horses after,' said Gi.

After stretching his legs for a minute, Haggitt sat on the back of the wagon, idly looking round at the trees and listening to the birds. He was enjoying the moment when two men emerged from the trees in front of him.

'Well, what have we got here?' said one.

'Oh, no,' said Haggitt. 'Father, we have company.'

Muto picked up a crossbow, slid off the wagon and moved quietly into the trees.

'It's a wagon,' said the other man. 'And an old man, and a younger man. What do you think they're doing out here all on their own, Trevor?'

'Asking to get robbed, I shouldn't wonder,' replied Julian.

'I warn you,' said Haggitt. 'We are not alone.'

'Shut up!' snapped Gi. 'You don't think they'll believe *that*, do you?'

'Course we don't,' said Julian. 'But you keep trying to convince me if it'll make you feel better.'

Trevor unslung his bow and notched an arrow. 'What have you got in the wagon?'

'Nothing of value, I assure you. We're just humble travellers,' said Gi. 'And if we had, we wouldn't give it to you.'

'What about… if there was *eight* of us?' said Trevor.

Gi looked him in the eyes. 'Then you will be the first to die,' he replied, calmly.

Trevor laughed. 'Did you hear that, men? Get out here now and show him we mean business.'

Six more men emerged from the trees and stood behind Trevor.

'I did warn you,' said Gi. 'Shoot him, Muto.'

Trevor's eyes scanned the trees. There was a dull thud. His bow slipped from his fingers and he stared down at the bolt sticking out of his chest. Then he fell face forward onto the forest floor.

'And then,' said Gi, 'there were *seven.*'

Julian swore loudly, drew his sword and charged Gi. He didn't get far, for the wizard was ready. With a wave of his hands, Gi sent a glowing blue fireball into the man's chest.

'And then… there were *six,*' he said.

'Wizards! Didn't anybody notice they were bloody wizards?!' yelled the new leader. Come on lads, I'm not messing with wizards.' He turned and started to run. Then he stopped.

Dash and Bayna were in his way. 'This does not appear to be your lucky day,' said Dash, as an arrow left his bow with such force it impaled the man to a tree. Bayna rode her stag into the clearing. The creature had gored two men to death on its antlers before they realised what was happening.

Haggitt grinned at Gi, had a quick count, and announced, 'And then there were… *three.*'

The three remaining bandits flung their weapons to the ground. 'We give up! We'll not cause you any more trouble,' said the third leader in as many minutes.

'Leave your weapons and go,' said Gi. 'And tell your friends to stay away!'

They ran back into the trees.

'I hope they come back for the bodies,' said Haggitt. 'Or this place will be attracting wolves and goodness knows what else by morning.'

'Brian! Can you and Maurice drag them into the bushes?' said Gi. 'About fifty yards would be good. We don't want to be looking at them while we're eating, do we?'

'It's not as if we're not used to dealing with the fallen,' sighed Brian.

The rest of them had their meals while the two guards were occupied. It took longer than anticipated, and by way of a thank you, Gi let them choose whatever they wanted to eat. Muto found himself preparing steaks, mushrooms and chips.

'Those bandits will know these woods well enough to track where we left their buddies, Mr. Mulderbish,' said Maurice, in case Gi cared. But he made no comment.

'So, you can conjure up anything we want?' said Brian.

'Within reason,' said Gi. 'There are, what I think of as, checks and balances in the realm of magic. It's an important part of what we learn. For myself, I like to keep it simple.'

'I like simple, too,' said Brian, tucking in, appreciatively.

'When you've finished, we'll clear up and go,' said Gi.

* * *

44

The forest was larger than expected. They wanted to follow the stream to the river, but the banks were overgrown further along, so they re-joined the rough track, and travelled at a sluggish pace for most of the rest of the day. Which was not unpleasant, but it didn't get them very far. And now evening was beginning to draw in.

'Let me know when you want to stop, Master,' said Muto.

'Soon. The next clearing. Preferably off the track again, if you can spot one,' said Gi. 'I saw you shoot that crossbow, earlier. You're very good.'

'Master, I was glad of the opportunity. It's been years since I killed anybody.'

Gi's chin moved up and down, while he thought of something to say to that. 'It was impressive. What were you before you became a cook?'

'*Always* a cook, Master.'

'Then how come you are so good with a crossbow?'

'Master, I'm a natural. Like I said, I'm the best ever,' he said, parodying himself.

'Muto, my friend, I'm beginning to believe you.'

Muto pulled back the reins. 'There's our clearing,' he said. 'If I can steer us through the undergrowth, we'll have a cosy place for the night.'

'Yes, I think so. Brian! Maurice! We're stopping. Can one of you get a fire going? Haggitt – tell Dash and Bayna.'

When the evening meal was over, Muto watched appreciatively as the magically produced plates and cutlery faded to nothing. 'Hope the food doesn't do that or we'll all be hungry again in a minute,' he quipped. Then as they lounged and chatted, he said, 'We used to sing songs round the campfire when I was young.'

'Thank goodness you're not young, then,' said Haggitt.

'Yeah,' said Muto. 'Everybody hated it. But I've heard elves can sing. They're pretty much singing when they talk, for goodness' sake.'

'Forget it,' said Dash. 'Not *all* elves can, and I am living proof of that.'

'Last time, his horse ran away,' Bayna laughed.

'I don't want to talk about it,' said Dash, but he was still smiling.

It seemed to Gi that, whilst the two elves bickered occasionally, they were devoted to each other. When they weren't in the saddle, they strolled hand in hand behind the wagon as they led their animals. Gi guessed they also stayed out of sight behind the wagon to back up Brian and Maurice in case of an attack. And now he was pleased to reflect that Muto had shown himself handy with a weapon.

Gi was getting tired. 'Right, lady and gentlemen,' he said, getting up, 'I'm going to bed. Don't make too much noise out here.' And he was gone.

'Mr. Haggitt,' said Brian, 'why is Mr. Mulderbish going to Gremanos?'

'There is a baron there. He was once my father's friend, but he cheated him out of a fortune. And to stop my father getting back at him when he found out, the baron imprisoned him. Now father's free, he wants to settle the score. Not only for himself, but for a lot of people the baron swindled.

Maurice took that in for a moment. 'But you're wizards. Your father could've escaped this baron, surely? Just as you both could have escaped the prison wagon whenever you wanted, I suppose.'

'We could,' said Haggitt. 'But that would have meant us having to walk. Not only that, we didn't have a clue where we were. So, staying captured made good sense.'

'Now I understand,' said Maurice. 'But not how the baron managed to imprison Mr. Mulderbish.'

'The baron is also a magician,' said Haggitt. 'He used a multi-dimensional pyramid capable of cancelling my father's powers to hold him.'

'Ah,' said Maurice, getting the gist of it, without understanding it.

'So, why are Fox and Reza going to Gremanos?'

'Couldn't say,' said Haggitt. 'It was du Merde who captured us. He hoped the baron would pay him a reward. Perhaps the new commanders would like to take us to the baron for the same reason, if they can. I'm not sure about Reza, but I think Fox has taken it upon himself to command the soldiers. He must be working for the baron.'

Everyone hushed at the sound of hooves coming along the track. Dash and Bayna picked up their bows and took cover in the bushes.

Before anyone could throw earth over it, the rider saw the campfire and reined in.

'Sivad?' said Maurice, 'what are you doing here?'

'Looking for you.' He was almost gasping for air.

'Are you alone?'

'For the moment,' he said, in a non-committal way.

'Get down, and tell us what's happened,' said Haggitt. 'Muto, get Sivad a drink.'

'Fox and his men ran into trouble two days ago,' said Sivad. 'He sent a rider for Reza. But by the time he arrived, the barbarians had done their worst, and run off. Half of Fox's men were dead or wounded. The rest joined Reza. Which didn't go down well with Fox, who had no choice but to flee.'

'Where is Fox now?' asked Haggitt.

'Just down the track. He wasn't sure he'd be welcome here. We got off the main track, and we've been running for two days.'

'Go and get him,' said Haggitt, 'he can ride with us.'

Gi heard the noise and stuck his head out. 'What's going on, Haggitt? I told you not to make too much noise.'

'Sivad's found us, Father. He says Fox has split with Reza. Reza's taken Fox's men, and he and Sivad are on the run.'

Gi looked about, sleepily. 'I don't see Fox.'

'He's back up the track.'

'Well? Somebody go and find him! I'm going back to bed. We can deal with it in the morning.'

Sivad rode back to fetch his sergeant.

The two elves took up stations in the bushes. They'd only known Fox a short time, and didn't consider it long enough to trust him. Dash had noticed the way he looked at the white horse and the beautiful white stag and wasn't happy about it. They heard the two horses cantering towards them, and stood to watch in the moonlight, but they remained out of sight.

* * *

45

'Welcome, Fox,' said Brian. 'Muto, get him a drink, please.'

Around the fire, Fox told them he'd been attacked by a horde of about a hundred barbarians. 'They were dressed like they'd come down from the north. I only had twenty men, and we were no match for them.'

Sivad retold them how they sent a man to get Reza and his troop.

'Yes, we know,' said Gi. 'He passed us on the road.'

'Reza didn't hurry. When he eventually caught up, half our men were dead or wounded.' Sivad told them.

'Then Reza attacked the last of the barbarians,' continued Fox. 'They didn't kill many, and the rest rode off. It was then Reza told me that Baron Striper had no use for me anymore. He said I should go, or his men would kill me. I looked to my men for support, but the few who were left went over to Reza. My only option was to leave fast. Sivad remained loyal and came with me. So, here we are.'

'You must be hungry?' said Gi.

'I could eat, thank you,' Fox replied. 'We both could.'

'Muto, bring some food for our.... are you guests? Or are you proposing to ride with us?'

Fox and Sivad looked at each other. 'We had hoped that if we found you, we could ride with you,' said Fox.

'We don't really know you well, Fox. And you will need to gain the trust of Dash and Bayna. They're concerned at your presence.'

'There is no need. I like to think I'm a good man,' said Fox. 'But if I do not prove my worth, then we will ride on and leave you in peace.'

Sivad nodded in agreement. The young soldier's loyalty said more for Fox's character than he did. Fox was likeable, but he was a prideful man who needed watching.

Dash came into the camp with his arms full of logs for the fire. Bayna, was at his side, and glanced disapprovingly at Fox.

'I'll take 'em,' said Brian, holding out his arms for Dash to transfer them.

Dash and Bayna then retreated to the other side of the wagon.

Brian dropped a log on the fire and stirred it to life. 'We're going north to the river, then west to Gremanos,' he told Fox.

'I'm looking to recruit some men of my own. I should be able to find some at Cot Hill,' he said, and following a questioning look from Haggitt, added, 'It's a small town on the way. I have to stop Reza getting too powerful.'

'He did go crazy when we encountered those bandits,' said Brian. 'There was no need to kill them all.'

'I took my share,' said Fox, glumly. 'But regretted it afterwards.'

'If you think about it, Fox, he always left you with less than a quarter of the men when he planned something. It's as if he wanted to get you killed,' said Maurice.

'It crossed my mind,' said Fox. 'But we were good friends, so I let it go. I don't know what's come over him.'

'I think I do,' said Sivad. 'I heard du Merde was promising all sorts of things when we got to Gremanos. He told Reza that Striper was looking for another centurion to double the size of the Black-Guard. I didn't say anything, Fox, because I thought you two would somehow be in it together. Seems he wants it for himself.'

Fox reassured him. 'Neither of us saw this coming, Sivad.'

Gi was listening, although he looked asleep. 'Striper always wanted a bigger army,' he said. 'But he can only spread his rule as far as Corin. King Treadwell will stop him going any further.'

'I didn't think Treadwell had much of an army,' said Haggitt.

'He doesn't. But he has a lot of enterprising dwarves,' said Gi. 'Muto, be a dear and get me another drink, please.'

Muto scurried away and was back in seconds.

'Thank you.' He downed it in a few gulps. 'Now, I really must turn in. In the morning, we will continue down the track, which Muto assures me runs parallel with the stream we last camped by, and we will come to a lake, or so he says. Muto thinks the river we're looking for flows through it. And, for reasons I can't explain, I think he knows what he's talking about.'

The cook grinned.

'So, somebody sort out who's taking the first watch. And goodnight, all.'

* * *

46

Birdsong and the chittering of squirrels woke Muto. He hauled himself out from under his seat and went to start breakfast. Fox was next up. He was drawn by the smell of bacon frying.

'Muto, are these supplies from Reza's wagon?' asked Fox.

'Might be...' said Muto, guardedly, 'might not. What does it smell like?'

'It smells like it should not be missed,' said Fox. 'And where did you get that frying pan? There's room in there to feed all of us.'

'No, Fox, only seven. The elves eat... er,' he paused. 'I'm not sure what they eat. I know they like apples. Mr. Haggitt looks after them at meal times.'

Brian and Maurice walked into camp. 'Haggitt's keeping watch, with Dash and Bayna. That smells good, Muto,' Maurice remarked.

'You can have an extra sausage for saying that, Mr. Maurice,' said Muto.

'I said it smelt good, too,' Fox reminded him, feigning a hurt face.

Gi was awake, but lay on his bed till the others had finished. The little cook knew his preferences well enough now to have his breakfast on the go when he emerged. He downed it in no time, and with relish. He could get used to having a personal cook!

'Everyone ready!' Gi shouted.

'They're always ready for you, Master,' Muto assured him.

'Then crack that whip, Muto.'

'I don't have a whip. You never said I needed a whip, Master. Shall I click my fingers instead?'

'Muto, you may click whatever you like, as long as it gets the horses moving.'

He produced the loudest finger-click Gi had ever heard, but it was the gentle tap of the reins that made the horses move.

Brian and Maurice rode up front. Then Fox and Sivad (after Haggitt had advised them that Dash and Bayna always rode at the back).

The party moved at a moderate pace through the forest, and at midday they came out onto a broad grassland, dotted with occasional groups of trees. And there, on their right, was the reflective splendour of a lake.

Gi smiled, broadly at the little cook alongside him. 'You were right, Muto. We've found it.'

'I knew you could rely on me, Master.'

Dash and Bayna walked their animals to the water's edge. Fox followed.

'I would like us to be friends, Dash,' said Fox.

'We will see,' said Dash. 'Let's start with mutual respect, and friendship may follow.'

What an interesting thing to say, Fox thought. 'I will do my best,' he promised, and turned to find Sivad.

'Take the wagon down to the edge, Muto. Let the horses drink, then we can have a look round and get our bearings,' said Gi.

'Father,' said Haggitt, 'you haven't got a clue when it comes to getting our bearings. It's better to ask one of the soldiers. Maurice is good at bearings.'

'I really thought I sounded convincing there, for a minute,' Gi moaned, 'I almost believed it myself.'

'We should get Maurice,' Haggitt insisted.

Maurice took a while to appear, and when he did, he was soaked through.

'Was it raining where you were?' asked Gi, looking him up and down.

Maurice grinned. 'No, Mr. Mulderbish, I've had a swim.'

'Muto! Fill the barrels from further up! Maurice has been swimming over there!' Gi shouted. 'And that might not be all he's been doing in it.'

'Just swimming, Mr. Mulderbish,' Maurice assured him.

'I think I believe you. Anyway, you are good at directions, I believe.'

'I know the direction you want to go, Mr. Mulderbish,' said Maurice. 'And so far, we're on track.'

'I'm trusting you, Maurice,' Gi whispered. 'As much as I might like Fox, Dash has misgivings. I want you to get us to Gremanos, by way of the northern snowline, then find this place called Cot Hill that Fox wants to visit. And regardless of your previous association with Fox, you and Brian will only take orders from me, and I will be advised by you. If Fox tries to give you orders, you let me know before taking action. Is that clear?'

'Crystal clear, Mr. Mulderbish,' said Maurice, almost saluting.

'Good,' said Gi, 'now, you have two options. You can carry on swimming, or you can get Haggitt to magically dry your clothes. Oh... and if you choose the latter, don't be wearing them when he does it.'

'Thanks for the warning, Mr. Mulderbish.'

Before he could do either, Brian alerted everyone to a column of smoke coming from a clump of trees by the water's edge a couple of hundred yards along the shore.

'We should check that out,' he urged them.

'Yeah. Send Sivad. It'll give him something to do,' suggested Maurice.

Brian found him sitting along the bank talking to Fox.

'Brian, what can we do for you?' said Fox, amiably.

'Mind if we borrow Sivad to go and see what's causing that smoke down there?'

Fox looked across at the trees with interest. 'Hmm. Sivad?' he said, leaving it to him. The young soldier nodded, and collected his horse.

* * *

47

Sivad dismounted early and approached with caution. Among the trees was a gaudily painted caravan. A multi-coloured horse grazed nearby. An elderly man was sitting on the caravan steps. He wore breeches and a shirt, and he was carving what looked like clothes pegs.

'A soldier,' said the man, looking up. 'I didn't expect to see a soldier today.'

'Good afternoon, sir,' said Sivad, breezily, despite his current misfortunes. 'I'm escorting a small party camped along the lake. We saw your smoke and I came to investigate. Have you been here long?'

'I never know how long I've been anywhere, young man. I don't really care. I'm in no hurry to go anywhere yet. I have grazing for my horse, there are fish in the lake. What more could a man ask?'

'This is an idyllic spot,' said Sivad. After a pause while the man carved some more, he ventured, 'Do you happen to know if there's a town or a village near here?'

'Anywhere particular?' said the man, not looking up.

'Cot Hill. Do you know the best way there? We are looking to employ some men for an expedition.'

'Hmm, expedition, eh. A long word, probably a long way then, I imagine,' said the man, sagely. 'No, I don't know the best way, except it would be better to ride than walk, if that's any help.'

'Not really,' he said, guessing the man was playing him along. 'I'm Sivad, by the way. Do you have a name?'

'Probably,' said the man. 'No, that's not right.' He grinned. 'Nobody's called probably, are they? Give me a minute, it's been so long since anyone used it, I've forgotten.'

Sivad waited, amused.

'Ah… got it. I'm called Kitsu, yes, that's me. Kitsu.'

'You're a traveller, Kitsu,' Sivad deduced from looking at the horse and van.

'Not in the true sense of the word,' he said. 'I just like to roam. Or, not. Depends how I feel.'

Sivad nodded, and having satisfied himself their neighbour was harmless, he re-mounted and bid Kitsu goodbye. 'Enjoy the rest of your day.'

Kitsu sat wondering if he should enjoy tomorrow as well.

Back in Gi's camp, Sivad reported to Brian. 'Just an old man. A traveller, of sorts. Hardly a threat to anyone.'

'Does he have a name?' asked Fox.

'Calls himself, Kitsu.'

'Kitsu?' said Gi, perking up. 'I knew a Kitsu, years ago.' This prompted him to go to the wagon and start searching for his staff. After a few fruitless minutes, he cursed. 'I left it in that damn cave, when I was trapped in that pyramid,' he remembered. 'Haggitt! Did you bring your staff?'

'Mine's still there, too,' said Haggitt.

'Would you like to borrow mine, Master?' said Muto.

'What? You have a staff, Muto?'

'Sometimes my left knee plays up a bit, Master. I have to lean on something,' he explained.

'Oh,' said Gi. 'I thought you were about to tell me you're a wizard.'

'I was,' said Muto. 'But I don't think I will, now.'

Gi let it go. 'Muto, come with me. I want you to meet someone.'

* * *

Gi and Muto strolled along the water's edge towards Kitsu's campsite. The water lapped gently from the river running into it.

'Is there anything else you're not telling me, Muto?' asked Gi.

'Lots of things, Master. But primarily, I'm your cook and I'm good with a crossbow, and on occasions, I've been known to talk bollocks, Master. So, don't believe everything I tell you.'

'You see that caravan?' Gi pointed. 'I think the man is familiar to me.'

When they walked into Kitsu's camp, he stood up promptly. '*Gi?* Is that really you?' he said, scrutinising Gi's face. 'A bit older, but I'd know that face anywhere. How are you, man?'

'Not bad, Kitsu. And you're looking… well… nothing like you used to,' said Gi. 'I heard your name from my scout and recognised it, but I don't recognise you.'

Kitsu's face changed, and Gi stepped back.

'Is this the face you remember?' Kitsu asked.

'That's more like it.' Gi held out his arms to embrace the man. 'It's good to see you, old friend.'

'Sit with me, Gi. Introduce your friend.'

'This is Muto,' said Gi. 'He's my cook, and probably a lot of other things, too.'

'You flatter me, Master. Cook will do. Nice to meet you, Mr. Kitsu.'

'We're going to Gremanos,' Gi told him. 'I could do with a man like you along. And you don't look especially busy.' He glanced around the quiet camp. 'How about it?'

Kitsu shrugged. 'Is this about Striper, Gi?'

'That obvious, am I?' said Gi.

'I get to hear things,' he said. 'And I know you of old.' He leaned back on the step, and looked to be weighing it up. 'Alright, I'll come. You may not notice me. But I'll be there when you need me,' Kitsu promised.

Gi and Kitsu talked for a while, shared a few memories and caught up. Muto half listened, his thoughts drifting across the lake, until the re-acquaintance was done.

'I'll watch out for you.' Gi stood up and shook hands with Kitsu, then Kitsu with Muto.

When they walked back, Muto was quiet.

'Something wrong, Muto?'

'Yes, Master. I saw him change into another person right in front of us. He's a shape-shifter?'

'Yes,' said Gi, 'and bloody good at it, too.'

'I can see he might be useful, Master. But that caravan... what *terrible* taste,' said Muto.

'It's a disguise,' Gi assured him. 'If you go back in the morning, it'll look totally different.'

As they got closer to the camp, Gi said, 'We'll keep Kitsu to ourselves, Muto. The others don't need to know yet.'

'No, Master. He will be our little secret.'

*

'Did you know the man, Father?' Haggitt asked.

'No. Interesting man, though,' Gi replied, avoiding Haggitt's gaze.

'I'll start getting food ready, Master. It'll be dark soon,' said Muto.

'Good idea,' said Gi. 'And cook a bit extra.' He winked.

Muto nodded that he understood.

* * *

49

Later that night, a small dog wandered into the camp sniffing the air, and found Gi.

'I didn't think it would take you long,' said Gi, quietly.

The dog yapped and sat on its hind legs with its paws in the air.

'Don't overdo it, Kitsu,' Gi whispered. 'Here boy, have another sausage.'

'Is that all? You're still as tight as ever, then.' said Kitsu, directly into Gi's mind.

'Muto, give the leftovers to the little dog, and send him home.'

After licking the plates clean, the animal scampered into the night.

'Is that how he's going to appear now?' said Muto.

'I wouldn't count on it,' Gi whispered, then yawned. 'It's time I went to bed. I haven't walked that far in ages.'

'Me neither,' said Muto. He tidied around and headed for his makeshift bed under his seat, peering around for anything that might be Kitsu.

* * *

50

Along the water's edge, the column of smoke was not over the clump of trees anymore. A closer look would have revealed a large boulder and two smaller ones where the trees, van and horse had been. Kitsu had obviously gone roaming again.

Fox was talking to Sivad. 'Did that old man know the best way to Cot Hill?' asked Fox.

'Yes, he said, riding is better than walking.' Sivad grinned.

'That's *so true*,' said Fox, 'but not really helpful.'

'Maurice reckons if we keep heading north, we should come to a proper road that will take us there.'

'What are you two plotting?' said Maurice, approaching them.

'We were wondering about a shorter route to Cot Hill, but yours is probably the best idea,' said Fox.

'Gi wants to stay on the flat,' said Maurice. 'He doesn't want to break the wagon, or get anyone injured.'

'He's a wizard. Surely he can fix things,' argued Fox.

Maurice shook his head. 'Since I've been keeping company with wizards, I've learned it's not always that straightforward. There are protocols – whatever *they* are.'

Fox shrugged. 'Okay. But if he stays out in the open, he's going to be a target.'

'He knows that, but he reckons we can deal with most things,' Maurice assured him.

'Try to get him to stay closer to the foothills,' Fox insisted. 'They give us somewhere we can retreat to and defend if we need to.'

'I'll mention it to him,' he said, and went off to find Brian to accompany him on the errand.

Gi had just surfaced, and was sitting on the wagon steps, scratching. When he saw the two soldiers coming, he got up.

'You're early,' said Gi.

'We need to talk to you, Mr. Mulderbish.'

'What's on your minds?'

151

'You told us to tell you if Fox comes up with any plans or ideas,' said Brian.

'Yes, I did,' said Gi. 'What's he suggesting, then?'

'When we move off, he thinks we'll be safer if we drive the wagon close to the foothills, rather than out in the open,' Brian told him.

'Hmm… sounds half-reasonable. Did he say why?' said Gi.

'He thinks there'll be places among the hills we could defend should we be attacked,' said Maurice. 'He says we're too exposed out in the open.'

'What do you two think?'

'Maybe we should get closer to the hills,' said Brian, then qualified it. 'But have a scout ahead to warn us of trouble, and check for defendable places for us to overnight, and make stops.'

'Sounds safe. But slow going,' said Gi. 'And I'm suspicious. I'm asking myself why Fox might prefer us to travel closer to the hills.'

Maurice voiced a troubling thought. 'We'd be more easily ambushed.'

'Hmm. Tell him, no. We're staying in the open.'

They went to find Fox and Sivad, and Gi went to find breakfast.

'Muto, will you start cooking, please. I want to see if we attract any animals,' he winked.

'You never know, Master,' said Muto. 'I'll get on it right away.'

Once the fire was going and the air filled with the aromas of frying bacon, eggs and sausages, Gi and Muto sat down to wait.

It wasn't long before the screech of a large eagle was heard overhead. 'You know him so well, Master.' Muto grinned.

'I just hoped, Muto. He lights fires, but I didn't see any evidence of cooking.'

Gi looked up and waved at the great bird, inviting it to come down. It dived behind the wagon, out of sight. Then a slightly hoarse voice called out, 'Gi, you'll have to come round here, I haven't got any clothes,' said Kitsu. 'That's the trouble with shape-shifting.'

Gi smiled. 'Muto, get him a cloak.'

Now he was decent, Kitsu appeared. 'I'll shift again if someone comes. Got a spare plate?'

Waiting for breakfast, Gi brought Kitsu up to date. 'So, I was wondering if, in your eagle guise, you could keep watch for us, and let me know if there is any danger ahead.'

Kitsu thought about it. He rather liked being an eagle.

'We can look after your horse and caravan,' said Gi, to help him decide.

'No, I'll do what you want,' said Kitsu. 'All you need do is feed and clothe me.'

'What about your horse?' asked Gi.

'It's wasn't real. Neither was the caravan. I shape-shifted the trees, too.' He grinned.

'Wow!' said Muto. 'That's a rare gift you have.'

'He's a rare one, alright.'

'Well, when you've finished being impressed, I could do with some food,' said Kitsu. 'Those worms I had earlier, were a bit off, I reckon.'

'You ate *worms*, Mr. Kitsu? Yuck! Have a sausage, quickly,' said a slightly green Muto.

'Thanks Muto, that should get rid of the taste.'

'What do you think of us travelling nearer the foothills, as Fox wants, Kitsu? Did you see anything or anyone over there?' asked Gi, in a low voice.

'You really don't trust him, do you? It sounds like he wants you over there for a reason,' said Kitsu. 'I'll take another look and get back to you. Thanks for breakfast, Muto. I'm going to undress. Leave some clothes out for when I see you again. I really must fly,' he said, to pained looks all round.

* * *

51

Two days had passed since Gi last saw Kitsu, and he was getting worried.

'What are you worried about, Master?' asked Muto. 'You don't know what he's been doing for the past twenty years, this might be normal for him.'

'You're right, Muto. He said he wouldn't be far away, so he probably isn't.'

'I'm about to send some breakfast smells into the air, Master. You never know, he might be fed up with worms.'

Kitsu appeared from behind the wagon. 'Somebody mention food?' he whispered. 'I'm starving.'

'Mr. Kitsu,' said Muto. 'Get back behind that wagon and put some clothes on. *Whatever* next.'

Kitsu looked down, 'Oh, sorry. Give me a minute.'

'Was he always like this, Master?'

Gi smiled. 'No, not always, Muto. He's better now.'

Kitsu emerged clad. 'Oh, is that for me? Thanks, Muto,' he said, taking a large sausage from the plate Muto proffered. Between mouthfuls, he said, 'A day up ahead, I flew over... about a hundred men... camped in the long grass. Gods, my arms ache,' he complained, making flapping motions.

'What are they wearing?' Gi asked.

'Wearing? All sorts of things, really... You know, furs, leather, bits of iron... all that kind of manly junk,' said Kitsu.

'Not soldiers, then?' said Gi.

'No, but there are soldiers in the foothills. About half a day further on. All in black – so must be Striper's Black-Guard.'

'We're going to have to revise our route,' said Gi.

'And don't worry Gi,' said Kitsu. 'They won't connect me with you. I rolled up in my caravan as my harmless old-fogey traveller. I told them the other crowd were camped along the way, and they seem to be waiting to ambush them.'

154

'Have another sausage, Mr. Kitsu,' said Muto.

'Who are the men on the plain, then?' Gi wondered. 'Are they barbarians?'

'Might be. But they had women and children with them. They looked more like a tribe of wanderers looking for somewhere to settle,' said Kitsu. 'And on reflection, I think I should have looked in on them before I went to the soldiers.'

'I think we should catch up with these people before something bad happens,' said Gi.

'It'd be quicker to send a rider ahead, Master. Get Brian, he'll know what to do.'

Gi approved, and Maurice went to fetch him.

Gi trod carefully when explaining his mission. 'Don't ask me how I know this, Brian, but about a day's ride ahead, there are a lot of people camped on the plain. I want you to find out whether they are hostile, or just looking for somewhere to settle. If you think they're barbarians, just come back. Do you understand?'

'I get it, Mr. Mulderbish,'

'But, if they are peaceful people, tell them to stay put until we get there. They might be in grave danger,' said Gi.

'Right. Shall I take Maurice with me?'

'No, but it might be a good idea to take someone. Dash or Bayna, maybe, if you can get them to use regular mounts.'

'Are you sure, sir? Splitting them up for two days may not be a good idea.'

'I hadn't thought of that,' said Gi. 'How well do you get on with Sivad?'

'We get on okay. He's a bit keen. Almost naively so. But a good soldier.'

'Check with Fox, then bring him here. I'll get Muto to pack some food for both of you.'

Half an hour later, when Brian and Sivad were on their way, Fox came to see Gi. 'What's going on, Gi?'

'I thought it would be a good idea to have scouts ahead, Fox,' said Gi. 'We don't want to travel close to the hills without knowing if there's trouble around, do we?'

'No, I should think not,' said Fox. 'We might even run into Reza and the Black-Guard, if we're not careful.'

'I'd expect them to stay on the main track to Gremanos, rather than wander around here. We may know when Brian and Sivad get back,' Gi, told him.

'Yeah,' was all Fox said.

When Fox had gone, Muto said, 'Can't help thinking he's up to something. He's trying too hard to appear genuine.'

'He's not fooling anyone, Muto. Tell Haggitt we're moving out, so he can go and find the elves. That shouldn't be too difficult for him,' said Gi.

'Very private people, them elves.'

'And we respect that,' Gi reminded him.

Up front, Maurice followed the tracks left by Brian and Sivad. The day passed uneventfully, and as dusk was drawing in, Gi called a halt for the day.

When Fox, Maurice and the elves had settled for the night, and Muto was dousing a lamp before turning in himself, a small dog appeared beside the wagon. It looked up a Muto, wagging its tail, and seemed to be grinning. The dog became a blur and unrolled into Kitsu – which was how what happened looked to Muto.

'Your clothes are at the bottom of Mr. Haggitt's bed, Mr. Kitsu,' Muto told him, averting his eyes, because some things are hard to unsee.

*

'Father?' said Haggitt, startled. 'There's a naked man standing at the bottom of my bed!'

Seeing a fireball generating in Haggitt's hand, Gi quickly placed an arresting hand on his arm. 'This is Kitsu. I want you to keep him a secret,' whispered Gi.

'The man you said you didn't know?' said Haggitt, slightly peeved.

'Yes,' said Gi. 'I've been keeping quiet about him. He's kind of my spy. I don't want any of the others to know about him. Understand?'

'I suppose you know what you're doing, Father,' said Haggitt, unsure, but relieved to see the intruder dressing himself.

'I saw the two riders you sent ahead, Gi,' said Kitsu. 'They're resting a few miles up the road, now.'

'Is there any change in the situation further on?'

'No, but there's the makings of big change,' said Kitsu. 'The soldiers are in for a surprise in a day or so. There are genuine, unmistakeable barbarians making their way down the mountain, just above where the soldiers might be thinking of ambushing the other crowd.'

'You've done well, Kitsu. When you've rested, go back and see what's happening, will you,' said Gi.

'Of course. I don't want to miss all the action,' said Kitsu. 'But it's dark now. There's hardly any moon out there tonight. I don't think anybody's going anywhere till morning. And I don't want to fly into a tree, either, if it's all the same to you?'

'I didn't know dogs could fly,' said Gi, settling himself down for the night. 'You learn something every day.'

Haggitt looked on, totally bemused.

* * *

52

Brian and Sivad approached the gathering of people camped in the long grass. The place seemed relaxed. They were not challenged, and entered easily. There were children chasing each other around the tents. A tall man emerged from one of the tents when he heard the sound of hoof beats. He had the friendly open face of a man one could trust, and the air of someone in charge.

'You look like soldiers,' he observed. 'Are you lost?'

'No,' said Brian, 'we came to see what was going on here. We intend to bring a wagon through this way, and we're checking to see if it's safe, or if we need to find another way.'

'No, please bring your wagon through, we mean no-one any harm,' said the man. 'Where are you going?'

'We're looking for Cot Hill,' Brian told him.

'We left there only a few days ago,' the man told him. 'The place is getting over-crowded, so we've decided to move east, and start again.'

'We've been scouting around here for a couple days, now,' said Brian, 'and I should warn you there's danger in the foothills ahead. It will be safer for you to stay here until we get back with help.'

'We are many,' said the man. 'Who would harm us?' He slapped the sword at his belt.

'Believe me, I'm reliably informed that you should not engage with whoever or whatever is up ahead. I say again, please stay here. We will bring help,' Brian assured him.

Sivad nodded enthusiastically. 'Absolutely.'

They rode back to Gi as fast as their horses would carry them.

Gi was travelling towards them, so the distance was less between them. A large eagle circled above the wagon. Gi acknowledged its cry with a wave, and saw the two riders in the distance.

When they arrived, Brian shouted, 'Gi! Those people are settlers, it's safe to go through!'

'Tie your horse to the wagon, Brian, and come up here beside me!' Gi called back.

Muto shuffled over to make room.

Sivad waved and fell in beside Fox at the rear.

'Tell me what you saw,' said Gi.

'The man we spoke to, said his people set out from Cot Hill, a few days ago because it was getting overcrowded. They're looking to settle further east,' Brian told him.

'Do they seem like barbarians?' asked Gi.

'They wear skins, and carry swords, Mr. Mulderbish, but they seem kindlier folk. There are women and children with them.'

'Any wagons?'

'Strangely, no. They have horses, though. We saw sort of sled arrangements with their stuff piled on them.'

'Do they know that if they travel further along by those foothills, they are in danger of being attacked by Striper's Black-Guard?'

'What?' said Brian. 'How do you know that? I didn't see any sign of *them*. We told them there's danger up ahead, and they should wait for us. But the Black-Guards...?' He was uncertain. 'Why would they be interested in settlers on the move? They're no threat to Striper?'

'Trust me,' said Gi, 'I'm a wizard. They are there. And they seem to be up to no good. We must make good time to get to them before anything bad happens.'

Brian jumped down and was quickly back in the saddle. 'Fox, Dash! We're stepping up the pace, be ready to follow.' He spurred his horse on to ride ahead with Maurice. 'We need to move it, Maurice. There are people ahead who need help. And soon.'

The wagon's horses baulked at Muto's shouts and slaps of the reins, but they soon understood to pick up the pace.

Fox looked at the grassy terrain, which was generally flat but with occasional hidden ruts and ridges, and complained, 'I thought Gi wanted to avoid damage to the wagon.' Sivad merely shrugged and spurred his horse.

It was early afternoon when Gi's party was in sight of the people on the plain, and he sent Brian and Maurice to let them know they were coming.

The tall man was sitting by a fire when they rode in. There was another man with him, and a woman.

The tall man stood up. 'Good, you're back. I was wondering when you'd get here.'

'Anything happening?' asked Brian.

'Two men rode down that hill earlier. They watched us for a while, getting the measure of us, I should think,' said the man.

'That doesn't sound good.'

'There are more of us than they think,' said the man. 'Other groups are nearby.'

Shortly, Gi's party showed up, and he and Muto got down off the wagon and introduced themselves. 'I am Gi Mulderbish, and this is Muto, my cook. Ah, and here's Haggitt, my son.'

'I'm Cardry. This is Puck. And that's Leoni, my wife. We don't see many wizards around here. Pleased to meet you,' he said.

There was a series of handshakes, then Fox and Sivad appeared. 'These are a couple of men that joined us a few days ago,' said Gi. 'They're going to Cot Hill.'

The trio's surprise at encountering wizards, turned to awe when Dash and Bayna walked their animals into the camp.

Dash urged Snow forward and dismounted. Some children saw the animals and ran over. 'It's okay to stroke them,' said Bayna, her melodic voice as enchanting as the animals. Ice, Bayna's white stag, lowered his head for the children to touch his antlers and stroke his head.

'What beautiful creatures,' said Cardry. 'And so gentle with the children.'

'They are gentle with everyone,' said Dash, smiling but making the situation clear. 'Unless we tell them to be otherwise.'

'I'll remember that,' said Cardry, smiling affably, unable to resist patting Snow.

Bayna introduced herself to Leoni. 'It's good to meet another woman,' Bayna said. 'I've had only male company for months, now.'

As they spoke, Bayna was distracted by movement in the long grass. She turned quickly, unshouldered her bow, and notched an arrow in one easy movement. 'Get behind me, Leoni. Is there anybody there?!' Bayna called.

'Bayna? Is that you?'

'Who's there?' she challenged again.

A dishevelled figure stood up. He was wearing a bandage on one hand. 'Badger? Is that you?'

'Lovely to hear your voice again, lady,' he said, then, 'Yeah, I've been trying to catch up for days. My horse died. Trouble was, I was still riding him when he fell and trapped my leg under him. He nearly broke it. It took me ages to get out from under.'

She lowered the bow. 'Find Gi. He'll want to see you.' Then taking in the state of him, she said 'But see Muto first. You look hungry, and in need of ointments and things.'

A little later when Badger had eaten and had his wounds treated, he went to find Gi. Maurice saw him first and greeted him with open arms. 'Where have you been?'

Badger had to think. 'Walking, mostly. Me horse died.'

'Sorry to hear that. Come on, I'll take you to Gi. He'll be glad you're back.'

Gi did indeed welcome him. 'Badger! What happened?'

They sat, and Badger retold his story. 'What's going on, Mr. Gi? Who are all these people?'

'They are settlers looking for a new home. They are in some danger, Badger. And getting them out of it, is where you come in,' said Gi.

'How's that? I've only just got here,' Badger complained, thinking more of sleep than work.

'When you've rested, I want you to go into those hills,' Gi pointed. 'And let us know what you see.'

'Oh, is that all?' said Badger, sneaking around being his speciality.

'No... Don't get caught,' said Gi.

'You know what's in there, don't you?' said Badger.

'Not for certain. I think the Black-Guard may be up there, planning to attack these people,' said Gi.

'Hmm... Give me a couple of hours Mr. Gi. It'll be dark by then.'

When it was dark, Gi sent for Badger. 'Do you want someone to go with you?' he asked.

'No, I'll be alright, two of us would make more noise,' said Badger.

'One more thing before you go...' said Gi.

'What's that, Mr. Gi?'

'At some point, you may find yourself accompanied by a wild animal out there. Don't be afraid. And don't try to kill it. It's a friend of mine,' said Gi.

'What's it look like?' asked Badger.

'I have no idea,' said Gi, truthfully.

'Hmm. Okay, then. Here's hoping I don't try and make friends with the wrong beast. If I'm not back in a couple of hours, I'd appreciate someone coming to rescue me.' So saying, Badger left the camp. Minutes later, he returned and everyone looked at him expectantly. He shrugged. 'Wrong way.' He grinned sheepishly and went off again.

'Do you think he's gonna be alright?' Maurice wondered, 'I think I should catch him up.'

'No, don't,' said Gi. 'He'll be perfectly safe.'

* * *

53

When Badger was nearing the hills where the Black-Guards were camped, something sniffed his leg.

He reached out in the darkness, without looking, for fear of what he might see. He felt the rasp of a canine tongue lick his hand. He hoped it was canine. His worst nightmare would be lupine.

Remember what Gi told you, said a quiet, soothing voice in his head that wasn't his own, *this wolf can help you.*

'What wolf? He never said anything about a bloody wolf.'

Try to moderate your language, please, said the voice.

Beginning to question his sanity, Badger risked a look. The dark shape was indeed a wolf. He wondered if it was licking his hand to make sure it was clean before he chewed it off. He wanted to jump back, but feared a sudden movement might not go well.

Do not step back. The wolf said. *There's a deep hole behind you.*

Badger turned to see a dark void. He looked back at the wolf.

'That's you speaking in my head, isn't it?' Badger whispered.

Well done, said Kitsu patronisingly. *I knew you'd work it out. We can speak with our thoughts. There's no need to say anything. I'm Gi's friend. A shape-shifter.* Kitsu let that sink in. *You stay here a moment. I'll enter the camp and get the lay of the land. Count to ten then follow me.*

The next thing Badger knew, the wolf had gone. He sat down, lost count at three, and followed on.

Kitsu saw a soldier guarding a few horses and crept forward. The horses became restless at the scent of a wolf, and he knew he'd have to change. To what? *A dog, everybody loves dogs.* He directed a thought to Badger: *I'll distract the guard. I'm the little dog trotting up to him.*

Badger thought he'd seen everything, but clearly not.

The guard smiled and rubbed Kitsu's ears. 'Are you hungry, little fella?'

Kitsu decided he wasn't and trotted into the main camp. Badger had slipped by.

'Those people haven't moved for a day and a half, now,' Badger heard one of the soldiers complain.

'If they don't head this way in the morning, I might think about attacking.' It sounded like Reza Lock, but Badger couldn't be sure, in the semi-darkness.

'But, Reza, they don't look like they've anything worth taking,' replied another man. 'They look poorer than us.'

'I don't need their stuff,' said an irate Reza, 'I need *them*! I need men. Recruits. The baron wants the Black-Guard to number in thousands, not the measly hundred he has now.'

'They're settlers,' said another soldier. 'They've got women and children with them. What do we do with them?' Badger heard Reza let out a long loud impatient breath. 'We'll see.'

Kitsu had heard enough and made his way further up the hill to find out what the barbarians were up to. After a few minutes, he sensed two men around the side of the hill, behind some bushes. 'Fanks for comin' wiv me 'arry, I 'ate going for a piss in the dark on my own.'

'So do I,' said Harry. 'Now, point that fing away from me, will you?'

Kitsu was surprised to find he could grin. He trotted quietly onwards for a minute or two more, then stopped dead in his tracks. *I thought there'd be a lot of 'em. But not this many.*

The barbarians' camp was quiet and dimly lit, not attracting attention from the soldiers below. He cursed himself for not having the night vision of a cat, then congratulated himself for having the hearing of a dog. As he crouched, taking in the scene, two scouts returned to the camp. 'They're going to attack in the morning,' said one. 'Shall I go down and tell Cardry?'

'Yes, and tell him to get the women and children away before dawn.'

'I'm on my way, chief.' The man disappeared into the night.

Kitsu gave him a moment, then crept away to become an owl. He took to the air, and swooped to where Badger was lurking. *Time to leave*, he thought towards Badger. *I'll distract the guard.* He did it by flying straight at him, screeching wildly. Badger slipped by again, to find the wolf waiting for him.

They walked together to the bottom of the hill, then raced back to Gi. The wolf won.

Kitsu jumped into the wagon. Fortunately, Haggitt wasn't in there. He dressed in the clothes Muto had left for him, and as he jumped down, Badger arrived.

'Who the Hell are you?' Badger demanded.

'I'm your guardian, but you may call me, Kitsu.'

'Thank gods,' said Badger, recognising Kitsu's voice. 'You were good out there. I'm impressed.'

'You're good yourself. But you ain't seen nothing, yet,' said Kitsu.

'I'm pretty sure of that,' he said, stepping back to take a good look at Kitsu. 'A shape-shifter. Wow!'

'Hush. Not everyone knows. Will you tell Gi I'm here?'

Gi was sitting by the fire with Cardry and a few others.

'Mr. Gi?' said Badger. 'Mr. Kitsu would like a word, over by the wagon.'

'Excuse me everybody,' said Gi, leaving the group.

'So,' said Gi. 'What do you have for me?'

'They might be barbarians up the top there,' said Kitsu. 'But they might not. But the soldiers are commanded by someone called Reza.'

'Fair-haired man with a plait, and too handsome for his own good?'

'It's him, alright,' said Badger.

'That's *not* good news. That man will likely kill everybody,' Gi told him.

'The camp above is quiet and dimly lit, like they're waiting to pounce. There could be quite a battle in the morning,' said Kitsu. 'They sent a messenger down to talk to someone called Cardry. He should be here soon.'

As predicted, a man in barbarian garb padded into the camp, and went straight to Cardry. There was a lot of agitated arm waving and pointing.

'What's going on?' Gi needed to know.

'The chief told him to tell Cardry to get the women and children out of the camp. The soldiers will attack in the morning,' said Kitsu.

'Get Fox and Sivad, Muto. We need a strategy.'

Fox and Sivad arrived promptly, with Muto close behind. Kitsu was introduced as an old wizarding friend of Gi's who'd shown up out of the blue. Which was, in fact true, and they didn't question it.

Without preamble, Gi said, 'It's Reza's men up ahead. He's going to attack these people in the morning, and we need a plan of defence. What Reza doesn't know is that there's a host of barbarians in the hills above him who seem to favour these people, and who could descend at any time. What do you think we should do?'

Badger and Kitsu gave Fox as much information as they'd gleaned. It was short, but not sweet. 'We don't have time to get the women and children far away,' said Fox, 'but we can hide them.'

'Good. Sivad, take Fox and introduce him to Cardry, then I want us all to sit down and plan this out properly. Remember, Reza doesn't take prisoners.'

* * *

54

Gi watched the plan unfolding. The women had collected their children and were marching out of the camp towards a gulley where they'd be out of sight. Then a row of some fifty plains barbarians – as Gi was calling the settlers who hadn't yet settled – fanned out, facing the direction from which the soldiers would come. Further back, probably a hundred yards, the rest of the plains barbarians were strung out in a second line of defence along the edge of the camp. Gi and Haggitt would be stationed in the wagon, behind open windows. Muto would position himself in the well under the driver's seat with Badger behind to load crossbows for him. The elves would guard the gulley and protect the women and children, should any soldiers stray that way.

Fox and Sivad took up stations in the centre of the second rank of barbarians. Kitsu stood alone between the two lines, free to use his powers as he chose, as agreed with Gi and Fox – Fox having been made aware of his abilities.

Meanwhile, Brian and Maurice rode the long way round to take a message to the barbarians in the high hills. Upon arrival, the pair were taken prisoner, by a couple of guards taking their job very seriously.

'We've come in peace with a message from Cardry,' Brian told them, hoping the man's name might hold some sway. 'Who's the leader here?'

'That would be me,' said a man, who was probably carrying more knives and daggers on him than a circus knife-thrower.

Maurice recognised him at once. 'Huddy Mincing! I thought you were dead.'

'No, Maurice. I should be. But I had a bit of unexpected help when Reza ordered me dead. I'll tell you about it some time.'

'Well, it's good to see you again. We've come to help. We've got the rest of your men in defensive lines down on the plain. The women and children are out of the camp and hidden a mile back.'

'You do know Reza's down there, don't you?' said Huddy.

'Yes, but Fox Loer is with us. He's with your front line down there now,' said Brian.

'I'm glad to hear that. Looks like we're in this together,' conceded Huddy, shooing his guards away.

'Good. Let's talk about what we need from you.'

When morning broke, the Black-Guard rode down out of the hills and lined up in charge formation, with Reza Lock in the middle. The line of soldiers standing side by side, was nearly twice as wide as the plains barbarians' lines. Reza raised his head and drew his sword. He paused for a moment, flung his plait over his shoulder, then nodded sharply. That was the signal for the Black-Guard to charge. Swords drawn and yelling to intimidate, they galloped headlong after Reza at the front line of barbarians.

The soldiers were ready to engage, but not for what Kitsu had in mind. He spread his hands and immediately the grass in front of them went up in flames. He spread his hands wider and the fire spread in both directions on either side. Reza's horse reared and threw him. Plenty of other soldiers were unseated, too, as their mounts shied away from the flames.

While they scrambled to catch their horses to fall back and regroup, Huddy Mincing charged in with his barbarians, cutting down at least twenty of Reza's men. Reza managed to remount and retreated back to his men, some of whom were now being hacked down by Huddy's men.

'This was not supposed to happen,' said Gi. 'They weren't supposed to run!'

The plain littered with the bodies of the Black-Guard, the main fighting was over in hardly any time at all. It had been a complete rout of the soldiers, who were either dead or in disarray. As far as Huddy was concerned though, it wasn't over: this was an opportunity to settle old scores. He told his men to circle around what was left of Reza's men. He walked his horse through and inside the circle, looking for familiar faces. 'Where's Fox Loer!' he bellowed.

Reza Lock raised his hand, 'Fox has gone! Deserted. He's no longer with the Black-Guard. And not welcome anymore.'

'Huh,' snorted Huddy, dismissively. 'I remember you. You killed Harvey the Bear. He was my friend.'

'It was a fair fight!' Reza snarled.

'I suppose it was, but I can't help thinking that if I didn't have so many men, I'd be dead as well. So, here's what's going to happen,' said Huddy, remembering how he'd seen Reza treat others. 'You will take what men you have left, and if you can get beyond that wagon, I will let you let you live. We will be chasing you down and putting you to the sword, like the thieves and murderers you are.'

'Do we get horses?' asked Reza.

'One each. I've taken the rest,' said Huddy. 'Break the circle, men. Let them through. Sergeant Lock, I will get my cleverest man to count to ten. I don't know how long that will take, but when he gets there, we will run you down. Now go!'

Reza spurred his horse on, and the thirty or so remaining soldiers raced out with him.

The illusion of fire Kitsu had created had gone. Reza rode hard at the first line of defence, which parted before any of Cardry's men were injured. Before he and his men reached what they thought was the safety of the wagon, Gi and Haggitt released fireballs at them, taking out more of Reza's men. Muto downed more with bolts from his crossbow. Reza and his remaining men thundered towards Fox, Sivad and the second line of Cardry's barbarians.

More fireballs hurtled through the air, some finding their targets to yelps of pain. Badger wasn't loading the crossbows fast enough for Muto, so he grabbed a handful of bolts himself. When he looked up, there were no targets left. Cardry's men had cut down the few that remained.

Reza and two others managed to get to the other side of the wagon. But Muto wasn't of a mind to observe the rules, and brought one down. What looked like a wolf from a nightmare took the other man out of his saddle, and no-one could bear to watch what became of him.

Reza was in full gallop towards the gulley where the women and children were hidden. He saw the snow elf on his white horse, and incensed by his humiliation, he rode crazily at him. Dash sat calmly in Snow's saddle, waiting.

Reza drew level and he swung his sword. Dash avoided it, but lost his balance and fell to the ground. Reza reined in his mount and leapt across onto Snow, digging his heels into the horse's flanks. Dash would never do that. Snow reared, then bolted with Reza on his back. Dash lay still on the ground, slightly stunned.

'Dash! Are you hurt?! He's taken Snow!' Bayna yelled. She pushed her white stag into motion and galloped off in pursuit. She sang out to Snow and he slowed down. Reza kicked him to make him obey. Snow didn't respond, in fact he slowed to a walk. Reza yanked him around and tried to make him charge Bayna.

She told Ice to stop. Reza was raging that Snow refused to obey. He even threatened to strike the beautiful beast with his sword. Bayna had had enough. She unshouldered her bow. 'Get off! Or I will shoot!' she called, menacingly.

Reza raised his sword arm in defiance, but before he could bring it down, an arrow had gone so far into his chest that half its length protruded from between his shoulder blades. He fell from the saddle with a look of surprise, almost in slow motion. 'I did warn you,' she smiled, taking Snow's bridle.

Dash was on his feet. Snow pulled away from Bayna and trotted up to nuzzle his shoulder. 'It's alright, boy. It's over, now.'

'Are you alright?' asked Bayna, anxiously looking him over before holding him.

'I am in no real pain,' he assured her. 'Bruised.' He grimaced as he remounted Snow. 'I think I have pain in my pride.' He forced a grin as he got settled.

Bayna looked around. 'Leoni, keep the women and children here until Cardry sends for you. We're still not sure if it's safe yet. Someone will come back soon.'

Dash and Bayna raced back to Gi's wagon. 'Is everybody alright?' asked Dash.

'We're all okay,' said Gi. 'Fox's plan went well. Only two of Huddy's barbarians were injured, but they'll recover. We got off lightly.'

Cardry came forward. 'Are our families well?' he asked Bayna.

'They are all unharmed. I told them to wait until you sent someone for them.' She dismounted, and went to help Dash get down.

'Dash, were you injured?' asked Gi, concerned and a little angry. He felt very protective towards the elves.

'Not in battle, no. I slipped from my horse, avoiding a sword,' he explained. 'Just bruised. I will mend quickly.'

Cardry sent two men to bring back the women and children. The menfolk were glad to see them unhurt. But the reunions were cut short, and everyone went quiet at the sight of Huddy walking his horse into the camp. His face and arms were blood-splattered, his leggings were blood-soaked.

Haggitt and Muto rushed to meet him.

'Let me help you down,' said Haggitt.

Huddy didn't refuse. 'Take him to the wagon, Mr. Haggitt,' said Muto. 'I'll get him cleaned up and see what the damage is.'

'Would you like me to help?' asked Badger, joining them at the wagon.

'No,' said Muto. 'I don't want you passing out on me again.'

'I won't do that again, Muto. I'll see you coming next time,' said Badger, with a reproving look.

'Oh, alright. Hold his leg still for me,' said Muto.

'What are you going to do?' asked Huddy, his nervousness bordering on panic.

'I'm going to clean all this muck off, and then stitch you up,' said Muto, with utmost confidence. 'See, while we were chatting, I've got it cleaned up already. Now, would you like to be asleep, while I stitch it?'

'Yes. And if you're going to hit me, warn me first,' said Huddy.

'I'm going to hit you,' said Muto.

'Okay,' said Huddy. 'On three. One, two... ow. I said three...!' Huddy moaned, his voice trailing off as he lost consciousness.

A few minutes later, Muto was slapping Huddy's face. Some of his fellow barbarians, who were waiting around, looked away, not wanting to see what might happen to Muto when Huddy came round. 'Wake up, Mr. Huddy. All finished.'

Huddy sat up. 'What did you hit me with?' he said, rubbing his bruised brow.

'It was just a quick tap with my hand,' Muto assured him, as he secretly toe-poked a rock further under the wagon.

'Remind me never to get into a fist fight with you.'

'How's the leg? Mr. Huddy. Does it feel better?'

'It does. Thank you, Muto.' The little cook helped the strapping barbarian to his feet.

'Maybe you should go check on your men now, Mr. Huddy. They'll be waiting for you. And you should also go and thank Mr. Fox, for organising the defences for you,' said Muto.

'What? Fox Loer? Oh, yeah, I remember Brian saying Fox was here.'

'Yes,' said Muto, 'he planned everything. And apart from you and a couple of your men, nobody on your side was injured.'

'Where's Reza Lock?' Huddy wondered. 'Lucky bastard probably rode off without a scratch.'

'I think his luck ran out. I last saw him heading for Bayna who was guarding the women. And Bayna's here.'

Bayna came forward. 'Do not worry. I killed him,' she said. 'He is out there, with an arrow through his chest.'

'Shame,' said Huddy. 'I wanted to do that. Never mind, as long as one of us did it, I'm happy. So, my thanks to you, Bayna.' He limped away, looking for Fox.

He found him close by, sitting with Sivad and Cardry. Fox moved to stand up. 'Don't get up, Fox. I mean you no harm,' Huddy told him. 'I was coming to thank you.'

Fox stood up, anyway. 'No need, Reza was a dangerous man. He had to be stopped. I remember we didn't part the best of friends, Huddy, but he would have killed you if I hadn't thought to get you on that horse,' said Fox.

'Did you know that the horse would find its way back to the camp?' asked Huddy.

'No,' said Fox. 'I had to take that gamble.'

'Well, thanks again,' said Huddy. 'What are you going to do now? You've got no army to look after. And Striper will be after you now.'

'I'm going after *him*,' said Fox. 'I'm heading to Cot Hill, to see if I can recruit enough men to ride with me to Gremanos. I'm going with Gi to help bring down Baron Striper. Do you know him?'

'Only his treachery. I know that much. He burned Broosh Marteef's hovel down, while Broosh's mother was still inside. She got out okay,' said Huddy. 'But that's not the point.'

'Is du Merde among the bodies? Do you know?' Fox asked.

'He's apparently gone to Striper's Castle,' said Gi. 'To warn him I'm coming, I expect.'

'How many in your group, Gi?' Huddy wanted to know.

Gi had to think. 'Nine, mostly. Kitsu turns up when he's hungry. He's my dog, sometimes.'

Huddy let it go. He looked thoughtful. 'How many men are you looking for, Fox?'

'As many as I can get.'

'I was thinking that most of the people here have been robbed or cheated by the baron, at some time,' said Huddy. 'There ought to be enough here that would follow you. And I'm happy for them to go.'

'Would that include you?' Fox asked.

'Perhaps,' said Huddy.

'Why don't we call everyone together tonight?' said Cardry. 'We can see who's willing to go. Some of us will need to stay with our families, of course, but we could probably spare half our men. And we've got about a hundred more horses now, thanks to Fox.'

'If I come with you, Fox, this will be a joint venture. I won't give you orders; so don't expect me to take them,' said Huddy.

'I take it you've made your mind up,' said Fox. 'In that case, you can give the orders. But I'll be the one who sorts out the battle plans.'

'You know,' said Huddy, rubbing his bruised face, 'I think this might just work out.'

* * *

173

55

The area to the side of Gi's wagon was teeming with barbarians that night when the two clans met with Fox and he outlined his plans. They remained sitting quietly on the grass when Huddy got up to endorse Fox, and to tell them he'd be leading this small army, and he'd like volunteers to go with him.

'How many men are here?' asked Gi.

Fox looked across the assembly and did a rough head count. 'I'd guess maybe four hundred.' He turned to Huddy. 'We won't need that many.'

'There are nearer six hundred altogether,' said Huddy. 'Some are out scouting or hunting. Robbing as well, I shouldn't wonder – we *are* barbarians.' The crowd was restless and murmuring, and Huddy seized the moment. 'We need men to take down Baron Striper!' he shouted. 'You all know that! The more of you who can come, the better the outcome is likely to be. We are going to take down a castle, so the spoils will be rich. Oh yes… and *shared*, is that clear? All those willing to come, raise your hands.'

Suddenly, Fox was looking at a sea of hands. Huddy was troubled. Not by the number of men who would stand by him, but for those who'd be left behind.

'All those men with families, should stay. You will not miss out on the spoils. That's the rule,' Huddy told them. About a quarter of the hands dropped and he smiled. 'Now, get some rest. We leave tomorrow. Cardry, will you send a man to call back half the scouts, please. We won't leave you without protection.'

Cardry didn't have to ask, one of the men stood up. 'I'll go,' he volunteered. It seemed that since Huddy Mincing had joined the clan, they got on with one another far better and were more disciplined. How long it would last, might be another story, but for now it was working.

'Thanks for what you're doing, Huddy,' said Gi. 'I need sleep now. It's been a good day, but a long one.'

* * *

A hundred miles, or so, to the west of Gi's barbarian encampment, a rider approached Striper's castle. There was a note pinned to the drawbridge. Which was totally useless, as the drawbridge was up and there was about thirty yards of water in the way. There was a small unmanned gatehouse on his side of the moat. The rider dismounted his horse and tethered it to a ring on the wall by the door. The walker, as he was now, banged on the door. It swung inwards under the force of his fist and he peered inside.

All he could see was a table and two uncomfortable-looking chairs. He sat down in one and looked around. He noticed a rope hanging through a hole in the ceiling, which looked promising, and gave it a tug. Nothing seemed to happen, then eventually he heard the creaking and rumbling of some heavy machinery grinding outside. He went out to find the drawbridge being lowered. It moved ponderously until it was about a foot from the ground, when it dropped like a stone. Fortunately, he'd stepped back.

Craning over the battlements were two heads.

'It went well that time, Ollie!' said Skeet. 'You nearly 'ad 'im then.'

The walker became a rider again, and clopped noisily onto the drawbridge, where he paused to look up at the two men operating it.

'Oh shit,' said Ollie. 'Do you see who that is?'

'Er… yes, I can see 'im, but I don't know who 'e is,' said Skeet.

'It's Captain du Merde,' said Ollie. ''E's bin away for months. I 'eard 'e was posted to the Baron's little fort in the desert.'

'Is 'e important?' asked Skeet.

'He's the Baron's Centurion of the Black-Guard,' said Ollie, worriedly.

'He seems to have lost 'em, then. We'd better go down and let 'im in.'

Captain du Merde was waiting almost patiently at the bottom of the stairs when Skeet and Ollie finally appeared.

'Honest, Captain, we didn't know it was you,' Ollie lied. 'The local kids have been playin' pranks on us, and we were just gettin' our own back.'

'You are supposed to be soldiers, not children!' he blasted them. 'Now, grow up and take me to the baron.'

'Yes, sir. Of course, sir. This way,' said Ollie, executing some rare choreography, bowing and turning at the same time, and colliding with a wall.

''Ave you been here before, sir?' asked Skeet.

'Yes,' replied du Merde. 'So don't try and take me the long way round. Oh, and stable my horse and give him a rub down. I may need him again, soon.'

'Yes, sir,' said Skeet, 'doin' it now, sir.'

'Right, Ollie, is it?' asked du Merde.

'Yes, sir. Ollie is me alright,' he said. 'I'll have you at the baron's reception room in less time than it takes to get there.'

'What?' Then *Reception room?* thought du Merde, *it was more like an oversized cupboard...* Ollie opened the door. *Oh, it's still a large cupboard.*

The décor had changed a bit since du Merde was last there. There were a couple of padded benches with arm rests and a long low table with a pile of ancient magazines at each end.

'Please sit, Captain. I'll let the baron know you're waitin',' said Ollie. He tapped lightly on the office door and listened. Inside, there was the clinking of glasses, then silence. Ollie tapped again, and listened. A voice on the other side said, 'Quickly! Get dressed, and go out through Pinch's office.'

This was followed by a lot of scuffling and the sound of a door being slammed in the far wall. 'Come in!' yelled Striper, irritably.

* * *

57

Baron Striper sat behind his desk, resplendent – he thought – in his crimson baronial attire, and composed himself while he waited for his visitor. He could feel beads of sweat on his ample forehead, so he reached into his pocket and pulled out a handkerchief and mopped his brow. The red satin cloth with a white lace trim, seemed to unravel in his hand. He stared at it in horror, then opened a desk drawer and rammed the women's undergarment back as far as it would go and slammed it shut.

Ollie stood with a foot on each of the threadbare patches of carpet in front of Striper's desk, trying not to snigger.

'Yes, Ollie, what do you want?' the baron demanded. 'I'm exceptionally busy, you know.'

'I don't doubt it, my Lord, but Captain du Merde is here to see you,' Ollie announced.

'Is he alone?'

'Yes, my Lord.'

'Good. This office isn't big enough for his men as well,' said Striper.

'No, Lord. Definitely on 'is own.'

'Alright… send him in,' the baron sighed.

Ollie turned and almost ran into du Merde as he strode into Striper's office, his helmet under one arm. He nodded and stamped to attention.

'At ease, Captain,' the baron told him. 'Is this going to take long?'

'My Lord, I take it you know Gi Mulderbish escaped from the pyramid?' said du Merde. 'Well, he turned up near the desert outpost.'

'Did you apprehend him?'

'Yes, Lord. I was bringing him back here, but we were attacked by barbarians – hundreds of the buggers – and they kidnapped him.'

'And you allowed this to happen?' He pointed a baronial finger.

'They took us by surprise, Lord. But that's not all. They've released him… He's coming here, Lord, and he's very angry.'

'Well, he would be! Locked away for eighteen years!' the baron was starting to shout. Which meant he was either getting angry, or starting to panic. 'Is he alone?'

'No, my Lord. His son is with him, and my cook, and four or five of our men deserted to ride with him.'

'So, you still command over ninety men...' the baron assumed.

'Er... no, my Lord. It's just me. I... I came on ahead... to tell you...about the wizards,' du Merde blustered.

'I know about the wizards, du Merde. Where is my Black-Guard?!' Striper slammed his bony fists on the desk.

'They're out on the plain, Lord. East of Cot Hill. Reza Lock took command when I was injured fighting barbarians. Then he and the men mutinied, and he stripped me of my rank. When I saw he was surrounded by more barbarians, Lord, I slipped away. I'm not *stupid*.'

'No, I suppose not,' said Striper. 'But you are now without a command and worse still, I am lacking protection, du Merde. Any ideas?'

'What, Lord? You have no soldiers in the castle?' said du Merde, in disbelief.

'Not that I would hand over to you, Captain. You've already lost a hundred of my men,' Striper pointed out. 'You can join the ranks of the Second Black-Guard, commanded by the almost-as-useless-as-you Captain Chirgwin. Ollie! Take him to the captain, please, and shut the door.' Striper waved them out.

'Pinch! Are you out there?' the baron yelled.

'Yes, Lord,' replied Pinch, through clenched teeth, always dreading what Striper might want next.

'Were you ever in the army?' the baron asked.

'Yes, my Lord, for eight and a half years,' said Pinch, wondering where this might go.

'What rank did you achieve?' asked the baron, in a tone suggesting 'as if'.

'Major, sir,' said Pinch, lying as hard as he could.

'*What?*' said Striper. 'How did that happen?'

'I was very good at it, Baron,' Pinch continued to lie.

The baron finally caught up with where his thoughts were leading. 'Do you know anyone who can write and organise as well as you, Pinch?'

A wicked smile flickered on the clerk's usually glum face. *I've got you now, you bastard.* 'Oh, yes, Lord. Barter Stogie's son is almost as good as me.'

'When Ollie comes back, I'll tell him to find Barter's son and bring him here. You can show him the ropes for an hour or so, then you can take command of the Second Black-Guard. How's that?' said Striper. 'Chirgwin's long overdue for it.'

'I'm honoured, Lord. I will do my best to serve you well,' said Pinch, knowing the patter, and with crossed fingers behind his back.

'That'll be all then, Pinch. Send Maureen back in, will you.'

* * *

58

Dawn was breaking over the plains and people were starting their daily routines. Gi could tell, by the queues at the bushes a short distance away. That distance was too short when the breeze was blowing in the wrong direction.

'I'm sure it wasn't this bad yesterday, Muto. What have these people been eating?'

'Couldn't really say, Master. But some of the dead horses have been shifted.'

'I think we'll have breakfast on the move,' said Gi, waving the odour away from his face. 'I can't take much more of this.'

'I agree, Master. When we make camp tonight, I'll teach them the advantages of a shovel.' With that, Muto climbed onto his seat, flicked the reins, and they started to move on towards Cot Hill.

A mile up the track, the air was fresher. Gi, sitting up top with Muto, breathed deeply. 'You know, Muto, I think I was a little premature blaming the barbarians for that smell earlier.'

'What makes you say that, Master?'

'It was probably the bodies from the battle. It's a wonder we weren't invaded by all manner of creatures during the night.'

'Well, Master, those creatures will have full bellies for a few days.'

'Don't forget, Father,' said Haggitt, interrupting from inside the wagon, 'we've got to get Dash and Bayna back to the snowline.'

'I haven't forgotten. Where are they, by the way?' asked Gi.

Muto looked behind where the elves usually rode. They were there, and this morning they had company. They were deep in conversation with Fox. And, just coming up to the head of the horde, Muto saw Brian and Maurice riding with Huddy.

Gi stood up so he could see all around. 'Muto, come up here and look.'

'Goodness, Master, I've never seen so many mounted men at once. Isn't it exciting?'

180

'I don't know about that my friend, but it certainly looks impressive,' said Gi. 'I'm just glad we're not at the back eating all the dust getting kicked up.'

Gi sat down, his aging legs were aching from trying to keep his balance on the wagon as it jogged along over the rough ground.

Dash rode up beside the wagon. 'Gi, we are probably only a couple of days from the northern snowline now, but Bayna and I wish to continue travelling with you to Gremanos.'

'Only too pleased to have you with us!' Gi called down. 'Would you get Fox up here, please?'

Fox caught up. 'Do you still need to go to Cot Hill, Fox?' Gi asked him.

'I do,' said Fox. 'These barbarians won't all be staying with me after Gremanos. I'd like to quickly see what the place has to offer. But I think only six or seven of us should go in. I can't take four hundred barbarians with me.' Fox allowed himself a grin. 'Can you imagine the panic?'

'What do you need from us, then, Master Fox?' asked Muto.

'Well… it's somewhere I've never been,' said Fox. 'I'm curious, and there might be some of Striper's spies in there.'

Now we're getting to it, Muto thought.

'Who do you propose to take with you?' asked Gi.

'You, for a start, Gi. Muto, Haggitt and the elves. That should be enough,' said Fox. 'Huddy has control of the barbarians. Brian, Maurice and Sivad can keep an eye on things here, and get a message to us if need be.

'How long do you expect to be there?' asked Gi. 'I want to get to Gremanos soon.'

'Oh, only an hour or two,' said Fox. 'That should be long enough.'

'Right then. Let Huddy know. He can either rest his men outside the town, or continue on and meet us at the river, later,' said Gi. As an afterthought, he added, 'And tell him to try and keep them out of trouble.'

A few miles further on, the rough track joined a road, and soon it sloped up to Cot Hill. Muto drove the wagon along the main road through the town. Fox and the elves rode side by side behind it.

'What are you looking for, Fox?' asked Dash.

'I'm looking for spies, Dash, but we won't find any on the street. We'll have to find a tavern,' said Fox.

'Bayna and I do not go into such places. We attract too much attention,' said Dash. 'We will guard the wagon.'

'Okay. If you're sure. I can bring you out a drink, if you like, and some pork scratchings...' said Fox.

'What are pork scratchings?' asked Dash.

'I've no idea, but they sound disgusting. This looks like a tavern,' said Fox, thinking how timely it was. 'Can I help you down, Gi?'

'No, it's okay, I'll use the steps at the back,' said Gi.

'Are you coming, Haggitt?' Fox called out.

'No. I'll stay with the elves.' he replied.

Dash and Bayna took up station each side of the wagon, and waited for the curious to come and admire the horse and the stag. They didn't mind the children so much, as crowds made it difficult for would-be thieves.

Inside the tavern, Fox walked to the bar counter. Gi and Muto hung back. After all, it was Fox's idea to go in there.

'What'll it be gents?' asked the bartender.

'Just three flagons of ale, please,' said Fox.

'I'll just have two flagons,' said Muto.

'No,' Fox stopped him. 'I've ordered us one each. We can order more when we've finished these.'

'I'm not used to taverns,' said Muto. 'It shows, doesn't it?'

Fox looked sideways at him. 'Come, let's find a table.'

No sooner had they sat down, than a girl was at Fox's shoulder with a notepad and pencil. 'Would you like to order food, gentlemen?'

'What have you got?' asked Gi.

She hesitated for a moment, then read the blackboard on the wall behind the counter. 'Ham sandwiches, hot bacon sandwiches or a ploughman's,' she read.

'Oh,' said Muto, rubbing his hands together. 'I'd like the ploughman's, please.'

'Bacon all right for you, Gi?' Gi nodded. 'And two bacon sandwiches, please,' said Fox. The girl scribbled on her notepad and went to the kitchen.

'That must have been for show,' said Fox. 'Nobody could forget an order like that between here and the kitchen.'

'I think she's a bit flustered by you, Fox,' said Gi, amused.

He shrugged it off, a little awkwardly.

It seemed a long time before the girl finally brought the three plates to the table. 'Who wants the ploughman's?'

Muto raised his hand and she put the plate down in front of him. Then her powers of deduction kicked in and she gave the bacon sandwiches to Fox and Gi.

Muto looked at his plate. 'Is there something wrong, sir?' the girl asked.

'I asked for a ploughman,' said Muto. 'I appear to have bread, cheese and pickle,' he complained, with more than a hint of disappointment in his tone.

'That's what we call a ploughman's, sir,' she told him.

'Alright, I'll eat it. But I'm not happy,' Muto moaned. 'I was so looking forward to a nice ploughman.'

Fox and Gi ignored him.

While he was eating, Fox noticed a man watching them from the far end of the counter. Fox put his hand over his mouth and looked away out of the window. 'Do you know that fellow at the end of the counter, Gi?' said Fox. 'The Eastern-looking man with the red bandanna? Hang on, is that…?'

'Without looking,' said Gi, 'Probably. What's he drinking?'

'It looks like plain water.'

'Call him over,' said Gi.

Fox waved the man forward.

'Kitsu?' said Gi, 'What are you doing here?'

'Waiting for someone to buy me lunch. I'm fed up with chasing rabbits.'

'You can't have sausages here. It'll have to have a bacon sandwich,' said Muto.

'Thank you, Muto,' Kitsu said, disconcertingly baring his teeth in a canine grin.

The waitress was hovering immediately, and left in a dither.

'We're looking for anyone out spying for Baron Striper,' Gi told Kitsu.

'Well, you've come to right place,' said Kitsu. 'There's at least three in here, Gi. They're sitting at the table in the corner by the privy.'

'I was just thinking of taking a visit,' said Muto. 'I'll see if I can pick up anything.' He casually wandered across the room. The men stopped talking and watched him walk by.

Muto watched them, feigning disinterest, as he passed, and ducked into the privy.

'Did you see who that was?' said the man wearing a cloth cap.

'Nope, didn't recognise 'im,' replied the bald man.

'Me neither,' said the man with ginger hair.

'That was Muto Bright,' said cloth cap. ''E was cook for du Merde's Black-Guards.'

'What's 'e doing 'ere?' wondered the bald man.

'I'd have thought that was obvious,' said ginger. 'He's having a piss.'

'No, here – *in the tavern*,' said the bald man.

'He's with those three over there. Do you know 'em?' said cloth cap.

'No, er… yeah. 'Old on a minute, that's Gi Mulderbish, the wizard, ennit?' said ginger. 'And the one on this side's Fox Loer.'

'Alright, what do you fink they're 'ere for?' cloth cap wondered.

'Shall I ask 'im?' said the bald man.

'Do you fink he'd tell you?' said cloth cap.

'Don't see why not. Not as if we don't know 'im, is it?' said the bald man.

'I'll go,' said ginger. 'I expect he'll remember me.' He got up and walked across.

'Hi yuh, Fox. Everything alright?' said ginger. 'Me and my mates were wondering where you're going. They bet me you wouldn't tell me.'

'Then you lose,' said Fox. 'Why do you want to know?'

'My curiosity got the better of me,' said ginger.

Kitsu leaned in and mumbled through a mouth half-full of bacon sandwich: 'Shall I tell him to fu...'

'No, Kitsu,' Gi interrupted quickly. 'I was going to do that.'

The ginger haired man suddenly developed a faraway look on his face.

'You've hypnotised him, haven't you, Gi?' Kitsu knew. 'And *I* was going to do that.'

'You can tell him whatever you like now, Fox, and he'll believe every word,' said Gi.

Fox was mentally rubbing his hands together. *What can I tell him...* he thought.

'Tell him the four of us are going to Gremanos,' prompted Gi.

Fox repeated it, word for word, then added, 'We're going to visit Gi's grandmother, she's not been well lately.'

Gi nearly choked on his ale.

'We might call in on the baron, while we're there,' said Fox. 'We know he likes to keep in touch.'

'When are you leaving?' said glazed ginger.

'Day after tomorrow,' Fox told him. 'You should get back to your friends now, and collect your wager? You won, after all.'

'Oh, yeah. Fanks, Fox. Be seeing yuh.' He ambled back to the corner table, passing Muto on his way back, and stared right through him.

'Well. What did he say?' asked the bald man.

The ginger man related it, almost word for word.

'We'd better get the bill and get back to the baron,' said cloth cap. 'We could all get a promotion for info like that.'

The bald man called the girl with the notepad to their table. 'What's the damage, sweetheart?'

'You call me that again and the damage will be to your mouth.' She smiled. With her mouth, but not her eyes. There was clearly another side to her.

'Oh, come on. Only being friendly,' the man insisted.

'Give me seven brass and forty copper, please. That'll cover it,' she said, taking his money. As she turned, she felt a pinch. She squealed, grabbed a metal tray and instead of bringing it down, she swept it round and buried it in the side of his head, edge first.

'Bloody hell,' said Fox. 'I bet he didn't expect that!'

The bartender went to assist her, although she seemed perfectly capable of looking after herself. 'You!' he pointed at cloth cap and ginger. 'Out. Now. And take your friend with you!'

They picked up the bald man and started helping him to the door. 'Wait!' the girl shouted, as she stormed across the floor. She stopped in front of them yanked the tray out of the man's head.

That's when things got mucky. A man sitting at the nearest table got showered in blood-flecks and stood up. 'My wife's gonna be mad when she sees this!' he fumed, pointing at the blood on his shirt.

He did appreciate where the blame lay, though. The girl caused the blood spatter when she extracted the tray from the man's head, but if he hadn't given her the lip in the first place, none of this would've happened. So, he punched the comatose bald man. Ginger took offence and swung at the man, who fell back into a table, knocking a round of drinks over.

'Oh dear,' said Fox. 'I might've known… Come on, Gi, let's get you outside.'

Like all tavern brawls everywhere, everyone else joined in. Men were getting slammed against walls, knocked to the ground, and thrown through windows. Any left standing, ran for the door. And remarkably, one man seemed responsible for most of it.

'Ah, Muto,' said Kitsu. 'I thought that might be you.'

'Er… Mr. Kitsu. I thought you were outside with the others.'

'No,' said Kitsu. 'I was waiting for an opportunity to join in, but you left me nothing to join in with.'

'You won't tell Master Gi, will you? Please, Mr. Kitsu,' Muto pleaded. 'I'd rather he didn't know this about me.'

'If you ask me to keep it secret, Muto, I will. I'd be foolish to get on your wrong side, seeing what you just did to these men littering the floor.' He looked incredulously at the little cook, his smile widening.

'Come on, let's go,' he said, putting a friendly arm around Muto's shoulders.

Flat cap and ginger carried the bald man outside, and dumped him in the gutter. He was beyond repair. 'I expect someone'll clear him up later,' said flat cap.

'We should get back to the baron,' said ginger, as they made their way to the tavern's stables, 'before someone catches us littering the place.'

* * *

Ollie found Barter's son, Gripper, and told him to report to Pinch.

'I understand you can read and write,' said Pinch.

'Yes, Mr. Pinch.'

'You call me Major, now. Who taught you to read?' asked Pinch.

'The old woman that owns the sweet shop in Chit's alley, Major. She said if I didn't learn to read and write, I'd finish up like my dad.'

'Your dad seems to get by,' said Pinch.

'That's because he doesn't get caught, Major.'

'What does your mother call you, young Stogie?' asked Pinch.

'Mostly "You little shit," Major.'

'No, you must have a front name.'

'Oh, yeah, it's Gripper.'

'Hmm, okay. Well, Gripper,' said Pinch, getting down to business. 'The accounts are in the top drawer over there. It's basic double-exit bookkeeping. You're familiar with that?'

Gripper was unsure. 'Well, I know double-*entry*.'

'That's the usual way, I know, but the baron's accounts are more about exits.' He continued, 'Copies of the baron's letters, if you get any, go in the second drawer. And watch out for the mouse traps. Any questions?'

'Yes,' said Gripper, 'where's the privy, and where can I hang my coat?'

'Hang your coat over there. But don't leave anything in the pockets when you leave the office,' Pinch told him. 'I found a secret place to hide my stuff. You'll have to find one of your own. Oh, and if the baron asks if you smoke, tell him no, or he'll keep scrounging off you till you have to buy him some.

Gripper sighed. 'There's so much to learn, Major. Do you think I'll be able to manage?'

'Of course you will. You don't have to do that much. Just sit at your desk and look busy till he calls you. And don't let him see you roll your eyes when he does.' Gripper started to protest he never would, but Pinch was getting up to leave. 'I'll be in the officer's mess if you need me. Have fun.' He left at considerable speed before Gripper or the baron changed their minds.

When the baron heard Pinch's door close, he shouted, 'Stogie! Are you in there?'

Gripper walked into Striper's office. 'You called, my Lord?'

'Yes, Stogie. Do you smoke?' the baron asked.

Gripper thought, *my gods, that didn't take long.* 'Er... no, my Lord,' Gripper replied.

'Shit,' murmured the baron. 'Okay, that'll be all.'

'Thank you, my Lord.' Gripper moved towards the door, and Striper called him back.

'Have you got a sister?' Striper asked him.

'No, my Lord. I've got a little cat,' he replied. Striper sighed and shook his head. 'Shall I go now, my Lord?'

'You might as well,' said Striper, glumly.

Gripper sat behind the desk – *his* desk. *What shall I do now?* he wondered. *Twiddle my thumbs? Clean my ears out? All these executive decisions I'm having to make, it's making my head hurt.*

Striper called him again. 'Can you ride, Stogie?'

'Yes, my Lord.'

'Ride into town and get me something to smoke,' the baron ordered.

Gripper came back and held out a hand, palm up.

'Yes? What is it?' said Striper.

'I don't have any money, my Lord. I haven't been paid yet. Do you have accounts in the shops?' asked Gripper, naively.

'Just say they're for me,' said the baron. He was not used to this. When Pinch was in the office, everything usually went *his* way.

Gripper went to the stables to find a horse. First he found Ollie, mucking out.

'Oh, hi, Gripper, what're you doin' down 'ere?'

'The baron wants me to get him something to smoke,' Gripper told him.

'Did 'e give you any money?' Ollie grinned.

'No, and I haven't got any. Does he expect me to steal it? I'm known around here!'

'Just do what the rest of us do,' said Ollie.

'What's that?'

'Ride into town, ask in a couple of shops, and tell 'em they're for the baron,' said Ollie. 'They'll throw you out. Then go back to the baron and tell him they didn't have any.'

'Is that what you do?'

'Yep. In the end, he'll get the message and ride into town himself,' said Ollie.

'It's a pity we haven't got any fag papers, Ollie. We could make some out of that stuff you're piling in the wheelbarrow,' said Gripper, grinning, half serious.

Ollie liked that. 'Tell you what – go into town and see if you can get hold of any empty fag boxes. The tavern's probably got loads in their bins. As they know you, you could get lucky and one of the shops'll give you some papers.'

'If I say what we're planning, they might be happy to give me two packets.' Gripper smiled.

'I wouldn't be surprised,' said Ollie. 'And while you're gone, I'll start drying out some of these horse apples so they stay alight. You'd better see if you can scrounge a box of matches, too. I don't suppose Striper's got any. You know, for someone who's swindled so many people out of so much money, he never seems to 'ave any!'

'Just a miser, maybe. Hoards it all up.'

'I'd love to know where it's stashed,' said Ollie. 'Right, the horse in stall number six should be ready. Bring 'im back in one piece, please.'

Gripper arrived in town and went to the nearest shop to check the baron's credit-worthiness. The proprietor was very understanding of Grippers situation, and sympathised, but it ended with him being told to piss off, as expected. It was not a good start. The next shop was equally fruitless. He could understand why they were like it, but it did hurt his feelings. He'd known some of these people all his life.

Gripper decided to tell the next shopkeeper what he and Ollie were planning.

'Does your father know what you're about to do, young Gripper?' said the man, unsmiling.

'No,' said Gripper. 'Not yet,' half expecting a ticking off.

'Well, he'll be proud of you when he finds out. I'll let you have one pack of ten cigarettes, two packets of papers and a box of matches. Now, go down to the tavern and speak to the bartender, tell him I sent you, and you want as many empty cigarette boxes as he's got. He'll be glad to get rid of them.'

'Thanks, Mr. Sayer. 'I'll let dad know you helped.'

The man in the tavern was equally as helpful, and even gave Gripper a bag to carry everything. It was halfway through the afternoon when Gripper got back. Ollie had left the drawbridge down for him, and Gripper rode straight round to the stables where Ollie was waiting.

'How did you get on?' he asked.

'I got everything,' Gripper announced proudly. 'How's the shit coming on? Got any dry enough, yet?'

'The smithy was a bit awkward about using his forge, till I told 'im what it was for. Then 'e couldn't 'ave been more obliging.' Ollie grinned.

The pair started to make cigarettes and pack boxes with different brand names. The most abundant was *Desert Gold*. The box said it was a really smooth smoke with a hint of cactus flowers and Aloe Vera.

'These will do,' said Gripper. 'The horses probably eat all that stuff. I'll take a pack of the real ones and a pack of *Desert Gold*, and leave the rest here where the smell won't be out of place.'

'Can you think of an excuse for me to be in your office when 'e calls you, Gripper? I'd love to see his face.'

'Just bring me my afternoon tea, Ollie. That'll be a good excuse.'

Gripper went up to his office and slammed the door to make sure that Striper knew he was back.

'Stogie! Is that you?' the baron called out.

'Coming, my Lord.'

'No, *don't* come in for a minute!' Striper called. Then to Maureen, 'Get dressed, and go out through reception,' he whispered. Then, to himself, *I really must get another door in here.*

Maureen dressed, picked up her shorthand notepad and pencil and left.

'You still there, Stogie?'

'Yes, my Lord,' Gripper thought about rolling his eyes.

'You can come in now. Did you get me anything?' Striper asked.

'Yes, my Lord. I've got a pack of that *Old Camel Stranded* that Major Pinch used to smoke, and a packet of *Desert Gold*. Which would you like?' asked Gripper, holding the *Desert Gold* box further forward.

The baron looked and thought, *I know the stuff Pinch smokes, it's bloody awful, but it was free*. 'I'll take the *Desert Gold*. Got a light?'

Gripper struck a yellow-headed match and it flared dangerously into life. Striper drew life into the cigarette. The smoke filling the air around him was an odd colour, and smelt a bit foreign. He breathed in deeply and choked loudly several times. 'My word, these are good,' he declared, and sat down. Very quickly.

'Are you alright, my Lord?' said Gripper, with mock concern.

'Never better,' Striper wheezed, then he had another bout of painful coughing.

'I'll leave the rest on your desk, my Lord.' Gripper slammed his door and ran to the other side of his office, trying to stifle his laughter.

Ollie wandered in. 'I've brought your afternoon tea, Mr. Stogie,' he said, grinning like a cat.

'Thanks Ollie. You're a bit late. And you'd better take it to the baron. He needs it more than I do.'

Maureen walked into Gripper's office. She didn't look happy. 'I hope you lads aren't up to something. I'm earning good money out of 'im.'

'Don't worry, Maureen. He'll be alright,' Ollie assured her.

Maureen left, flint-faced.

'Are you sure?' said Gripper.

'No,' said Ollie.

'Well, I don't suppose anyone will care,' said Gripper.

'Except the lovely Maureen, of course.' Ollie sniggered.

* * *

Kitsu and Muto came out of the tavern and strolled to the wagon. 'That was close,' said Kitsu. 'Muto and I only just made it out of there.'

'Yes,' Fox grinned. 'I can tell by all the cuts and bruises you almost got.'

'We ducked a lot, Mr. Fox,' said Muto, cheerily.

Fox laughed, then, 'Look, our spies are heading out. That worked well, Gi. They'll tell Striper we'll be a couple of days behind them and, knowing him, he'll wait until the last minute to sort out his defences. He might still be doing it the day after we've entered the city.'

'Do you think we should send someone ahead, Fox? To see if there's anything we should know, before we go crashing in,' said Gi.

'I'm ahead of you. I plan to send Badger. He's proving useful,' said Fox.

'I'll go with him,' said Kitsu. 'We're good together. And I can be whatever I like.'

'Don't scare him too much,' said Gi.

'Great.' Fox was satisfied. 'We'll get back to the others and brief Badger.'

'Dash, Bayna!' Gi shouted. 'Get rid of all those kids. We're leaving.'

'Just pull out, Muto!' called Bayna. 'We will follow. If the children don't move, then our beasts will move them. They've *been* warned.'

Worried, Muto got down off the wagon and went to speak to one of the children. The child listened intently. Suddenly her face froze and she ran, calling all the others to follow. Muto climbed nonchalantly back into the wagon.

'You never cease to amaze me, Muto,' said Gi.

'When I stop being amazing, Master, I will steal away like a thief in the night, and you will never see me again.'

'I trust not,' said Gi. 'Come on, let's catch up with the others.'

The grinning little cook slapped the reins, and the group rumbled up the street and out onto the plain.

'What happened in the tavern, Muto?' asked Gi.

'I'd rather not talk about it, Master. All I'll say is that one of those nasty men in there, tried to lock me in the privy,' said Muto.

'I shan't pursue it, Muto,' said Gi, avoiding eye contact for fear of bursting out laughing.

'No need, Master. Justice has been done. Gee-up, horses!'

'Where's Kitsu?' Gi wondered, aloud.

'He stole a horse, Master. Said he would send it back when we catch up with the rest of the men. If he remembers,' said Muto. 'That's not nice.'

'Did anyone see him take it?' Gi asked.

'Probably not, Master. He was invisible the last time I saw him. That didn't come out right, but you know what I mean.'

'Would you like to be a shape-shifter, Muto?' asked Gi. 'All the tricks you could play, and the fun you could have?'

'It is appealing, Master, and if I ever decide to be one, you'll be the first to know.'

'You can't just decide it, Muto, you have to be born one.'

'Well, I won't then, Master. I'll just be amazing this shape.'

Gi threw his head back and guffawed. 'You'll do, Muto.'

'Camp's ahead, Gi!' Fox called out.

'Go and find Badger. We need to talk to him. Is Kitsu back yet?' asked Gi.

'Right behind you,' said a voice.

Gi turned and looked down into the wagon. There was a large brown and yellow dog laying on his bed.

'I hope you haven't got fleas, mister!' said Gi, tetchily. 'I thought you'd stolen a horse.'

'I thought better of it, and flew.'

'The flying dog again, eh?'

'Oh, ha-ha.'

Muto steered the wagon into the camp and drew up by the river to let the horses drink while he busied himself with cooking.

Gi and Kitsu went in search of Badger, and Fox went to find Brian and Maurice. As he strutted around the sprawl of tents and tethered horses, he spotted Sivad talking intently with Huddy, and wondered what it was all about.

'Problem?' said Fox, approaching.

Sivad pointed across the river. 'Two riders, Fox. They've been watching us for a couple of hours.'

'Not a friendly thing to do.' Fox squinted at them, but they were too far away to identify. 'I'll ask Kitsu to go up and take a look.' Which he went immediately to do. Finding Brian and Maurice could wait.

'You want *me to fly over there* and see who they are?' said Kitsu. 'I've just landed from getting back from the tavern. Have you any idea how much my arms ache? No, of course you haven't. Muto, get some sausages on the go, please. I'll be back in a minute.'

'Thanks, Kitsu. I owe you one,' said Fox, with a wry smile and an appreciative glance towards the food sizzling, and back to Kitsu. 'That was quick.'

'Oh, do shut up, Fox. I haven't been yet. You don't think I'm going to shift in front of you all, do you?' said Kitsu.

'Not shy, are we?' said Fox, a smile playing around his mouth.

'My reason,' he said, with strained patience, 'is that I'm told the sight of me shifting is beyond weird, and you'll find it hard to forget. So, if you want to watch, be my guest, but I don't advise it.

'Get in the wagon, Mr. Kitsu. It's more private,' said Muto.

Kitsu agreed, and after a few grunts and groans, an eagle took to the sky from behind the wagon and soared over the river. It circled the two men a couple of times, then returned to perch on the back of the wagon.

Muto was waiting inside. 'I really liked it when that beak turned back into your nose, Mr. Kitsu. Did it hurt?'

'Not so much as turning my nose into a beak. Now, where are my clothes?'

'I straightened them for you, Mr. Kitsu. You managed to get them all creased up. Have you been sleeping in them?'

'More *on* them, than *in* them,' he explained.

195

'Are you normal?' called Fox from outside, eager for news.

'Never have been,' said Kitsu. 'But I'm not likely to offend at the moment, if that's what you mean.'

'What can you tell us about the riders?' asked Fox.

'They're the spies from the tavern,' replied Kitsu.

'That's not good. Not if they saw us join up with the barbarians,' said Fox. 'We can't let them take word back to Striper.'

'What do you want to do?' asked Gi. 'Send Brian and Maurice to kill them?'

'No, Gi,' said Fox. 'That's *not* what I do. I'm *not* Reza Lock.'

'That's good to hear. So, did anyone find Badger?' asked Gi, looking about.

'He's with Huddy and Sivad.'

'We need him here, please,' said Gi.

'Your sausages are done, Mr. Kitsu,' said Muto.

'Where do they keep coming from, Muto? You don't seem to have any stores to speak of, and suddenly there's stuff frying. Like magic,' said Kitsu.

'That's exactly what it is, Mr. Kitsu, I've tried other ways, but magic works best.'

'Looking for me, Mr. Mulderbish?' said Badger, on his arrival at Gi's wagon.

'Yes, thanks for coming,' said Gi. 'There are two of Baron Striper's spies across the river.' He pointed in the general direction. 'They've been watching us.'

'It's what they do,' said Badger, chirpily. 'Do you want me to go and kill 'em, Mr. Mulderbish?'

'*No*,' said Fox, intervening. 'What is it with you people? We don't have to kill all the time,' he said, open-mouthed at what he was hearing. 'I want you to get to Gremanos ahead of them. Or, go with them, even. Kitsu will be around, so you won't be on your own.'

'Yeah, I'd prefer to go alone with Kitsu,' said Badger. 'We can leave in the morning. They won't move off before then.'

'Find out if they've put two and two together, and if our element of surprise has gone. We need to know if we'll be walking into a trap, Badger,' said Fox. 'Kitsu can bring a message back.'

'I'm an eagle, not a bloody carrier pigeon' retorted Kitsu, affecting deep hurt.

'Muto,' said Gi, 'will you pack some food for them, please?'

'Of course, Master.'

* * *

Shortly after Badger awoke next morning, Sivad brought two horses over. One had a sack slung each side of the saddle. *Ah*, Badger thought, *breakfast*. He glanced across to the spot where Striper's spies had been, but they were gone. Kitsu arrived promptly.

'When you were flying around, Kit, did you see a bridge, or a ferry along the river?' Badger asked him. 'Those spies must've got across somewhere.'

'There's a ferry about a mile upstream,' said Kitsu. 'Looked like it'd take the horses.'

'Right, let's tell the others we're off, and head up there,' said Badger.

'Fox and Sivad are the only ones about,' said Kitsu.

'Yeah, I saw Fox polluting the river a few minutes ago,' said Badger.

'We might need to do the same before we get too far.'

Then Fox showed up and gave them a hearty send-off. 'Be careful out there, you two. We're depending on you.'

Kitsu and Badger set off at a brisk trot. Once clear of the camp, Kitsu confessed, 'You know, I try to dislike that man, but I can never quite manage it.' Badger knew exactly what he meant.

When they arrived at the ferry crossing, there was nobody about. There was a small shed-like building at the side of a wood-plank jetty. 'I'll see if there's anyone home?' said Badger, dismounting. He banged on the door.

A muffled voice from within, told him to wait. Badger stood patiently watching the river flow.

'Call him again,' urged Kitsu.

'We haven't got all day you know!' Badger shouted.

'Well... bugger off, then,' was the comeback.

Not the response Badger was expecting. 'What're you doin' in there?'

'If you must know, I'm having a crap!'

'Oh... sorry,' said Badger, wondering why he needed a privy beside a sizeable river.

Kitsu grinned. 'Must be that time of the morning.'

'We'll give 'im a few more minutes,' said Badger, loudly, 'then we'll steal the boat and take ourselves across.'

Immediately, they heard the noises of a man hurriedly making himself presentable.

'You've done this before, haven't you?' said Kitsu.

'Yeah, once or twice,' said Badger.

The door opened and the man came out. 'You touch my ferry and I'll kill you. You undo the ropes and I'll kill you. If you do anything without my permission, I'll kill you.'

Kitsu laughed. He'd never been threatened that many times in such a short space of time before, especially by an armour-clad dwarf with his trousers round his ankles.

'Are you the ferryman?' said Badger, not even trying to keep a straight face.

'Do I look like the ferryman?' said the dwarf. 'Course I'm not. He's tall and skinny, wears a black hooded robe and carries a scythe.'

'Well, where is he?'

'Sitting on the end of the jetty, soaking his feet,' said the dwarf.

'Thanks for your time,' said Badger. 'Now pull your trousers up.'

Badger followed Kitsu onto the jetty. 'How much?' Kitsu asked the black-clad figure with the dangling feet.

I DON'T CHARGE. IT'S A FREE SERVICE, said a voice like doom.

The men led their horses onto the ferry. The ferryman mysteriously produced a long pole, which He pushed into the river, and proceeded to propel the flat-bottomed craft through a sluggish crosscurrent to the other side.

WILL YOU BE COMING BACK? He asked.

'Er... thank you, no,' said Badger. 'We're going further north.'

NO, YOU ARE GOING TO GREMANOS. I WILL SEE YOU AGAIN.

The ferry gently bumped the landing stage on the other side of the river and Badger and Kitsu led the nervous horses to firm ground.

'Thank goodness that's over,' said Badger. 'He was a laugh a minute.'

'Probably bored out of his skull,' said Kitsu. 'I don't know why I said that,' he shrugged.

They spurred their horses on and soon picked up the fresh trail of Striper's spies.

'What kind of spy leaves a trail this easy?' said Badger. 'Do you think they guessed they'd be followed, and they're setting us up?'

'No, I think they're just stupid.'

'Do you want to fly around and see where they are?' asked Badger.

'Maybe, when it's darker and there's less chance of me being spotted,' said Kitsu. 'Trouble is, night-flying is dangerous.'

'For an eagle, yeah,' said Badger. 'Try an owl.'

Kitsu conceded the point. The two men rode in silence for the next few hours, until the watery sun was as high as it would get before starting its long slide into sunset. But shady trees were plentiful.

'Shall we see what Muto's packed for lunch?' asked Badger, eventually.

'I expect he's given me sausages,' said Kitsu.

'I don't know 'ow 'e does it,' said Badger. 'He just seems to conjure things up out of nothing.'

'I think Gi does the conjuring. Muto just cooks,' said Kitsu. 'And it works well.'

'I've got bread and cheese, and a bottle of ale,' said Badger. 'Looks a bit flat, but it'll do me.'

'Yep,' said Kitsu, grinning. 'Sausages.'

*

When men and horses were rested, they got back on the road. By late afternoon, they were closing on the spies. Badger could tell from their tracks that the riders were in no hurry. Too clear. Not scuffed enough.

'We should catch them soon,' said Badger. 'If you're worried about being recognised, just turn yourself into a dog or something. I can lead your horse with mine.'

Shortly after, they saw Striper's spies about a hundred yards ahead. 'Gimme your clothes,' whispered Badger.

Kitsu passed his clothes to Badger and disappeared into the trees. The clothes went in the empty saddle bag, and Badger continued to close with the spies.

One of them turned, having heard him coming. The man stopped and waited for him to approach. *I hope you can hear me, Kit. This might not go well.*

'Hmm, a barbarian,' flat cap observed. 'What're you doing in these woods?'

'Not that it's any of your business,' replied Badger, 'but I'm going to Gremanos.'

'We're going there,' said ginger. 'Want company?'

'No, I travel alone, thanks. It's quicker.'

'Then why've you got two horses?' asked flat cap.

'In case I get hungry,' said Badger, thinking on his feet. Or on his butt, in this case. 'Now move aside.'

'We might get hungry, too,' Flat cap insisted.

'Do I have to set my dog on you?' Badger threatened.

'What dog?'

'That one,' said Badger, pointing out a large wolf that had prowled into view, baring its fangs.

'Oh. Perhaps not, then,' said flat cap.

'Heel boy!' Badger called meekly, and, snapping and snarling, the wolf trotted obediently to him and followed at his horse's side.

'So glad that turned out to be you,' said Badger, when they were far enough ahead, still taking deep breaths to slow his heart-rate.

Kitsu had shifted back into human form and was putting on his shirt. 'Well, we're ahead of them. Now what?'

'I should've killed 'em last night,' said Badger, ruefully. 'But, Fox said no.'

'Any idea why?' Kitsu wondered.

'He wants them to tell Striper we're coming. He reckons, on the quiet, that the centurion who commands the Second Black-Watch is so useless he'll panic, and it'll spook the lot of 'em. But I reckon they'll panic a lot more if we just show up unannounced, like.'

'Good point,' said Kitsu. 'I've made an executive decision. If those two catch us up, which one do you want to kill?'

'Flat cap,' said Badger, without hesitation.

'I was hoping you'd say that.' Kitsu grinned. 'I *hate* gingers.'

The pair rode in silence for a few yards, then Kitsu stopped.

'You know what, Badger? We should deal with 'em now.' They turned their horses and galloped back.

The spies, who were trotting along in no hurry, saw them coming. 'It's that barbarian again, Ginger. Perhaps he wants to ride with us after all.'

'He's got company already,' said Ginger. 'I know 'im... We saw 'im in the tavern!'

Badger and Kitsu drew their swords and came at them at speed. The spies saw what was happening and pulled their horses aside. They were a fraction too late. Flat cap fell first, and slid from his saddle, one foot caught in a stirrup and the horse dragged him a hundred yards or more before it stopped.

Ginger's horse reared away from Kitsu's charge and he fell to the ground. He drew his sword as he got to his feet, cursing and threatening as he went for Kitsu. Kitsu jumped from his horse and sprang to face him. Ginger parried the first blow, but didn't notice the long dagger in Kitsu's left hand, which he rammed hard under his chin until it protruded from the top of Ginger's head.

'That was exciting,' said Kitsu, retracting his dagger and wiping it on the dead man's clothes.

'I expected more of a fight from spies,' said Badger. 'They're supposed to be trained killers. We did well.' He sheathed his sword and stood stretching for a few moments. 'Anyway, I think I need to eat, now.'

'Me too,' said Kitsu.

Badger wondered if they should bother with a fire. 'We're not cooking, and it's not that cold. Let's just eat, rest the horses and push on.'

The pair reached the edge of the woods by nightfall. They camped rudimentarily, and Badger took the first watch. They switched at midnight, and again in the small hours. Nothing happened apart from badger needing to relieve himself in the pre-dawn.

Kitsu stirred. 'Is that a waterfall I can hear?'

'No, it's me.'

'I feel I need one as well now,' said Kitsu, hurriedly getting up.

'Now you're up, we might as well get going,' said Badger. 'I can ride and sleep at the same time. Just catch me if you see me sliding off.'

'Don't worry, my friend. I'll keep an eye on you.'

The pair rode at walking pace for half the morning, till a small village lay in the valley ahead of them.

'I wonder where we are,' said Kitsu.

Badger just grunted, still half asleep. He opened one eye and announced, 'I haven't got a clue. I don't even remember *getting* here.'

They allowed their horses to trot into the village, and they stopped outside the tavern. There was a man sitting in a rocking chair.

'You staying?' he asked, 'or just passing through.'

'Just passing through,' replied Kitsu. 'What's this place called?'

The man spat something brown into the road. 'This is Havrom,' the man told him. 'Where are you goin'?'

'Gremanos,' said Badger. 'We're looking for work,' he lied.

'What do you do?'

'Clean windows,' said Badger, dismounting. 'Lots of windows in Gremanos. Fancy a drink, Kit?'

'I do,' Kitsu replied, and they went inside. 'What a boring conversation that was.'

'Let's not stay long. Just fill the water bottles and go, eh?' said Badger.

The tavern was empty. No customers. No barman. No atmosphere, unless you count musty. They turned and walked out. 'Is

203

there a well, or a pump?' Kitsu asked the man in the rocking chair. He spat something else into the road. He didn't answer, just pointed. Kitsu followed the man's arm. He was pointing at the river. They got back on their horses and walked them down to the water's edge.

'Not exactly an 'oliday destination, is it?' Badger remarked.

'If we ever come back again,' said Kitsu. 'I really will have to kill that man.'

'I doubt he'll last that long, looking at him,' grinned Badger.

They filled the bottles while the horses drank.

'You gonna fly off and tell Fox he don't have to worry about the spies anymore?'

'What?' said Kitsu. 'And let him know we ignored his orders to let them live?'

'Oh, yeah.' Badger thought for a moment. 'We should keep on to Gremanos. Let Fox catch up. With a bit of luck, he might 'ave forgotten by then.'

* * *

Fox and Sivad weren't the only ones up and about when Badger and Kitsu left that morning. Gi and Muto had watched them ride off.

'Do you think they'll be alright, Master?' said Muto.

'No doubt about it,' said Gi. 'They are both a lot more capable than they'd have us believe. It can be wise sometimes to keep your full potential to yourself.' Muto didn't rise to the bait.

'I'm going to miss them, Master. Can't rightly say why, but since they joined us, things have felt better.'

'Well, if we get going, we won't be far behind. It's only a couple of weeks to Gremanos.'

'Yes,' said Muto. 'Lots of interesting things can happen in a couple of weeks.'

Fox and the elves rode up. 'We're ready to move out, Gi,' said Fox. 'Are you taking the lead?'

'Of course,' said Gi. '*I'm* not eating the dust from that lot all day.'

Gi and Fox's barbarian army of volunteers followed the course of the river as close as the forest permitted.

'We need to get to the other side, Master,' said Muto.

'I know, but it's too deep here to ford, and it'll take too long to get everybody across on the ferry,' said Gi. 'We need a bridge.' He looked around for Huddy. 'Brian!' he shouted, 'Have you been this way before?'

'No, Mr. Mulderbish!'

'Find Huddy, he might have. If not, he might know somebody who has.'

'I'm on it,' said Brian. He dropped back to the front of the horde where Huddy and Sivad were.

'Huddy! Mr Mulderbish wants to know if you've been this way before?' Brian asked.

'What's the problem?' asked Huddy.

'I think he's looking for a bridge.'

205

'Okay,' said Huddy. 'Hardly surprising. I'll go up and see him. Is Fox there as well?'

'He's riding with the elves behind the wagon.'

Huddy picked up speed and joined the wagon. 'Brian thought you might be looking for a bridge, Mr Mulderbish.'

'Yes,' said Gi. 'Is there one?'

'Yes, about four miles on past the ferry, if I remember rightly.'

'I was thinking we might take the wagon and the elves across on the ferry, and the main body of men could go on and cross at the bridge. The ferry would take too many trips. It would take ages, and probably cost too much as well,' said Gi.

Muto remembered the chest full of gold under Haggitt's bed, but thought it best not to mention it.

Gi could see the shed and the jetty up ahead, but the ferry was on the opposite bank. He hoped it would be on this side by the time they got there.

He hoped in vain. 'Muto, can you attract the ferryman's attention?' said Gi.

'Not from here, Master.'

'I just knew you were going to say that,' Gi smiled.

'You could send up a fireball, Master.'

'That's more likely to encourage the ferryman to stay put.'

'I'll see if there's anyone in the shed, Master.' Muto climbed down, and hammered on the door. 'Anyone in!' he called.

'Round the back!' cried a voice.

Muto went around. 'I'm looking for the ferryman.'

'Well, 'e ain't 'ere,' the dwarf told him.

'Who are you, then?' asked Muto.

'Albert. Thanks for askin',' said the dwarf.

'Well, Albert, do you know how to get the ferry back to this side?' asked Muto.

'Yes, I know how, but I'm not strong enough,' said Albert.

'I'm not suggesting you carry it,' Muto told him.

'That'd be a good trick, wouldn't it? No, you need to attach a rope to it and pull it back.'

'Really? Do you have any rope?'

'It's in the shed,' said Albert. 'Help yourself.'

Muto went round to the door and turned the handle. The door didn't budge. 'Albert! It's locked!'

'It sticks a bit when it gets damp. Give it a good yank.'

Muto gave it too good a yank. 'Albert! I've pulled the door off! But the good news is, I've found the rope.'

Albert rolled his eyes.

'Don't worry. I have a wizard friend who can restore it. You have a privy in here,' said Muto, having almost stepped into it.

'Yes,' said Albert, 'my bed's in there as well.'

Muto pulled a face. 'That's handy. Why don't you fix a partition in here?'

'It's a shed. Not, a bloody hotel.'

'Ah, well. You know best,' said Muto, taking the coil of rope off its nail. He carried it down to the jetty and dumped it on the boards. 'Master!' he called. 'Will you pass me a crossbow and bolt, please?'

'Are you going to tie that rope to a bolt, Muto?' asked Gi. 'It'll be too heavy.'

'I was hoping you could magic the rope into thinking it was a piece of string, Master,' said Muto.

'I've got string here!' said Gi, tossing the ball at Muto. 'And don't think I doubt your skill as the greatest crossbowman the world has ever seen, but I think Bayna may be the one for this job.'

'You think so?' Muto stared out across the river, this time noticing how small a target the ferry was from there. 'Bayna!' he called.

'Where's the best place to hit it?' asked Bayna, without a trace of conceit.

'I love your confidence,' said Muto. 'Just anywhere along this end of it. Though the centre would be handier for hauling it back.'

Muto didn't see how she nimbly attached the rope to an arrow, but when she positioned herself and let it fly, it hit the end of the ferry dead centre, and so hard it almost went right through. 'Give it a tug, Muto. It should be firm enough,' said Bayna.

Muto looked at her in disbelief, thinking, *what is that bow made of?*

He picked up the rope's end and wound some around his hand a couple of times before giving it an experimental tug. The arrow held firm. He wound more rope and started walking slowly towards the shed.

'Feel free to join in, gentlemen,' he said.

Brian and Maurice came forward and took the rope. With their combined effort, the flat-bottomed craft slipped its mooring and began to glide across the river. As soon as it bumped the jetty, Albert did his duty and gave the mooring line a couple of turns over a short post, and went to secure the other end.

Now, Muto could steer the wagon aboard. With Dash and Bayna, there wasn't room for Brian and Maurice, so, they had to wait for Gi and Muto to get over, and drag the ferry back.

'Hold on! Hold on!' yelled Albert frantically, just as they were ready to leave. 'It's not going to push itself along, you know!' He scurried behind his shed and appeared with a long stout pole in each hand. 'You're gonna need these. Unless you want to float down-river a couple of miles and take a chance which side you finish up.'

Everyone found that funny, except Albert himself, which made it even funnier.

When the ferry bumped the jetty, Muto urged the horses forward, and with the help of Dash and Bayna pulling on their bridles, the wagon rolled safely off and along the jetty. The elves' own mounts seemed unperturbed by the crossing.

'Right, Muto. Signal Brian and Maurice to haul it back,' said Gi.

He did, and remembered to stow the poles on board where they wouldn't roll off, or Albert would never have forgiven him.

'Is Fox coming with us?' asked Dash.

'He'll probably ride with his new army, Dash,' said Gi. 'We'll have to see who comes across with Brian.'

Dash accepted that, and walked his horse back to Bayna. 'You look concerned, my love, is everything alright?'

'I don't know. I keep feeling we are being watched.'

'It occurs to me,' said Dash, 'that we are vulnerable now. Stay closer to the wagon.'

'Has that ferry reached the other side yet, Muto?' asked Gi.

'Just reaching the jetty now, Master. Oh, my word, it's rammed it. Albert's going to be *very* annoyed about that,' said Muto. 'As he'll be about me forgetting to ask you to fix his door.'

'Door?'

'Don't ask, Master.'

'Is the ferry still afloat?' asked Gi.

'Yes, Master. It looks like four riders have managed to jump aboard and it's coming over.'

'Can you see who they are?'

'Wait a minute.' He let them get closer. 'It's Brian, Maurice, Fox and Sivad, Master. Brian and Sivad are using the poles. Struggling a bit with the current, but they'll make it.'

After a long-drawn-out five minutes, they guided the ferry to the jetty. Four riders spurred their mounts forward without waiting for it to be secured, and galloped to catch up with the wagon. Albert held the rope on the other bank and had the presence of mind to wind it on to the mooring post. It drifted in a long arc downstream to his side.

'Everything alright, Dash?' asked Fox.

'Bayna senses we are being watched, but I can't see anything,' Dash replied.

'There's something in the water,' said Muto, casually, as if this was an everyday occurrence. There was a V-shape on the surface of the water, rapidly approaching the jetty.

'I think we'd better move away from the river, everybody,' said Muto. 'Especially the horses.'

The cause of the V-shape was now dragging itself onto the jetty.

'Anybody know what that thing is?' asked Brian, with a deep frown.

'It's a bloody Sulamoth! Oops, excuse my language,' said Muto. 'It's sort of a cross between a lion and a fish. Very dangerous.'

'If I'd known it was in there, I'd have taken the bridge,' said Gi, flexing his fingers in readiness to defend himself.

The Sulamoth reared up onto its tail and lunged forward. It was frighteningly quick, and had repeated this action several times before the riders realised how agile it was. Bayna's stag reared and jumped away before turning to face the beast. Its head moving from side to side, looking for a chance to impale it on its antlers. Bayna was not prepared to allow the thing that close and drew her bow. She moved so swiftly and efficiently, no one saw her fit the arrow and draw the string. Her arrow hit the beast in the eye. It squealed and reared up enraged to throw itself at the stag, only to receive another arrow to its head. As it fell, the stag charged with his head down and tossed the beast back into the river.

When the beast hit the water, it started to drift downstream. In seconds, the river around it turned red and started to boil, and the tails of several more Sulamoths breached the water in their frenzy to feed on the remains of their dead colleague. Gi and his party couldn't help but stand and stare in shock. This was something none of them had ever witnessed before, and hoped they never would again.

'We should move away from the river now, everybody,' said Gi. 'We don't want those things coming after us again.'

Muto noticed more Sulamoths swimming downstream. Occasionally a head would rise out of the water to see where the travellers were. Muto steered the horses along the river as far from it as he could, and finally came to a well-used track. They entered a small forest, which looked free of any signs of danger.

Brian and Maurice had taken up their stations escorting the wagon from the front, while Fox, Sivad and the elves took the rear. The next few miles proved uneventful and as the travellers neared the bridge, they saw that some of the barbarian army had crossed, and others were queueing. Muto halted the wagon at the bridge. He felt uneasy and picked up the crossbow he kept under his seat. Gi watched him, knowingly.

A couple of barbarians had decided to allow their horses to drink while they waited. Without warning, a Sulamoth surfaced and lunged, almost taking a horse's head off. Muto guessed it was coming but was powerless to stop it. He hit the creature with a bolt, forcing it to let go and slip back into the water, where the blood and thrashing drew several more. They finished off the horse, then attacked the wounded beast.

Bayna was poised and ready for another of the beasts to poke its head up. When it did, she let an arrow fly. It struck the beast in the neck, causing major blood loss, and attracting more of its own kind. Bayna readied her bow again. Two heads bobbed up. Two arrows flew. They moved so fast she only winged them, but each Sulamoth thought it had been attacked by the other, and they began to fight. The river ran red. Crows were dropping to the river banks waiting to pick up the pieces. Literally.

While the animals fought, the barbarians made their way hastily over the bridge. Muto moved the wagon on, while Bayna and Dash hung back to pick off any more Sulamoths that might follow. It seemed like an age before the last of the barbarians had crossed over, and once the elves were satisfied that everybody was safe, they galloped to catch up with Gi at the head of the column.

* * *

En-route to Gremanos, Badger and Kitsu arrived at a tavern called the *Wayside Inn*. They tied their horses and went in. 'Got any money, Kit?' asked Badger.

'I took some coins off the spies, but I didn't stop to check it,' said Kitsu.

'Whatever it is, I don't think there's anything in here we can't afford,' said Badger, looking at the rundown state of the place.

'Oh, I don't know. That tall blonde sitting in the corner looks a bit pricey.' Kitsu grinned.

'I was referring to the stock.' Badger smiled.

'And you don't think she's stock?' said Kitsu. 'I'll wager the landlord makes more from her than he does from his ale.'

'I expect you're right,' Badger conceded.

'Landlord, two pots of ale, please. And how far is it to Gremanos?'

The landlord filled two pots and banged them down on the counter. '*Gremanos?*' he said, scratching his head. 'It's been a while since I went there, but it took me three weeks to get there and back with my wagon, so I reckon you two gents could probably get there and back in two, maybe two and a half.'

'Thanks,' said Kitsu. 'How much for the ale?'

'Three coppers, please,' said the landlord.

'In that case, landlord, we'll sit by the window, and you can oblige us with two more pots, please,' said Kitsu.

Badger picked up his ale and made his way to the table. Kitsu paid, went to join him and sat down, just as two riders thundered passed the window.

'Where do you think they're goin'?' Badger wondered.

'Must be very urgent,' Kitsu murmured. 'Landlord, what's going on out there, do you know?'

'I did hear say there's a horde of barbarians coming this way.'

'Is that a fact?' said Badger. 'We just came from that direction and only saw an old man driving a wagon.'

'I think we'll finish our ales and see if we can catch 'em up,' said Kitsu. 'Just in case.'

The two men sat looking out of the window, downing their drinks and enjoying a brief respite, not even feeling the need to converse. Once refreshed, they slammed their pots down on the table. Badger belched, a little louder than necessary perhaps, and stood up. 'I'm ready Kit.'

Having popped out the back briefly, Kitsu waved at the landlord, and they wandered out. 'Sky's a bit grey,' he observed, 'could be coming in to rain.'

'I hate rain,' said Badger.

'It makes tracking riders easier,' said Kitsu.

'Huh,' Badger scoffed. 'The way those two were riding, it won't be difficult anyway.'

They loosed their horses, eased themselves into the saddles, and set off in pursuit of the riders.

Further down the road, they found a loose horse, grazing on the grass verge. 'Looks like one of the horses those men were riding,' said Kitsu.

They pulled up and approached the animal on foot.

'Gods, Kit, look at that,' said Badger, pointing at a deep gash in the horse's flank. 'I wonder what did that.'

'Looks like a slash from a big cat of some sort,' said Kitsu, looking around. 'I wonder where the rider is,' he added, pulling a face showing he didn't think it bode well.

'We must have past him,' said Badger. 'Let's go back and take a look.'

Kitsu drew his sword and they led their horses back a couple of hundred yards down the road, where they came upon a blood trail leading off into the trees.

'You sure you want to go in there, Kit?' whispered Badger.

'I feel I should,' said Kitsu. 'But something's telling me I shouldn't.' He peered through the trees and could see nothing to worry about that wasn't his imagination on overdrive.

'If we catch up with the other rider, he'll tell us, I'm sure,' said Badger, hopefully. 'Come on, let's get out of here.'

'Are you afraid?' smiled Kitsu.

Badger didn't answer for a moment, then said, 'Yep. If there's a cat out there big enough to drag a man down, I think it makes good sense to be afraid.'

'I hadn't considered that,' said Kitsu. 'Yeah, we should try and catch the other rider.'

'Take the horse or leave it?' asked Badger.

'Take it. I don't think it's safe to leave here,' Kitsu replied.

The pair continued on their way, until they came to the spot where the loose horse had been grazing. 'Well, I'm not going to walk through the woods whistling for it,' said Badger, sizing up the situation.

'Me neither. We need to push on.'

They galloped hard for the next few miles, then slowed to a walk, while their horses got their breath back. Neither man spoke until Kitsu broke the silence.

'When this is done, Badger, I'm going back to that inn.'

'The ale wasn't that good, Kit,' Badger remarked.

'I'm thinking we'll get enough out of sacking Striper's castle to finance me for the rest of my life,' said Kitsu.

'What? Are you going to buy that tavern?' asked Badger, surprised.

'No, but I think I'll be able to afford that tall blonde girl in the corner.'

Badger laughed. 'Do you think she's got a sister?'

'Let's get this done, then we'll go back and find out,' said Kitsu.

They spurred their horses on again in the hope of finding the other rider, but he must have been too far ahead. At least, that was the best-case scenario.

Later that day, almost evening in fact, they saw lights in the distance.

'Could be a tavern,' said Badger. 'Shall we stop for the night?'

'Only if they've got a stable,' said Kitsu. 'I'm not leaving the horses unattended.'

A fifteen-minute ride got them to the building, which turned out to be a tavern that, according to the board outside, had a few rooms for rent and a stabling for six horses. Kitsu went in.

'Landlord, we need to stable two horses for the night. Can this be arranged?'

'That's not a problem, sir, but I've got no empty rooms.'

'We can stay with our horses, if that's alright,' Kitsu told him.

'Will you be wanting food?' asked the landlord.

'Yes, for two, please. Can you bring it to the stables? We'll eat there,' said Kitsu.

'That'll be eight coppers, then,' said the landlord, holding his hand out. 'Please.'

'Here's ten,' said Kitsu. 'And thanks again.'

Kitsu joined Badger outside with the horses. 'Everything alright, Kit?'

'Yes, we can sleep in the stable, and he's bringing food out in a while – not sure what, but I'm not fussed.'

*

The stable was roomy enough if you didn't need much room. They unsaddled the horses and gave them a quick rub down. There were a couple of sacks of grain and some hay stacked at one end, and when the landlord came in with the food, he told them to help themselves to feed for the horses.

Kitsu told him, 'We don't help ourselves, landlord, we pay. So how much?'

'Oh... just give me two coppers, then. I wish all my customers were like you.' He smiled appreciatively as he backed towards the door, and closed it behind him.

Kitsu lifted the top of his sandwich and looked inside.

'Hmm...' he murmured. 'Muto's favourite – a nice ploughman.'

'I don't think Muto's as daft as he'd have us believe, Kit.'

'No,' said Kitsu. 'And he's a good man in more ways than anyone might imagine. Gi's a good judge of character. Apart from being fooled by Striper, that is. So, let's just leave it at that.'

Badger nodded thoughtfully, then switched the subject. 'When we've finished this food, I think one of us should go into the tavern, and ask if that other rider came in here.'

'I had that in mind,' said Kitsu. 'I'd like to know what that animal was – if it was an animal – that killed his partner.'

* * *

64

'Stogie! Are you there!' shouted Baron Striper, then he coughed.

'Coming, my Lord,' said young Gripper. He sauntered into the Baron's office and stood on the two bare patches in front of the desk.

'Do you know where your father is?' Striper asked him.

'What time of day is it, my Lord?' asked Gripper, in mild retaliation.

'Er... I don't know,' said Striper. 'That's what I keep you for. I never had this problem with Pinch, you know.'

'No, my Lord? Well, it's early morning, just after dawn,' said Gripper.

'What makes you think that?'

'It's no longer *dark*, my Lord.'

'Ah... open the curtains then, and blow out that candle. I'm not made of money,' Striper snapped. 'Now, what were we talking about?'

'You asked me if I knew where my father was,' Gripper recalled.

'Yes. I remember. Well?' said Striper.

'He's not very well, my Lord.'

'Well, I need him to get a message to Lord Welkin,' said Striper, huffily, then added, 'What's wrong with him?'

'He's got sore feet, my Lord,' said Gripper. 'From all the walking. You could give him a horse, you know. Messages would get delivered much quicker.'

'I can't afford to *give* him a horse,' said Striper, incredulously.

'Then I fear you must wait until he recovers, my Lord.'

'I have an idea,' said Striper, undeterred.

'What's that, my Lord?'

'I'll send you.' Striper grinned, pleased with himself.

'My Lord? You *do know* I've got a wooden leg, don't you?' Gripper lied, skilfully coordinating the tapping of his leg with tapping the cabinet beside him.

'Have you?' said Striper. 'I thought it was the way your trousers hung, or something,' he winked.

'No, my Lord. I will take your message, but I'm not walking.' Then he had a thought, 'Wasn't Lord Welkin here a few days ago, Lord?'

Striper didn't answer, he was still thinking, 'Oh… Let me think about this.'

'Has Lord Welkin got any pigeons?' asked Gripper.

'I don't know,' said Striper, honestly, for a change. 'I'll ask him if I ever find someone to deliver a message.'

'You could ask Major Pinch if he can spare a man for a few days?' suggested Gripper. 'I'm sure he'd be only too pleased to help out.'

'That's not a bad idea,' said Striper. 'Do you know where he is?'

'Yes, my Lord, he's in the officer's mess.'

'Officer's *mess*? I never knew we had an officer's mess,' said Striper. 'How do I afford that?'

Gripper shrugged. 'Maybe somebody helping to run your affairs has been taking backhanders or creaming a bit off the top now and then, my Lord.'

'Am I supposed to understand what you're saying, Gripper?' he asked, waiting for a translation.

'What I mean, my Lord, is that someone has had their hand in your pocket.'

'No, I would've felt something, I'm sure,' said the baron.

'Okay, my Lord, let me put it this way. You're being robbed, and you haven't realised it yet.' Gripper hoped this would sink in.

'Do you think so? I could be. I used to have loads of money. Where's it all gone?' said Striper, almost in tears.

'How much do you give Lord Welkin?' asked Gripper.

'I can't tell you that!' said Striper.

'You don't have to. Just sit and think about it,' Gripper advised. He turned laboriously on his imaginary wooden leg and went back to his office.

'Stogie! Before you vanish, have you got any of those *Desert Golds* left?' Striper called after him.

'They're downstairs, my Lord. I'll bring them up later.'

'How long is 'later'? I need them while I think about how much my son might be screwing me out of.'

'I'm on my way, my Lord,' Gripper lied, and went and sat down in his big comfy office chair.

There was gentle tap on his door. He crept across and opened it a tad to see who was there.

'Come in, but be quiet. The baron's still in there,' whispered Gripper.

'I'll be as quiet as a mouse,' whispered Maureen. 'This'll be our little secret.'

'I can't afford what the baron pays you,' said Gripper.

'Who said I was going to charge you?' She smiled mischievously. 'I only charge him because he's got the kind of face I'd like to slap with a... a...' she searched for something appropriate.

'Wet *kipper?*'

'Exactly.'

'We'll have to be quick. I told him I had to go downstairs and get his smokes for him,' Gripper explained.

'What? Not those awful-smelling, foreign things he had the other day?'

'Yes, but they're not foreign, they're horse shit rolled in fag papers. Ollie and me put them in empty boxes we got from the tavern,' Gripper whispered.

He got his hand over her mouth just in time, before she broke into fits of laughter. 'Quick, let's go out through reception,' he hissed, 'he'll hear us in a minute.'

Maureen also doubled, or perhaps moonlighted would be a more accurate way of putting it, as Striper's receptionist, and she'd just got back into her chair when Striper's door opened.

'There you are. I called just now, but I didn't get an answer,' said Striper, quietly.

'I was er... powdering my nose, my Lord. I'll get my notepad, shall I?' she said, patting her hair back into place.

'No... the moment has past now. Just go and tell Ollie I'd like morning tea, now,' said Striper. 'I can drink and smoke while I think.'

219

'What are you thinking about, my Lord?'

'My son… Lord Welkin.'

'What's he been up to, now?' asked Maureen, trying to sound interested.

'I'm not sure. But my money's been dwindling fast, and he's high on my list of suspects. Well, he's the only one, actually,' said Striper, grim-faced.

'Oh. Anyway, I'll send Ollie back with your tea, my Lord. I've got a couple of things I need to do for Mr. Stogie, so I'll see you later.' She left Striper's office, slamming the door behind her.

Gripper had wandered down to the stables. 'Ollie? Are you in here?'

'Over 'ere, what do you want?'

'The baron wants another pack of *Desert Gold* and his morning tea,' said Gripper.

'You're jokin',' said Ollie. 'I thought that last pack would've killed him.'

'No, he's still kicking, and now he thinks someone, probably Welkin, is stealing from him.'

'What gave 'im that idea?'

'I did,' said Gripper.

'For an evil man, he's not very bright, is 'e?' said Ollie.

'And for a bright man, I'm not very good,' Gripper answered, smirking.

'You know, he tried to get me to walk to Welkin's castle with a message. I told him to get one of Pinch's men to do it,' said Gripper, 'because of my wooden leg.' He tapped it while tapping the stable door.

'No!' exclaimed Ollie, hardly believing Gripper's nerve. 'Why won't 'e send your dad?'

'I told him father is unwell,' said Gripper.

'Is 'e?' asked Ollie. 'I'm sorry to 'ear that.'

'No, he's fine. He's missing because I convinced him to go and see the old woman in the sweet shop down Chitts alley and ask her to teach him to read.' Gripper smiled.

'Good idea. We'll know what Striper's up to all the time, then.' Ollie rubbed his hands together.

'Well, I suppose I'd better get back now, Ollie. Got those cigarettes?'

'Uh, yeah, here you go.'

'See you later,' said Gripper, and made his way back to his office.

When he got there, Maureen was sitting on his desk, legs crossed waiting for him. 'Did you get the tea?' she asked, not seeing it.

'Damn. I forgot. I'll just nip down and tell Ollie.'

'It's alright. Pinch always kept some in his desk. I've already made the baron a cup.'

'Better take these in too,' said Gripper, showing her the smelly cigarette pack.

Gripper knocked on Striper's door. 'Come!' he shouted.

'I've brought you a pack of *Desert Gold*, my Lord. Is there anything else?' enquired Gripper.

'No, I don't think so,' said the baron, taking a cigarette out of the packet and putting it to his lips. He patted his pockets.

'Top drawer, my Lord,' said Gripper, referring to the yellow-headed matches the baron was looking for.

'Oh. Yes. Alright, you can go, now.' Striper waved him away.

Gripper closed the door on the baron's latest coughing fit, and sat at his desk. Maureen shook her head. 'The baron always asks me to lay on the desk,' she told him, 'It's much more comfortable.'

Gripper's face reddened slightly. *I wasn't expecting this today*, he thought rather smugly. In fact, he was feeling *very* smugly.

* * *

Kitsu picked up the empty wooden tray and went back inside the tavern.

'Ah, landlord, I was wondering – have any lone riders been in this afternoon?'

The landlord looked around the room, there were a number of empty tables, but there was one occupied by a pale-faced man in his mid-thirties, poorly dressed, nursing a pot of ale. The landlord pointed him out.

Kitsu nodded and walked over to him.

'Mind if I join you?' he asked.

The man looked up, assessed Kitsu to be okay, and said, 'Be my guest.'

'I think I saw you earlier,' said Kitsu. 'I was at a tavern way back down the road, you rode by with another man.'

'So?' said the man, wondering where this was going.

'My companion and I were travelling the road behind you and came across a loose horse, in some distress, which we thought belonged to your friend.'

'It did,' said the man, beginning to look even sadder than when Kitsu came in.

'What happened?' asked Kitsu.

The man stared into his drink, and, as if speaking to it, said, 'We saw a horde of barbarians headed this way, so me and Jamie thought we'd better get to the city as fast as we could. We know a quick way through the woods, cuts a corner off, but the moment we turned off a huge black cat sprang out of nowhere, and savaged Jamie's horse. It knocked him to the ground, and before I knew it, the cat had Jamie's head in its mouth. He didn't stand a chance. It was nothing like anything I'd ever seen around here. I could only ride like hell.'

The man sobbed, and Kitsu put a hand on his shoulder. 'Alright, friend, thank you. That's all I wanted to know.'

There was nothing else to say. Kitsu turned and went back out to the stables and found Badger arranging his bedroll.

'Was the rider there?' said Badger. 'Did you find out what that thing was?'

'Yes, and yes. It was a big, black cat – bigger than a man, apparently – attacked his friend.'

'Wow. Are you going out to look for it?' Badger asked him.

'No,' said Kitsu, quietly. 'Not tonight. The creature's something never seen around here before. I've decided to go back and talk to Gi about it.'

'What's the rider going to do?' Badger wondered.

'I didn't ask, but I think I'll persuade him to ride with us,' said Kitsu.

'Can we trust him?'

'He needs the company. And he's too shaken up to be a threat,' said Kitsu. 'I'll go back and talk to him.'

'I'll bolt the door after you,' said Badger. 'Knock three times – twice then once – when you want to come back in.'

The man was sitting, alone where Kitsu had left him. He took a chance and sat down. 'People call me, Kitsu,' he said, 'do you have a name?'

The man stirred. 'Er… I'm Rodney.'

'Rodney? Good. Well, Rodney, my friend and I are going to Gremanos – why doesn't matter, it's a long story. And I can tell you all those barbarians you saw, are not barbarians. They're travellers looking to settle somewhere and build new lives. I'm going to make you an offer. You can sit here for a few days and wait for them to come through, or you can ride back with us and join their march. It'll be a lot safer than riding on your own,' Kitsu warned him.

'I won't ride through those woods on my own again, ever,' said Rodney.

'Tomorrow's our best time to go. I doubt that the animal will be hungry enough to kill again for a few days. By which time, me and my friends will have found it, and hopefully dealt with it,' said Kitsu.

'How can you be sure?' said Rodney, seeming desperate for reassurance.

'When you meet my friends, you'll know, I promise,' said Kitsu. 'Are you coming or not?'

'It may be for the best,' said Rodney, cracking a weak smile.

'Have you got a room here?'

'No, I only had enough money for a pot of ale.'

'Then, where's your horse?'

'Hitched round the side. It's free.'

'Well, we can't fit another horse in our stable, but we can fit another man in with us, at a push,' Kitsu reckoned. 'Right, drink up and come with me.'

Rodney followed him around to the stable. Kitsu knocked three times as instructed, and after a few seconds, the bolt slid back and Badger opened the door.

'Badger, we've got company. This is Rodney. It was his friend's horse we saw on the way here,' Kitsu told him.

'Sorry to hear that, friend,' said Badger. 'We looked for it, but it was gone.'

'Yeah, I heard,' said Rodney.

'So, Rodney, you'll be coming with us to Gremanos. Do you live there?' Badger asked him.

'Sometimes. I've got a brother there. He's a blacksmith.'

'I think our friends could use a good blacksmith,' said Kitsu. 'Do you have any more useful friends or relatives?'

'Not really,' said Rodney. 'A couple of my friends are in Baron Striper's Black-Guard.'

Kitsu and Badger looked at each other and went quiet. That revelation was a real conversation killer.

'Do you have a problem with the Black-Guard?' asked Rodney. 'I think most people do, but they're not *all* bad.'

'In our experience, most of them are. Worse than barbarians, in fact,' said Badger.

'Well,' said Rodney. 'I can only speak as I find.'

'Fair comment,' said Kitsu. 'But wait till you meet our friends. Badger here's an ex-barbarian.'

Rodney's chin dropped.

'Don't worry, he's quite tame.' Kitsu grinned.

'And this ex-barbarian's tired. So, shut up, now, while I sleep.'

Badger stretched out and turned onto his side. It wasn't long before he was gently snoring. Kitsu yawned and checked on the horses. He told Rodney to take some grain out to his, and then turned in. Rodney was tired, too, but they guessed that after what he'd witnessed today, it was going to be a while before he closed his eyes.

* * *

Light began to penetrate a dusty window near the roof of the stable. Kitsu opened an eye and, like most days recently, he was anxious to feel if he had fur, feathers or skin. This morning, he sighed with relief: he was wearing skin. Human skin, that is. Next, test the vocal cords. Would he bark or screech? 'Are you awake, Badger?' he asked. That was a good sign.

'Not yet,' said Badger.

'Just checking.'

'I am,' said Rodney. 'What time is it?'

'Look outside, see where the sun is,' suggested Kitsu.

Rodney scrambled to his feet. He slid the bolt back and opened the door slightly. 'It's just coming up through the trees.'

'Right,' said Kitsu, stretching. 'Badger, come on – on your feet. I'm going to get some food to take with us, while you two saddle the horses. I'll be back in a minute.'

'Is he always this bossy?' said Rodney, when Kitsu had left.

'He's eager, that's all,' said Badger. 'But I'd trust him with my life.'

Rodney went to bring his horse round, and he and Badger had barely finished tightening the girths when Kitsu returned. He was carrying three packages that smelt of fresh bread, which he handed round before leading his horse outside.

'Be right with you, Kit.' Badger led his horse out into the yard, and sniffed the morning air. 'It smells better out 'ere. That place must be full of horse shit,' he complained.

Kitsu slowly shook his head. 'I can't think why.'

Rodney thought he was beginning to like these two.

'We have a choice, gentlemen,' said Kitsu. 'We can ride back and tell our friends to beware of that cat. It might not be the only one. Or, we can head for Gremanos, and let them find out for themselves.'

'We should go back,' said Badger. 'What do you say, Rodney?'

'I'm okay with that,' he agreed. He seemed to have recovered somewhat from yesterday's ordeal.

'Good,' said Kitsu, 'that's settled then. I think we'll come back with Dash and Bayna, and hunt that thing down. I'd wager they're quicker than any cat!'

'And we can tell Fox that the thing killed the two spies, not us,' said Badger, pleased with his idea.

'I'm a bad liar,' said Kitsu.

'Yeah, so am I,' said Badger, smirking, 'a very bad one sometimes.'

It wasn't long before they were passing through the wooded area where the loose horse had been grazing. Subconsciously they pushed their horses even harder. And, as with all journeys, it didn't seem to take so long going back as it had taken getting there in the first place.

They emerged from the trees when the sun was halfway high, and soon came to the *Wayside Inn*.

Kitsu remembered the leggy blonde he'd seen in there before. 'Come on you two, let's get a drink,' he said, pulling over and dismounting.

'I think one of us should stay out here,' suggested Rodney. 'And as I'm the one with no money...'

'Okay, but we'll bring you a drink out,' insisted Badger. 'What do you want?' They've got ale, or *ale*.'

'Er... in that case, I'll have ale,' said Rodney.

'Packet of salt and vinegar?' asked Kitsu.

'No, thanks,' said Rodney. 'I have trouble passing them.'

Kitsu and Badger went inside. 'What do you think he meant by that?' Badger wondered.

'Oh, come on, man. I shouldn't have to explain it to you.'

Then the penny dropped. 'I *see*,' Badger grinned. 'Our friend may have a sense of humour.'

'I know what he hasn't got,' said Kitsu. 'Haven't you noticed? It's very odd.'

'What's that?' Badger was intrigued.

'A sword!' said Kitsu. 'He doesn't carry one. And I'm certain I know why.' He turned to go back outside. 'Just get *two* pots of ale, and stay in here. I won't be long.'

Kitsu drew his sword and held it behind his back. He stepped silently out of the inn and went quickly to where Rodney was waiting with the horses.

'Rodney,' he said. And as the man turned, Kitsu brought his sword around so quickly that by the time Rodney saw it, it was too late. His head rolled to a standstill on the ground, and his body fell back like an ironing board. Then, Kitsu saw what he was expecting, Rodney's facial features morphed, and slowly he became the large black cat that he'd spoken of. Kitsu wiped his blade on what remained of Rodney and went back inside.

'Are you alright?' asked Badger.

'You'd better come and see this, my friend.'

Badger eyed the headless black beast on the ground that was once Rodney. 'How did you know?' he asked.

'Just little things,' said Kitsu. 'Like not eating vegetables. The way he lapped his ale, when he thought I wasn't looking.'

'Lapped his ale? I didn't notice that,' said Badger.

'You pick up on these things when you go through similar things yourself sometimes,' said Kitsu.

'Takes one to know one, like.'

'I suppose it does,' Kitsu agreed. 'Now, I think we'd better hide the body and go and finish our drinks, don't you?'

'Okay, I'll take the head.'

Kitsu promptly kicked the head like a football, right over the bushes and into the long grass behind the inn. 'Now, do you want the tail, or the soggy end?'

'The tail end,' said Badger.

They walked crablike to the bushes, where they swung Rodney's body to and fro to get some momentum, before Kitsu gave the signal to let go.

It was lighter than both men thought, and once the body was airborne, it seemed to travel a great distance before it landed almost silently in the long grass.

'I hope the crows get here soon,' said Badger. 'That thing's going to stink later on.'

'Don't worry, Badger. We won't be around. When we've finished our drinks, I'm going to use the privy, and then we'll be on our way to Gremanos.'

'I just need to know something first, Kit,' said Badger.

But Kitsu had gone. He was ambling over to the leggy blonde in the corner. 'What's your name?' he asked her.

'Lily,' she replied, smiling.

'Well, Lily, I'll be back in a few weeks to take you away from all this,' said Kitsu.

'Really? All of it?' she said, sweetly.

Badger caught up and was looking over Kitsu's shoulder. 'Have you got a sister?' he asked eagerly.

She raised an eyebrow and nodded once.

'Good. I'll be back in a few weeks, too. Let her know a handsome lad is coming.'

The men disappeared through the door, leaving Lily staring after them.

The landlord came over. 'What was all that about?' he asked.

'I have no idea,' she lied.

* * *

67

'It's been ages since Badger and Mr. Kitsu left, Master,' Muto moaned.

'I'm sure they're fine, Muto. They're just getting on with the job in hand,' Gi assured him.

'I feel safer with the river right over there, Master. I never realised such creatures lived in there,' said Muto.

'Neither did anybody else,' said Gi.

'I believe Bayna killed them all, Gi,' said Dash. 'Those that didn't kill each other.'

'Can we get Huddy and Fox up here later?' said Gi. 'I would like to discuss how things are going.'

'I'll see to that, Father,' said Haggitt.

'I'm concerned that the horde is getting strung out,' said Gi. 'I don't like that. If people are hanging back, they could get picked off by bandits – or they could be plotting something.'

'We're in the middle of nowhere, Father. No one will attack. And what would they plot?

'All sorts of things – murder, treason, things like that,' said Gi.

'They can't commit treason, Father. We don't have a king,' Haggitt pointed out.

'I know. It was a wrong choice of word. I meant treachery. I should remember *that*, I've been victim to it enough,' Gi murmured.

'Do you suspect anyone, Master?' whispered Muto.

'That's why I want to call a meeting. Depending on who says what, I can put my own counter-plot into operation.'

'There are one or two who could lead, Master, but I don't think any of them are quick enough to harm you,' said Muto. 'Especially while I'm around.'

*

The evening found Gi sitting by his campfire. Haggitt was to his left and Muto to his right. Dash and Bayna sat next to Haggitt. They were all waiting for Fox and Huddy. Apart from the crackle of the fire, the only sound was Muto cleaning and oiling a crossbow.

'Do you want Brian and me to sit in, Mr. Mulderbish?' asked Maurice.

'Yes, I think so. Get Sivad as well, then I'll know where *everyone* is,' said Gi.

Almost half an hour passed before Fox and Huddy arrived. Neither man offered an apology or explanation for their tardiness.

'Looks like we're the last to arrive,' said Huddy, sitting opposite Gi.

Fox sat beside him, expressionless. 'What's on your mind Gi?'

Gi locked eyes with Huddy. 'I'm thinking we should split the horde,' said the wizard. 'It's a practical thing. Some men are travelling slower than others, and they're getting left behind. Or they're choosing to.' Huddy's face seemed to redden slightly. Was the firelight reflecting on him, it was difficult to tell. But Gi noticed his eyes darting back and forth from Fox to Sivad.

'Is the horde loyal to *you* Fox, or just him?' asked Gi, pointing at Huddy.

'The question has never arisen,' said Fox. 'But keeping control of an army of so many men with no proper training and discipline behind them is not easy.'

'I agree,' said Gi. 'But I don't need all those men. Only the good ones. So, bearing in mind that in a couple of weeks they'll be fighting Striper's Black-Guard, I want you and Huddy to sort out who's really up for it. I think we must assume that the men hanging back don't have their hearts in this campaign, so I suggest that once you've sorted them out, Huddy can take them back to the women and children. And you, Fox, can train the remainder to fight. Not like soldiers, but to fight to win. Are you both clear on that?'

'What?!' Huddy was barely containing his anger. 'I promised all the men a share of the spoils, Gi. What am I gonna tell 'em now?'

'Tell them they still might. But leavers will get a lesser share, if anything,' said Gi. 'If they've lost interest, we don't need them. Take them home!'

Huddy's expression twisted into a snarl. He sprang to his feet and drew his sword, swiftly raising it double-handed above his head – and slowly fell forward into the fire, with a bolt from Muto's crossbow in his forehead. Fox rushed forward and rolled Huddy's body out of the flames.

'I told you there are none quick enough to harm you while I'm here, Master.'

'Thank you, Muto,' said Gi. He turned to Fox. 'Who have you got who can lead those men back now, Fox? I need you here, leading the ones who can fight.'

'Once they know Huddy's dead, they'll drift back home anyway,' said Fox. 'But they might need my boot in their rears to send them on their way. Do you want me to go tell them?'

'No, you stay here. Send Sivad. Once he's got them moving, he can catch us up,' said Gi.

'No. I'll go,' Fox insisted. 'They might not take kindly to losing Huddy *and* me.' He stood up and walked away from the meeting.

'It's such a shame,' said Gi. 'He can be so good, but...' said Gi, not knowing how to finish.

'I have never trusted Fox,' said Dash. 'I have often seen him looking at Snow, enviously. And I can tell his friendship towards me is false. Given the opportunity, I know he would steal Snow.'

'Surely not,' said Gi.

'I give you fair warning, if Fox does take Snow, Bayna *will* kill him,' said Dash.

'Why not kill him yourself, Master Dash?' asked Muto.

'Snow was given to me by Bayna's father. She would not think kindly of anyone who took him,' Dash explained.

Bayna sat beside him, nodding her agreement.

'Aren't you afraid that Ice might get stolen?' asked Muto.

'Always, but only Bayna can ride him. No-one else would get very far. Or ever ride again.'

'Is there any ale left, Muto?' asked Gi.

'No, Master. Unless you conjure some up.'

'Never mind,' sighed Gi.

Fox came back with a small party of barbarians. 'We've come to collect Huddy,' one them announced.

Gi didn't speak, he just pointed at the body by the fire. The men silently picked it up and left.

'They're not happy,' said Fox. 'There are rumblings of unrest...'

'Do they have a new leader?' Gi asked.

'At the moment, they seem to think it's me,' replied Fox.

'Have you said anything to make them think otherwise?' asked Gi.

'Not yet, Gi. And I'm not sure I need them as much as I first thought. The ablest fighters are sat here, around this fire. I'd be foolish to turn my back on you.' He may have been trying too hard to be affable, because there was an edge to it.

'Well,' said Gi, 'if you want to ride with us, you can ride up front with Brian. Maurice and Sivad can ride each side of the wagon.' He looked around at everyone. 'We leave at first light.'

'Thank you,' said Fox, without much expression. 'I'll go and see how they're sorting themselves out, and come back.'

When Fox was out of hearing range, Muto said, 'Do we trust him, Master? He may come back with a few chosen men and make his move on us.'

'I have to agree, Muto.' said Gi, resignedly. 'Dash, take Bayna and stay out of sight behind the wagon, will you? And *keep an eye on your animals*. Brian, Maurice, get each end of the wagon. Muto, get to your seat and have a crossbow ready.'

'Yes, Master.' The little cook was all enthusiasm.

'Haggitt, stay in the wagon and keep a couple of fireballs warming,' said Gi.

'I wish Badger and Mr. Kitsu were here, Master.'

'So do I, Muto,' said Gi. 'But we can handle this. I have every confidence in you, my friend.'

An hour passed uneventfully. The first hint of the trouble was an axe thrown at the side of the wagon. It sliced through the air, tumbling and glinting in the firelight, and thudded into the timbers.

'Did you see who threw that, Haggitt?' asked Gi, seeing a mob approaching.

'Could be any of them. It came from somewhere near the back,' Haggitt replied.

'I saw him, Master. When I see him again, he'll be dead shortly after.'

'Ready, Haggitt?' asked Gi.

'Yes, Father.'

'Four hands, four fireballs – now!'

The glowing balls lit the whole area as they arced from the wizards' fingers and exploded in the midst of the press of men who were edging forward, threatening Gi and his friends. A dozen barbarians fell dead or maimed.

The mob edged forwards, some carrying torches, all carrying weapons of some sort. Two more axes tumbled through the air towards the group at the wagon. Both were deflected magically. An arrow thudded into the wagon door.

'Brian! Maurice! Get to the back and shoot at will,' said Gi. 'There's another crossbow in the back.'

'It's okay, Mr. Mulderbish, I took a longbow off one of the dead,' said Brian. 'It's not my favourite, but they're so bunched, it's difficult to miss at this range.'

Fox was nowhere to be seen, as yet.

Gi and Haggitt launched another quartet of fireballs into the crowd, killing and injuring more. And, what with the damage Muto was inflicting with his crossbow, the slain were beginning to pile up in front of the wagon, and hindering the advance of the barbarians.

The attackers fell back briefly, but moments before an all-out charge on the wagon, someone at the back of the mob shouted for them to stop. They did, for a moment, unsure what to do, waiting to find out.

Those at the wagon paused, too. 'Hold on a moment, let's see what's happening,' ordered Gi.

Fox Loer shouldered his way to the front and planted himself firmly between the wagon and the barbarians, a sword in each hand. He turned to face the mob, defying anyone to move. 'Stop this insanity! You people are never going to win this!' Fox shouted. 'You might as well go home. All of you!'

'They killed Huddy!' someone shouted.

'Yes! In self-defence!' yelled Fox. 'He attacked Gi. That was stupid. Look at the bodies here! You've lost about forty men this evening. How many has Gi lost? *None!* Do you really think you can defeat wizards, elves and professional soldiers just because you outnumber them?! Go home. It's over!'

There was a lot of muttering and looking from one to another in the mob, but reluctantly they started to drift back to their campfires, some dragging bodies, some supporting the injured.

Fox sheathed both swords and strolled to the wagon.

'Couldn't you have stopped that sooner, Fox?' Gi asked him.

'I would have, but I was set upon by a dozen of them when my back was turned. "Never trust a barbarian with a pulse," as the saying goes. They held me back while that lot came after you. Now they all have serious headaches.' He half smiled.

'Well, at least you stopped it in the end,' said Gi, glancing around. 'There must be about forty unclaimed horses out there now and we could do with three more for ourselves.'

'No problem, Mr. Mulderbish, said Brian, not needing to be asked.

'Sivad and me can collect what weapons and arrows and stuff they've left behind,' said Maurice.

'Do you want saddles? Mr. Mulderbish, asked Brian.

'Only for one,' said Gi. 'I want to double the team pulling the wagon so we can travel faster. The one with the saddle can be tied to the tailboard as a spare.'

Gi climbed into the back of the wagon and sat on his bed. 'Are you alright, Muto?' he asked, noticing how quiet the cook had been the last few minutes.

'We'll need longer reins, Master. And harnesses. And shafts.'

'There is a box bolted under the wagon, Muto. I'm guessing it contains spare wagon bits and tools. They usually do. Let's have a look.'

There was indeed a box under the wagon, not very deep, but about three feet wide and almost the length of the wagon's floor.

'I didn't know it was there, Master,' said Muto.

'I've never bothered to check it out, but I knew it had to be some sort of storage container,' Gi said. 'Can you see a handle to pull?'

'No, there's just this small hole near the top.' Muto poked his finger into it and felt around. 'This is fun, Master.'

Gi looked away to grin, not wanting to encourage him. There was a click and the side of the box swung down.

'Can you hand me a torch down, Master, or make one? It's dark in there.'

There was a gentle popping sound. Gi passed him a small flaming stick.

'*Amazing*, Master. As always.'

Gi thought it was about as basic as magic could get, but didn't argue.

Holding it close to the box, Muto saw a coil of rope, two longbows, two quivers of arrows and some lengths of black leather, which, when pulled out, turned out to be the long reins and harnesses he needed. He found poles, too, for shaft extensions.

'Master, there's a partition in here, shall we see what's on the other side?'

'What else do you need?' asked Gi.

'A couple of blankets would be nice,' said Muto.

Gi muttered something under his breath and stretched his fingers. 'Is there a hole to stick your finger in Muto?'

'Not as often as I'd like, Master. But this one will do for now.'

The other side of the box dropped down. 'Would you believe it? – there are blankets in here, Master.'

'*Noo…* you're joking,' said Gi, smugly.

'No, Master. And they're fit for a king's coach, not a bloody prison wagon!' said Muto, incredulously.

'Take what you need, Muto. When Brian gets back with the horses, will you organise the shafts and reins so we're ready to leave at first light?'

He was already examining the pieces to see how it all went together. 'What? Oh, yes, Master.' They both looked up at the sound of hooves. Maurice and Sivad had returned with a collection of arrows, knives and swords. 'I'll tell him to put them in the box. They'll be safe there. Oh, and here's an axe,' he said, gleefully, working it free from the woodwork of the wagon. 'Aren't we doing well?'

Gi grinned to himself, thinking *how can this genial man be so bloody dangerous at times?*

* * *

Badger and Kitsu trotted their horses on to Gremanos. Badger was uncomfortable.

'I need to stop for a minute, Kit,' he said, reining in his horse.

Kitsu reined in his horse and waited for Badger to catch up. 'Something wrong?' he asked.

'No, just need to relieve myself,' Badger told him. 'Just a thought, Kit. When those two riders went passed at the *Wayside Inn*, they weren't together, one was riding for his life.'

'That had crossed my mind,' said Kitsu.

'Do you think there's any more of those cats about?' Badger wondered.

'It's likely, Badger, but I'll give you some advice. Don't trust any man who isn't carrying a weapon. If they can shapeshift into an animal like that – they don't need one.'

'You carry a sword, Kit. And you can be anything you want,' said Badger.

'Yes. And that's the point. I can be other people who also need a sword. Shifters like the cat-man have only one option, like werewolves, they can't be anything else. And their best form of defence and offence is never a weapon, it's shifting.'

Badger took it all in, and something occurred to him. 'I told Gi I wanted you with me on this errand. He wanted you to stay, but I insisted. I hope you don't mind,' said Badger.

'Not at all,' said Kitsu. 'We work well together. And...' he paused to think how to say what he wanted to. 'I've been thinking I could show you a few things.'

Badger's interest was roused. 'Such as?'

'Don't take offense, but I can help you become a better fighter.'

'I'd like that,' said Badger 'I'm reasonable, but could be better, I suppose.'

'That's a part of your problem: you write yourself off as reasonable – and it's all you'll be if you don't change how you think.'

Badger pulled a face. 'Yeah, I've heard that stuff,' he said dismissively.

'Not from me, you haven't, Badger. You don't realise this, but you're the only man, apart from Gi, who's capable of hearing my voice in your head.'

'I thought you could do that to anyone, when you're something else,' said Badger.

'Very few people I've met,' said Kitsu. 'And with practice, you'd be able to send your thoughts to me anytime. You'll see. We could practice while we ride.'

'Woah!' said Badger. This was all moving a bit fast.

Shortly they arrived at a fork in the road. There had been a signpost, but a stump and some rotten pieces of wood were all that remained.

'Which way, Kit?'

'Straight on. That looks like it takes us up into the hills.'

Badger was thinking hard, *this road does look creepy, Kit.*

'You picking up my thoughts?' said Kitsu. Badger could somehow hear him smiling.

I didn't think I'd be doing it as soon as this, Badger thought.

'It's mostly a matter of being made aware you can,' Kitsu said vocally, then added in thought, *Well, my friend, take a deep breath and tell me what you smell.*

'Whatever it is,' said Badger, 'it smells delicious.'

'It's well-cooked meat. Probably goat, or sheep,' said Kitsu.

'I didn't notice any smallholdings round here, so where's it coming from?' Badger wondered.

'I think it's time for me to take to the air to see what's about. I'll scout the road ahead, as well, to see where this road leads.'

'Give me your reins… and clothes,' said Badger.

'Get under the trees and stay on your horse. And if either of them gets agitated, ride back the way we came. I can catch up,' said Kitsu.

Kitsu became an eagle and was aloft after a few strong wingbeats. He circled around, getting higher on the thermals, until he felt cold and glided lower. He saw a narrow plume of smoke to his right and dipped a wing. Circling overhead, he saw the smoking carcasses of a couple of sheep. Oddly, they were on the ground, not over a fire. Something else he spotted with the benefit of the bird's vision, was a large, black cat creeping forward on its belly. Just as it crouched ready to dart in and grab a carcass, it was hit by a flame so hot it turned the cat into a smoking mess.

A dragon, greyish brown and easily fifteen feet long, hauled itself out from the trees and promptly started eating the cat's remains. Kit thought... *it's using other dead animals to attract the ones it wants. I've never seen that before. Badger, can you hear me?*

Faintly, yes. What's wrong?

Go back the way we came, and be quick, said Kit. *I'll catch up in a few minutes.*

Seeing Kitsu's shadow, the dragon looked skywards. It saw the eagle and made a running take off to intercept it.

It beat its leathery wings to gain height, and remarkably quickly managed to get above Kitsu before dropping down to glide beside him. A throaty voice came into Kitsu's mind.

Is that you Kitsu? asked the dragon.

Kitsu folded his wings and dropped to the ground, like falling on prey. *Badger, quick! Bring my clothes!*

Badger saw Kitsu down the road – a pale, nude Easterner, with his hands strategically positioned – and spurred his horse on. He supressed a smile, pulled up beside his companion and threw down his clothes. 'Get behind me, and get dressed!' he called, drawing his sword. Though he had no idea what he was with dealing with yet.

The dragon settled clumsily on the dirt road, brushing the trees and bushes on its way. Badger was about to sheath his sword, turn tail and ride, when he heard the beast say, 'Ouch! Bugger that... I caught my wing on a bramble then.'

Kitsu emerged dressed and smiling from behind his horse. 'You can put your sword away, Badger, this is a friend of mine,' Kitsu grinned.

'I hope you don't get it into *your* head to change into a dragon, Kit, or I'll be changing my underwear,' said Badger.

The dragon looked hurt. 'Are you saying that *I* haven't scared the crap…'

'That's enough,' said Kitsu, smiling.

'Badger, this is George. George, this is Badger. He's a very good friend,' said Kitsu.

This was turning into quite a day, Badger thought: first he'd learned to send his thoughts to someone else, and now he was getting formally introduced to a dragon.

'You can change back now, George, we're all friends here.'

'No,' said George, sadly. 'I can't do that. Can't change at all. I'm stuck like this.'

'What happened?' Kitsu asked.

'Ever heard of Bob?' asked George.

'No,' said Badger and Kitsu in unison.

'He's a giant, and a bit of a wizard… lives in the castle over that hill. He's like a wizard gone mad. He fixed me like this. The only way he's going to let me change again, is if I take him my weight in gold,' said George. 'Where am I going to get that?'

'Is he a gloater, or just cruel?' asked Kitsu.

'He's a gloater,' said George.

'That's in our favour then. He's not a thinker,' said Kitsu. He turned to Badger. 'We have to do something for George, Badger… well, I do. I can't expect…'

Badger held up a hand to stop him. 'Count me in, Kit. Any friend of yours…'

'Thanks. Shall we try something on our own, or go back and get Gi?'

'Whatever you want to do is fine by me Kit, you know that.'

'Before you make too many plans,' said George. 'I should tell you he's not averse to eating humans.'

'Well, we'll just have to make sure he goes hungry then, won't we?' said Kitsu.

'Can you change into anything else at all, George?' asked Badger.

'No, just bigger or smaller versions of dragon,' said George. 'But I can change colour, if that's any help.'

'It may be. Does he expect you back at any specific times, George?' asked Kitsu.

'No, whenever I feel like it really. He told me not to come back unless I've got some gold,' said George. 'That's why I've been trapping big cats. The locals leave money out for me each time I catch one.'

'Well, at least you're performing a service,' remarked Kitsu.

'If you can change your size, George,' queried badger, 'why don't you make yourself smaller and get Bob to weigh you, again?'

'There's a problem with that,' said George. 'No matter how big or small I make myself, my weight doesn't change.'

'That's odd.'

George snorted, smokily. 'Everything's odd about shapeshifting, my friend.'

'We'll, we're never going to find that amount of gold, and you can't spend the rest of your life like this, George,' said Kitsu, pondering the situation.

'Maybe Gi is our best hope?' Badger offered.

'Maybe,' said Kitsu. He patted the dragon's scaly shoulder, as you might console an anxious pet. 'Don't worry, we'll get you right.' He stood and stroked his bare chin with his other hand and thought around the problem until something occurred to him. 'I may have a sort of a plan. How far is the castle?'

'It's a good three or four miles,' George replied.

'Can we get there on horse?' asked Badger.

'It's better to fly,' said George.

'Badger can't fly,' Kitsu was sorry to say. 'He's gifted, but not a shifter.'

'I could carry him,' George suggested.

'Whoa, I don't know about that,' said Badger, fending off the idea.

'You can ride, can't you,' said George.

'Horses,' Badger pointed out.

'Same difference,' said George, confusingly. 'Come on, put your saddle on me. Just don't make it so tight that I can't breathe.' He cocked his head sideways and waited for Badger to move, which he finally he did. 'And if you dig those spurs into my ribs, you're toast. Understand?'

'Clearly,' said Badger, removing them.

'Right, let's saddle you up, George,' said Kitsu, helping, and grinning, mostly at the look on Badger's face.

George obliged and made himself smaller for Badger to buckle the straps. When they were ready, Badger put one foot in a stirrup and hauled himself on board.

'As you'll be flying, you'd better give me your clothes, Kit.'

Kitsu tied the horses up out of sight, then undressed and put his clothes in the sack, which he tossed to Badger. What happened next, was too painful to watch. Badger was used to seeing his friend change into a dog, wolf or bird, but this was the first time he'd seen him morph into a sizeable dragon.

Kitsu unfurled his wings and stretched them out fully. He was pleased, and gave them a gentle flap to get the feel of them. He unexpectedly lifted off the ground a couple of feet. *Why didn't I do this before?* he wondered. 'Are you two ready?'

'You could have ridden *him*,' said George, eyeing Kitsu's dragon appreciatively.

'Not safely,' said Kitsu. 'You're used to flying one of these, I'm not.'

'Fair enough. Let's go. You just hang on, Badger. I'll do the steering!' said George, making that last remark very clear by adding, 'Do NOT try yanking me in any direction, or you may get your first and last solo flying lesson.'

'Now – let's get up there and see where we are,' said Kitsu. 'After you.'

George made a lumbering run along the track and beat the air with his wings, and with one final bound he was airborne, with Badger hanging onto a couple of horn-like protrusions on his shoulders.

Now Kitsu had seen how it was done, he performed an even more ungainly take off. He climbed to a short distance from George, very aware this shape wasn't as manoeuvrable as an eagle's.

Badger wasn't afraid of heights, but it took a while to get the feel of moving swiftly at this height. He was first to see the towers of a castle on the horizon. 'Is that it, George?' he shouted. 'To our right?'

George dipped a wing and banked slightly, taking them in the general direction. Kitsu managed to stay with them, and they landed without incident behind a copse of trees a short distance from the castle. But Badger didn't need to see the backs of his hands to know he'd had just had a white-knuckle ride.

Kitsu changed back into his human form, and Badger tossed him his clothes as he got down from George's back.

'I'll have a scout round while you get dressed, Kit,' said Badger.

'I'll make myself smaller,' said George.

'Not too small,' said Badger. 'We may need to leave in a hurry.' And he went quietly through the copse to get a closer look at the castle. For a giant's place, it didn't look large. There weren't more than four men patrolling the battlements. He hurried back to Kit to tell him.

'Just four?' said Kitsu, surprised. 'Do you know who they might be?'

'I didn't have any friends in there, if that's what you mean,' said George. 'They might not even be real.'

'How's that?' asked Badger.

'They could be anything,' said George. 'He changes small animals into things and controls them with his mind.'

'He sounds cleverer than I thought,' said Kitsu. 'Can he see remotely what they're seeing?'

'No, he just sets them up to walk the battlements and leaves them to it,' said George.

'Do they know fear?' asked Badger, hopefully.

'I don't think they've ever been tested, at least not by me,' said George.

'I think today's the day they get tested,' said Kitsu. 'Probably to destruction.'

'Okay, what's the plan, Kit?' asked Badger.

'Bob is going to be attacked by two large dragons,' said Kitsu. 'But first we'll take out the soldiers on the battlements, to make sure he can't see with their eyes.'

'Okay,' said George. 'I'll kill two, you kill two, that's fair.'

'What about me?' asked Badger, feeling left out.

'You're our diversion. I want you to hammer on the door, and tell whoever answers, that you're lost and need directions,' said Kitsu.

'Then you'll come and rescue me, yes?' said Badger, hopefully.

'I told you,' said Kitsu. 'You're better than you think you are.'

Badger huffed, still not convinced.

'George, you need to make yourself as big as you can, and get up there in time to meet those two soldiers when they reach that corner,' said Kitsu, pointing up at the right-hand turret. 'I'll take the other two, when they reach this end.'

'And turn 'em to ash?' enquired George.

'Yep. That's it. Then, when Badger's inside, we drop down into the courtyard and set the whole place on fire, before your magical giant knows what's hit him,' said Kitsu. 'He can hold a bit of control over one shapeshifter – now let's see how he copes with two, plus Badger. And keep your eyes open for Badger!'

* * *

Badger took a deep breath and strode up to the main gate. When he got there, he found a smaller door set into it. He took another breath, squared his shoulders and banged on it. That was the signal for Kitsu and George to take to the air. Badger waited and listened. He heard heavy footfalls approaching. A small hatch opened and a pair of shifty eyes peered out. The hatch was higher than Badger's head.

'Down here!' he called.

'What?!' said a gruff voice on the other side.

'I said, *down here*,' Badger repeated.

'No. What you want?' said the deep, gruff voice.

'I'm lost. Can you give me directions to…?'

'No. Sod off!' boomed the voice, and the hatch slammed shut.

Bingo! thought Badger, whatever that meant. *Bob himself, from the sound of him.*

Badger banged again, harder.

The hatch slid back more violently this time. 'Look. I gave my last directions to the man before you! I don't 'ave any left!'

'Can I use your privy, then?' asked Badger.

The man hesitated. *Supposin' it was me*, he thought. 'Nah! Sod off!' and he slammed the hatch shut again.

Badger was struggling for excuses. Though this was handily prolonging the diversion. He banged on the hatch again, and shouted, 'Oi! Yer cat wants to come in!'

The hatch door was rammed back again. 'My cat's in the kitchen. Go away!'

Badger had a brainwave. 'Before you close it, would you like to meet my sister?' he asked.

There was a pause. 'What's she like?' came the cagey reply.

'Well, she's my sister. Open up and take a look. You won't see her from in there,' Badger reasoned.

While the usual panoply of bolts was being slid back, Badger picked up a bigger than fist-size rock and ran to the end of the wall.

The door opened. 'Where is she?'

'She's shy,' called Badger. 'She's waiting for you just around this corner.'

Bob looked both ways before leaving the door and, satisfied there was no danger he couldn't handle, he stepped out walked to the corner where Badger was waiting.

Badger glanced out quickly and ducked back. 'Oh, no. He can't be real,' he said to himself. 'No wonder I heard heavy footfalls. The size of those boots!' Not only were they more than a foot longer than Bob's actual feet, they were also made entirely of iron. He was wearing a fur-trimmed coat with gold buttons and a large red, woolly hat with a pompom hanging down one side. His cheeks were ruddy, his eyes bulged, and his lower face seemed all teeth. As giants went, he wasn't the hugest or the most presentable.

Badger waited until he got closer, then knowing he could outrun this red-hatted little giant, he raced past him to the castle gate, slammed it behind him and slid most of the bolts back into place.

Bob steered his iron boots through a many-point turn and shuffled back to the gate, grunting. He paused and listened, then banged on the hatch.

'Yes? What do you want?' asked Badger.

'I wanna come in. This is my 'ouse!'

'Sorry?' said Badger.

'I wanna come in!'

'Step closer to the hatch!' Badger called. 'I can hardly hear you.'

The man put his head squarely in front of the hatch.

'I wanna co...' was as far as he got before a fist-sized rock smashed into his face. He fell back and wacked his head on another rock by the gate.

Badger waited a moment then undid the bolts and looked out. The man was lying unmoving in a pool of blood that ran from the back of his head, and a deep gash on his forehead. Unexpectedly, the body started to grow longer, until it was at least fourteen feet long. *If this man stood up, he'd be a giant*, Badger thought. A cat squeezed between his legs and ran out onto the road. Badger was sure he heard it say 'thank you' as it ran away. He closed the door, thought of something, then opened it again and went outside.

There seemed to be no-one else in the entire castle. 'Kit!' he called, 'can you hear me!' He waited in silence, then heard the tell-tale beat of leathery wings.

Kit alighted clumsily, still needing some practice. 'What happened here?' he asked, pointing at the fallen giant.

'He wasn't as tough as we thought.' Badger grinned. 'Where's George?'

'Well... fortunately... he was landing on the battlements when the two men he was about to incinerate turned into white rats... and George turned into a man. It's a good thing he wasn't flying.'

'And that I wasn't on his back,' said Badger, horrified. 'Where is he now?'

'He's looking for some clothes,' said Kitsu. 'He seems to know his way about.'

'Does he think he'll find anything that fits in a giant's wardrobe?' Badger said, shaking his head. 'Come on, let's go inside and have a look round. Who knows what we might find. Glad you didn't burn the place down after all. It's not a bad castle, really.'

'George talked me out of it. He said it was a bit wanton.'

Kitsu and Badger, left the gate and walked across to the main keep.

'I might've guessed,' moaned Badger. 'A bloody great portcullis.'

'Let's have a closer look. It might not be that much of a problem.'

'Kit, it's made of iron!'

'Yes, I know. But is it locked?' asked Kitsu.

'You don't lock a portcullis,' said Badger. 'It's so bloody heavy, you don't have to.'

'So, it's not locked then,' said Kitsu.

'Well, no. I suppose not,' Badger agreed.

'Look for a handle or a lever of some sort,' said Kitsu.

'Is this what you're looking for?' said a voice in the dark on the other side of the grill.

'Is that you, George?' asked Badger. The voice was familiar, but lacked a certain smokiness.

'Yes… who were you expecting?' George looked pleased with himself as he stepped into the light in a well-fitting, smart set of clothes. He looked at Badger and Kitsu. 'Were you trying to lift this up?'

'That's the usual direction these things go,' said Badger.

'Did you take a really good look at it?' said George. He sighed. 'Come here, I can't reach it from this side, but there's a knob on the right, about chest high. Turn it to the left.'

Badger did as instructed. The portcullis was in fact, a hinged iron gate, and after a firm push, it swung inwards on well-oiled castors. 'I was expecting lots of creaks and groans,' said Badger.

'Well, if nothing else,' said George, 'Bob kept the place in good repair. Let's take the tour, shall we?'

'Where shall we start?' asked Badger. 'Up top?' With a spring in his step, he found the stairs. 'Does this mean we own a castle now? And everything in it?'

'Nothing of the sort,' said George, emphatically.

At the top of many flights of stairs was a room some twenty feet square, with two wood-plank doors on each side, and with a single arch in each of the other facing walls, that led out onto the battlements. Kitsu and Badger went out to look, and were taken aback by the grandeur of the view.

'I really didn't expect this,' said Kitsu. 'Giants aren't known for their love of scenery.'

'He probably stole the place from someone who did love it,' said George, joining them.

Badger was keen to check the rooms. 'Let's see what we have in here,' he said, trying the handle of the nearest door. 'We could do with a light. Any torches out there?'

George handed Badger a torch and a box of yellow-headed matches, he'd found on a shelf, just inside the arch.

'What's in there?' asked George.

'It's like a small armoury. There must be about a hundred bows in here. Thousands of arrows, as well,' said Badger, eyes everywhere. 'It's pretty dusty, though.'

'There hasn't been a standing army here for years,' said George.

'You know, George?' said Kitsu. 'I'd forgotten you had that long, brown curly hair. Are you going to do anything with it?'

George gave him a sideways look. 'And I'd forgotten how personal you can be with your remarks. Like what? It'd look stupid in a ponytail. And everybody knows what's under a pony tail.'

'I don't,' said Badger.

'What do you think is under there?' asked Kitsu.

'The only thing that comes to mind is a... oh, yeah,' replied Badger.

'That's exactly right,' said George, just in time.

Kitsu moved to the other door of the pair on the wall of the main room. Badger followed him in.

'Whoa...! Get that torch out of here. Quick! This room's full of black powder.'

'I'll find a lock for this when we've finished,' said George. 'Let's have a look in the rooms opposite.'

Badger pushed a door open. His face lit up. 'Hey! A dart board!'

Kitsu smiled. 'Okay, leave it for now. There's more to see.'

'I vote we look for the kitchen now,' said Badger.

'I agree,' said George. 'It's off the main hall on the ground floor.'

They went back down the seemingly interminable staircases, with landings every twelve steps, until they reached the ground floor. 'The place don't look this big from outside,' complained Badger. He and Kitsu, stood in awe at the size of the main hall. Looking around, they could see shields, banners and tapestries hanging from the walls and ceilings, and in some of the recesses were the statues of long dead heroes.

At the far end of the hall, was a long table with at least a dozen chairs along either side. At the head was an ornate armchair that looked more like a throne. Behind the throne-like chair was a walk-in fireplace with a roasting spit, and a small treadmill that could be worked by dogs in relays. To the side, was an open door, through which they could see huge copper pans and saucepans hanging from ceiling-hooks. There were cauldrons and ovens, and a water pump over a large iron sink.

'This was never Bob's,' said Badger. 'Who do you think lived here before? He must've had more money than everyone else in the world.'

'Not quite,' said George, seeming to know. 'Let's see if Bob left anything to eat that's not human.'

The others looked disgusted as they all trooped into the kitchen. 'Try the big cupboard,' said George, pointing at a door in the corner.

Badger opened it, and went inside. 'There's whole sides of cows in here. And pigs and sheep hanging up. And it's damn cold.'

'That's why it's called the cold store,' George told him.

'How do you know all this?' said Badger.

George stood and stared at the pair of them. 'I'm surprised you two haven't worked it out,' he said, holding out his hands in an expansive gesture. 'It's my castle.'

'No,' said Kitsu. But saw he wasn't joking. 'Really? You never said anything about a castle when we used to hang around together.'

'Nobody needed to know,' said George. 'How many *real* friends do you think I'd have had? None, apart from you. Everybody else would've been consumed by jealousy and probably would have tried to steal it from me.'

'How true that is,' said Kitsu.

'We're an ancient family, as you can see by all the trappings in the main hall. Not powerful any more, though. And I didn't inherit a title. But somewhere down the line, I inherited the gift of shapeshifting.'

'Or curse,' said Kitsu quickly.

Badger, was curious. 'Don't you need people to run the place? What happened to the staff?'

'They didn't stay around when Bob showed up and started eating them,' he said.

'Uh,' said badger.

George said, 'I turned dragon to kill him, but he fixed me so that if I did, I'd be stuck as a dragon. I was sure that his hold would die with him, but not sure enough to risk it. Seems I was right.'

Badger was quietly horrified that killing Bob might have fixed George forever as a dragon.

Guessing his thoughts, George reassured him. 'You weren't to know.'

Kitsu was still adjusting to the new George. 'Well, if we could just scrounge lunch off you, me and Badger will be on our way. We're not going to take advantage of our new friendship.'

'No,' said George. 'I'd still be trapping cats if it wasn't for you two. I insist you help me start the fires, then we will eat properly. Badger, I expect there will be ale in the room by the cold store, bring a barrel in here, please.'

'I need to get our horses,' said Kitsu. 'So don't be alarmed when a naked man rides through your front gate.'

George laughed. 'We'll get things going while you're gone, my friend. Try not to be too long.'

Less than fifteen minutes later, an eagle arrived at the spot where they'd left the horses. They stood with bored expressions, and he was glad he hadn't spooked them by arriving as a dragon. He shifted back into human form, patted their necks and gave their ears a friendly tug, untied the reins and got into his saddle. 'Damn, that's cold,' he muttered, when his bare skin touched cold leather. He grabbed the reins of Badger's horse, and rode back to the castle.

There was no need for the usual formalities. He rode straight through to the keep. 'Badger!' he called, 'Throw my clothes out here, will you!'

'Coming!' yelled Badger. 'Keep an eye on the sausages, will you, George. I won't be a minute.'

Badger took charge of the horses while Kitsu dressed. 'George!' he shouted. 'Where's the stables?!'

'*Stables?*' echoed George. 'I've only got *one*. Face the main gate and turn right. You can't miss it. Just follow your nose.'

* * *

70

Dawn was breaking when Haggitt peered out of the back of the wagon. There were no fires, although there was a light smoke haze hanging over the plain where the horde was camped the previous night.

'Father, wake up,' said Haggitt. 'The barbarians have gone.'

'What?' said Gi, suddenly conscious. 'On to Gremanos, or back the way we came?'

'I don't know, Father… I've just woken up,' replied Haggitt.

Dash and Bayna appeared. They looked concerned. 'Fox and Sivad took about fifty men and rode for Gremanos,' said Dash.

'The others turned back,' Bayna added.

'What's Fox up to?' Gi wondered. 'He said he would ride with us.'

Bayna started to say something, but she was upset and Dash took over. 'Bayna and I drove him away, Gi. He and two others were trying to steal our animals. Bayna killed one, but Fox and the other man ran off into the night. They probably thought I did not recognise them.'

'You were right not to trust them, Dash,' said Gi. 'He had me fooled for a while… but only *for a while*.'

Haggitt climbed down out of the wagon, 'Father, there are two bodies back here.'

'My apologies, Gi,' said Dash. 'I caught them trying to creep up on the camp.'

'Thank you,' said Gi. 'Let's wake Muto. We'll eat and be on our way. I just hope nothing else goes wrong. The day's hardly started!'

It was another hour before Muto urged the horses into action. Although now a foursome, the horses initially strained on the incline ahead of where the wagon was parked overnight. But once they picked up some momentum, the wagon moved at a good pace.

The sky was overcast, but there was no rain, which was kinder on the eyes than the glare of the sun they'd endured for the past few days.

'We could do with it being cooler, Master,' said Muto, using a crude fan.

'Wherever did you find that?'

'I made it, Master.'

'I can believe that.' Gi chortled, and scanned the roadsides ahead. 'Keep your eyes open, Muto. If Fox and his men have tried to steal the elves' animals once, they'll probably try again.'

'I should have shot him when I had the chance, Master,' Muto grumbled. 'I won't let the chance slip by again.'

'Fox will be expecting us to send a couple of scouts out, and no doubt he'll pick them off, reducing our numbers again.'

'What numbers?' Muto couldn't help challenging him. 'We've only got Brian and Maurice, Master. And I think we're better off keeping them here, rather than sending them out looking for trouble.'

'We don't *look* for trouble, Muto,' Gi grinned, sourly. 'But it always seems to know where we are.'

'Yes, Master. It's been quiet, but I expect Old Man Trouble will show up soon.'

'Ever the optimist,' said Gi.

Brian pulled over, waiting for the wagon to catch up.

'Gi! These tracks show that Fox and his men went straight on. But I'm pretty sure we can cut a corner off by going northwest through the woods. There's a trail just up there that looks like it gets a bit of use.'

'Sounds okay to me,' said Gi. 'It might speed us up a little.'

Muto was okay with it, too. 'The quicker we get to Gremanos, the better. Mr. Kitsu and Badger don't know Fox isn't riding for us anymore. They may be in danger.'

'I think they'll realise something's wrong when they see we're not with him,' said Gi.

'That's what I'm hoping, Master. Perhaps they're already there by now.' He drove the wagon behind Brian to the turn-off. He paused and peered down the narrow trail through the trees. For safety, he suggested that the elves separate, one ahead and one be behind, each with one of the soldiers. 'It'll even up the strength front and back in case of ambush.'

'And we thought Fox was the strategist,' said Brian, good-humouredly.

Bayna joined Brian at the front. Maurice went back to ride with Dash.

'You seem worried, my friend,' said Maurice, 'Do you think Fox would dare try again?'

'Yes. Maybe not for a couple of days,' said Dash. 'I think he will probably attack with most of his men to create a diversion while he tries to steal them.'

'I don't understand the man,' said Maurice. 'They're just beautiful animals, they're not magical in any way. They don't have any special powers – *do they?*'

'No. There's nothing special about them. In our own dimension, a black horse or a brown stag are considered rare,' Dash explained. 'Back home, nobody would give us a second glance.'

'Do you think Fox wants to ride them or sell them?'

'He is vain. He will want one for himself.'

Maurice had to agree, and the pair went quiet to watch the trees.

Gi started wondering about the wisdom of this shortcut through the woods. It shortened the journey, but the ground was lumpier, and it slowed the wagon. So, what was the point? 'We'll go left at this crossway coming up, Muto. It should take us out of the woods sooner.'

Muto yelled an instruction to Brian and Bayna up front. He was pleased to be getting back on the main road to Gremanos. 'Trees can be so *boring* at times, just one after another for mile after *bloody* mile.'

'I'll feel safer in more open country,' said Gi. 'Not so many places for would-be attackers to hide.' He looked about him as he said it.

'Father, there are at least four riders behind us,' said Haggitt, softly.

'I *thought* I heard something. Thank you, son.'

'Shh.' Dash put a finger to his lips to quieten everyone. Bayna stepped aside and let the wagon pass. Then she urged Ice into the trees and stopped. Waiting.

The men following the wagon, didn't notice her and carried on by. She gave them some twenty yards start, then emerged back onto the road. She could see from their clothes they were barbarians, and knew instinctively they meant to attack. Fox wasn't among them, but probably waiting in ambush up ahead. She tensed as one of the four pulled a double-edged battle-axe from his belt, and swung it over his head, aiming to throw it at the wizards in the back of the wagon. Bayna was ready, and released an arrow.

'Damn!' she cursed under her breath. 'I hit his shoulder.' But the man fell from his horse from the impact and hit the ground while his axe was turning through the air and, as bad luck would have it, it finally thudded into his forehead, splitting his skull in two. She allowed herself a wry smile, 'I couldn't do *that* again,' she whispered.

Two of the attackers turned to face the threat from behind and hesitated when they saw a beautiful woman on a white stag, and that was their undoing. Bayna was swifter than the eye when loading her bow, and her favourite trick was releasing two arrows together. Moments later, both men received their share. The last man turned to run. Dash saw him and released an arrow, bringing the man down in the deep undergrowth beneath the trees. He stopped Snow, and waited for Bayna to catch up.

'A good morning's work, my love,' he said, as he reached out to touch her hand. 'I really liked that trick with the axe.' He smiled.

'It was nothing,' she lied, lifting her chin imperiously, but spoiling the effect with a grin.

'Is everybody alright back there?' asked Gi.

'All is well, Gi,' said Dash. 'The danger has passed... for the moment.'

Bayna returned to her place up-front beside Brian.

A mile further down the track they re-joined the main route to Gremanos. The elves and soldiers returned to their usual formation of Brian and Maurice leading and Dash and Bayna following. The threatened rain had not come, though the sky was still overcast. A light breeze made travelling more comfortable, especially for the elves who found the heat more of a challenge, though they rarely complained.

A couple of miles up the road, they came upon the *Wayside Inn*. They drew up to take a look, tempted by the thought of a drink or two. There were no horses outside and no noise from within.

'Can you see anything, Muto?' Gi said.

'No people, if that's what you mean, Master. No horses, either.' He cracked the reins to attract Brian's attention and beckoned him back. 'We think it could be a trap, Brian. Let's ride on.'

Brian nodded and caught up with Maurice. 'Gi thinks it might be a trap, so we're moving on. Keep your eyes open.'

Bayna slipped an arrow into her bow. 'Just in case, my love,' she whispered.

Dash nodded and stared at the windows of the inn as they rode slowly by.

The place seemed deserted and Gi had every intention of leaving it that way. A door slammed somewhere around the back, but no other sounds followed.

'Mr. Haggitt,' whispered Muto, 'have you got your crossbow handy? Or are you going to use that wonderful magic again?'

'That depends on how close anyone gets, Muto,' replied Haggitt. 'But I will use magic first.'

'Good,' said Muto. 'I do so like to see a good fireball.' He rubbed his hands together at the thought.

The party were some hundred yards past the inn, and everything was calm, but Muto felt something was amiss because there was no birdsong in the air. Then he worked it out. *Perhaps it's because of us*, he thought, and tapped the reins against the horses' backs again.

They travelled another mile in silence watching for any suspicious movement in the roadside trees and bushes.

Then, something they didn't expect happened. A short distance ahead of them a solitary rider stood in the middle of the road.

'Anything behind us, Haggitt?' asked Gi.

'Not that I can see, Father,' came the whispered reply.

'Shall I run him down, Master?' said Muto, watching the man blocking their path.

'It remains an option. But let's see what Brian and Maurice do first.'

Brian and Maurice drew up either side of the man. 'What's your business, friend?' asked Brian.

'I have no business, I'm waiting for you to pass, so I can be on my way,' he replied.

'Better stand aside, then. Can't you see we have a wagon?'

'Where are you going?' Maurice asked him.

'I'm told there's an inn down the road. I plan to stay there for the night.'

'We just passed it. It looks closed,' Brian told him.

'Well, I'll check it out and move on then, I expect.' Then he caught sight of Bayna and Dash's animals. 'Nice beasts,' he commented. 'Are they for sale?'

'Absolutely not!' Brian snapped.

'Oh,' said the man, 'pity.' And he started to ride on.

'Hold fast!' said Brian. 'If you've come that way what's up there?'

'Now you mention it,' he said, suddenly serious. 'Many riders. I had to get off the road to let them pass. They seemed to be on a mission. If I hadn't moved, I would have been trampled. They didn't seem to see me. It was as if I wasn't there.'

'Thank you, friend, have a safe journey,' said Brian, and he moved his horse away to allow the man room to continue on his way.

When he was past the wagon, Dash said, 'What did you think of him, my love?'

'I think he was lying. If he comes back, we may have to kill him,' she said, bluntly.

Brian watched the man until he was out of sight around the long curve of the road. 'Do you think that's Fox's men he was talking about?' Brian wondered.

'Almost certainly,' replied Maurice. 'From what he was saying, they seem desperate to get to Gremanos ahead of us.'

Before they got moving again, Dash rode to the back of the wagon. 'Haggitt, can you lend me one of your cloaks, please? I wish to scout ahead a short distance.'

Haggitt took one from the wooden chest he kept under his bed and handed it to him, neatly folded. 'Try not to get it dirty. Or covered in blood. It's a bugger to get clean.'

* * *

Dash grabbed the reins of the spare horse and rode back to Bayna. As he passed Gi, he called, 'I need to see what's up ahead. I won't be long.' He passed Snow's reins to Bayna, and jumped nimbly onto the spare horse. After wrapping the cloak around him and pulling the hood over his silver hair, he trotted the horse up the road, not so much looking about him, but relying on his keen hearing to listen for things his eyes might not see.

When he'd gone, the others all looked at Bayna, who shrugged. 'He sometimes gets notions about things.'

The woods were quiet and the only movement was the uppermost branches swaying slightly in the light breeze. Dash rode at a canter, and was about a mile ahead of Gi's wagon when something caught his attention. He slowed to a walk as he approached a sharp bend, and stopped to listen. He could hear two unusual voices. He dismounted and led the horse off the road and into the trees, where he looped the reins over a bush and went on foot to see who was on the road.

The voices grew louder, so he stepped behind a tree and waited. He wasn't sure if they were arguing or complaining, but one seemed to be trying to placate the other.

As they got closer, Dash realised they were dwarfs. One looked a fraction taller than the other, but it could be that he had a taller helmet. They both had extremely overgrown beards. The taller one was saying, 'It's your own fault. If you hadn't given him so much lip, he wouldn't have run you into that ditch.'

'He even had the cheek to try and pick me up. Huh. Didn't think I was going to be that 'eavy.'

'You're not. It's all that scrap-iron you wear. Look at you! It's a wonder you can walk.'

Dash stepped out in front of them. His hood had slipped onto his shoulders, revealing his long, silvery hair. 'Who are you?' he demanded, struggling to keep a stern expression.

'Shit, Ben, it's a bloody great ghost!' yelled Thadax, the smaller, by an inch.

'Nah, I can't see through 'im,' said Ben, the other dwarf, knowledgeably. 'He's just a bloke who's a bit on the pale side.'

'What are you both doing out here, miles from anywhere? And who are you?' Dash repeated.

'See,' said Ben, 'if 'e was a ghost, 'e would've remembered 'e'd already said that.'

'Well,' said Thadax, trying to look tall. 'I'm Thadax, from the court of King Treadwell, of Corin.'

'And I'm Ben. Ben de Little, to be precise, also from where 'e said,' said Ben. 'So, who are you?'

'My name is Dash, and, as you don't seem to know, I'm a snow elf,' said Dash, mentally struggling not to squat down.

'Are you going to kill us?' asked Thadax.

'Have you done anything that would make me want to do that?' said Dash, grinning slightly.

'Dunno. Does arguing with barbarians, count?' asked Thadax.

'Of course not,' said Dash. 'Everyone argues with barbarians. That's what they're for.'

'See, I told you, you were getting too personal. That's why you got run into that ditch,' said Ben.

'Well, 'e did *stink*. I was only tellin' him in case he didn't know,' argued Thadax.'

Dash's back was beginning to ache from stooping forward, so he finally sat down in the road. 'What are you doing this far from Corin?'

'We're spies... ouch,' said Thadax, as Ben kicked him.

'See, now you've told 'im. Now we're not spies any more, you fool,' snapped Ben.

'Easy, now,' said Dash, quietly. 'Your secret's safe with me. Where are you heading?'

'We're looking for Gremanos,' said Ben, lowing his voice. 'Do you know where he is, have you seen 'im?'

'Gremanos?' said Dash, raising an eyebrow. 'Gremanos is not a man, Ben, it's a city. And you're going the wrong the way.'

'See...' said Thadax, 'our stupid king's got it all wrong again. Fancy sending us to arrest a city. How did he think we were going to bring it back?'

Dash tried to follow this. 'How did you get here?' he wondered.

'By wind. We flew. Teeter, the king's clever bugger, made this huge bag of air wiv a basket 'anging under it, to sit in. It went for miles,' said Ben. 'Then we ran out of coal and we crashed. Pretty impressively, in fact.'

'You shouldn't 'ave told 'im that, Ben,' said Thadax, quietly. 'He might tell the king *we* broke it.'

'How long were you flying?' asked Dash, regretting keeping this conversation alive, but curios.

'About two months, maybe three,' said Ben.

'Three months! You must be starving,' said Dash.

'It does have its upside,' said Ben. 'You don't eat, you don't need a privy.'

'You look a bit tasty, mister,' said Thadax, licking his lips, his brain clearly addled by hunger.

'Don't even consider it,' said Dash. 'Look, I can get you food. Whatever you want, in fact.' He stood up. 'Get off the road, and wait. I'll be back soon. You'll see a few riders with a wagon: that will be me and my friends.'

He remounted and galloped back to the wagon.

'Anything wrong up ahead, Dash?' Brian asked, as he approached the wagon.

'Not as such,' said Dash. 'I found a couple of men looking for travelling companions.' He grinned. 'They are quite hungry. I don't think they've eaten for a few days.'

'Might they be a danger to us?' asked Gi, joining in.

'I do not know, Gi. One of them thought he might like to eat me, but I convinced him otherwise,' said Dash. 'I would also consider them to be formidable fighters,' he added, testing his new found sense of humour.

'And yet not a danger?' said Gi, unsure of this. 'Okay, Dash. I trust your judgement. Swap your horse and tell Brian and Maurice to be on the lookout for them.'

Dash changed mounts and rode with Bayna to Brian's side.

'Brian, there are two men waiting just around the next bend that I want you to meet,' said Dash. 'We will be giving them a lift to Gremanos. But be careful. They may not be as big as they think they are.'

'What?' said Brian.

'Do we need to have our swords ready?' Maurice wondered.

'That might not be a good idea,' said Dash, quite enjoying this. 'We don't want to anger them. But if we feed them, they should remain calm.'

'What are you up to?' whispered Bayna.

'I am trying to be humorous, my love. Watch, when we get round this next bend,' Dash whispered, behind a hand.

Brian led the party around the bend and pulled up sharply. At the roadside, trying to look as tall and as threatening as they possibly could, were two heavily armed dwarfs.

'Brian! Maurice! Do not laugh,' Dash instructed. 'They might be what you call, evil little shits.'

'Whoa!' said Muto, hauling on the reins, 'I haven't seen the likes of them for a few years, Master.'

'Nor me, but I think I recognise one of them, even under all that beard. Help me down, Muto,' said Gi.

When he was on the ground, he strode forward to meet the newcomers. Thadax took a step back when he saw a wizard in flowing robes coming straight at him. But, Gi wasn't interested in him. 'Ben? Is that *you?*'

A grin spread across Ben's face. 'Gi Mulderbish, as I live and breathe. What the fu… nniest of things to happen, finding you here!' he recovered, lamely.

'Indeed, old friend. We're on our way to Gremanos, to pay our respects to Baron Striper,' Gi replied, 'and from what I heard, you're coming with us.'

'Respects?' interrupted Thadax. 'To Striper?'

'He's kidding,' said Ben. 'I hope,' he added quickly, looking to Gi's face for reassurance. 'And, yes, it was unexpected, but here we are. Oh… this is Thadax, he's… he's… well… he's… Thadax,' said Ben, by way of an introduction. 'Back when you knew me, I was just a humble palace guard. And back when you didn't know Thadax, he was just a humble palace servant. And now we're both spies. Though we don't tell anybody that, of course.'

'Of course,' said Gi.

'Your tall, pale-faced friend said you'd give us food,' said Thadax, his eyes darting everywhere. 'Only I don't see any.'

'What would you like? Muto does a really nice sausage,' Gi told him.

'I want more than one,' said Thadax.

'You can have as many as you want, my friend,' said Gi, with a smile.

'Six should do for starters,' said Thadax, already salivating.

'Muto, will you look after our new friends, please?' asked Gi.

'Certainly, Master. Sausages coming up.' Muto moved the wagon forwards a few yards to a spot he could park, climbed down from his seat and set about making a fire. Haggitt brought the huge frying pan and enough sausages for all of them.

Ben and Thadax were impressed. 'We were going to carry on by ourselves, Gi.'

'In the wrong direction,' interjected Dash, with a smirk.

'… But, being as you've got this excellent cook, I think we'll be staying with you,' finished Ben.

'You're both welcome. We could do with the help,' said Gi. 'I know you can handle that sword as well as any man. Dash says you ran into some barbarians, Ben. Can you tell me how many? They're a bunch who were supposed to be our friends, but they want to rob us now. Well, the elves, really. They're after the stag and Dash's horse.'

'They're nice-looking animals,' said Ben. 'But you'd never get us on one of those. Their bodies are too wide for our short, little legs.'

'Ben, you're the tallest man I know,' said Gi, putting and arm around his shoulder.

'Don't give me that bullshit, Gi… it's me, Ben, remember?'

'Come and get 'em while they're hot!' Muto called. 'Mr. Haggitt, will you rustle up some food for Dash and Bayna, please.'

'You were asking, how many barbarians we saw,' said Ben. 'Well, I reckon there must've been about fifty, maybe sixty. Enough for a small army, probably.'

'I was hoping for less,' said Gi. 'But now we have you and Thadax, it evens the odds a bit.'

'Just a little,' grinned Ben.

'You haven't told me what you've been up to for the past few years,' said Gi, 'I imagine it was full of adventures. And in places without scissors, by the look of you.'

'That was just the last couple of months up in the air.'

'Speak to Muto. I'm sure he'll sort you out.'

'Well,' said Ben, 'where to begin?' He looked about for inspiration. 'I know – I went to help some new wizard get back a magic drum that some high wizard called Dennis, stole from her.'

'Her?' queried Gi.

'Oh, yes. Eydith. She's pretty powerful. Pretty, too, as I recall. She was with another young wizard, called Linkwood. She'll probably marry 'im I reckon. The lucky bugger,' said Ben, with a hint of envy.

'Did she get her drum back?' asked Gi.

'Oh, yes. And I heard she helped get rid of that Dennis, too,' said Ben.

'Describe this Dennis for me,' said Gi. 'There was an Archchancellor at Havrapsor of that name a while ago, I'm sure. There can't be two wizards with a name as unusual as Dennis.'

'He was a bit stupid. Treated his men badly and he wore this big white robe with gold braid on the shoulders. And it had hundreds of pockets,' said Ben, pushing his memory to its limits.

'It sounds like the man who broke through into the snow elves' dimension,' said Dash. 'He had demons with him.'

'That's the one,' said Ben. 'I'd forgotten about the demons.'

Dash took a long breath. 'Gi,' he said, 'When we have helped you deal with the baron, I will make it my duty to go back and help rid my dimension of this Dennis and his demons.' He looked across to Bayna, who was nodding vigorously.

'I'm sure you will, Dash. And perhaps it will work out that some of us can go with you,' said Gi. 'Don't be too hasty to confront a high wizard. I wouldn't do that lightly, and I'm almost one myself. You need to fight fire with fire. Which is what we'll be doing shortly at Gremanos.'

'We will see,' said Dash. 'I will keep your offer in mind.'

* * *

72

'Thank you for your hospitality, George,' said Kitsu, 'but I think Badger and I should push on to Gremanos in the morning, if you don't mind.'

'Why should I mind?' said George. 'I'm coming with you. I'm not staying here on my own, it's too bloody creepy, till I get some staff again.'

'How will you travel?' asked Badger, 'we've only got two horses.'

'I can change into other things now,' said George. 'I just won't choose to be a dragon for a long time, yet.'

'It's good you have your powers back,' said Kitsu. 'I'm pleased for you.'

'I'll just need Badger to look after my clothes sometimes, that's all,' said George.

'No problem,' said Badger. 'As long as you put 'em in a different sack from Kit's. I don't want to be on the wrong side of either of you if I mix 'em up.'

'We should be worried about getting on the wrong side of *you*, my friend. You killed a giant, remember?' said Kitsu.

'Hmm... Yes, I did, didn't I?' said Badger, quietly. 'I'd rather that stayed between us, though, if you don't mind. I don't want young hot-heads coming after me to boast they killed the giant-slayer.'

'Agreed, Badger. This will not be discussed outside the three of us ever again,' said Kitsu.

'Thanks.' Badger stood and yawned. 'Well, gentlemen, I'll be asleep shortly, so wake me if you're up before me.'

* * *

267

73

The next morning, the three men strolled out of George's castle gate, and were preparing to leave.

'There's no need for you to fly all the way to Gremanos, George. It's tiring,' said Kitsu. 'Give your clothes to Badger, turn yourself into an eagle or owl and sit on my shoulder.'

'A parrot might be more appropriate.' Badger laughed.

'No. Eagle it is,' said George, passing his shirt to Badger.

'But you dig those claws into me just once, my friend, and you'll be flying all the way,' said Kitsu, sounding like he meant it.

'I'll try not to, Kit. But I'll be a bit bird-brained,' said George.

'Why don't we steal a horse from a tavern on the way?' Badger suggested.

'There speaks the ex-barbarian,' said Kitsu.

In his defence, Badger pointed out that more than half the horses outside those places were already stolen.

'I know just the place,' said George. 'I'll go and see what's on offer.' He gave a squawk like an eagle and ran along the road to gain enough speed and momentum to get airborne.

When he was above the trees and out of sight, Badger said, 'You really didn't know about George's castle, Kit?'

'As my gods are my witness, he never said anything about it to me.'

'What do you think he'll do with it when this is over?' Badger wondered.

'Find some staff, maybe – and a wife – and go back to it. But I think he likes his freedom too much,' said Kit. 'Mind you, he may have changed since being stuck in Bob's spell.'

'But it's so big, Kit. How many people would it take to run a place like this?'

'You're asking *me*?' said Kitsu. 'I don't know – probably a dozen, then he'd need about forty men on guard duty, plus a couple of servants.'

'Servants?' said Badger. 'Make the lazy sod fetch his own ale.'

'Yes, there is that. And someone to make his bed – the list goes on.'

George the eagle squawked to let them know he was descending, and, without thinking, Kitsu held up his forearm. 'Not too hard, George. Remember what I told you.'

George settled on the road and began the laborious change back into human form. Badger had the presence of mind to throw George's trousers over and look the other way.

'It's alright, I've finished now,' said George.

'Well… if you say so, but you're going to have to do something about that fine head of feathers, my friend.' Kitsu grinned.

'Damn! The times I used to do that,' George grumbled. 'Anyway, as I thought, the tavern up the road has six… yes, I'm sure it was six, I have trouble counting with a bird brain… six horses outside. I can walk that distance.'

'You can get up behind me,' said Badger, offering George his hand. 'We can be there in a few minutes.'

Sure enough, there were six bored-looking horses standing at the hitching-rail outside the tavern. George slid down the back of Badger's horse.

'Pick one and free the others,' said Badger. 'It'll stop anyone chasing after us.'

'Ah, the voice of experience,' said Kitsu.

George double-checked there was no-one about. He gathered up the reins and climbed onto his chosen horse, and the three of them galloped up the road to Gremanos. After a few minutes they let the five unwanted horses go free. Annoyingly, they didn't run off. They were used to running in a group, and stayed with the riders.

'What shall we do, Badger?' asked George.

'Just leave 'em. When they get tired, they'll give up.'

A mile up the road, that's exactly what happened.

'They looked like barbarian horses, Badger,' said Kitsu. 'Do you think some of Fox's men have deserted?'

'No, they might just fancy a drink,' said Badger. 'Though we must be way ahead of Fox's men by now. I reckon they're scouts.'

'Yes, we can't be far from the city now,' said Kitsu. 'A couple of days, at most.'

'That's about right,' said George, who knew the region. 'Any idea how we're going to play this when we get there?'

'I've a few thoughts,' said Kitsu. 'When we get past the city gates – assuming there *are* city gates – we ride straight to Striper's castle. We tell his guards that we have news of Gi Mulderbish, so we're bound to get to see him. Then we tell the baron that Gi's on his way, and that he's not a happy wizard.'

'I thought we weren't going to tell him until Gi gets there,' said Badger. 'Surprise him.'

'No. It's better we tell him straight away. Striper will send a company of soldiers out to arrest him, not realising there are about fifty barbarians between here and Gi. So, he'll soon be very short of soldiers to protect him. Which will make the odds a lot more even,' said Kitsu.

'It's a good start,' said Badger.

* * *

74

Two days slipped by without mishap...

Arriving at a hilltop about a mile off, Kitsu, Badger and George saw the walled city of Gremanos spread before them. Baron Striper's castle was perched on a hill in the centre. From there, if he had a mind to, the baron could see all that was happening, but as he was so effectively isolated, he couldn't hear anything apart from the persistent drone of people going about their business.

A shadowy figure moved cautiously up the stairs to the baron's office and tapped apologetically on the door.

'Just a minute!' Striper shouted, then in a quieter voice said, 'Pick up your clothes and go, quickly.'

There was a brief interlude of scurrying behind the door and, eventually another door closed somewhere. 'Come in!'

Barter, the baron's messenger, went to stand on the two bare patches in the carpet in front of Striper's desk.

'Ah... Barter. What news?' the baron asked, discretely smoothing his breeches.

'Some riders are requesting an audience, my Lord,' said Barter from somewhere in the depths of his black hood. 'They claim they've seen Gi Mulderbish coming this way and they thought you ought to know.'

'What? How far away is he?' asked Striper, in a sudden panic.

'I don't know, my Lord. It wasn't me what saw 'im,' said Barter, truthfully.

'Well, bring them in, bring them in. I need to know,' said Striper, getting agitated.

'Yes, my Lord. Give me a minute,' said Barter, purposely scuffing his feet in an effort to add more wear to the baron's carpet as he left.

At the bottom of the stairs was a small waiting room where Kitsu and his friends sat.

'Taking his time, ain't 'e,' said Badger.

271

'Patience, my friend,' said Kitsu. 'And when we meet this baron, I'll do the talking.'

'Okay by me,' said Badger. 'I wouldn't know how to talk to him anyway. I'm not used to talking to royalty.'

'Hardly royalty,' said George. 'Kings, queens and their ilk are royalty. He's just a thief and a bully who got his title from some king who was too weak to tell him to go and...'

The door opened. 'The baron will see you now, so follow me,' said Barter.

After trudging up the stairs twice in succession, Barter was puffed out. He knocked on Striper's door and, without waiting for a reply, virtually pushed the men into the office and went for lie down.

'That'll be all for now, Maureen. Gentlemen, be seated. What can you do for me?' asked Striper, smiling patronisingly, resting his elbows on his desk and staring at each of them in turn.

'Well, your Lordship. We passed Gi Mulderbish on the road here, and we heard you might be interested to know he's coming. That was about two days ago,' said Kitsu.

'Is he alone?' the baron asked.

'Nope,' said Kitsu. 'There must be about thirty men with him. Barbarians I would say, from the look of them.'

'Which way?' the baron asked.

'They're coming from the east and they're armed to the teeth. Looked like big trouble. Pardon me for saying so, sire, but it might be a good idea to send some soldiers out to tackle them before they get here,' suggested Kitsu.

The baron sat quietly, brooding... 'Right – I'll get one of my officers and twenty well-armed soldiers to sort him and his rabble out.' He opened a drawer in his desk and lifted the lid on a small black box. 'Here's a silver for each of you. Don't spend it all at once.'

Kitsu picked up the coins and gave one to each of the others.

'You can go now,' said Striper, rudely waving them away. He stood up and went to the door at the back of his office, 'Gripper! Come in here.'

Three or four moments later, Gripper had positioned himself on the two bare patches. 'Yes, my Lord. What can I do for you?'

'You always ask the right questions, my boy. I like that. I want you to go to the officer's mess and tell Major Pinch I want to see him, now,' said the baron, leaning back in his big chair. 'Well? What are you waiting for?'

'Er... I don't know where the officers' mess is, my Lord,' said Gripper.

'Well... *ask* somebody,' said the baron.

'Okay – where is it, my Lord?' asked Gripper.

'How would I know? I'm not the one going.' He waved Gripper out of the room.

Gripper went back to his office and slammed the door. He went through to Reception. 'Come on Ollie, get off. Maureen, get off my desk, please. This is not the baron's office.'

'Sorry, Gripper. What did you want?' asked Ollie, adjusting his clothes.

'Do you know where the officers' mess is?'

'Yeah, why?' asked Ollie.

'I need to go there. His baronial self wants Major Pinch, for some reason.'

'Come on, then. It's not far,' said Ollie.

Ollie led Gripper out into the quadrangle, and diagonally to a small door in the corner. 'Mind your 'ead,' said Ollie, ducking under the granite lintel. Gripper couldn't help noticing the blood smears of those who hadn't. 'It's up two flights. Do you want me go with you?' asked Ollie.

'I wouldn't mind,' replied Gripper.

'Good. They have some really nice wines up there and the ale's pretty good too,' Ollie beamed.

'Will they give us any?' Gripper wondered.

'If there's somebody in, they will. If not, they won't mind if we help ourselves,' he said, cheerfully.

Ollie knocked: two quick raps followed by three drawn out taps. A hatch slid aside.

'Who is it?' came a solemn voice.

'It's me, Ollie, from the stable.'

'What's the password?' asked the voice, gravely.

'Is it the same as last time?' Ollie tried.

'Yes.'

'Then it's, *Can I come in, please*,' said Ollie.

The door opened, allowing them in. 'What's it to be, lads?' asked Major Pinch, greeting them from across the room.

'Surprise us,' said Gripper. 'You've certainly changed a lot since you've been up here, Major, if you don't mind me saying.'

'I have a senior position now, my lad,' said Pinch. 'Here, ale for each of you. Now, what brings you two up here? It can't be just the ale.'

'Er... the baron would like you to go to his office, Major,' Gripper told him, briefly standing to attention without knowing why.

Pinch almost choked. 'You sure that's what he said? Not: go and find Pinch and tell him to get his backside in here? Am I right?'

'Pretty close, Major.' Gripper smiled.

'What does he want? Any ideas?'

'It's probably about the three men who were in his office earlier. He gave them money for information,' said Gripper.

'That can only mean trouble,' said Pinch, thoughtfully. 'Right lads, when you've had your drinks, we'll go and see what the fool wants. No point hurrying. He'll bawl us out however quick or slow we are.'

In less than good time, Gripper and Major Pinch were outside Baron Striper's door. Gripper knocked and waited in case Maureen had to vacate, but the baron yelled, 'Come in!' and looked up from something he was pretending to write. 'Ah, Pinch. About time!'

Pinch glared at him. 'It's *Major* Pinch, now my Lord,' he corrected him.

'Of course, Major. At ease.'

'I am at ease, my Lord,' and under his breath he muttered, 'You don't think I'd stand to attention for riff-raff like you, do you?'

'I have received information that Gi Mulderbish is coming this way from the east,' the baron announced.

'Yes, my Lord. I heard the rumour, too,' said Pinch.

'It's not a rumour, Major. It's a fact.'

'What do you expect me to do about it, then, my Lord?'

'Well, Major, I thought it would be nice if you sent about a dozen men to arrest him, and bring him back here so I can put him back in my dungeons,' said Striper, sarcastically.

'I don't even know what he looks like,' said Pinch, defiantly. 'But I believe he's a wizard, and...'

'Pah! You must have somebody in your troop, or whatever it is, that knows what he looks like. So just do it! I will expect you back in four days,' said Striper, waving him out. 'With Mulderbish in chains!'

Gripper followed. 'I don't think we've got any chains, Major. Do you know anybody who'd recognise him?' he asked.

'Yes...' he grinned. And when Pinch grinned, he looked quite evil.

'Who's that then, Major?'

'The man who lost a hundred men – du Merde, by name' said Pinch, with a scoff bordering on hatred.

'I know of him,' said Gripper. 'The centurion in command of the outpost, he was.'

'That's the one,' said Pinch. 'Well, this time, including himself, du Merde will be in command of a baker's dozen.' Pinch sounded almost triumphant.

'Do you want me to help you find him, Major?' asked Gripper.

'No, that's alright, lad,' said Pinch. 'I know exactly where he'll be, but you can come and savour the moment with me, if you like.'

Gripper fell into step beside the Major and they marched to the practice yard. This was somewhere else Gripper had never been. 'Which one is he, Major?'

'He's the one slashing away at invisible enemies and that unlawful incursion of weeds,' said Pinch.

'Does he always practice swordplay like that?'

'What? In his imagination, you mean? Oh, yes. That way he's only a danger to *himself*,' said Pinch.

'Catscart!' Pinch yelled across the yard. 'Over here, please.'

'Coming Major,' du Merde called back, and hurried across the yard. He stopped in front of Major Pinch and saluted smartly. 'Sir?

'I have a mission for you, Sergeant,' said Pinch, smirking a little.

'Yes, sir. Whatever, sir. When, sir?'

'I'm trying to tell you, so do shut it. I want you to pick twelve men, get them provisioned and kitted out for a four-day trip,' said the major.

'Four days?' said du Merde.

'Yes, Sergeant. Two days out, and two days back,' said Pinch.

'May I ask why, sir?' said du Merde.

'Well,' said Pinch. 'You're the *Sergeant*. I'm the *Major*. That'll do for a start.'

'You're not coming with us then, Major?' said du Merde.

'You've got it in one, Sergeant. The baron wants you to take your men, ride out to arrest Gi Mulderbish, and bring him back. He's supposed to be coming from the east, wherever that is. So get to it. I'll see you at the end of the week.' Pinch saluted, turned on his heel and marched back to the officers' mess, with Gripper half running to keep up.

'Do you think he's the right man for the job, Major?' Gripper puffed.

'No, son, he's the *only* man for the job,' said Pinch.

'Are you going to tell the baron you sent du Merde?' asked Gripper.

'Not unless he asks. Between you and me, I think he wants du Merde out of the way,' said Pinch, quietly.

They arrived back at the mess. 'Coming in for another, lad?'

'Thank you, Major, but I should be getting back,' said Gripper. 'But now I know where you are, I'll come and visit.'

'Good lad. Don't forget, the baron doesn't need to know,' said Pinch, tapping the side of his nose. Gripper smiled, stabbed himself in the eye saluting, and went back to his office.

* * *

75

Kitsu, Badger and George, made their way down from Striper's castle and looked for a tavern.

'Are we going to spend it all on ale?' asked Badger, flipping his silver as they walked.

'No, my friend, we pool it to buy food for the next two days. And if there's enough left over, we'll drink,' said Kitsu.

There was no shortage of taverns in Gremanos.

'This looks as good a place as any,' said George. It was part-full, and free of barbarians and trolls, so would be quiet.

The three filed in, and after negotiating a price for the takeaway food with the landlord, they had enough money over for a decent jug of ale (as opposed to a jug of decent ale). By luck, they found a table adjacent to one occupied by two of Striper's Black-Guards. The soldiers were discussing the orders from Sergeant du Merde about shipping out the following morning. Kitsu leaned in closer, but they twigged and soon left.

'Did you catch any of that?' asked Kitsu.

'Enough,' he said.

'We can't wait till morning,' said Kitsu. 'We need to be ahead of them. I say we finish our ale, get the horses, and be on our way. All agreed?'

The others nodded. When they'd drunk their ale, Kitsu signalled the landlord they were leaving and he brought three packages over and laid them on the table.

Once outside, Badger asked, 'Anyone remember where the stables are?'

Kitsu looked left and right, and decided on left. 'That way.'

Two of them were staggering slightly. 'What was that stuff we drank?' said George, leaning on Badger, who was leaning on Kitsu.

'I dunno,' said Badger. 'But it must've been cheap.'

'It was all we could get for the money,' said Kitsu. 'And it wasn't cheap. It was competitively priced.'

'It was sh… rubbish, I nearly swore then,' Badger complained, and promptly threw up violently in the gutter, proving that whatever it cost, it was only rented.

Unaccountably, it had no effect on Kitsu, and now Badger had expelled it, his head was clearing. By the time they reached the stable, George had sobered up enough to get on his horse. The second time, he managed to stay on it.

'Will you be alright, George?' said Kitsu, concerned. 'We can wait awhile, if you like.'

'I'll be fine. You two ride either side for a while, though, in case I start to fall.'

From the motion of the horse, George soon deposited his share of the ale onto the street. Almost immediately, he felt much better.

'There's a lesson to be learned from this,' thought Kitsu aloud.

'Yeah,' they all agreed.

'I wonder what it is,' said Badger.

They shrugged, galloped out of the city gates, and were shortly on the road they knew Gi and the others would be taking.

They rode for most of the day, until both men and horses were tired and hungry. They sat at the roadside with their food-packs and watched the horses munching. They'd almost finished, when Kitsu heard something.

'Let's move off the road,' he said. 'I can hear horses.'

No-one argued. They hastily led the horses into the woods and watched. Soon after, a large band of riders went past. They were riding at a steady canter, slow enough for Kitsu to recognise a few of the men.

'Badger, did you see that?' said Kitsu.

'Yeah, it looked like Fox Loer.'

'That's what I thought.'

They watched and waited ten more minutes, but no wagon came by.

'Well, Fox is obviously not looking out for Gi,' said Badger.

'Then we'd better go and find him,' said Kitsu.

The other two stared in disbelief. 'Much as I love your enthusiasm,' said Badger, 'the horses need more rest, and so do I. But you two can fly on ahead, if you want.'

'No, I'm not sure that was all of Fox's men. There may be stragglers, so we'll stay together,' said Kitsu.

They didn't leave for another hour. There was still no sign of Gi. When it got dark, they came off the road, and slept until sunrise. Then, they were back on the road.

'Gi can't be far away, now,' said Badger. 'My bum's killing me.'

'Try standing in the stirrups a while,' George suggested.

'I tried that and it didn't help. I think I'm getting too old for this stuff,' Badger complained again.

Nobody took any notice. He'd get over it.

They took a couple more rest breaks, and finished their food. It was nearly midday when Kitsu slowed his horse and stopped them. 'I heard voices up ahead,' he said. They pulled into the shade of the trees.

Fifteen minutes later, Gi's party turned the bend and came into sight. 'You've got damned good ears,' said Badger, nudging his horse onto the road.

'It's from spending too much time as a dog.'

'Kit! Badger! It's good to see you again,' said Gi. 'Did you run into any trouble?'

'No, but we passed Fox and a lot of riders, yesterday,' Kitsu told him. 'We didn't show ourselves. Why isn't he with you?'

'He tried to steal Dash and Bayna's animals,' Gi explained.

'Bayna killed some of his men,' said Dash. 'They ran off, taking the rest of the men with them. But we have two new friends,' said Dash, with his now familiar grin.

'Yours outnumber *ours*, we've only got one,' said Kit. 'This is George, an old friend of mine, we had the good fortune to meet up with. I'll tell you about it later. George, this is Gi Mulderbish, he's a wizard.'

'Good to meet you at last, Mr Mulderbish.'

'Mr. Kitsu!' shouted Muto. 'Welcome back. Our new friends are in the wagon, sleeping probably, the lazy beggars. I'll wake them later and introduce them.'

'Did you see Striper, Kit?' asked Gi.

'Oh, yes. He gave us a silver coin each for telling him you were coming,' said Kitsu.

Gi liked that. 'What's he going to do?'

'He's sending a dozen Black-Guards to arrest you.' He paused. 'I can see how terrified you are. They might be here tomorrow, but they're going to run into Fox's men long before they get to us,' said Kitsu.

'Only twelve,' said Gi. 'That's disappointing, I thought I'd be worth more than that.'

'I told him to send twenty, but he thought twelve was enough to take down a few barbarians, and bring you in,' said Kitsu. 'I didn't tell him there were about fifty, though. Is he mad, or what?' he added.

'He might be, by now. I used to think he was just stupid,' said Gi, sadly.

'We might as well camp for the night now we've stopped,' said Brian, appearing. 'Oh… nice to see you back,' he said, looking at Kitsu, Badger… and George.

'Haggitt! Get a fire going will you? Muto, break out the sausages. I'm sure Kit's having withdrawal symptoms by now.'

'You don't know how true that is. George, you are in for a treat. Nobody cooks sausages like Muto,' said Kitsu.

'I look forward to them,' said George.

As the evening wore on, Kitsu and Badger related the story of George and the giant. It was much romanticised by all three tellers, but they were all careful not to mention that the castle belonged to George, or that it was Badger who killed the giant.

'So, it was just a couple of fairly uneventful days, then,' said Gi, as he got up to retire. He stopped momentarily and turned, 'Well done,' he said, quietly.

He arrived at the steps leading up into the wagon and opened the door and looked inside. He took a deep breath and sighed. *Gods*, he thought, *these little buggers have been farting in here all day by the smell of it.* He fanned the door for a moment, then let it drift shut.

'Muto! Get me a blanket, please.'

'Yes, Master, are you sleeping outside tonight?' he asked.

'Yes. And unless that smell goes fairly soon, I'll be out here tomorrow night, too,' he said, with some resignation.

'I can't let you do that, Master,' said Muto, with concern. 'Those little buggers are our guests; they will sleep where I put them. Not where *they* decide.'

'Leave them for tonight, Muto. We'll sort it out in the morning.' He took the blanket, and laid down by the fire. Muto threw on more wood, and helped Gi get wrapped in the blanket.

'Has anyone seen Haggitt?' said Gi, glancing around.

Muto had. 'Mr Haggitt took his sleeping things from the wagon – which wasn't easy with one hand on his nose – and he magicked himself a sleeping pod that's parked under those trees.'

'Oh, yes, I see it,' said Gi. It glowed softly from Haggitt's nightlight. 'It'll be interesting to know at what point during the night the magic wears down.'

When Muto was sure that Gi was sleeping, he got a blanket for himself and laid down close, but not too close, to Gi.

'Are you pleased to see me, Muto?' asked Gi.

'No, Master, it's my dagger. Sorry, I didn't think I was so close.' And he moved away a few inches. 'And I didn't think you were awake,' he whispered.

*

Muto was first to wake. He went to the back of the wagon and threw back the door.

'Right! You 'orrible little buggers… on yer feet!' he snapped. 'I want you *and* your smell, out of 'ere in two minutes, or I'll drag you out!'

'Are you awake, Ben?' said Thadax, quietly.

'I am now,' said Ben, still in his sleep haze. 'What's up?'

'I think we slept in someone else's beds last night,' said Thadax.

'Oh, shit. Why didn't they say something, then? Come on let's get out. I reckon this Muto might just carry out his threat,' said Ben, with some urgency.

'No, he wouldn't, would heee... Ouch!'

'Hmm... I think he would,' said Ben, peering through the gap in the door and grinning at his colleague spread-eagled on the ground.

'Are you coming?' said Muto. 'Or do I have to drag you out as well?'

'I'm coming as quick as I can,' said Ben, but it wasn't quick enough for Muto.

He grabbed Ben by his shoulders and pulled. Nothing happened.

'You'll have to wait for 'im,' said Thadax. 'You'll never lift 'im. He's wearing more lumps of iron than you can find in a blacksmith's shop.'

Eventually, Ben stood up and walked to the top of the steps.

'Muto, why didn't you say we were in someone else's bed?' asked Ben. 'I don't want other peoples' *fleas.*'

'You probably have enough of your own,' snapped Muto.

'Stop, both of you,' said Thadax. 'Let's start again, shall we?'

'Alright,' said Ben, looking at his feet. 'I'm sorry if 'e is.'

'Likewise,' said Muto.

Gi stretched and yawned, fed up with the early-morning chatter. 'Alright, Muto? Give me a hand up, and we'll sort this out.'

Muto obliged. He also picked up Gi's blanket and shook the grass and leaves out of it.

'You dwarfs will ride in the wagon during the day,' said Gi, 'but I sleep in my bed at night. Understand? Good. We'll see how that goes, shall we?'

Muto had revived the fire and the pan was hot. 'Master, can I have sausages, please!' he called.

Gi waved his hands arcanely, and breakfast was on the go. He sat by the fire and waited for the others to wake up. Kitsu first, then Badger.

'What's the plan for today, Gi?' asked Kitsu.

'I'm still thinking,' said Gi. 'I'm still half asleep, you know.'

'Well,' said Kitsu, 'hopefully, nothing too ambitious. We three haven't had a lot of sleep lately.'

'The only plan is to stay on the road to Gremanos, and be prepared for anything we might meet.'

'Sounds good to me.'

Badger was happy with it, too. 'And I think George can sleep and ride if we tie his ankles under his horse,' he said, grinning.

'I'm not deaf, Badger,' said George, arriving.

'I don't want you to fall off, George,' said Badger.

'I'll take my chances,' said George.

Remarkably, Haggitt's ovoid pod was still intact, though flickering slightly. Muto looked across from his cooking. 'I'm very tempted to go over and prod it to see if it bursts.'

'You have my full permission,' said Gi.

'No, I couldn't, Master.'

'Leave it to me,' said Ben, overhearing. Before anyone could stop him, he'd produced one of his knives, skipped the distance, and they heard a loud POP.

Everyone waited for Haggitt's reaction.

He sat up and looked about, rubbing his eyes. 'Oh, it's gone, has it,' he said simply, and started gathering his things.

Nobody spoke, or even dared look at one another for another minute.

The circle of friends at the fire for breakfast grew wider as Brian and Maurice joined in, then the two dwarfs approached, clanking and rattling as they walked.

'Is everybody here now?' asked Gi.

They looked at each other, thinking that if one of them wasn't there, how would they answer. So, nobody did.

'Good,' said Gi. 'This is what's going to happen. After breakfast, do what you have to do to make yourselves comfortable. Then, form up as usual. Now Kitsu and Badger are back, and we have George with us, they can take the rear. Brian and Maurice up front as usual. Dash and Bayna, I'll leave you free to keep a general eye out. Badger

283

can scout around, too. Ben and Thadax will sit in the back of the wagon.' He turned to them directly. 'And if you two keep farting in there, you'll be walking. Do you understand?'

Ben and Thadax put their hands behind their backs and looked down, while scuffing a foot moodily along the ground. 'Yes, Gi,' they mumbled.

'Right, gentlemen – and lady, of course – meet back here in ten minutes. Then, we're off.'

Down the road the travellers came upon the *Wayside Inn*, and Kitsu remembered the long-legged blonde. He also noted that there were a number of horses tied up outside. 'Do you want to stop, Gi?' he asked.

'It looks a bit run down,' he said, 'and going by all the horses, it's probably crowded. No, maybe the next one. This one looks like trouble.'

'I've told you, Master. Old Man Trouble always seems to know where we are,' said Muto.

'Well today, Muto, we'll press on, and perhaps he won't stir himself.'

'I hope you're right, Master.'

They passed the inn without incident. But then Badger rode up beside Gi's wagon.

'Is something wrong, Badger?'

'Probably not, but last time Kit and I rode through here, we ran into a big black-cat, shape-shifter. It killed a man and, for all we know, it ate him, as well.'

'That was not pleasant,' said Dash, showing up. 'What did you do?'

'I did nothing. I didn't know it was a shape-shifter, but Kit guessed. He killed him,' said Badger.

'Let's hope he was the last of them,' said Gi. 'Is that a rider coming this way?' he added, looking up the road.

'Not Old Man Trouble, is it?' said Muto.

'No,' said Kitsu, 'it looks like one of Baron Striper's Black-Guards.'

'Now, *he's* Old Man Trouble.'

The rider was agitated when he pulled up in front of Brian and Maurice.

'What's the hurry, friend?' Brian asked.

'We ran into barbarians... about fifty of 'em. They took the others prisoner. I rode into the woods and lost them,' he said panting. 'Am I glad to see you people!'

'What was your troop doing heading this way?' asked Kitsu.

'We were ordered this way... to arrest Mr. Mulderbish. But that's not gonna happen now, is it?' said the soldier, looking across to the wizard on the wagon, and assessing things remarkably well.

'Er... no,' said Kitsu. 'I'd say the odds against you here are worse than they were with the barbarians.'

'Who was your commander?' asked Gi.

'Sergeant du Merde, sir. I think the leader of the barbarians will use him as a ransom hostage.'

'Oh dear,' said Gi. 'In that case, du Merde and his men are going to die. The Baron won't pay to get a few men back.'

'How far up the road are they?' asked Kitsu.

'Two – maybe three hours,' the soldier replied.

'Well,' said Gi, 'du Merde is just following orders, he doesn't deserve to get killed for it.'

'He's a soldier,' said Kitsu. 'Soldiers die. The Baron won't care if he loses a few.'

'You sound as though you know Striper better than I do,' said Gi. 'But I'm thinking we should rescue du Merde and take him with us to Striper as *our* man.'

'You've just given me an idea,' said Kitsu.

'I've just given myself one,' said Gi. 'And I think it's the same as yours.'

'Yes. We'll rescue du Merde – for which he will be eternally grateful. We'll tell him the Baron expected him to get killed. He'll want revenge. And he knows the castle so well he'll help us get in,' said Kitsu.

'That's more or less what I had in mind.'

'What's your name, soldier?' Kitsu asked.

'Stanley, sir,' the man replied.

'Well, Stanley, you can call me, Kit. I'm not a sir. And you can ride ahead with Brian here and show us where you were ambushed.'

'Yes, er… Kit,' said Stanley, still taking in his revised circumstances.

A couple of hours up the road, they found the place. There were certainly a lot of tracks from horses milling around, but if there was a skirmish, there was little evidence of it. du Merde had obviously thought discretion better than valour, as he was outnumbered about four to one.

Further up the road, the tracks veered north off the main route, showing the route Fox had chosen to take du Merde and his men.

'Wait up, Stanley! Gi, it's getting dark. Do you want to do this tonight, or wait till morning?' Kitsu asked him.

'What's your plan, Kit?' asked Gi.

'I want Badger to ride in and identify du Merde and his men, while me and George take care of the barbarians,' explained Kitsu.

'As simple as that, eh?' said Gi. 'There are about fifty men in those woods. Three of you can't defeat them.'

'Better give me the dwarfs as well,' said Kitsu.

'What? *Both* of them?' queried Gi.

'One would do, but if they come as a pair… I'm okay with that,' said Kitsu, grinning.

'I was joking, take them both,' said Gi.

'Good,' said Kitsu. 'This is what I'd like you to do…'

* * *

76

Muto drove the wagon up the road and stopped where it would effectively block the track Fox took. Brian and Maurice stood their horses either side of the wagon, while Bayna and Dash stood firm between them, their snow-white animals shining in the dusky light.

Ben and Thadax followed Badger up the track just in time to see Kitsu and George disappearing into the trees. 'Turn away!' said Badger. 'Watching those two change will give you nightmares.'

Moments later, two dragons took to the air and circled around, looking for signs of a campfire. 'I'm grateful the moon's almost full,' said Kitsu. 'I'd hate to fly into a tree up here. To your right, George.'

'I see it,' replied George. 'Must be a clearing.'

'Just need to circle till Badger finds the soldiers,' said Kitsu.

'How are we going to know?'

'Badger and I can thought-speak,' Kitsu told him. 'I sensed he could do it, and with a little work it happened. When he's found them, he'll let me know.'

Down on the ground, Badger heard voices ahead and raised a hand, indicating they should stop. He dismounted. 'One of you to mind my horse; the other to come with me,' he whispered.

'I'll mind the horse,' whispered Thadax.

'Good. Ben, come with me,' he said, thankful the dwarf had managed to silence his mobile armoury.

They crept along the track until they saw the barbarians spread around three campfires.

'Ben, can you get through the undergrowth and see where the soldiers are?' whispered Badger.

'I can see 'em from 'ere,' said Ben, who'd shinned partway up a trunk. 'They're over there.'

'Can you see where their weapons are?' asked Badger.

'Could be the pile on the right. It's got a guard, so probably weapons.' said Ben 'Do you want me to 'it 'im?'

'What? *How?*' said Badger.

Ben bobbed down and up and pirouetted in one blurred move. Something struck the guard's head and he collapsed to the ground. 'Like that,' said Ben.

'Did you just throw a stone?' asked Badger.

'No… a rock. Let's go see if he's alive, shall we?' said Ben.

'Alright, but keep low,' said Badger.

'Ha, bloody ha, as if I haven't heard that one before,' said Ben.

'Sorry, Ben. I wasn't thinking,' said Badger, apologetically.

'Can you do that again to the guard with the prisoners?'

'There's only one?'

'Yeah. They're all roped together. Have you got a knife?'

'You're full of funnies tonight, aren't you?'

'What…? Oh.' Badger covered a laugh. 'I'll be grabbing the swords.'

Ben chose a rock and performed again. The soldiers saw the guard drop, and an armoured dwarf approaching them brandishing an evil-looking knife. 'Which one of you is du Merde?' asked Ben.

'I am,' said du Merde, not sure he should have.

Badger appeared and dumped the weapons. 'Free them and get them going while I contact the others.'

Ben quickly slashed at ropes amid a wincing group of soldiers. 'You heard him, du Merde. Grab your weapons and get your men out of here. That way. Fast!'

'Can you hear me, Kit?' asked Badger.

'Yes, my friend. Are the prisoners clear?' Kit replied.

'Yes, but don't forget they need horses. Kill barbarians only, please,' said Badger.

Kitsu banked and flew higher to where George was circling. 'All clear, George. Kill as many as you can, but avoid the horses. We'll need a dozen or so.'

George climbed higher, then stalled and fell into a steep dive. When he was tree height, he roared fire into the camp and swerved away steeply into the air as Kitsu came in from the other side raking the ground and lighting up a scene of utter panic.

Both dragons beat the air to gain height and see what damage they'd inflicted. From Fox's point of view, the sight of most of his men lying blasted on the ground was calamitous, but it was a good result for Kitsu and George.

'Set a ring of fire around what's left of Fox's men,' called Kitsu, 'then we can find Badger... and our clothes.'

'We need to round up horses first,' said George. 'Any more fire's going to scatter them further. Speaking of fire, we need to check it's dying down. We don't want the whole bloody woods alight!'

The dragons circled low, checking the area and looking for the horses in the moonlight. Soldiers' horses were preferable to barbarians', as they were less wild. But when they stampeded from the fires, they'd all run together.

'George, we're not helping like this. We need to change back to humans and mount a couple of them, and see if we can get more to follow?' suggested Kitsu.

'It's worth a try. They've stopped running,' said George.

'Have you tried shifting into something else while you're flying?' said Kitsu.

'No... does it hurt?' asked George.

'I don't know, but I want to be closer to the ground before I try it.'

He found shrinking to the size of an owl a strain, especially on the wings. He was aware that if things didn't occur in the right order, he might plummet. But he sorted it out, if a little frantically.

When George saw that Kitsu had achieved it, he made the change himself, and both men settled on the upper branches of a tree.

'They've calmed down now, Kit,' said George. 'And some of the soldiers' horses have stayed together.'

'I'll take those,' said Kitsu. 'See if you can get some of the others.'

The owls swooped to the ground and changed into humans.

'Bugger!' muttered George. 'I wish I had my boots on. Now, I've got to get muck out of my toes.'

'That's the trouble when you grow up in a castle like a prince – not used to a bit of dirt,' observed Kitsu.

'I'll have you know...' started George.

'Only kidding,' Kitsu assured him, sniggering.

'Not totally wrong, though,' said George, hauling himself onto a barbarian's horse and distastefully scraping some mess off his foot. He reached out and gathered the reins of a couple of other mounts. Kitsu climbed onto a Black-Guard's mount. A couple followed and he reached for their reins.

'Circle behind, George. When I lead off, start nudging them after me. It might work.'

It worked well. Kitsu found himself leading about twenty horses, and he no longer needed to hold the reins of the ones beside him. George was even able to join him up front. They were only a short distance behind the rescued soldiers.

'This is embarrassing,' said du Merde. 'Being rescued by a dwarf.'

'Two dwarfs and a Badger, to be exact,' said Ben. 'But if you're not happy, you can always go back.'

'No, this is the better option,' said du Merde. 'At least you're not going to kill us, *are* you?'

'Our friends won't, but at this rate, we might,' said Ben.

'Oh… where are you taking us?' du Merde asked him.

'Do pay attention. To our friends. The people who organised your rescue,' said Ben. 'Then you can tell 'em how grateful you are.'

'LOOK OUT!' shouted Kitsu, as twenty horses came galloping down the track. 'Help us stop them, Badger!'

To their credit, the soldiers instantly grasped what had to be done and grabbed for bridles, bringing all but a few to a halt.

'Well done, lads,' said Badger, riding up. 'I was thinking these men might have to walk back to Gremanos.'

'Did you see what else we got?' said George, with a satisfied grin.

Badger looked around and saw du Merde's two pack-horses still loaded with supplies.

'Pure luck,' said Kitsu.

'Don't knock it,' George countered.

'Excellent!' Badger rubbed his stomach. 'Something for Muto's stores and our bellies.'

'Where's the Sergeant?' asked Kitsu.

Badger glanced about. 'Ah… Sergeant! Will you come over here, please? And, Kit… do you want your clothes back now?'

'Of course. George, too. But he'd like you to hang on to his boots for a while,' said Kitsu.

'Oh dear,' Badger sounded concerned, but didn't look it. 'What's he trodden in?'

'Horse shit!' snapped George.

'You'd better wipe some off George, or you'll spread it down the inside of your trouser leg,' Badger warned him, while noticing he already had.

'Give them to me, Mr. George,' said Muto, holding his hands out, one for the trousers and the other holding what passed for a towel.

While George was cleaning his feet, Muto disappeared momentarily and returned with the trousers freshly-laundered and pressed. He passed them to George, who wondered how that had happened.

'Don't ask, Mr George. Just be grateful, and put them on.'

'I'm most grateful, Muto. Thank you,' he said, and bowed respectfully. Muto blushed slightly.

'Sergeant du Merde,' said Kitsu. 'I believe you know Mr. Mulderbish?'

'I do,' said du Merde, 'it would seem that I am in your debt again, sir.'

'That would be a yes,' said Gi. 'But I would like this to be the start of a good friendship. My companions will vouch that I have mellowed somewhat since I was in your little prison,' said Gi.

'I was merely acting under orders, sir. Nothing personal. I hope we can put that in the past.'

'Were you acting under orders this morning when you were ambushed on your way to arrest me?' said Gi.

'Yes, sir, but…'

'Did the Baron tell you there was a horde of barbarians in your way?' asked Gi.

'No…' said du Merde. 'Are you saying Striper knew we'd meet them? He could've got us all killed.'

'Did you know that I have several guards of my own, who, I hasten to add, are capable of making short work of the few men you were given?' said Gi.

Looking around him, du Merde saw Brian and Maurice, the two dwarfs, Dash and Bayna, and the three who came to his rescue, and he had no choice but to agree with Gi.

'And I tried to tell Striper that a dozen guards were useless against two wizards, but... but what are you two doing here?' asked du Merde, looking at Brian and Maurice.

'We didn't get paid for months, so we considered ourselves unemployed,' Brian told him.

du Merde's head dropped. 'I can't blame you. The Baron never sent money to pay any of you. I'm surprised you stayed as long as you did. What happened to all the men I left in the hills by the river?' du Merde went on.

'Fox Loer took some of them, and we killed the rest,' said Gi.

'What? I had about a hundred men in those hills,' said du Merde, in amazement.

'Yeah, we know,' said Badger. 'So, whose side are you on now?'

'I can only offer meals and relative safety,' said Gi. 'But if you can help me, I will make sure you and your men are well paid.'

'I will speak with them, if you don't mind,' said du Merde.

'I think you should,' said Gi. 'I need all of them with me.'

The Sergeant called his men together and walked them a short distance from the wagon. 'What I'm going to tell you is not pleasant,' he began. 'The Baron sent us on this mission knowing full well we were riding into an ambush, and if it wasn't for these people...' he said, signifying Gi and the others, 'we'd all be dead. We're now being given the chance to work for Mr. Mulderbish and help him get back at the Baron.'

'You mean we're not working for Striper anymore?' said Stanley.

'That's exactly what I mean. I'm taking up Mr. Mulderbish's offer. Are you with me?' asked du Merde.

'No, Sarge, we're with Mr. Mulderbish,' said an ad-hoc spokesman.

'Thank you, men,' said du Merde. 'I'll tell Mr Mulderbish.'

When du Merde and his men returned, Muto had a fire going and food cooking. 'I hope you don't mind, Sergeant, but I thought I'd share your supplies,' said Muto.

'No, that's fine… do I know you?'

'Probably Sergeant, I've been everywhere,' said Muto.

'You remind me of someone. Your wagon looks familiar, too…'

'Of course it does, Sergeant. We've been together a long time,' said Muto, avoiding eye contact.

'Well… I'll leave you to it,' said du Merde.

'Right you are, sir. I'll call you when it's ready.'

Haggitt joined the elves and conjured them some food. 'We'll be in Gremanos in a couple of days,' said Haggitt. 'Have you any plans after we take the castle?'

'We will consider our options, Haggitt. But eventually we must return to our own dimension. It's too dangerous for our animals here,' said Dash.

'And I would like to see my parents again,' added Bayna. 'They must be very worried about us.'

'I will be at a loose end, as we say,' said Haggitt. 'Though I don't imagine my parent will be too worried about me.'

They laughed, but weren't sure they should have.

* * *

77

The next day, everybody in Gi's camp awoke refreshed. The Black-Guard tended to keep to themselves, although a few renewed their friendships with Brian and Maurice, which Gi approved of. It was going to be a lot easier if they all got along. Gi asked Kitsu to find du Merde and bring him over to discuss the remainder of the journey.

'Thank you for coming, Sergeant,' said Gi. 'Please sit. Kit and I want to go over the plan with you.' du Merde sat down and before he was settled, Muto brought all three men a hot drink.

'This is very civilised,' commented du Merde. 'Thank you.'

'Yes, thanks, Muto,' said Gi. 'Now, Sergeant...'

du Merde raised a hand and stopped him. 'I'm working for you now, Mr. Mulderbish. I no longer have a rank,' said du Merde.

'What's your name, then?' asked Kitsu.

'Just call me, Cat,' said du Merde. 'Although Sergeant might be better in front of the men.'

'Cat, I doubt that will be necessary...' said Gi. 'I fully expect you'll *earn* their respect over the next few days. Now, to business. So that we keep some order now there are more of us, l want you to split your men into two groups: six riding in front, ahead of Brian and Maurice, and six behind the wagon. You, Cat, can ride free, keeping a watchful eye on them. Though, when we reach Gremanos, I want you at the front, leading *all* your men. I'll move Brian and Maurice to the rear with the snow elves.'

'What do you need from me, Gi?' asked Kitsu.

'When we're close to the city, I want you, Badger and George, to ride up to the castle and tell Striper I'm coming with four hundred barbarians.'

Kitsu smiled. 'He'll probably shit himself if I tell him that.'

Cat laughed at the thought. 'He has nowhere near enough men to defend against those numbers.'

'Thanks, Cat,' said Kitsu. 'That was my next question. Just how many does he have?'

'Two hundred... no more. Fewer, in fact, with my men taken out of it.'

'What do you think he'll do,' asked Kitsu, 'after a visit to the privy?'

'Knowing him, he'll pull all his men together and march to Lord Welkin's castle. There's more men there, and it's easier to defend.'

'Against a regular assault,' said Gi. 'But we have Kit and George.'

'The shapeshifters who helped rescue us,' said Cat, acknowledging them appreciatively.

'The very same,' said Gi, proudly.

'It seems we have an abundance of horses, Mr. Mulderbish, are you planning on keeping them?' asked Cat.

'Well, we only need fifteen. Obviously, mostly for you and your men. Plus a couple for the dwarfs. Do we have two small ones among them?' Gi queried.

'The pack-horses are small. They should do nicely,' said Cat.

'Ideal,' said Kitsu. 'We can adjust the harnesses – and redistribute the supplies. Most of the men made a start on that over breakfast.' He smiled. 'Okay, Cat. Will you go and get Ben and Thadax.'

'Must I?' moaned Cat. 'I've done nothing to make them like me, yet.'

'Well, when you give them the two pack-horses, that should change their minds,' said Kitsu.

After some persuading, Cat managed to convince the dwarfs to come and see the horses.

'They're more like mules,' Ben complained.

'Yes, Ben,' said Thadax, 'but not so wide. We could ride them.'

'Can you ride?' Ben asked him.

'I don't know,' replied Thadax. 'I've never tried.'

'No, neither have I,' said Ben.

'Do you know why that is?' asked Thadax.

'Course I do!' said Ben. 'Nobody's ever given me a bloody horse.'

'Are you actually giving us these, then, Sergeant?' asked Thadax, glaring from under his bushy eyebrows.

'Yes... they're yours to keep.'

After a pause, Ben turned to Thadax and half whispered… 'See, I told you… he's not *that* bad, is he?'

One small remark like that was enough to put a spring into du Merde's step.

Later that day, Cat and a couple of his men fashioned two serviceable saddles for the dwarfs, and they now sat bolt upright on their horses, looking terrified out of their minds.

'I think I need the stirrups higher please,' said Ben, through gritted teeth.

'You've only got an inch to play with…' said Stanley.

'Don't be bloody personal!' snapped Ben. 'Just sort these stirrups out.'

Stanley did his best, but had the feeling that whatever he did for the dwarfs, it would never be right. 'Is that better?' he said, making sure Ben's riveted boots were into the stirrups as far as they could go. Taking in all Ben's armour and weaponry, he was thinking it was just as well the horse was used to carrying a burden.

Ben tested the stirrups, and grudgingly supposed they were fine. 'What about you, Thadax?'

'Mine are alright,' said Thadax. 'I'm shorter than you.'

At last, thought Stanley. 'Okay, do you know where you'll be riding?'

'Wherever it takes me,' said Ben, having not tried the reins.

'I think we'll probably be safest with the elves,' said Thadax.

'Well, don't get in their way,' said Stanley, climbing onto his own horse, thinking, *Yeah, riding with the elves, probably is the safest place.*

'Sergeant!' yelled Gi.

'Coming, sir.'

'All, ready. Take the lead, and get us to Gremanos.'

The Sergeant galloped to the front and his men followed.

They put a lot of miles under their hooves that day. And unexpectedly, the dwarfs didn't complain, but actually enjoyed the novelty of riding. Though they'd be whingeing about sore butts for a while. In the late afternoon, they reached the hill overlooking the city. With Muto's help, Gi climbed down off the wagon to join Kit and the

Sergeant. Muto stared across in awe at the size of the city, and the castle with its huge curtain walls on the hill right in the centre. The rest of Gi's party clustered to look, too, though the soldiers were familiar with the place.

'We'll stay out here tonight.' Gi announced. 'Muto, get a fire started. The rest of you men, see to your horses.'

'Kit, I want to go into the castle looking like we're Cat's prisoners. Once we're in, I'll repeat Kit's news about the four hundred barbarians ready to storm the castle, whenever I give the signal.'

'Are you sure he'll fall for it?' said Kit. 'There'll be lookouts on those turrets.'

'Remember, I know your capabilities, Kit. I want you to create the illusion of about a hundred campfires up here. He'll go for it all right.

'No problem. I'll let them burn for a couple of hours, then let them die down one at a time. It's more realistic.'

'Have you done this before?' asked Gi.

'Many times.' He smiled. 'I'll find George.'

* * *

78

Inside the steep stone walls of Baron Striper's castle, the Watch Commander knocked on the mess room door.

'Who is it?' called a voice from within.

'It's me, Major, the Watch Commander.'

'I'm just off home, man. Can't it wait till morning?'

'I don't think so, sir. You should come and see this.'

'Oh… alright,' sighed Pinch, and hung his coat on the back of his chair again. 'This had better be important.'

'It is, sir. You need to come out to the front battlements, sir.'

'And throw myself off,' he muttered to himself. Outside, he found himself staring into the gloom at a hundred points of light.

'What do you think they are, Commander?' Pinch wondered, curious, but unconcerned.

'I know exactly what they are, Major. They're campfires. And that many would mean four to five hundred men.'

'Shit,' Pinch cursed. 'You'd better warn the Baron.'

'No, sir. You're in charge… you do it.'

'Alright, Commander, come with me,' said Pinch.

'Yes, sir…' came the deflated reply.

They trudged through low-lit passages and empty courtyards until they reached the Baron's office door, and Pinch knocked. It had been a busy day, so Striper was stretched out on his shabby leather couch by the window. 'Come in…' he yawned.

Pinch did – and suddenly found himself alone. The Watch Commander had sprinted back to his post.

'What is it Major?' Striper sighed.

'There are numerous campfires across on the hill, my Lord. The Watch Commander estimates there's about five hundred barbarians up there,' Pinch informed him.

'Can I see them from here, Major?' asked Striper, through half-closed eyes.

'No, my Lord. Perhaps if you stood up, you might,' said Pinch, the sarcastic.

'Oh… if I must.' Striper struggled to get upright and looked out the window. '*Shit*, Major, are you sure there's only five hundred?'

'Could be six by now my Lord. They're arriving all the time,' Pinch lied.

A sound like silk ripping came from Striper's direction.

'Are you alright, my Lord?' asked Pinch. 'You seem to smell a bit unwell.'

'I think I need the privy,' said the Baron, urgently. 'I won't be long.'

When the Baron had left the room, Pinch pushed the window up a bit, and smiled to himself. *When he comes back, I'll tell him there's seven hundred up there now. That should get him thinking.*

He paced the room, waiting for Striper's return. Which seemed like forever.

'Pinch! I was having a think…' said the Baron, striding back into the room.

'Yes, my Lord, I'm sure you were.'

'I don't have enough men here to protect me. And if they see six hundred men…'

Pinch interrupted. '*Seven* hundred now, my Lord.'

'What? Another hundred while I was in there?'

'Yes, my Lord.'

'Do we have a bugler?' Striper demanded to know.

'Probably, my Lord.'

'Well, get him to bugle all the men into the courtyard. I need to address them,' demanded Striper. 'And do it now!'

Pinch didn't stop to salute. He swivelled on his heels and marched out of the office. Back on the battlements, he found the Commander of the Watch. 'Do we have a bugler?'

'We did have, Major, but he rode off with du Merde some time ago and we haven't seen him since.'

'Well, Commander,' said Pinch, 'the Baron needs one to call all the men into the courtyard. Now! He wants to speak to them.'

'I'll get someone on it immediately, Major.' He ambled along the battlements and down the steps to the stables. Ollie would know.

Ollie greeted him cheerfully. 'Hello, Nobby. Don't see you down 'ere very often.'

'Ollie, do you know if we have a bugler?'

'Only Gripper's dad, as far as I know,' Ollie replied.

'A *bugler…* not a burglar,' said Nobby.

'Yeah, Gripper's dad's quite good at the bugle, too. So am I, come to that. I'll even do you a request, if you've got one,' Ollie boasted.

'I do have one, actually, son,' said Nobby.

'What's that?'

'Get your bugle, then get your arse up on those battlements and play the tune called *Everybody assemble in the courtyard*,' Nobby ordered.

'Right-ho, Nobby… you hum it and I'll play it.'

'Oh, don't bother… just get around to all the men and tell them to get down there, on the double,' he said, hurrying away. 'Baron's orders!'

Ollie didn't fancy searching out two-hundred men. And he wasn't about to. He went out into the courtyard, and looked up at the battlements to see who was about. He saw a guard leaning against the wall, puffing on a home-made pipe. 'Is that you, Jimmy?' Ollie called up.

The guard peered down over the parapet wall. 'Oh, hi, Ollie, what do you want?'

'Baron wants all the men assembled down 'ere in ten minutes, can you tell whoever's next along from you to pass it on, please.'

'Will do, Ollie…' Jimmy cupped his hands round his mouth and shouted… 'Wayne!'

Ollie went back up the steps to the distant sound of news spreading. 'Nobby!' he called. 'You can tell the Baron they'll all be here in ten minutes!'

'How did you make that happen?' said Nobby, quietly impressed.

'Wasn't easy,' he said, deadpan. 'I asked 'em.' He turned back down the steps. 'Give me a shout if you need anything else.'

* * *

79

The agitated Baron paced to a window overlooking the courtyard and saw all his men standing shoulder to shoulder. *I must be going deaf,* he thought. *I never heard that bugle.* Pinch knocked. 'Come in!' the Baron shouted.

'All in the yard, my Lord,' said Pinch, proudly.

'I know that, Major. I can see them.'

'They're waiting for you to address them, my Lord,' Pinch told him.

'Lead the way, Major. I'm right behind you.'

Emerging into the courtyard, the Baron had forgotten how small it was. There were two hundred men rammed into about two hundred square feet of space.

'Can you all hear me?' he said, in a slightly raised voice. The reply was a mixture of 'yes' from the front, and 'whad 'e say?'' from the back.

'Right. Let's go up a floor, Major, and open a window. It'll be easier to talk down to them from there,' said Striper.

'You've never needed to go up a floor to do that before,' Pinch whispered to himself.

'No... I haven't, Pinch. I'll remember that.'

'Yes, my Lord. I'll remind you,' said Pinch. 'In case you forget.'

The Baron threw open the window. 'Can you hear me now!' he called.

'Yeah!' came a solitary reply from the back of the crowd.

'Good!' Striper studied them briefly. 'I want you, you, you and you, in my office in five minutes. And I want you two to bring the small wagon round and leave it outside that door there.' He pointed to the bottom of the stairs. 'The rest of you get your horses and form up behind the drawbridge. We're moving to Lord Welkin's castle tonight and I want to be there by sunrise. Understand?'

There was much grumbling, and much arguing over who he'd meant when he said 'you' Which Striper didn't hear. He shut the window and hurried back to his office, with Pinch keeping pace behind him.

'Aren't you going to tell them why?' asked Pinch.

'Certainly not,' said Striper. 'If I tell them there are seven hundred barbarians waiting to attack, you and I will be going to Lord Welkin's castle on our own, Major.'

'Do you honestly believe they would desert you, my Lord?'

'Like a shot, Pinch. Same as you. There'll see an excuse, they'll find an opportunity, and they'll be gone,' said Striper, being morbidly realistic. 'Now help me get this chest out of the cupboard.'

'I've never seen in there before,' said Pinch.

'I should hope not, Major. And from that remark, I can only assume you've looked in the others?' said Striper, accusingly.

'No, my Lord. They're *all* locked,' said Pinch.

'Ah… so you tried them, then?' said Striper.

'Oh, yes, my Lord. Looking for a new pencil,' Pinch lied, hoping his smirk didn't betray him.

'I take it you didn't find one.'

'No, my Lord, I had to ask Maureen for a favour,' said Pinch.

'Did she give you one?' the Baron asked.

'Oh, yes, my Lord, she's a very obliging young lady.' Pinch smiled.

The Baron was thinking: *she never gave me one… she always charged.* He didn't say a word. There was a knock on the already-open door. 'Come in!' snapped the Baron, eyeing the four burly soldiers blocking the light from the doorway. He'd chosen well.

'I need this chest taken down and loaded onto the small wagon,' said Striper.

'Oh, yeah,' said the biggest man in the group, 'what's the magic word?'

Striper thought for a moment. 'Is it… *abracadabra?*'

'I think he's expecting you to say, *please,*' said Pinch.

'*Please?*' said the Baron. 'What's that mean?'

'It means you're grateful for… Oh, don't bother.' Pinch turned to the men. 'Please, men. For me,' he almost pleaded, exasperated.

'Anything for you, Major,' said the biggest of them.

'Why do they do things so willingly for you, Major, but not for me?' the Baron whined.

'Do you want the honest truth, my Lord?'

'Yes, Major,'

'They think you're an ignorant shit, my Lord,' Pinch flinched, waiting for the outburst. It never came.

'Oh. I didn't realise they thought that highly of me, Major. Perhaps I should try being a bit more tolerant. Come on, let's go downstairs with them, I don't want to lose sight of my luggage.'

When Striper and Pinch emerged into the courtyard it was empty but for the small wagon and four soldiers pushing the chest into the back.

'Do you want to drive, my Lord? Or shall I?' said Pinch.

'You'd better do it, Major. I'm rubbish with machinery.'

They climbed aboard and Pinch took the reins. He looked down at one of the men. 'Who's in charge tonight, Jason?'

'Nobby's the Watch Commander, Major,' replied Jason.

'No, who's actually in charge?' asked Pinch.

'I don't know whose turn it is today, Major. Give me a minute, and I'll check.'

'Don't worry,' said Pinch. 'I need to get this wagon moving.'

'They've left a space for you, Major, halfway up the line,' Jason informed him. 'They're waiting for you.'

Pinch steered the wagon out of the courtyard and into the main square, where he joined the rest of Striper's Black-Guards.

'Give the order to lower the drawbridge, please Commander,' said Pinch, as he continued to drive up the line to his allocated place.

'Yes, sir,' said Nobby, as he saluted and rode to the front.

'You're really good at this, Major,' said Striper. 'I didn't realise.'

'I know,' said Pinch. 'Sometimes, I even surprise myself.'

The drawbridge clanked and lowered majestically and the lines moved off in two columns. 'My word, Major, don't they look impressive.'

'They do, my Lord. And that's about all they are,' said Pinch, as he drove the wagon under the portcullis and rattled across the drawbridge. 'When the last of the men are through, Ollie, will you raise it, please.'

'No worries, Major, I'll see to it.'

'And put the lights out,' he murmured to himself, feeling there was something final about this.

* * *

'Oh dear, Kit, have you seen this?' said Gi, as he watched all the Black-Guards leaving the castle.

'Are they coming out to meet us do you think?'

'Battles rarely start in the evening. Let's see which way they go,' said Gi.

After a short time, it became obvious that the Black-Guards were leaving for Lord Welkin's castle.

'Damn...' Gi cursed. 'That's ruined things.'

'Cat was right,' said Kitsu. 'We'll have to re-think this. We can't meet them head on. We're badly outnumbered.'

Badger walked over. 'Gi, the buggers are leaving the castle undefended. Shall we go in and take it?'

'No... but take Brian over there and see if you can find out what's going on,' said Gi. 'I don't see any point in us all going, yet.'

'Let the fires go out, George,' said Kitsu. 'They don't matter now.'

'If the soldiers are all out in the open, Kit, why don't we send in the dragons?' suggested George.

'It's a thought. What do you say, Gi?'

'I don't want to incinerate everybody,' said Gi. 'But if they all make it to Welkin's castle, that's what may have to happen, because of the sheer weight of numbers we'd be up against.'

'We wouldn't have to burn them, Gi,' said George. 'Dragons sweeping low and breathing fire is enough to unnerve most people. They'd scatter.'

'And you'd only have to scatter half of them,' said Cat, joining in. 'the rest will take flight of their own accord. I know these men of old. Very few are that loyal to the Baron.'

'Are any of them archers?' Gi wondered.

'No, sir,' said Cat. 'All swordsmen. The archers will be at Lord Welkin's castle.'

'Yes, of course...' said Gi, thinking aloud. 'That puts a different light on it. Kit – you and George shift yourselves into the biggest, scariest beasts you can come up with, and scatter Striper's men – not all of them. Leave him just a few. I need him to get to Welkin's castle. But I don't want him putting another two hundred men on the battlements,' said Gi. 'For what I have in mind, I want Striper and Welkin in the same place.'

'One thing, though, Gi.' Kitsu looked troubled. 'Striper's a wizard, isn't he? Won't he be sending fireballs up at us?'

Now George looked troubled, too.

Gi shook his head. 'Trust me, if he sees two monstrous dragons swooping around spitting fire, he won't be drawing attention to himself by lobbing fireballs at them. Every ounce of his magic will go into shielding himself.'

Cat nodded vigorously to this.

'Okay…' said Kitsu. 'Ready, George?'

Moments later, two of the most evil-looking dragons imaginable took to the sky and circled the night sky above the Baron's men.

'They haven't noticed us yet, George. Shall we drop down and introduce ourselves?'

'Yes, and if there's any resistance, we can flame them,' said George.

'Okay, but remember what Gi said. Leave the wagon and some of the Baron's men,' said Kit. 'We only need to scare the shit out of the rest of 'em.' Kitsu could hear George laughing. *Oh dear*, he thought, *he's going to have too much fun…*

Next thing Kitsu knew, a red-hot shaft of fire streaked through the middle of the men following the wagon.

'George, what are you doing?'

'Sorry, Kit, I get carried away when I look this mean. We need to scare them,' he confirmed, all apologies. 'But you have to admit, that certainly did the trick.'

Striper's men were in disarray. 'Won't this thing go any faster!' the Baron yelled, keeping one worried eye on the dragons, the other on the box in the back.

'No, my Lord,' said Pinch. 'But the horses will.'

'Well, get them going as fast as you can!'

George had circled around and was coming head on at the soldiers leading the Baron's column.

'Don't burn them, George!' Kitsu shouted in his head. 'That wagon's got to get through!'

George veered away, brushing the heads of some of the soldiers, knocking them to the ground. Some with their heads missing. Loose horses were running in all directions, fleeing the dragons. Most of the remaining Black-Guards were doing the same.

Kitsu made a quick assessment of how many were left and considered they'd left the Baron with about twenty. He and George made one last flypast to help those retreating on their way back to Gremanos.

Pinch drove his team like a maniac, accompanied by a small band of soldiers who'd stuck blindly with the wagon, not knowing what the hell else to do.

* * *

Badger and Brian rode down the hill to the sprawling city. A group of men were idling outside the first tavern they came to inside the gates.

'Why would two strangers be riding into our city when all the guards have gone?' asked one of them, raising suspicions.

'We saw them ride out and wondered what was going on,' replied Brian.

'There's supposed to be seven hundred barbarians coming down off that hill to sack the place,' said another.

'Strange,' said Brian. 'We've just ridden down from there and we didn't see any.'

'Do you think he means us?' murmured Badger. 'I used to be a barbarian, after all.'

Brian grinned. 'That would be funny. We're a few short of seven hundred.'

'We're just travelling through,' said Badger. 'Hoping to find somewhere to sleep the night.'

'Help yourselves. With all the guards gone, there'll be plenty of room in the barracks up at the castle. You two don't look the sort for hotels.'

'That's a bit cheeky,' said Brian. 'But dead right. Can you point us in the right direction?'

'You really want me to tell you where the castle is?' the man said, not believing his ears. One of his companions sniggered.

Brian looked up the hill at the grey-stone building that loomed against the night sky over most of the city. 'So that's where it is.'

Their hooves echoed across the empty market square. 'They must be new in town,' said Brian. 'Most people know me and Maurice.'

They rode up to the castle, and detoured towards the rear where the moat became more of a culvert. Here was the stable entrance. Brian pounded on the solid wooden door.

'Just a minute,' said a cheery voice on the other side. Footsteps got louder, a bolt slid back, and the door squeaked open slightly – then flung wide. 'Brian? Where have you been?' Ollie welcomed him with his usual chirpy enthusiasm.

'I didn't think you'd still be here,' Brian smiled. 'It's good to see you.'

'You, too. Now what can I do for you?' Ollie asked.

'My friend and I need a place to bed down for a few hours,' replied Brian.

'The horses could do with some feed as well,' Badger prompted him.

'I'll see to the horses,' said Ollie. 'If you go up the stairs over there, you'll come to Gripper's office. He'll find you somewhere to kip. Tell him I sent you.'

'Who's Gripper? I thought that was Pinch's office,' said Brian.

'You must remember Gripper – Barter Stogie's son? He's taken over from Mr. Pinch,' Ollie updated him.

'What's happened to Pinch?' asked Brian.

'He's in command of the Black-Guards. It's Major Pinch, now.'

'What?!' He cried in disbelief. 'Where is he? I'd love to see him.'

'He rode out with the Baron. You wouldn't believe it. I heard Pinch winding him up, saying there were hundreds of barbarians outside getting ready to storm the castle. We almost laughed our socks off,' said Ollie, grinning. 'So, you must be them!'

'Apparently. This is my friend Badger. He's part-qualified; he used to be a barbarian,' said Brian.

'Nice to meet you Mr. Badger,' said Ollie. 'Have you come to storm us on your own, then?'

Badger smiled and patted Ollie on the shoulder. 'Well, it's quiet enough for it, son. But not tonight, no.'

'Upstairs, you said, Ollie?'

'Yeah, just knock and wait, Gripper might be busy.' He winked, though it was lost them.

At the top of the stairs, Brian knocked on the office door. 'Anybody in?'

He tried the handle and the door swung open. Brian peered inside, just in time to see a young lady disappear through the door opposite.

'What can I do for you gentlemen?' said Gripper, tucking his shirt into his trousers.

'We'd like somewhere to stay the night. Ollie said you could help,' said Brian.

'No problem, the barracks are pretty much empty right now, what with all the guards shipping out to Lord Welkin's castle. The Baron thinks this place will be overrun by hundreds of barbarians…'

'That would be us two,' confessed Brian.

'Huh? …And he didn't want to be here when it happened. The bastard,' said Gripper, with all the conviction as he could muster.

'Are there many soldiers at Lord Welkin's castle, do you know?' asked Badger.

'Not as many as you'd think… about a hundred, no more. Welkin's the Baron's son – and a true Striper – he won't spend more than he has to,' Gripper told them.

'You've been most helpful, Gripper. Give my regards to your dad when you see him,' said Brian.

'That might be a few days. He's delivering a message to Lord Welkin,' said Gripper.

'Well, whenever,' said Brian. 'Let's find somewhere to bed down, shall we, my friend?' Badger followed Brian back down the stairs and across the courtyard, then had second thoughts. 'I don't think we need to stay now, do you?' said Brian.

'No, we've got what we came for. Might as well get the horses and go and tell Gi what's happening.'

'Thanks for everything, Ollie, we've decided to move on, after all,' said Brian.

Ollie was fine with that, and ushered them to the stable door. 'Can't tempt you to stay for a bit of sacking?' he asked Badger on the way out.

Back on the adjacent hill, Badger found Gi. 'Looks like Kit and George were successful,' he said.

'What did you find out?' Gi asked.

'Mostly what we already know, really, Gi. The Baron took fright and left the castle with all his men for Lord Welkin's place. Oh, we did learn that Welkin has fewer than a hundred men. Do you plan to use Striper's castle tonight, Gi?' asked Badger.

'Yes, I think so,' said Gi. 'We can go to Lord Welkin's in the morning.'

* * *

82

Elgett Chirgwin walked the battlements on Welkin's Castle. This was something he did most days routinely, but this morning, as he strolled alongside Barter Stogie, there was actually something to see from up there.

'Do you see what I see?' said Elgett.

'Probably,' said Barter. 'Where are you looking?'

'Up the road. It's a wagon,' said Elgett. 'In quite a hurry.'

'Then I suggest you get down there and open the door before it crashes into it,' said Barter, but he was talking to himself. Elgett had already taken off down the steps. 'Drop the drawbridge while you're at it – it's the Baron!' Barter yelled after him.

'Oh, shit. That's all I need,' moaned Elgett.

Now Elgett Chirgwin was confused. Should he open the door first, or drop the drawbridge? He decided to find Lord Welkin and let him sort it out. He ran to Welkin's private quarters and hammered on the door.

'Wake up, my Lord, quick. Your father's coming up the road!' Elgett shouted.

'What? Shit! Get down there and stall him. I'm not dressed yet!' Welkin shouted at the door.

'The drawbridge is up, my Lord. That should slow him for a while, but he's already smashed the gatehouse door down,' said Elgett, frantically.

'Well get down there and open the front door… It's already got one hole in it, I don't want another one!'

'Yes, my Lord. Shall I take my time?'

'No, he'll only get angrier the longer we keep him waiting,' said Welkin, pulling on his boots.

Elgett fled to the front door and opened it as far as it would go, then he ran to the drawbridge. 'You still up there, Barter?' he called.

'What do you want?' Barter replied.

'I need someone to help me get the drawbridge down? It's a bitch trying to do it on my own.'

'There's nobody else up here, Elgett. So… it's going to be a bitch!' Barter called down.

'The Baron will be sooo mad if we keep him waiting, Barter. Please, help me,' Elgett pleaded. 'I'll owe you.'

'Oh… alright, wait a minute.' The minute dragged on until Barter arrived.

'What do you want me to do?'

'Can you reach up and swing off that lever? It should dislodge that pin or whatever it is, so the wheel can spin and the chains should unwind,' said Elgett.

'Fascinating.' Barter looked skywards. 'And what are you going to be doing while I'm swinging, then?'

'I'll be ready to catch you when you fall off the stool,' said Elgett.

'Is that what usually happens?' said Barter. 'Why don't you get someone taller to do it?'

'I can't do that. I won't be so indispensable if others can do what I do?' said Elgett.

'Don't be daft, man,' said Barter, 'anyone can do what you do.'

Elgett tapped the side of his nose. 'You know that, and I know that, but Lord Welkin doesn't.'

'He can't be that blind,' said Barter.

'Oh… I assure you he is. Watch your fingers! It's coming down,' said Elgett, somewhat relieved.

The drawbridge bumped the ground on the far side, and half a minute later the Baron and Pinch thundered across and onto the small parade ground. The remaining members of the Black-Guard had fallen behind long ago, when they realised they were no longer being pursued by dragons.

'Get my son down here, Major,' said the Baron. 'We need to talk.'

Ouch….! Pinch thought, *I hate that when my wife says it.* 'I've not been here before, my Lord. What room does he use?'

Striper nodded across the front lawns towards the keep. 'Go to that door, the front door with the *hole* in it, and shout his name. He'll come down.'

Pinch jumped from the wagon and walked purposefully to the open door. 'Lord Welkin!' he shouted. 'Your father's here! He wants to see you!'

Welkin was finishing dressing while striding down the stairs two and three at a time. 'Oh... and who are you?' he asked, when confronted with Pinch.

'Major Pinch, Lord Welkin. This way, please.'

'Oh, no...' sighed Welkin, 'he's not going to bollock me in public again, is he?'

'Not for me to say, Lord. I was just told to get you down here.'

Striper was strutting towards the front door. 'Father, how nice to see you...' said Welkin, with open arms.

'Yes, I know,' said Striper. 'Now, get four strong men to get that chest out of the wagon and up to my room!'

Welkin rushed out onto the lawn. 'Elgett, find four men and get my father's luggage in, please!'

Without thinking, Elgett agreed. Then realisation hit home. *What's 'e on about? There's only me and Barter here.* 'Barter! The Baron wants 'is luggage brought in.'

'Well... I'm not doing it. Get Striper's men,' said Barter.

'That's what I was doing when I asked you,' said Elgett.

Barter huffed, and strolled over to the wagon to look inside. One look at the chest, and he flatly said, 'No.'

'Why not? You're one of the Baron's men, ain't you?'

'Not that sort,' said Barter. 'I deliver messages. And anyway, 'ave you seen the size of it? There's no way you and me are goin' to shift it.'

'Let's just drive it into the stable and tell him to use his Black-Guards to shift it,' said Elgett.

That done, the pair went back inside. 'Well? Where is it?' asked the Baron.

'We couldn't move it, my Lord. We had to leave it on the wagon. But we've put it in the stable till you can get your men to move it,' Barter told him.

'Where are your men, Welkin?' Striper demanded.

'Er... things have been a bit slow lately, Father. So I gave them a few days off,' then quickly added, 'without pay, of course.'

'Hmm...' breathed Striper. 'How many men have you got, now? Three, four hundred?'

'Not exactly. Sixty-five, Father,' said Welkin, sheepishly.

'What? Sixty-five *hundred*?' said Striper, in astonishment.

'No, just sixty-five, Father. That's all I can afford,' said Welkin staring at his boots.

'What? So, what have you done with all the money I've sent? The gold? The silver? Where is it? Tell me!' Striper was beginning to rant.

'I thought that was for me, personally. I didn't think you'd want me wasting it paying soldiers,' Welkin whined.

'Well, you'd better get your army of sixty-five back here now. Gi Mulderbish is coming with an army of seven hundred barbarians and two bloody great dragons.' Striper was getting redder by the moment. 'Do you want to keep this castle, young man? If so, you're going to have to fight for it.'

'But Father, this *is* my castle. You gave it to me,' Welkin pleaded.

Striper breathed a long, deep sigh. 'You don't understand. I took this place from Gi Mulderbish.' He let that sink in, and by the look on Welkin's face, it did. 'And now he wants it back. What have you done with all the gold? You've still got it, I trust?' said Striper, ready to explode.

'This is getting a bit intense, my Lord,' said Pinch. 'I think I'll wait outside.'

'As you wish, Major. But don't go far,' said the Baron.

'No, sir.' Pinch quietly made his exit.

Elgett and Barter were waiting around outside. 'Barter... where's the wagon?' asked Pinch.

'We put it in the stable, Major. Out of sight,' he replied.

'Good thinking,' said Pinch. 'There don't appear to be any guards here. And I know you're not guards, but can you two share the watch tonight? – keep a lookout for the barbarians, and let me know when you see them?'

They looked unsure.

'It's as much in your interest,' said Pinch, 'as anyone else's.'

'We'll sort something out,' said Barter.

'Good. Thanks. I'm going to find something to drink. When I come back, I'll be sleeping in that wagon if anyone wants me.'

* * *

Gi's small troop transferred to Striper's castle that night. There was no resistance from the few staff in residence. Brian and Badger were good ambassadors.

Kitsu and George chose to enjoy their really scary dragon shapes for a while longer, swooping around isolated farmhouses and lighting up the night sky. When they neared Gremanos, Kitsu learned of the move to the castle from Badger.

Muto and Badger were waiting on the castle battlements when the two dragons flew in and settled impressively on the walkway.

'Wow,' said Badger, 'You wouldn't want to meet those two on a dark night.'

'That would seem to be exactly what we're doing,' observed Muto.

'Yeah, you're right.'

Moments later, having retrieved their clothes, Kitsu and George walked back to their two friends.

'Mr. George! What's happened, your arm is cut in several places. Goodness… look at all that blood,' said Muto, with concern.

'I got cut hitting Striper's men on their helmets as I flew passed. It will heal,' said George, confidently.

'Better let him see to it, George. He'll have you better in no time at all,' Kitsu assured him.

Down in the courtyard, Muto climbed into the wagon and rummaged for bandages. Then, he remembered where he'd put them – in the box underneath – and climbed out again.

'Are you afraid of pain, Mr. George?' asked Muto.

'Depends,' said George, warily.

'Well, just hold your arm out, and look the other way,' Muto advised him.

George didn't feel any pain, just a warm sensation of something wiping the dried blood away. 'Ah… that's good,' said Muto, 'just superficial. I won't need to sew you up, Mr. George. Just be still a little while longer. I'll just splash a little cleansing spirit on it.'

'OW!' George jumped. 'I wasn't expecting that.' Then he felt something being wound around his arm and the sting of the spirit, and, indeed, from the cuts themselves became just a fading memory.

'How does he do that?' he mouthed at Kitsu.

Kitsu shrugged, 'I have no idea… he's just that good.'

'That's so soothing, I've half a mind to cut myself again,' George grinned.

'Please, don't. Mr. George, I'm not *made* of bandages…' He shuddered at the thought. 'That's a creepy image, isn't it?'

'Don't go there, Muto,' said Kitsu. 'I've encountered beings like that in the Eastern desert, and I couldn't get away quick enough.'

'Okay,' said George. 'Let's go and report to Gi, now, shall we?'

'Where is he, Muto?' Kitsu asked.

'He's taken the Baron's old rooms,' said Muto. 'Don't look at me like that Mr. Kit, I changed the sheets first.'

'You think of everything, Muto. If you were a lady, I'd marry you,' Kitsu smiled.

'You're not my type.' Muto grinned. 'But, maybe in another life, who knows?'

'You forget, I can be almost any type,' Kitsu countered. 'It's alright, my friend, I have my eyes on another.' His mind wandered momentarily to the leggy blond in *The Wayside Inn*.

'Shall we go and wait for Gi in Striper's office,' Badger suggested. The others agreed and followed him to the Baron's dingy office.

'Oh dear,' whispered Muto, 'just look at all the dust in here.' He ran his finger along the mantelshelf, then wiped it on the knee of his trousers. 'It's worse than I thought.' He started opening cupboards.

'What are you looking for?' Kitsu asked him.

'A duster and some polish, for a start,' Muto snapped. 'I can't have the Master staying in here, it's filthy.'

'I'm sure Gi won't mind a bit of dust for one night,' said Kitsu.

Muto tried a drawer and a bottle clinked against a glass.

'*Hello*... what have you found there?' said Badger, holding up an expensive-looking bottle with a smooth-looking amber liquid in it.

'Any more glasses in there?' asked George.

'No,' said Muto, 'but I can see a few in that cupboard by the fireplace. How many do you want?'

'Five?' said Badger.

'No, not for me,' said Muto. 'I need to have a clear head in the morning.'

'I'll go and get Gi,' said Badger. He didn't have far to go. The wizard was in the next room. He tapped gently on the door.

'Just coming, Badger. Give me a minute,' said Gi.

Badger was taken aback. How did Gi know it was him at the door? 'Right you are, sir. We're in Striper's office... next door.'

'I know,' Gi replied. 'I can hear you.'

Badger started running through the conversations of the last few minutes, trying to remember if anyone had said anything detrimental about the old mage. Then he thought. *No. We never have; why would we start now?* He shrugged, and walked back to the office.

Gi entered through an adjoining door. 'Oh, sorry, I thought this was the privy.'

'I think it's on the other side,' said Badger.

'Well, I don't need it yet, so let's get on with it,' said Gi. 'Are the remainder of Striper's men back yet, does anybody know?'

'Only about twelve of them,' said George. 'I think the rest deserted.'

'Did any of them go to Welkin's Castle?' asked Gi.

'We saw twenty, unless any of them deserted on the way,' said Kitsu.

'So, we'll be facing up to a hundred soldiers,' said Gi, quietly.

'That's not bad, Gi,' said Kitsu. 'Me and George frightened a lot more than that on the road. If we send the dragons in again, I don't think they'll be brave for long.'

'I would rather win them over to our side, if I can,' said Gi. 'I want to isolate the Baron and his son, so it's just me and them. Others shouldn't have to die because we are fighting.'

'That's always the way with war,' said George, sadly.

'What about Haggitt? You'll want him by your side,' said Kitsu.

'I'd rather not,' said Gi. 'I don't want him getting hurt, either. No… Just me.'

'Let's think about that in the morning when we're travelling,' said Kitsu.

Muto woke next morning feeling lonely. It seemed that last night, everybody decided to sleep alone and they were in rooms spread all over the castle. *Well… gentlemen, I'm not spending half my morning looking for you lot,* he thought. *Now, where did I see that kitchen?* He found it on the ground floor, in the opposite corner from the stables, and inside he saw what he was looking for. A huge brass gong with a long handled hammer.

Fortunately, it was on castors. Muto wheeled it out into the courtyard. He spat on his palms and rubbed them together, then picked up the hammer. 'Are you ready?' he whispered.

A very loud and resonating *Boing!* echoed around the courtyard. 'Wow,' said Muto. 'That was impressive. Now, will you go any louder?' He struck it again, and yes, it would. *BOING!* it rang out again. Then, unexpectedly, there was a metallic clink, as something hit the gong.

There was an arrow stuck in it and it was now beginning to droop. The archer ducked back behind a curtain when Muto turned his way. Maybe somebody didn't appreciate an early-morning call. He took no notice. He couldn't see who it was, but he knew he would find out in a very short while.

'Breakfast!' he shouted, and stood back in a shadowy doorway. The first person to appear was Ben de Little.

'Oh, no… not you again,' Muto muttered to himself. 'Be professional Muto, it's not for much longer,' he added.

As Ben went into the kitchen, Muto stepped out of the shadows and followed him in. 'Take a seat,' said Muto, icily. 'This won't take long.'

Ben sat on the bench and heaved his legs over. 'Hmm… nice boots…' commented Muto, 'a bit impracticable though, I imagine.'

'Don't know what that means,' said Ben, 'but they fit all right.'

'That's all that matters, then, isn't it,' said Muto, trying to be positive. 'Did you manage to wake anybody else while you were clanking over here?'

'Not as many as the bastard hammering on that gong,' Ben replied, with some serious grumpiness.

'I take it, that it was you who shot the arrow into it, then,' said Muto.

'What?' said Ben. 'Me? No. Do I look tall enough to handle a bow?'

'No, perhaps not.'

'No, it was one of Baron Striper's soldiers,' said Ben. 'He was aiming at you! Anyway, he's dead now. I got to him before he took his second shot.'

'Oh,' said Muto. 'It would appear you have saved me from serious injury. Thank you, Ben.'

'Death's pretty serious,' said Ben. 'No thanks needed, just give me some food, and so much for there being no archers among Striper's men.'

It seemed like a long time before the rest of the men arrived in the dining area. Then everybody was talking at once.

Muto stood on a chair and banged two empty metal jugs together. 'Can I have your attention, please? This is important!'

'What's going on, Muto?' said Gi.

'I'm coming to that, Master.' He had their attention. 'One of Baron Striper's loyal guards entered the castle late last night, or earlier this morning. This man made an attempt on my life, but thanks to Ben he is now dead. What I'm saying is... that you should all be vigilant – *That means 'keep your eyes open', Ben,*' he whispered – 'in case there are any more out there.'

Everybody looked around at the few of Striper's men who'd returned and were now among them. Kitsu stood up and did a head count. 'It looks like everybody's here, Gi.'

'I don't see Haggitt or the elves,' said Gi.

'They're in the stables,' said Kitsu. 'Dash and Bayna don't leave the care of their animals to anyone else.'

'Of course,' said Gi. 'But I value their company, as I do all of you. Once Muto has fed you all, get mounted and ready to go. We'll come back and occupy this castle when we've defeated the Baron!'

A cheer went up from all concerned. Even Striper's former men.

'Now,' said Muto, 'get in line, there's plenty for all of you. So, no pushing!'

* * *

After twenty men had visited the privy, Gi and his men, and the small troop of ex-Black-Guards formed up in front of the castle gates. Cat was at the front, assuming his old role and looking pleased with life, even though hardly a centurion. He stood up in his stirrups and looked over his shoulder. 'Ready, Stanley?'

'Yes, sir!'

Cat waved them forward and shouted, 'Ho!'

'Ho?' said Brian, 'What's that all about?'

'It means move out,' said Maurice, vaguely remembering it.

'Well, we *are* moving out,' said Brian. 'So, it obviously works.'

A few hours up the road, they came upon debris from Kitsu and George's attack. Most bodies were charred remains, some were decapitated, but one man was sitting up, with a hand raised.

'See what he wants, Stanley,' said Cat.

He dutifully rode ahead the short distance. 'What do you want?'

'What? Can't you see, man? I'm mortally wounded.'

'Right,' said Stanley. 'Hold on.' He rode back to Cat. 'Sarge, he says he's mortally wounded.'

'I don't think so,' said Cat, reacting swiftly. He jumped down and raced to meet the man, who had miraculously recovered and was running at Stanley with a long bladed dagger in his hand. Cat drew his sword, nimbly side-stepped him, and caught him with a solid blow to the back of his head as he stumbled by. '*That's* mortally wounded, son!' said Cat, rolling the body over to look at his face.

'Do you know him, Sarge?' asked Stanley.

'Nope, never seen him before,' said Cat, getting back on his horse.

'Is everything alright up there?' Gi called out.

'All's well, Mr. Mulderbish,' said Cat, arriving back at the head of the small column. He raised his arm. 'Ho!' he shouted, contentedly, and they all moved off again.

* * *

Later that morning, the front riders saw Lord Welkin's castle. Just before midday, Cat held up a hand. 'Halt!' he shouted.

Everyone stopped while he rode back to Gi's wagon. 'The castle's just below the hill, Mr. Mulderbish. Do you want to go directly there, or camp here for the rest of the day and attack in the morning?' asked Cat.

Gi called Kitsu, 'Kit, would you fly over and see what's happening, and how many we're up against?'

'Shall I take George with me?' asked Kitsu.

'No… one eagle won't draw attention, but two might,' said Gi. 'There's something else that George can help me with, if you wouldn't mind.'

'Sure,' said George, 'what's on your mind?'

Muto helped Gi down off the wagon while George dismounted. Then Gi took George's arm and they walked to the top of the slope that led down to the castle. Gi was waving his hands and pointing at different parts of the castle, while George was copying some of Gi's gestures and nodding his head, showing he understood.

'Do you think that's possible, George?' Gi asked, at last, not totally sure.

'Don't see why not, Gi, I know how those things work,' said George. 'And I've fixed a few in my time.'

'You can take Badger with you.'

'I was going to suggest that, in case it turns out to be a two-man job.'

'Do you want to wait until Kit gets back, or go now?'

'I'll get Badger. If he agrees, we'll go now. The sooner we start; the sooner we finish,' was George's view.

'Good man,' said Gi. 'Try not to break anything beyond repair, please.'

'Huh.' George was only mildly reassuring. 'We'll do our best.'

Badger was keen to be involved, before he even knew the plan. And before long, he and George were riding together at walking pace down the slope.

'I can't see many guards,' said Badger. 'I don't know if that's a good sign or a bad one.'

'For what we're going to do, Badger, the fewer the better,' George told him.

'There goes Kit,' said Badger, seeing the bird high over the castle, out of bowshot range, relying on the bird's exceptional eyesight.

'I might have to resort to a change, Badger, if things don't go well,' said George.

'So, what exactly are we going to do?' asked Badger.

'Gi wants the gatehouse door jammed open and the drawbridge down. And he wants us to fix it so it'll take a few days to get back up again,' George explained.

'Oh... is that all?' said Badger, with a wry smile. 'Well, we can do that... can't we?'

As they drew closer, they could make out a single guard watching from the battlements. He seemed inattentive, just having a quiet smoke, judging by the grey clouds forming around his head.

'He'll see us in a minute,' said Badger.

'Probably... but two riders coming down the road won't give him much cause for alarm,' said George.

'I'd rather he didn't see us,' said Badger. 'But I can't see how we avoid it.'

'Can you talk to Kit from here?' George asked him.

'I don't know. What do you want me to say?'

'Ask him if he can drop down hard enough to knock that guard over the battlements,' said George.

'I'll see what he thinks.' Badger closed his eyes, '*Kit... can you hear me?*' he thought.

'*I'm counting – can it wait?*'

'*Yes, let me know when you're done,*' Badger replied, mentally.

'*Sixty-nine... right, what's the problem?*'

'Me and George are on the approach road. He wants to know if you can knock the guard stationed over the drawbridge, into the moat.'

'It would be one less soldier to worry about, Badger... and Gi said to keep the killing to a minimum. Hitting the moat will be better than hitting the stone floor,' said Kitsu.

'He said he'll try and force him into the moat, George,' said Badger.

'Good, let's get a move on, then,' said George, and both men rode their horses at speed down to the gatehouse.

Unexpectedly, considering they should have been readying for an assault, the gates were open, and there were no guards on duty. What's more, the drawbridge was being lowered – and the body of the guard on watch was sprawled on the leading edge. Oops. When the drawbridge hit the ground, two riders thundered across from the castle on stolen horses.

The leading rider was Barter Stogie, hotly followed by Elgett Chirgwin. George pulled out into their path. 'Whoa... Stop!' said George, raising his hand.

'Sorry, mister,' said Elgett, urgently, 'gotta go. There're seven hundred barbarians coming this way.'

'Then I suggest you go that way,' said George, pointing in a different direction from the one Gi was coming.

'Thanks, mister!' And off they rode.

'I wonder if they were in Kit's head count,' Badger grinned.

'How many did he see?' asked George.

'He said sixty-nine, but it's looking like sixty-six, now,' said Badger. 'The odds are improving.'

An eagle screeched overhead. Kitsu was flying back to Gi.

Badger and George, hardly believing their luck, walked across the bridge and located the mechanism that raised and lowered the drawbridge.

'Don't do too much damage, Badger. Gi wants this back up and running in a day or so,' said George.

'What about... if we just levered the chains out of the main cogs?' said Badger. 'That's not too much, is it?'

'That would be perfect,' said George. 'Give me a moment and I'll slacken them so you can lever them off.' Chains began to clank, but they weren't getting any looser.

'How're you doing?' asked Badger.

'I think these chains have been repaired so many times, I'm not getting any slack at all,' said George.

'The only other thing we can do then, is find a way to lock them where they are, then,' suggested Badger.

'Can you see anything we can use?' asked George.

'Is this any good?' said Badger, offering George the lance that the guard was leaning on when he fell.

'That'll do fine,' said George, snapping the metal point off the shaft. He wedged it into the chain and knocked it in the rest of the way with a rock.

Badger tested George's handiwork and was satisfied that it would do the job as Gi had intended. 'What's next?' he asked. 'Ride back and tell Gi we've done it, or wait here for him?'

'You stay, I'll go back,' said George. 'Just make sure no-one tries to fix the bridge.' He re-mounted his horse and trotted back over the bridge. He dismounted on the other side, and pulled the remains of the dead guard away from the bridge and rolled him into the moat, where he was immediately attacked by a shoal of alarmingly ferocious fish.

Bloody hell, he thought. *He'd have been better off hitting hard stone after all!* The turmoil in the water ceased almost as soon as it started and all that was left was a skull and a battered rib-cage. George purposely walked his horse away from the water's edge before remounting.

When George reached the top of the adjacent hill, he was greeted by Catscart du Merde.

'Come, George,' he said. 'Gi is talking with Kit.'

George followed as Cat turned his horse and walked down the short line of soldiers.

'George! Are you okay, where's Badger?' asked Gi. 'Is he injured?'

'No... he's alright. I left him guarding the drawbridge.'

'Good. You were successful, then,' said Gi. 'Kit tells me there are now sixty-six soldiers in there, as far as he can tell. Does that include the Baron?'

'I didn't see him, Gi.'

'Well, we know he must be in there, so we'll have to be careful,' said Gi.

'Are you ready to go now, Mr. Mulderbish?' Cat asked.

'Yes, I think we are, Sergeant. Move 'em out,' said Gi.

Cat rode the short distance back to the head of the column.

'Wait for it…' said Brian, almost whispering.

'Ho!' shouted Cat.

'Ah… told you.' Brian grinned.

At the bottom of the slope, the soldiers fanned out each side of the wagon and stood waiting.

After a while, when it was apparent that they were not going to be challenged, Brian and Maurice walked their horses across the drawbridge.

'Oh… Hi, Badger, everything all right?' asked Brian.

'I must say I'm a bit worried, lads,' said Badger. 'I've been here for ages now, and I haven't seen a soul, so watch your backs, it might be an ambush.'

Brian and Maurice rode on to the open front door. A man was standing in the shadows by the stables. 'Psst… over 'ere,' hissed a voice.

'Hold my horse, Maurice, and wait here,' said Brian. 'I'll see what he wants.'

'Careful, Brian.'

Brian drew his sword and walked towards the man in the shadows.

'Thank goodness,' said Pinch. 'Brian – am I glad to see you.'

'Mr Pinch? What are you doing here?'

'I'm trying to escape,' said Pinch. 'The Baron's in a rage and he's looking for somewhere to hide. I convinced him that seven hundred barbarians are coming to storm the castle. He doesn't know yet, but half the men he had left have gone, the other half have barricaded themselves in the main hall and they're not going to let him in.'

Brian laughed. 'Come and see the barbarian horde, Mr. Pinch, you'll be surprised how little room they take up.'

Pinch walked to the drawbridge with Brian and saw the men standing in front him. 'Where are they?'

'This is it,' said Brian. 'But we have big plans afoot. Come on, I'll introduce you to Mr. Mulderbish.'

Pinch arrived in front of Gi and waited for him to speak.

'Do I know you?' Gi asked.

'We met briefly, Mr. Mulderbish. I was the Baron's secretary,' Pinch replied.

'What are you doing here, then?' said Gi.

Pinch told Gi how he'd exaggerated the barbarian horde, and about Striper's men deserting, which resulted in the Baron running to Lord Welkin's castle… and the dragons… Pinch tailed off the saga.

Gi was smiling broadly at the Baron's series of catastrophic events.

'How many men has Striper got now, Mr. Pinch?' asked Kitsu.

'At the moment, sir? None… at least, none loyal to him,' said Pinch. 'And those still here have barricaded themselves in the main hall.'

'Where's Striper now?' Gi wanted to know.

'He was in the top tower, overlooking the parade ground, sir,' Pinch told him.

'Muto, drive the wagon into the castle, please. Cat… you and your men follow me, and when we're inside reform the line.'

'Yes, sir,' said Sergeant du Merde, still relishing his command.

* * *

Muto drove the wagon to the centre of the parade ground and stopped. du Merde's men re-formed the line behind him. The others in Gi's band took their horses to the stable and looked for somewhere safe to stand. Everything was quiet, even the birds were silent.

Gi got down from the wagon. 'Muto, move the wagon out of the way, please.' Then he turned to Cat, 'Send six of your men to hold the doors on the main hall, Sergeant. I don't want any of Striper's men getting out of there until we're ready. Then, tell your men to get their horses out of the way and come back here.'

Cat saluted smartly and made various hand gestures to his men that relayed Gi's orders.

Now Gi stood alone in the middle of the parade ground. The stage was set. He cupped his hands to his mouth and shouted.

'Striper! Come down and face me! Or I will come in and find you!'

The threat was met with silence, until a fireball hurtled noisily down from the tower. Gi saw it in good time and a mere motion of his hand steered it away. 'I can do this all day, Baron… now get your backside down here!'

Another fireball buzzed Gi's way from a top window, and met the same response as its predecessor. 'All right…' said Gi. 'I'm coming in. This is between me and you, nobody else needs to die today.' Another fireball buzzed down. Gi didn't bother to deflect it, as it was hopelessly off target. He reached the open front door and ducked inside.

Due to his concentration on the Baron, Gi didn't notice when Muto and Haggitt slipped inside ahead of him.

'What are you doing in here?' he hissed.

'We're watching your back, Father. If you insist on fighting him on your own, we will make sure the Baron is on his own too,' said Haggitt.

'Well, stay behind me,' said Gi. 'I don't want you two getting injured.'

'Don't fuss so, Father. Dash and Bayna are already upstairs somewhere,' Haggitt told him.

'Alright, but keep out of the way,' said Gi, a little irritated by their concern, which he mistook for interference. He started to make his way cautiously up the stairs. A door slammed ahead of him and he heard footsteps running along a passageway on the next floor. 'I can hear you, Striper!' Gi called out. 'I know exactly where you are. This is my castle... remember, Striper? Remember when you tricked me into your black pyramid and stole it from me. I've come to take it back, Striper.' Gi's anger echoed around the tower.

Gi trod warily, on full alert, edging his way to the next floor. He heard a noise and ducked around a corner as a fireball spun along the passageway. 'It'll go worse for you if you damage *my* castle, Striper.' Gi moved quickly in the direction the last fireball had come from. 'Come on, Baron... let's not play cat and mouse... meet me on the parade ground... just the two of us,' said Gi, calmly. 'I promise you it'll be quick.'

A key turned in a lock. A door opened with a squeak. It groaned again as the Baron tried to close it quietly. He turned the key on the inside and locked it again. Gi knew exactly where the Baron was now.

The armoury.

'That's all I need,' he said to himself. 'He's got to get by me when he comes out of there. There's no other way out.'

The tip of a crossbow bolt came through the door with a thud about head height. *Well,* Gi thought, *I'll have to replace that door now, so it won't matter if I damage it some more.* He stood back and raised both hands. Three fireballs burst into existence in front of him. He threw the first two at the door, making a hole big enough for the third to hurtle though. It exploded inside in a shower of light that temporarily blinded the Baron and blasted the damaged door back towards Gi, catching him a glancing blow on his shoulder. It was enough to knock him to the floor and give the Baron a chance to barge and stumble by in his haste to escape.

Striper ran along the passageway, occasionally twisting to send a fireball back at Gi.

Haggitt had been watching from the far end and sent two fireballs back at Striper. One burst by his shoulder and the other just above his head. Not enough to penetrate his magical shielding.

Striper was getting confident. He didn't think Haggitt's aim or power was going to improve and started throwing fireballs at him two and three at a time.

Haggitt waved them away as his father had shown him and started to come forward. He wasn't throwing fireballs anymore. He was just walking towards the Baron.

Then the Baron shouted, 'Get him, Welkin!'

A dagger flew by Haggitt's head. He turned instinctively and unleashed two fireballs at Lord Welkin, who had no chance to evade them. Both hit him squarely in the chest, and he fell slowly forward onto his face.

'No...!' shouted Striper, in anguish. 'What have you done!?' He ran to his stricken son, throwing a quick succession of fireballs at Haggitt and Gi. He had a sword now, which he must have picked up in the armoury, and was bearing down on Gi as the old wizard struggled to get to his feet. Then, with the sword raised triumphantly to bring down hard on Gi, the Baron's face turned abruptly from anger to surprise and he fell to one side, with one of Bayna's long arrows through his neck.

'Damn,' muttered Muto. 'The Master wanted to do that.'

'Help me up, Muto,' said Gi, struggling to his knees. 'It doesn't matter, now. It's done.'

'No, Master, but I know you were so looking forward to it,' said Muto, in a commiserating tone.

'I must go and thank Bayna. Striper had the better of me just then. I'm getting too slow for all this.'

'Never, Master,' said Muto. 'You've only suffered some bruises. I'll have you as good as new in no time.'

'I know you will, my friend. So, let's go. Do whatever it is you do, and help me find my way around my castle again,' said Gi.

* * *

87

Down in the stables, Brian and Maurice were talking to Pinch, who was getting ready to take the small wagon back to Gremanos.

Brian lifted a corner of the canvas and peered in. 'What's in the chest, Mr. Pinch?' he asked.

'I don't know… all I can say is, it's very heavy, and it's the only luggage the Baron brought with him,' said Pinch. 'I'm taking it back to Gremanos to get a locksmith to open it.'

'No need to do that, Mr. Pinch, we'll get Muto to take a look,' said Brian. Pinch didn't argue. He had a good idea what was in the chest, but wasn't certain. 'Muto is good at everything,' Brian added, proudly.

'I think we should see the Sergeant first, Brian – see if there's anything we can do while we're waiting for Gi and Muto to come back,' said Maurice.

They found Cat walking across the parade ground with his helmet under his arm. 'Brian… Maurice,' he said, when he came closer, 'everything all right?'

'Yes, Sarge. We were just thinking that Muto would probably be able to open Striper's big chest in the wagon,' said Brian.

'Show me,' said Cat. The three of them went back to the stables.

Cat eyed the locks and then felt in a small leather pouch attached to his belt. He extracted a selection of keys on two rings. He separated one of the keys and tried it. 'No… too small,' he muttered, then he tried another… Click! The lock released. The men looked at each other in anticipation. Cat tried the other lock… Click! But the box still didn't open.

There was another lock in the top of the lid, but the hole was square. Cat checked the key rings again and there it was… a square key. He inserted it into the lock and turned it. Something inside moved… he turned it twice more and the lid raised, just enough for him to get his fingers under it. He looked at the others. 'Ready?'

'Yes…' came the chorused reply.

For reasons known only to himself, Cat stood to one side as he lifted the lid. There was a small crossbow inside. Turning the key had wound the string back, and the bolt was about to fly when Cat showed just how quickly he could move by snatching it from the stock like a cobra striking. 'That could've hurt somebody,' he said, frowning.

'Yes… you Sarge. Well done,' said Brian. 'Now, what's in it?'

Cat took the crossbow out and lifted an empty tray that hid the contents below. 'Gold coins…' said Brian.

Shit, thought Pinch.

'There must be *thousands* in there…' said Brian. 'Better find Gi, they're probably his, knowing how Striper was stealing from him.'

'Somebody mention me?' said Gi, entering the stable.

'Yes, Mr. Mulderbish. Look,' said Brian, standing aside to reveal the open chest.

'I wondered where that went. Where did you find it?'

'It was here. Striper brought it from Gremanos,' Brian told him.

'There's a lot of gold coins in there, whose are they?'

'We thought they must be yours, Gi,' said Brian.

'No, the chest is mine,' said Gi.

'The coins belonged to the Baron,' said Pinch.

'Well he won't be needing them anymore, then,' said Gi.

'I'll take them back to Gremanos, then, shall I, Mr. Mulderbish?' said Pinch, hopefully.

'Not yet, Mr. Pinch. Before you do anything else, I want you to get me a list of all the people who worked for Striper. And for how long, please,' said Gi.

'I can do that in an hour or so,' said Pinch.

'Then do it, please,' said Gi, waving him away. 'And don't forget to include the Sergeant and his men.'

'Muto, come with me, please. I want to show you something,' said Gi, hushed and a little conspiratorial. Muto followed Gi out through the front door. Gi looked at it and shook his head. 'Can you write, Muto?'

'Why, yes, Master. Would you like to dictate a letter?'

'No, as we go around the castle, I'm going to tell you the things that need mending. Will you write them down, please?' asked Gi.

'Of course, Master. Give me a pencil and a paper,' said Muto.

Gi waved his hands and muttered something that sounded a bit obscene, then passed a small pad and a pencil to Muto. 'We'll start with the front door.' Then instead of going upstairs, Gi turned to a cupboard under the stairs. He opened it and went inside. 'Bring a torch, Muto,' he whispered, and when Muto followed him in, Gi moved a stone in the wall. A door section opened into a room like a cellar. 'Raise the torch higher, Muto.'

Muto took another couple of steps into the room and held the torch over his head. And gasped. 'Master... is all this yours?'

'I hate to say it, Muto, but, yes. And this is not even half of it,' said Gi. 'There's another room on the ground level, somewhere. All we have to do is find it.'

'I've an idea, Master. Are you willing to trust Mr. Kit? If you told him there's so much gold hidden around here?' said Muto, quietly.

'Not completely,' said Gi. 'What are you thinking?'

'Get him to change into a dog. Ask him to smell the gold, and see if he can sniff it out,' Muto suggested.

'Does gold have a smell? Gi said, doubtful.

'Not to us, but I bet it does to a dog – especially a magical kind of dog like Kit.'

'Okay. I'll take a few coins, and we'll try it. We'll get Kit to search the castle on that side,' said Gi, pointing away from the stable area.

'Right, Master. You tell him while I get my crossbow.'

'What for?'

'Master... it's easier to kill a treacherous dog, than a dragon if our trust is misplaced.'

They left the secret room and found Kit. He agreed to try, and had a good sniff at the coins. He led Gi and Muto through the passages, sniffing at every door. Gi was beginning to think it wasn't working, but then... Kit smelt something. He stopped and gave a toothy canine smile. Gi felt around the for an entry point.

Muto noticed a slightly darker stone and pushed. A door sized section of wall slid smoothly back with a quiet hiss. Gi grabbed a torch from a wall-bracket and went inside. Muto followed and slammed the door shut behind him, leaving Kit outside.

'Master… are you now the richest man alive?' asked Muto.

'Hmm… could be. But not for long. Come, I'll tell you what I want to do with it,' said Gi.

* * *

'Mr. Pinch!' Gi called as he walked back into the stable. 'Have you got that list for me?'

'Yes, Mr. Mulderbish,' said Pinch, handing it over. 'I was looking for you.'

Gi looked at the names and the lengths of service. 'Excellent, Mr. Pinch. And, I see you've been there the longest… almost *twenty years*, I see.'

'Yes, Mr. Mulderbish.'

'What did Striper pay you?'

Pinch looked embarrassed.

'Come and whisper it,' said Gi.

Pinch whispered.

The old mage raised his eyebrows. 'Come with me, Mr. Pinch, we'll talk in private.' Gi led him away from the others into a small side room that appeared to be where the stable hands took their tea breaks. 'Write forty thousand next to *your* name, and twenty-five thousand against Sergeant du Merde's. Brian and Maurice, ten each. And du Merde's men five each. Do you think that's fair, Mr. Pinch?'

'I do, sir. I really do. Thank you so much,' said Pinch.

'Now go back out there and say nothing. Just ask the Sergeant to come in.'

Cat marched in and stood to attention before Gi. 'You want to see me, sir?'

'Yes, Cat. Close the door… That chest of gold coins belonged to me, but I'm going to carry out my promise and pay you and your men like I said. I want you to give each of your twelve men, five thousand coins, each.'

Cats grinned. 'It'll give me the greatest of pleasure, sir.'

'Then, tell Striper's men who are holed up in the main hall that it's over. Get them out and tell them if they stay and work for me, I'll give them a thousand golds each.'

'I'll get on it now, sir,' said Cat.

'Wait a minute, Cat. Don't you want to know what I'm giving you?'

'Sorry, sir. I was carried away by the generosity you're showing my men.'

'I think you were badly treated by the Baron, Cat. You always followed his orders faithfully. So, I'm giving you twenty-five thousand,' Gi told him.

'Sir?' said Cat, 'I think I should sit down...' Then he had a thought. 'Do you remember when we first met in the desert, sir? I got so drunk, and the next morning I promised myself that when I could afford it, I'd buy my own pot to piss in and never have to wash my helmet out again.'

'Ah,' said Gi, 'All that money's gone to your head already, has it?' He grinned. They both grinned.

'I don't know what to say,' said Cat.

'I haven't finished yet,' said Gi. 'I want you to remain a member of my household as Sergeant – no, make that Captain – of the men who decide to stay with me. You can pick your own team... you know: Sergeants, Corporals... that sort of thing. And you can use the main hall as your mess room. If any of your men get out of line, feel free to get rid of them. Permanently, if necessary. I don't want anybody who's not prepared to get along with everybody else. And I want good discipline. Can you do that?'

'The way these men will be treated, sir. I don't see a problem.'

'When you go back out, send Mr. Pinch back in, will you,' said Gi.

Pinch stepped livelier than he'd stepped for years and stood before Gi. 'What can I do for you, Mr. Mulderbish?'

'Do you have a family, Mr. Pinch?'

'A wife, sir. No children.'

'Then I'd like you to go and fetch your dear wife, Mr. Pinch. Bring her here. I will give you as many rooms as you *need*. The downside is that I want you to look after all the gold that's in this castle, regardless of who it belongs to. I want to make one or two rooms as safe possible, so the men here can leave their money in them. You will keep records of how much each man has. And for that, you can work out how much you want me to pay *you*, but don't get too ambitious,' said Gi.

'Thank you, Mr. Mulderbish,' said Pinch, bowing slightly. 'If I may borrow a wagon and horses... oh, and a couple of men... I'll leave in the morning, if that's all right?'

'I'll see you back here in a week then, Mr. Pinch.'

Gi went outside. 'Brian, Maurice, Muto... do you think you can move that chest?'

'If the Sarge locks it again, Mr. Mulderbish, I'll get some of the lads to shift it, said Brian.

'Where do you want it?'

'Inside the front door and round to the right,' replied Gi.

The day had gone well. Gi was pleased beyond measure and almost as tired. He made his way to his old bedchamber wondering what state the late Lord Welkin had left it in. Hoping there wasn't a wife or mistress waiting there.

* * *

Over the next few weeks, the two strong rooms were completed, and Pinch asked for a long counter to be built in one, with an iron grill running its length. Mrs. Pinch had chosen a suite of four rooms plus a kitchen and a privy, and was decorating them in her spare time. Gi had convinced her to be the one to sit at the counter, receiving and paying out the money. Gi considered she would get less aggravation than Pinch, as she was easy on the eye and she would command more deference. Pinch hadn't seen her looking so happy in years.

Captain Cat had made Stanley his sergeant, and a couple of the other men were promoted to Corporals. Ben and Thadax volunteered to guard the safe rooms until Gi could find permanent replacements. Gi asked Brian and Maurice to be his personal guards, to which they agreed, provided they didn't have to wear silly hats.

The men who had previously barricaded themselves in the main hall had seen sense and were now happily serving in Gi's little garrison. Each of them with the most gold they'd ever had, and they didn't have to carry it around with them. In conversation with Muto, Gi commented that if the men had something worth fighting for, they would fight well.

Everything was going how Gi had planned. He knew that Kitsu and George wouldn't stay. George had his own castle to run, and Badger was going to follow Kit on his quest to find the long-legged blonde and her sister back at the *Wayside Inn*.

Haggitt was standing with his father, looking out over the battlements. 'Are you sure this is what you want to do, son?' asked Gi.

'I've thought about it a lot,' said Haggitt. 'Dash and Bayna have been very brave… helping to take care of *us* all this time, now they feel it's time to go back to their own dimension.'

'So, you want to go with them and help them get rid of that wizard, Dennis, is that it?' said Gi.

'Yes, Father, and as soon as it's done, I'll come back.'

The elves were hovering nearby. 'Dash... Bayna! Come to me!' Gi called out.

When they reached Gi, they each took one of the old mage's hands. 'Thank you, sincerely, my friends.' Gi told them. 'I will miss you. And look after my son, please.'

Bayna put her arms around Gi and gave him a long hug. 'I expect we'll see you again, Gi,' she whispered, the melody transporting him momentarily.

Haggitt and the elves walked wordlessly back to the stables. Haggitt had managed to beg a light grey mare from one of Striper's ex-soldiers and was now riding out through the gate with Bayna on Ice, her white stag, and Dash on Snow, his larger-than-life white stallion. Haggitt was told his horse was called Doris. He shrugged. *It's a good name*, he supposed.

When the three friends reached the end of the drawbridge, they turned and waved sadly to Gi, still standing up on the battlements, where he waited with Muto, watching until the trio disappeared over the hill.

The End

CAST OF CHARACTERS

Badger Hercop	Barbarian (reformed) working for Gi
Baron Striper	Owns a castle in Gremanos (also a wizard)
Barry	Barbarian Scout
Barter Stogie	Striper's errand runner
Bayna	Female Snow Elf
Ben de Little	Dwarf
Brian	Soldier
Bob	A Giant
Broosh Marteef	Barbarian Chief
Cardry Hiprat	Barbarian settler
Catscart du Merde(a.k.a. Cat)	Striper's Centurion
Dash	Male Snow Elf
Dennis	Evil Wizard
Elgett Chirgwin	Lord Welkin's Servant
Fox Loer	Soldier
Gennett the Weasel	Barbarian Spy
George	Dragon – Shape shifter
Gi Mulderbish	Wizard – Haggitt's father
Gripper Stogie	Barter's Son
Haggitt Mulderbish	Gi's Son
Harvey the Bear	Barbarian
Huddy Mincing	Barbarian
Ice	Bayna's White Stag
Kirsten	Broosh Marteef's Mother
Kitsu	Shape Shifter

Leoni	Cardry's wife
Lord Welkin	Baron Striper's Son
Maureen	Striper's Receptionist (sometimes)
Maurice	Soldier
Muto Bright	Gi's Cook
Nigel	Barbarian Scout
Ollie	Stable hand
Puck	Barbarian
Reza Lock	Soldier
Sivad Snod	Soldier
Skeet	Stable hand
Smokey Kole	Barbarian – Deserter
Snow	Dash's White Horse
Thadax	Dwarf

Plus, many more with no script, and whilst all the characters are fictitious, you may spot someone you recognise. Happy hunting!

www.ingramcontent.com/pod-product-compliance
Lightning Source LLC
Chambersburg PA
CBHW020641030726
47498CB00002B/315